"Steinke's book reminds us why Elsa's frenetic, avant-garde world is worth remembering."
—*Time Out* (New York)

"Rich, honest prose, lush imagery, and wit. . . . This lovingly constructed novel gives the Baroness a proper place in history."
—*New Orleans Times-Picayune*

"Steinke brings the Bohemian world of the Village to life with vivid description and inventive language, capturing the quirks and giddiness of the Baroness's antics."
—*Rocky Mountain News*

"René Steinke's fictional reimagining of Man Ray and Duchamp's mad muse is wonderfully insightful about the self-absorption required to be a fashion avatar."
—*Atlantic Monthly*

"Steinke opens the world of the fearlessness of the artist, the urge to create that never surrenders, whether by madness or genius or both. Baroness Elsa von Freytag-Loringhoven came long before we had Björk—*Holy Skirts*, with a narrative as mesmerizing as its subject, honors a woman who risked all, survived defeat, and proved art can conquer all."
—J. T. Leroy, author of *The Heart Is Deceitful Above All Things*

"In this exquisitely written novel, René Steinke has created a feast for the senses. *Holy Skirts* is a banquet of language, smell, touch, sound, and taste that readers will emerge from, as if from a long, satisfying, slightly debauched night— staggering, completely satisfied, back into the light of day."
—Dani Shapiro, author of *Family History*

"René Steinke's *Holy Skirts* is a wonderfully vivid and convincing rendering of the distant era it reanimates—and a captivating portrait of a woman generations ahead of her time."
—Madison Smartt Bell, author of *The Stone That the Builder Refused*

Also by René Steinke

THE FIRES

HOLY SKIRTS

A Novel of a Flamboyant Woman

Who Risked All for Art

RENÉ STEINKE

HARPER PERENNIAL

NEW YORK • LONDON • TORONTO • SYDNEY

For my parents, Peter and Kelly,

and for Craig

HARPER ● PERENNIAL

Grateful acknowledgment is made to reprint from the "Canto XCV" excerpt by Ezra Pound from *The Cantos of Ezra Pound*, copyright © 1934, 1937, 1940, 1948, 1956, 1959, 1962, 1963, 1966, and 1968 by Ezra Pound. Reprinted by permission of New Directions Publishing Corp.

A hardcover edition of this book was published in 2005 by William Morrow, an imprint of Harper-Collins Publishers.

P.S.™ is a trademark of HarperCollins Publishers.

FIRST HARPER PERENNIAL EDITION PUBLISHED 2006.

Designed by Claire Vaccaro

The Library of Congress has catalogued the hardcover edition as follows:

Steinke, René.
    Holy skirts / René Steinke.—1st ed.
      p. cm.
      ISBN 0-688-17694-1 (acid-free paper)
      1. Freytag-Loringhoven, Elsa von, 1874-1927—Fiction. 2. Greenwich
Village (New York, N.Y.)—Fiction. 3. Germans—New York (State)—Fiction. 4. Artists'
models—Fiction. 5. Women artists—Fiction.
    6. Bohemianism—Fiction. I. Title.

PS3569.T37926H65   2005
813'.54—dc22   2004052783

ISBN-10: 0-06-077801-6 (pbk.)
ISBN-13: 978-0-06-077801-9 (pbk.)

05 06 07 08 09 ❖/RRD 10 9 8 7 6 5 4 3 2 1

With a royal gesture she swept apart the folds of a scarlet raincoat. She stood before me quite naked—or nearly so. Over the nipples of her breasts were two tin tomato cans, fastened with a green string about her back. Between the tomato cans hung a very small bird-cage and within it a crestfallen canary. One arm was covered from wrist to shoulder with celluloid curtain rings, which later she admitted to having pilfered from a furniture display in Wanamaker's. She removed her hat, which had been tastefully but inconspicuously trimmed with gilded carrots, beets, and other vegetables.

GEORGE BIDDLE, *An American Artist's Story*

The immense cowardice of advertised literati
& Elsa Kassandra, "the Baroness"
von Freitag etc. sd/several true things
in the old days/
driven nuts,
Well, of course, there was a certain strain
On the gal in them days in Manhattan
the principle of non-acquiescence
laid a burden.

EZRA POUND, *Canto XCV*

PART ONE

1

Elsa had never been like the other girls she knew, modest and squeamish about their bodies. Men seemed to sense this. When she was twelve, the doctor, while examining her, had winked and pinched her breasts, and she had been stunned at the sweet stars of pain there, the moist heat between her legs. She had been infatuated with him for weeks, inventing fevers and asking him about his ornithology prints on the examining-room wall. Then there had been the fisherman's son who met her twice at a certain spot in the woods and, laying her down in the leaves, had let her touch his penis, the little eye with its crumpled pink hood. It amused her the way it stiffened and grew in her hand as if she had commanded it with a spell, and when the semen spilled on her arm, it felt like tears. There was the shy milk boy, whom she took behind the house to a little shed where the shovels and gardening tools were kept, and when she put his hand under her skirt, on her thighs above her stockings, he pushed her up against the tines of a rake, but she did not mind. She had a theory that she simply had more heat in her limbs, more blood than most girls, and sensitive skin (she was also prone to hives and blushes), and so her body's chemistry gave her these pleasures other girls were not so lucky to feel.

At home she had been warned about the sailors who roamed the streets near the marina, that they were dangerous and wily. And so at night she would put on her red chemise and imagine them climbing through her bedroom window, one by one. They would admire her, touch her pale skin, slip a thumb beneath the strap on her shoulder, keeping their voices low so that no one would hear. She fantasized about being kidnapped by a sailor with green eyes and sunburned skin. As he was taking her off to China or India, he would tell her about volcanoes, zebras, and pygmies, about the monkey's brains and grasshoppers he had eaten. The ocean would spread ahead of them in its dark infinity, the moon winking, as he slipped his hand inside the secret spot where her bodice met the chemise.

She finally lost her virginity one night on a rowboat with a boy who smelled of salt and grunted into her hair. The boat rocked, and water splashed over them. Afterward she put her hand in the cool sea and, opening her fingers, imagined her virginity floating away like a lock of hair in the waves.

When she stepped off the hot train, after the five-hour ride from Swinemünde to Berlin, she realized she had no idea where to go. It was a gray day in January, the air cold and still. As Elsa wandered the streets, her duffel bag slung over her shoulder, she kept an eye out for landmarks from her earlier visits—that giant pockmarked door that opened onto a courtyard of discarded wheels, the candy shop with the bonbons like tiny breasts. She looked for the dark cathedral with its low, despairing bells but found herself on a strange street of vegetable carts and stores selling pots and pans.

She was nineteen years old, tall and long-limbed. In a hat that fell low on her brow, she walked with a gangly abruptness that made her skirt appear to stop and then start again suddenly, sweeping the pavement in odd bursts of movement. People rushed past her, their faces pressed into mufflers and coat lapels, and on the street smoky plumes rose up from the horses' nostrils. She had not thought it would be so difficult to find a place to stay the night, having imagined she would stay at the Bristol Hotel, where she had always stayed before with her mother, but now she couldn't find it.

When her fingers turned numb and her nose was running, she hurried into a café, the door's bells clattering after her. Green and red bottles behind the bar gleamed, and the air smelled of licorice. "I need a boardinghouse," she said to the woman.

"Down that way," the woman said, pointing toward the church. "Is Frau Hoffman's. She might have a room."

Elsa went to the address and knocked on the door of a tall, narrow house with pointed eaves.

Elsa had assumed she could survive for a year or more on the money she had brought. She also had her notebook, three books of poetry, an extra dress, her favorite yellow shoes, and that last gift from her mother, which she didn't have a name for yet—all that she could fit in the bag when she climbed out the window of her bedroom and ran for the train.

She was shocked when Frau Hoffman asked for almost all the money remaining in her purse.

"For the first month's rent." Her loose cheeks flapped like dog ears around her mouth, but her face turned hard when she spoke of money. "And after this, always on the first Friday."

She showed Elsa to a small room with a bed, a dresser, and a chipped washstand. The bedspread was gray with city ash. "You'll share the toilet and bath with the two others on this floor—they're nice girls, seamstresses."

In the parlor, crowded with dark furniture and black-faced china dolls, Frau Hoffman sat in a chair with a high back like a throne. She took Elsa's money and put it in an envelope that she sealed. "Now, don't tell me where you go at night. If someone comes looking for you, I don't want to have to lie."

Elsa's throat clenched. She had never known a woman as old as Frau Hoffman who did not watch girls, waiting for them to make a mistake. "*No one* will be looking for me." She tried not to think of her father's threats.

Frau Hoffman seemed to study Elsa's face, then nodded. The orange cat jumped into her lap and curled its tail over her large bosom. "Well, no men of course, even here, in the parlor. And no girls overnight. I had an unfortunate experience with that once."

She wrote on the envelope: *Elsa Plötz, Nov. 12, 1904.*

Frau Hoffman apparently had no trouble filling her rooms. People swarmed into Berlin for jobs and luck. Hansom cabs crowded the streets, the horses in such close proximity that they bit one another on the tail and neck. Elsa quickly learned that the drivers were notoriously crooked, and if a passenger did not know the way, he would be given an unnecessary turn around the Tiergarten. People came from towns with one beer hall and a single church and from farms abutted by forests. They came for work, and they came for excitement—a dinner of snail's tails, the parade of beautiful prostitutes in wigs along Potsdamer Platz, the department store with bear rugs beside harps next to lamps shaped like trees. Almost everyone in Berlin had come from someplace else, though few would admit it, and Elsa saw people walking down the street in clothes that did not quite fit or in suits extravagant as costumes. It was said that in order to survive in the city, one had to have a Berliner *Schnauze*—tall, straight, turned up.

That first week Elsa was afraid to go into the fancy shops on Leipzigerstrasse, which were ruled by shopgirls with circles of rouge and hair coiffed like little shiny cakes. She walked up and down the street, trying to muster enough courage to go inside one of the boutiques she had visited so often with her mother. As she looked through the white glare of the windows at unmoving dress forms and frilled hat stands, she rehearsed the question again and again in her head—*Is there a sales position available?* The clerks were all Berlin women, and they would see her detachable collar and lumpy serge skirt and know that she was from someplace where there wasn't even a decent hat store.

Finally she made it inside the door of a shop that sold hair combs, where the clerk was counting bills, touching a cut lemon to moisten her fingers. "What would you like to see?"

Elsa opened her mouth but could not make herself ask, not in this place with its velvet-lined display cases and gleaming, closed cabinets. She felt awkward and sloppy and imagined the clerk trying not to laugh. "I thought you might have a spotted tortoiseshell comb."

"No. Just ivory," the clerk said, slamming shut the cash register. She had a perfectly neat fringe over her eyes.

Elsa left, trembling. All the way back, in a cloud of defeat, she berated herself for losing her nerve again. Women who were cowards ended up married to brutes, their teeth falling out, their backs bowed. If she didn't find work soon, she would have to go home to Swinemünde. She'd have to return to that dull house, where, in the months since her mother had died, her father barged through doors, calling hearty greetings to the cook and maid as he never had before. Her stepmother, with her nutcracker mouth and sharp eyes, sat at Elsa's mother's crystal-knobbed dressing table and gazed at herself in the oval mirror, as if it had always been hers, and Elsa's sister, Charlotte, frantically needlepointed designs of the local seascape and lighthouse.

Her mother's death lingered in all the rooms, like an object she'd left behind: the kitchen with clanging copper pans hung from the ceiling; the pantry, where meat dangled over sacks of flour; the empty parlor, where the piano stood silent and nobody read in front of the fire; the hallway, where, one afternoon after the doctor's visit, her father, smelling of sour beer, had stopped her and put his burly arms around her so tightly she could not breathe. She had seen him in the alley the day before with the woman who kept a room above the tavern. "You're a good girl," he said. This made her want to belch rudely or run screaming into the street.

"Am I?" She pulled herself out of his arms and went back to her room.

She could not remember when there had not been an alarming absence inside of her. She felt it most acutely when she woke in the middle of the night, not knowing who or where she was, her body melding with the dark. But also in that gray light just before morning, when voices spoke in her inner ear, slow and taffy-pulled, or yammering like a faucet. She knew that it meant there was not enough of her somehow, that she could so easily be snuffed out.

The sensation made her want to create evidence of herself. As a girl she had taught herself to paint, studies of her mother's face with its secretive smile, the heavy black eyelashes, and blond hair like a golden waterfall down her back. She painted birds that landed on low branches in the woods and sea flowers that washed up on the beach. In her notebook she wrote poems with cornflowers and dew—because all the poets she knew wrote about spring.

The day her mother died, it was so windy that open books fanned and ruffled their pages and cups fell off the kitchen shelves, and when Elsa went outside, her hair fell out of its pins. The cold air clamored through the poplars, blowing down the hill, howling.

Sometimes now at night, Elsa dreamed she stood at the lip of the grave, the coffin still wet from the ice, a lily against the black wood. Her toes grazed the edge of the hole, the freshly turned soil slippery under the soles of her shoes. She would feel herself about to fall and catch herself just in time, waking up with her breath suddenly short and clamped.

After three weeks of surviving on just bread and milk and a small cake Frau Hoffman gave her, Elsa resigned herself to writing to her aunts to ask for a loan, though she dreaded their tight disapproval. They did not believe in running away from one's lot in life, and they did not believe, despite how much they disapproved of him, that Elsa should ever disobey her father. They would point out that she should have learned to cook, that at least her sister would surely marry soon, that if only Elsa could keep her dresses clean and her hair under her hat, she might do all right for herself.

Then one day, as if by a miracle, Elsa saw the advertisement in the newspaper: "Firm seeks girls with good figures."

She found the address on a little street off Dorotheenstrasse. The door opened to a dim basement, where a man sat on a wooden desk, wearing a top hat and white socks showing under too-short pants. He was tall and rangy, with a scruffy beard and thinning light brown hair. He said he was Henry de Vris and worked for the Wintergarten Cabaret. He turned to his assistant: "Remove her dress." And then, to Elsa, "You're healthy, I assume. No diseases?"

"Yes," she said, trying to hide her shoes, curled up at the toes from walking everywhere. She felt the woman's fingers spidering at the top of her back, unbuttoning.

Last year Elsa had decided she wanted to be like those women she had seen at the Freyburg Theater with their spun-jewel dresses and limpid eyes, the ones who had found secret escapes from the mundane, sparkling ways to avoid marriage, the ones who knew Shakespeare and Goethe by heart. They were women who, she imagined, were so passionate they were prone to rashes and hives, weeping fits and nightmares, as she was. Actresses were women whom ordinary people constantly nagged to calm down.

She was nervous about being undressed, but if that were all she had to do to get a position at the Wintergarten Cabaret, then it would be worth it. Standing there on the cold, gritty floor, she watched the way de Vris gazed at her, his eyes flicking up and down her body.

He smiled slightly. "We're seeking living statues, Miss Plötz. Will you be able to stand absolutely still?"

"Of course. I can dance, too." She would find herself in a pink, wispy future, smoking with the director at a late-night restaurant and giving her opinion of the play, bells ringing nearby, oysters about to be served in their cragged shells.

"We don't need dancers," he said. "But if you can stand still, I will hire you."

She had always been teased about the way she liked to pop up and down on her toes, how she fiddled with her hair, tapped her finger on tables. "I can stand still," she said.

He circled her, and her skin began to warm and tingle, as if the basement had suddenly filled with sunlight. Being admired made her feel more solid somehow, more rooted in the bright springs she conjured in her poems.

When she was dressed again, de Vris gave her the house rules on a stiff piece of paper and told her not to lose them. She was required to make her whereabouts known, even on the evenings she was not scheduled to perform; she was to refrain from slamming doors or stomping her feet or raising her voice backstage; she was not to draw attention to herself if she entered the auditorium when she was not onstage; she was required to wear the theater apparel chosen by the manager. If she broke any of these rules, she would be "released from employment."

That night she took out the last gift her mother had given her in the asylum. This was after she had begun to speak in that childish voice, after she had begun to call her husband "that man," after she'd stopped combing her hair so it lay matted on the sides of her face, after the blue of her eyes had started to fade. Elsa's father, thinking it might comfort her mother to do something "useful," gave her his good tweed suit to mend, the expensive one he saved for special occasions.

The hundred small pieces she had cut from the suit lay strewn around her on the dusty floor of the asylum, scissors splayed next to her leg. She had sewn two scraps together in broad crosshatched stitches. It crinkled like a piece of ham or bacon and was adorned with a little wooden whistle, its snail shape embedded in the tight weave of the fabric, surrounded by haphazard beads. "Here, Elsa." Her mother handed her the piece, giggling. "You can use it to handle hot things."

It was useless as a pot holder, and besides that, Elsa could not cook. "How could you cut up his good suit?"

Her mother's lopsided grin widened. "Oh, he doesn't need it. It's much better for me to have all this lovely material, isn't it?" Elsa stared at the crumpled thing, the beads and painted whistle gleaming in the lamplight. Her mother, gathering the scraps in her lap, wore a dirty dress that hung loose on her wasted frame. Elsa watched her carefully fold each frayed piece, the bare room so quiet Elsa could hear her own ragged breath.

Her sister, Charlotte, pretended that nothing had changed. "Mother isn't feeling well," she would say. "Mother has a bad headache," and if Elsa protested, Charlotte would turn, twisting the swirl of her bun at the back of her small head, and march away. Her father, his frown hidden behind his beard and mustache, slammed doors and ate his meals at the tavern.

After Elsa's mother was sent away, Elsa's easel looked ridiculous there, blankly waiting for her. Ordinary objects—the bookcase in the parlor, the little brass bucking horse on top of the mantel—seemed to waver and dissolve when she looked at them, while the walls remained solid—corners pointed and precise, loud, mocking flowers in the paper. During the day she was under the watchful eyes of the servants, but at night she began to sneak out to walk in the silent woods or linger near the marina, where she watched the sunburned sailors in their crisp uniforms, shouting cheerily to one another across a deck, tossing ropes or duffel bags, while the water lapped at their boats, rocking them back and forth.

2

Black curtains with silver tasseled swags hid the stage of the Winter-garten Cabaret. Below the balcony there were several archways, each guarded by the figure of a small naked woman, her breasts thrust forward, as if she might pull herself from the plaster.

When Elsa went into the dressing room, nude women walked among the mirrors and open trunks. One had tall legs and an egg-shaped belly, the space above her sex hairless and pink. Another had short, round legs and a tiny waist that gave her the figure of a bottle. The woman next to her had narrow hips and huge breasts that she had pressed down with a wide, thick bandage. Elsa was mesmerized by the row of women at the mirror, all those pink buttocks, like so many pretty hams.

A woman asked her if she had any cologne. She was tall and big-boned, with little clocks of black hairs around her nipples.

Elsa told her she did not have any, just as the tiny, bony-faced assistant darted over to her. "Plötz, right? Padding for you."

"What?"

She handed Elsa an armful of fleshy material. "Your tunic and stock-ings," she said, pursing her lips. She pulled out two cardboard cones and a thin, rounded cotton pillow attached to a belt. "Here are your breasts," she said, handing her the cones. "And here are your hips." She handed her the pillows and shrugged. "Not enough of you there, I guess."

Elsa felt a flame rising up from her neck. None of the other women were wearing this padding. Wasn't her figure good? She remembered the way de Vris had stared at her body, how giddy she'd felt. She looked down at the stiff cardboard mounds. "Do I have to wear them?"

The assistant glanced back at her with tired eyes. "If you want your wages, you'll wear the titties and the bottom."

The pillows hung limply over her backside and hips like a saddle. She pulled up the stockings, fastened their elastics, then pulled the tight tunic over her head and adjusted it over her new hips. As she stuffed the cones into two empty pockets over her chest, a woman with blond ringlets, who said her name was Natalye, told her, "Don't pout. You're lucky."

Elsa walked back two steps to check her reflection in the mirror. From a distance she supposed she might have been mistaken for a voluptuous woman, but when she stepped closer, her body resembled a cushion mistakenly stuffed with wine goblets.

"At least you're covered. With me—in the front rows at least—they'll see everything," Natalye said. "Anyway, here's the powder for your face and arms so you'll look like a statue." She pointed to a broken box on the table, white powder spilling through the tear. She showed Elsa how to drape the white robe over one shoulder and the opposite hip. "Just do what de Vris tells you and don't laugh. He gets furious when a girl laughs."

The women filed onstage, and de Vris grabbed Elsa's arm, pulling her to a red X on the floor in the back. He pulled her arm one way, prodded her hips to the left, touching her as if she were a chicken he was about to cook, and then he stood back, his forefinger over his lips as he studied her. She was suddenly glad for the upholstery.

He posed her in three positions, then said, "You'll hear a bell and then, ve-ry grace-ful-ly . . ." He turned to the second position, one hand in the air, the other extended behind him. "You change your form." One of the women began to giggle. He glared at her, and she stopped. "We have a performance momentarily, Frau Schmidt."

Then his voice half sang, as if he were casting a spell. "You are Greek statues this evening, girls, beautiful living statues, feminine perfection created to tantalize and torture mortal men." He flung his hands out and wiggled his fingers. "I've just changed you into stone. Blink if you must, but not rapidly, and otherwise remain still until you hear the bell."

Elsa closed her eyes and imagined cement hardening in her blood. Behind the curtain she heard rushed voices, the skid of a chair. The show was about to begin, and beyond the heavy curtain, the murmurings in the audience grew rowdier. Standing still was only the beginning. When she became an actress, her photograph would appear in little cameo circles on the theater page, and the critics would write about her voice and her grace, and she would become so famous that her father, just for a chance to see the play, would apologize for all that he had done. She would give him a seat in the audience, but she would not forgive him.

When the curtain lifted, the audience applauded. She blinked in the bright yellow light, then tried not to blink, and felt her eyes tearing. She looked up at the happy glitter of the balcony railings above the dark crowd and then thrilled to the mass of them, all that breath and pumping blood, all those eyes.

The musicians in the orchestra pit played slow, plaintive flutes. When the bell rang, she moved to her next position, one arm crooked behind her as if it had been broken off. The applause was thinner. In the front row, the robe slipped off the shoulder of one of the girls and dropped to the floor. When the girl bent down to grab the robe and cover herself, there was laughter and heckling.

In Elsa's effort to stand still, her mind wandered, caught on the memory of the cross-stitched embroidery on the sheet, the yellow sores on her mother's abdomen, the pale dryness of her arms, the piss in the bedpan, how she hated even lifting her nightgown. When the bell rang again, Elsa put all of this out of her mind, moving to the next position, her elbow bent just above her head. There was another brief round of applause, then she accidentally hit one of her cardboard breasts, which fell to her waist and hung there. The weight pulled at the mesh tunic around her midriff, but she knew that if she tried to move, she would attract attention. So she stood there with the cardboard cone protruding from her side like a tumor. In a flash she saw her mother's face grimacing in pain, then focused again on the audience out in the dark. The breast was edging its way down, and if it fell any lower it would look as if she had grown a swollen male member. She held still, waiting, but saw, with relief, that the traveling breast was probably not visible behind the statue in front of her. She was sweating so much under the lights that the powder mixed with her perspiration made a paste on her skin.

When the last bell rang, Elsa panicked. Henry de Vris had instructed them to "float" offstage—as if floating were an action as natural as walking. Elsa, not knowing what it meant, assumed he wanted the girls to walk slowly, with a certain grace, but she tripped near the curtain.

Once she passed the stage edge, Natalye pulled her aside. "Don't worry. I don't think he saw you do that. Look, this is how you float." She walked languidly a few paces to show her. "You point your toes and walk as if you don't have any bones in your legs, but hold up your head like a soldier."

Elsa tried it, and for years afterward, whenever she exited a room full of men, she would be floating.

There were three shows a night at the Wintergarten, a cycle that varied only slightly each day of the week. To begin, there were the Albanian brothers, Jed and Cornelius, jugglers who caught one another's oranges and shoes and bottles but backstage argued viciously. There were the Chinese acrobats, who'd arrived from Shanghai with their potent medicinal teas and magic shark's fin. They tied their limbs into pretty knots and swung from a rope ladder, pointing their pink-slippered toes. For the next act, one of the couples alternated singing with short skits full of jokes about either sex: "Men are like hot soups—you have to blow on them or they'll burn you." "My wife is so fat the Kaiser wants to use her dress as the new flag!" There was the dwarf man and wife, the fat man and wife, and the tall man and wife, who balanced on stilts and were really brother and sister. Then one of the Beauties sang, usually Theodora, who, rather than enter the chorus's dressing room, kept to herself backstage with the jugglers or acrobats. In her filmy dresses, which in the stage lights looked as if they were made from soap and rain, Theodora sang sad songs about dying youth and abandoned girls. She softened men's hearts, prepared them for the twelve half-naked chorus girls about to traipse onstage. They struck poses like Greek statues—*The wonders of ancient art brought right here to you, sir.*

In the beginning Elsa accepted every invitation, unless the man was very fat or smelled of onions. They waited at the stage door; they followed her on the street and tried to strike up a conversation; they offered to buy her coffee in cafés. She dressed in red and yellow, wore lace bodices and huge sleeves, high-heeled shoes, rouge and kohl. Signals that she was no one's wife. The men bought her dinners and clothes; they took her on carriage rides through the Tiergarten, and they took her to concerts and cabarets.

She liked having to choose between one or the other when she went out at night, and she liked it when they begged her to go to dinner with them or said that of all the living statues, she was the one who most resembled the *Venus de Milo*. She liked men's smells, shaving soap and mint and hair oil, the funny things they said to try to charm her, and the way they looked at her as if she were a thunderstorm or a pile of money.

There were parties in dark rooms where she was offered absinthe, and three or four men in natty suits vied for her attention. There were bouquets sent backstage to "the statue second from the right in the front row." Each time there was a man waiting for her at the stage door, he seemed more handsome than the one who had been there before. She went man-crazy up to her ear tips. Her father had called her *stupid, reckless, sloppy, ungrateful,* but his words dissolved each time one of the men told her she was beautiful.

She went to restaurants that served caviar, oysters, game hen, perfect tarts of vegetables and potatoes cut like coins. Sometimes she liked to sit and listen to the din of table talk and wait for a word or phrase to rise up out of the noise. There were always white linens and silver and crystal and occasionally, off the private dining room, a secret door in the paneling that led to a room with a bed. "You're too pretty—it isn't good for a girl," one man said to her.

She only went into the bachelor rooms with the ones she fell in love with, but there were dozens. One wanted her to pretend she was a virgin, one wanted her to wear black ribbons on her wrists, and one taught her how to lick his *Schwanz*. She was thrilled at the worshipful faces he made while he pushed at the back of her head, moaning.

The men's love made the house in Swinemünde distant, the locked doors and angry chairs, the helpless bedposts, all so far away they might have belonged to someone else's girlhood. In love it seemed as if her hair had been perfumed with clouds, as if the shoes she walked in were soled in silver, her fingers tipped with pearls, her breasts with rubies.

There was one stationery salesman who said to her one night, "You do not have any idea what you are doing, do you?" She was eating her duck, and he was staring at his fork, turning it over and over again on the table.

"What do you mean?"

"I think of you when I'm at work, when I'm getting a shave, when I'm talking to my wife. It drives me mad that you walk on that stage every night. Let me buy you a proper apartment, where I can pamper you. Quit the Wintergarten. I'll arrange to come to Berlin every Saturday."

Looking at his unhappy mouth, at his dark glistening eyes, part of her wanted to kiss him and nod happily, but she knew she could never sacrifice all the other men for just one. "I want to be an actress."

He pushed his plate away and wiped his mouth. "Then we cannot meet anymore." He gave her money for the cab home and left her there at the table. She finished her dinner alone, listening to the clink of silverware and the professor at the next table, who was talking about the little-known importance of dogs in history.

Sometimes she was still afraid that she might be caught, that somehow her father might find out where she was and come stomping into the boardinghouse demanding to take her back. With tears in his eyes, he would loudly announce that she was a girl who only needed to learn to be polite and run a household, and then, he'd cluck to Frau Hoffman, she wouldn't be so unhappy at home.

He'd married her stepmother, Lottie, just three months after they buried her mother, and Elsa bristled at Lottie's efforts to reform her. The night she ran away, her stepmother had found her smoking in her room, with the window open to chase out the smell. After her father had torn up her cigarettes and opened all her drawers to see if there were any more, he'd snapped, "Apologize to your mother."

She told him her mother was lying in her grave, and he reached over and slapped her. The rest shot out of her mouth before she realized it: "Because of you!" His jaw set, his cheekbones stony. Then she knew that what she'd overheard her aunts say was true—his rages had made her mother sick.

If he had wept, or said, "How can you say such things?" she would have
believed that their whispers had just been a symptom of grief, or their usual
mean-spiritedness. But he put his big hands around her neck and shook her
until her stepmother made him stop.

Natalye was the only one of the statues whom Elsa could consider her
friend. Natalye had not read many books—she mixed up her letters, as she
explained it—but she was smarter than Elsa about what the city required of a
girl. While the other statues were protective of their "gentlemen" and
laughed rather than dispense any advice, Natalye did her best to help Elsa
along. One night when they both had been reprimanded by Henry de Vris for
their lateness, Natalye snarled behind his back and whispered to Elsa, "He
likes it better if you hate him." She was not a Berlin girl either. She had been
in the city for years but remembered well enough what it was like to be new
there, and when Elsa told her she wanted to be an actress, she did not laugh,
but winked and said, "Well, you had better get to work on finding costume
money."

While they were getting dressed for the show one afternoon, Natalye
said, "You really like them, don't you?"

"Who?"

"The men."

"Doesn't everyone?"

She shrugged. "Once in a while, someone nice comes along, but he
always ends up being a brute. Maybe you have better luck—who knows?
But you seem to like even the ones without decent hats."

Frau Hoffman knew that Elsa worked at the cabaret, but even when Elsa
came in an hour or two before dawn, she did not complain, because Elsa
never brought any men back to the boardinghouse. Frau Hoffman only
requested that Elsa take the back staircase so she would not wake any of the
other boarders. But one day a man came to the house looking for Elsa—she
never found out who it was. Frau Hoffman slammed the door in his face and
said Elsa did not live there anymore. "What do you think?" she lashed out at
Elsa, who was coming down the stairs. "I've got five young women living

here, and if the neighbors see men going in and out, they'll say I'm running a business. So, like I told you, no men."

"I didn't invite him. He must have followed me."

Frau Hoffman came over to her, her loose cheeks trembling as she grabbed Elsa by the arm and shook her. "Wake up, girl. Wake up, or you're going to end up a whore."

3

There was a cabaret called Heaven and a cabaret called Hell. There was one designed to look like the Catacombs, with shackles on its stone walls and bars over the windows, and another one designed to imitate a criminals' headquarters—on the tables, open suitcases of fake money and the waiters carrying knives or toy guns. Unlike the Wintergarten, these cabarets were alternate worlds, and the performers made fun of men who cared only about making a profit and getting fat in one way or another. Flashing gilt and lace and bruises, the performers sang sober songs for the socialists or acted out satires of factory owners.

Elsa felt suddenly sophisticated when her date explained the system. One had to know the secret names for the Kaiser and the police in order to laugh at the jokes. Then there were the female performers, Rose the Siren, who told a story about being seduced by her boss at the factory, and sang:

> I am a piece of meat,
> Blush pink and bloody,
> Eat me, if you like, boys.
> I'm already long dead.
> I won't make any noise.

She was quite beautiful, with her paper-white skin and abandoned-kitten's eyes. There was Karla, a man dressed as a woman in a blond wig and a grape-colored dress with a tight velvet fishtail hem. She sang about back doors and secret windows, and her laughter was like glitter up and down the stage. Elsa was mesmerized by the faint shadow of beard under the powder, by her thick barrel chest and sweet mocking voice. The man she was with eyed her and said, "Don't tell me you're insulted."

"Not at all. I love the way she sings."

This made him laugh so hard he shook the table where they sat and spilled their drinks. Afterward, in the alley, he started to pull up her skirt but seemed to change his mind and hailed her a cab instead.

One night in the dressing room, Elsa and Natalye shared a mirror, a flourish of rust hanging just above Elsa's head in the reflection, rust freckles on Natalye's shoulder. "What are you doing later?" Natalye asked. "The man I'm meeting has a friend."

"I'm not sure," said Elsa, crimping her hair with an iron. They performed as wood nymphs now, *Living Pictures*. They were supposed to look like part of the painting, a countryside backdrop full of trees, and they wore their hair loose around their shoulders, with small bits of fur pinned to their body stockings. A few of the girls wore horns in their hair or tails on their bottoms. Elsa unclasped the iron and pulled it gently from a lock of hair. "I was hoping George would be back tonight." George was a sweet man with a limp who had hard blue eyes.

Natalye powdered her nose with a pink puff. "Does he give you more than Max did?"

Elsa placed another lock of hair between the scalloped rods of the crimping iron. "George hasn't given me any presents yet, but he buys me bottles of champagne."

"You mean you haven't come to an agreement with George yet? You'd better hurry up."

Elsa smelled her hair beginning to burn and quickly pulled the iron from her hair, the lock curled and shiny with heat. "An agreement about what?"

"The money, silly girl."

Separating the crimps in her hair with her fingers, Elsa glanced at Natalye's small, exquisitely pointed chin.

"Elsa," Natalye said, "you don't know anything about it, do you?"

Staring at her face in the mirror, Elsa saw how obvious it was that she was too stupid to live in Berlin.

"Of course you don't come right out and say it like a whore does, but how do you think we all get along? You find a way to casually mention that with fifty marks or so, you could dress so much better or with a hundred more marks a month you could finally take acting lessons. Then, when you excuse yourself and go to the powder room, you leave your purse there for him to fill. You have to come to an arrangement and hope that he won't be too stingy or vulgar about it."

"But . . . I like them," Elsa stammered. Quickly and sloppily, she rubbed the rouge on her cheekbones and then realized she had made herself look feverish.

"That's fine," said Natalye. "All the better. I hate the one I'm meeting tonight. He wheezes and squints, but he gives me lots of cash. Don't give yourself away for nothing."

Elsa stood up and pinned the fur to her body stocking.

"Don't worry," said Natalye, squeezing Elsa's shoulder. "I'm sure it only makes you all the more charming to them. Just make sure they pay."

The Swinemünde women wore practical dresses in blue, gray, or black, with modest bustles, nothing that distracted one's attention. But Elsa's mother wore a dress with the largest leg-of-mutton sleeves, striped to exaggerate their size, and a velvet overskirt that was trimmed with gold netting. It was an evening dress, and as there were few evening occasions, Marie wore it even to the autumn parade and the market. She liked to make occasions. Some evenings, drinking wine, she would recite poems for Elsa and her sister.

> Let me appear this way until I become real
> Do not take off my white robe!
> I hasten from the beautiful earth
> Down to that secure abode . . .

Then I shall leave behind this pure covering,
The belt and the garland.

Elsa still had her mother's Hölderlin, a cloth-covered book with a broken binding, and whenever she opened it, she heard her mother's voice, remembered the firelight in her blond tresses and the drops of wine that would spill on the floor.

Her mother spent afternoons in a chair angled toward the window, one hand caught in her hair, a book in her lap. She would sit for long moments before she turned the page, and, watching her, Elsa had the sense that it was filling up under her mother's gaze, as if she looked the words onto it, all the phrases that should have been there but weren't. When Elsa threw her own notebook of verses into the fire because the cook had teased her about them, her mother had wept, but they couldn't be saved. Her mother had praised the poems too easily, in a way that made Elsa feel small and silly.

In the Wintergarten dressing room, there was talk about the girls who had not been careful where they went at night, girls who had been beaten up or raped or murdered. There were jokes about the pox, about a rich woman in the society pages who had paid a doctor to construct a new nose for her after she had lost the old one, and gossip about the actress who had contracted the syph from her leading man and then killed herself, and the other actress, so beautiful and talented she filled the Royal Theatre each time she performed, who was rumored to have given a dose to every wealthy man and baron in the city. Elsa always tried not to listen, turning the pages of her book but quickly losing her place in the story.

There were tonics and prophylactics, charms and superstitions. But, some said, sooner or later everyone would get it.

Natalye disagreed. "A girl just has to be sensible," she said. "You make them cover themselves, and you look at their *Schwanz* in the light before you let them touch you."

Another girl in the chorus, who was always red-eyed from something she had drunk or smoked, said, "You're dreaming, Nat. Unless you wear a chastity belt, you're going to get it. But then after a while it goes away—it stiffens up your blood."

When George mysteriously stopped waiting for Elsa at the stage door, she went out with Oscar, who seemed to have plenty of money and slipped it under her napkin without her even asking for it. He took her to a dark restaurant where there were only a few other diners and the waiters appeared to know him. Elsa noticed that when he turned his back, one of them grinned.

"I want to know all about you," Oscar said, taking her hand in his and rubbing it.

It made her uncomfortable. "What do you want to know?"

He raised his eyebrows. "Your pathetic girl story, how you ended up in the Wintergarten wearing fur."

"I'm not poor."

He chuckled. "Of course not. I was being sarcastic. Listen, have you ever had snails?" He opened the menu.

There was a kind of concentration in his expressions that fascinated her. He was a law student, and he seemed surprised that she had read so many books—"A pretty girl like you does not usually lock herself up in a room reading." He had ideas about the justice of the courts, and she could not understand why his talk seemed tedious one moment, sunny the next—like certain train rides through the country.

She went with him to a room in Potsdamer Platz, and after a little while, he took off her clothes. The variety and color of men's desires always made her curious to know what she could learn from their coos and gropings. Oscar laid her down on the bed, whispering that she was lovely, and she closed her eyes.

He took one hand and then the other in his soft fingers. He nuzzled his stubbled cheek against her neck, nibbled at her ear. As he moved to hover over her, she smelled the stale talc beneath his undershirt, the wine on his breath. Then she felt the rough weave of the rope and screamed.

He covered her mouth with his damp hand. "Hush. I gave you the money, didn't I?" He was looking at her neck. She thought of the girl who had been found dead under the carousel, her throat cut in two places.

His fingers pressed under her nose, dug into her cheek, and she couldn't breathe. She bucked up, drew in her leg, and kicked him in the thigh. He stumbled back.

She tore off the rope, picked up her dress from the floor, and pulled it down over her head. Shaking, she grabbed her shoes. "I should have my brothers hunt you down and carve you up," she lied. "They'd do it in a second."

He was smoothing his hair, rebuttoning his shirt. "Oh, get out of here! I thought you were a professional. And give me back that money." She ran out of the room, hiding her tears.

He's a known pretend torturer," Natalye said of Oscar later. "One of the girls said he doesn't even touch you. He just ties you up and asks you to beg. It's pretty easy really. He probably thought you already knew all about him."

Elsa thought of the way he'd tilted his head at her, narrowed his eyes as if she were too tiny to see clearly. "I don't ever want to beg."

Natalye laughed when Elsa told her how she ran out of his room. "He's harmless."

To be a woman was to be looked at. But what was seen was partly up to her. Elsa found that simple, straight fashions suited the sharp angles of her frame and face. She began to go around in a blue straight skirt and colt-hide belt with a red blouse. One day the wife of the tall man asked her where she bought her red gloves, and even Theodora, sighing, lowered her eyes and said, "Chic skirt—who is your dressmaker?"

Then, on Liebenstrasse, Elsa saw a pretty woman in a tailor-made man's suit, her hair cropped and pushed behind her ears. As she walked, people turned to stare, and Elsa recognized her. She was Clothilde, the actress who was said to have the ability to make men swoon or weep at her will. And she did look like no other woman on the street. Her earrings and lip rouge confused the sharp lines of the suit, which somehow hid her body's curves and suggested them at the same time. It was like a dream Elsa sometimes had, when she was both the princess and the prince, the beauty and the hero.

Elsa went to a consignment shop and bought a man's suit for herself, and not long after that, there was an article on the ladies' page about the actresses who were chic and scandalous in "tailor-made." When Elsa felt rakish, she put on the suit. Sometimes she even wore a monocle around her neck because it implied studiousness. On the street—as if she were already famous—people stared.

One night the jugglers got into a bloody fight, after Jed called Cornelius a bore and had his head smashed with a beer bottle. Backstage the floor was slick with beer, Theodora was weeping into her sleeve, the fat wife was yelling about cooperation, and Elsa commiserated with Cornelius, whose head had been beaten with a broomstick. Kristen, one of the girls from the chorus, came over to them. "Want to come to dinner with Marc and me?"

Cornelius lifted the bandage from his head. "What was that?"

Elsa handed him the cold, wet cloth. "You're in no shape for dining, my friend."

She had planned to meet a man who owned a china factory, but he had sent a note that he was called away on business. "It's an invitation to Elsa only," said Kristen. She was new to the chorus, and the other night when Elsa had forgotten to bring her bag, she had lent Elsa her powder. She had dark, thick eyebrows and a voice that suggested she knew more about everything than she let on. She had been with a circus troupe before and claimed to have slept with the dwarf.

"It will be a fancy dinner. Marc just got paid, and he wants to go to Kempinski's."

Elsa was disappointed at the restaurant when people did not stare at her suit. After a heavy meal of lamb chops, they sat listening to the orchestra, drinking. Marc seemed annoyed that Elsa was there, but Kristen ignored him.

"Shall we dance?" He stood up, offering his hand to Kristen.

She shook her head and leaned over the table to Elsa. "So how long are you going to be at the Wintergarten? It won't be long, I think, before they force us to get rid of the body stocking and just go bare-legged and bare-bottomed on the stage."

"As long as it takes before I get an acting assignment." Kristen had been to Paris, St. Petersburg, and Prague, seen things that Elsa wished she'd seen—and Elsa wanted to make it clear that she was preparing to have adventures of her own.

"Oh, are you auditioning?" Kristen touched her arm.

"First, you have to learn the roles. I practice on Tuesdays with Natalye." Elsa finished her third glass of wine and began to feel pleasantly dizzy.

"You know, you could even play a boy. There was a girl in the circus who fooled everyone until the night there were no toilets and she was forced to pee in the bushes with the strongman."

When Kristen danced with Marc, Elsa got fascinated with the way the bouquet of roses blurrily twirled on the table, and as she watched the dancers, the ladies' skirts seemed to expand, filling with air like parachutes. The music sounded like men complaining and whining, and then like a military parade for dogs. She realized she was very drunk.

As they left the restaurant, Kristen said, "You understand, Marc—Elsa will have to spend the night with me. It's too late for her to wake up her landlady." Marc gave her a sharp look, but Kristen ignored him, taking Elsa's arm as they passed between the green velvet curtains.

In Kristen's room they got undressed and lay on the bed, and Kristen sent Marc home, but he wouldn't leave the building. Outside the bedroom door, there was a crashing sound and a thump.

"Just ignore him," Kristen said, bending so her lip grazed Elsa's ear.

"Let me in!" he wailed.

"Don't worry. I locked the door." Kristen giggled. The walls turned half circles.

Kristen's skin felt hot. Elsa closed her eyes and suddenly felt Kristen's lips on hers. There was more banging on the door and Marc's wavering voice. "Kristen, you promised. I bought you that ring because you promised I could watch you." He began to weep. "What's wrong with you?"

Kristen sat up and called to the door. "Nothing's wrong. We're sleeping, Marc. Go to sleep!"

It seemed as if Kristen's skin were made of thick white velvet. Her hands were quick and warm, and her face appeared to sway from side to side. She pulled the blouse off Elsa's shoulder and touched her breast. "You like girls, don't you?"

Kristen's finger exquisitely traced the outline of Elsa's shoulder, the undercurve of her breast, the other hand warm in the fragile dip of her belly.

Marc's voice bellowed through the door. "I can't sleep—you're with that slut!"

After a moment Kristen sat up and screamed at the door. "Really, Marc, haven't you ever seen a lady wear trousers?" She came back to Elsa. "He's from Hamburg—what do you expect?" she said.

As Kristen's finger circled her nipple, Elsa smelled the orange water beneath Kristen's chemise. Her hand felt smooth and knowing. She unbuckled Elsa's belt. Elsa felt suddenly as if she were Kristen *and* a man lying on the bed. It was an odd, disjointed feeling, but pleasant—like touching herself in the bath or wearing silk.

Kristen knelt over her and kissed her stomach, her thigh. In the darkness of the room, the walls seemed to shudder, and there was a quake in the bed before the streetlight in the window silently exploded.

In the morning Elsa found Kristen curled around her, and she untangled herself and got dressed. Inside her head a dozen tiny hammers pummeled and only gradually in small flashes, did she remember the night before.

When she opened the bedroom door, Marc fell inside. He must have been listening at the door all night, and when he rubbed his eyes awake, he looked up at Elsa and said, "Oh, it's *you.*"

Though Elsa had found Kristen's attentions surprisingly pleasant, she was sure it was not love, but more like a strange inexplicable dream.

Going into the dressing room that night, Elsa noticed that Olga, a plump girl with arms like bread loaves, was already costumed and waiting near the backstage. Elsa was running late. She hurried to the bin where she kept her things and began to undress just before she opened the little door and saw that her costume was not there. She shut the door and made certain she hadn't mistakenly opened someone else's bin, noted again her initials, *EP.*

She turned to Eva, who was fixing her hat of antlers on her head. "Did someone take my stocking by accident?"

Eva shrugged, not turning away from the mirror.

If Elsa did not go onstage that night, she'd be fined a week's wages, and she'd just spent all her money on a new silk petticoat. She looked around the dressing room floor and chairs, wondering if she had left her costume out the night before, but there were only the street clothes of the other girls hanging limply on hooks and, on the table, a swath of white silk.

Marceline and Lisel were gossiping in the corner, and when she approached them, they stopped talking. "Did you see anyone go into my things? My costume's gone!"

Marceline said, "I didn't see anything," then giggled and covered her mouth.

Lisel, suddenly grand, raised her head. "Why don't you ask Kristen?"

"Where is she?" Elsa demanded.

"She's not here tonight." Lisel smiled broadly. "She's with her fiancé." Lisel and Marceline burst into laughter.

Elsa ran over to Penelope near the door and asked her if she'd seen anyone take her costume. Penelope shook her head, a laugh spurting between her teeth. She was a spiteful, snout-faced girl. Elsa wished Natalye were there, but she was out that night visiting her brother. Elsa started to rush over to Oda, who was preening at the mirror, but stopped herself.

What did they all have against her? As she felt them sneaking glances at her from around the room, her cheeks burned.

Running in a rage to de Vris's office, Elsa almost raced right by it. At first, she thought someone had tried to be helpful by placing her lost costume somewhere prominent, but as she got closer, she knew better. The tall man and short wife were examining the display: Elsa's body stocking, the fur piece, and antlers had been nailed to the wall in the area backstage. In the place where her body and face should have been, there was a chalked outline of a fish and below, it said, "Elsa Plötz, a fishy deer." Surrounded by the jugglers, acrobats, and Theodora, the tall man bent down to study the fish eyes. When he saw Elsa approaching, he stood up, covered his mouth, and stared. Elsa, her eyes stinging, pulled the costume off the nails and tore a hole in the fur that would cost her two marks to have repaired.

4

At night Elsa tried to recall the things her mother had said to her as they strolled through the woods finding mushrooms or walked along the shore getting sand in their shoes. Once on the train to Berlin, her mother had wanted her to denounce men altogether, to promise that she'd never stop "feeling things," and another time, at a neighbor's house, over coffee, she had said proudly, "I've spoiled Elsa on purpose, so she'll always know what's entitled to her." But she contradicted herself, too, as if she couldn't help repeating the laws she'd been raised under. *Women in the theater ruin themselves for others' profit.* Her mother had been a talented pianist and had been asked to tour with a company, but her parents had forbidden it, because a woman who appeared onstage risked her reputation. She liked to say that Elsa's sensibility had been refined, which meant that one day an educated stranger with a face "like a light" would want to marry her. When Elsa argued that she didn't want to be a wife, her mother wept. Usually it was Elsa's father who made her cry, and Elsa wanted to shake her, tell her to stop for God's sake, because crying only made her weaker.

Elsa imagined herself rehearsing a play into the famished evening hours, riding a carriage by herself all the way home. But some nights the fantasy broke apart. She would lie in the dark, feeling as if she had no face, as if she had accidentally given it away to someone or forgotten it on the trolley car, as if her memory would soon be lost, too, like a box that wouldn't open. She made too many mistakes. She said the wrong things.

A few days after her costume had been stolen, she was reading the play *Rose's House* backstage with Natalye, Elsa playing Rose, the silly lover, and Natalye the envious sister. "Does he make you swoon?" was Natalye's line. Natalye put down the book. "Do you still feel it?"

"What?" Looking at Natalye's kohl-smudged eyes, Elsa dreaded the revelation of some other Berlin secret she'd been too stupid to see. "You know, the climax. I certainly don't anymore." When Elsa didn't answer, Natalye sighed and explained that she meant the female version of completion in the sex act.

"Oh, that. Of course." Elsa experienced the ecstatic sweetness of first penetration. What more could there be? A woman couldn't ejaculate like a man; that was only a joke one heard around the dressing room.

"And is it the same with women?" Natalye fluttered her eyelashes. "All the chorus knows, Elsa."

Elsa thought of Kristen's pillowy alabaster breasts, her silky hands, the warm fog of that night and how the next morning she felt as if her skull were cracking open. Then, irritatedly, she remembered how the tall man had straightened up after laughing at that splay of her body stocking.

"It was Kristen who did that to your costume," Natalye said. "Olga told me she came backstage yelling that you were a woman lover and had tried to seduce her."

"That's not what happened." Elsa considered telling Natalye what *had* happened but did not know how to put into words those half-asleep caresses or the way she'd trusted them, and she felt cornered. "I'd like to throttle that girl, or at least make her pay for the stupid mending."

"You can't." Natalye snapped the book closed. "She married her fiancé and left the city."

One night Elsa and Natalye went out with two brothers, Karl and Daniel. Karl was round-headed and bespectacled, with a hoarse, booming voice. Daniel had delicate eyelashes, the nostrils of a pretty girl, and long, stalky legs. He kept his hand in the small of Elsa's back as if he were afraid he might lose her. Karl had a habit of turning to Natalye and making pronouncements: "Women shouldn't wear their hair that way—it suggests lewdness" or "At this hour one should drink only beer." But Natalye just laughed at him.

They were walking on Unter den Linden. "I like it when you girls take out the archery equipment," said Karl. "Those pretty pink bows and arrows."

"I heard that in a few months we're going to be bird women," said Elsa. "Rosa told me."

Natalye shook her head. "No, fairy queens. The wings are enormous. I saw them in the office. They look as if they weigh twenty pounds. Our backs will be aching."

Daniel smiled but didn't laugh. They passed a café where people were eating cakes, each one the color of a flower. Elsa heard violin music coming from an open window above them, the same plaintive bar over and over again.

Karl poked Daniel in the ribs. "We'll let you rest your backs. Women have naturally strong backs anyway, don't they?"

This led to an argument, which culminated in Natalye's drunkenly saying, "Let's go to the Avenue of Dummies. We'll ask Frederick I whether he thinks women are naturally frail."

She meant the Siegesallee, the avenue in the Tiergarten, where the Kaiser had arranged for a line of statues depicting Germany's forefathers to stand on either side of the lane: Albert the Bear, Kaiser Wilhelm I, Otto II, Margrave Heinrich dem Kinde.

"At this hour?" said Karl, pulling Natalye to him, licking her ear.

She shrieked. "Why not?"

"What do you think?" Elsa turned to Daniel, who was quiet, reedy, and raspy-voiced.

"I think it will be dark there."

They took a cab to the Siegesallee. The avenue was empty, except for a ragged woman who staggered down the row of statues singing about a boat, holding out to them what looked like some kind of fruit. The statues, on three-foot pedestals, stood palely on either side of the path, each soberly posed as if he were the only guardian of the property.

All night they had been drinking absinthe and beer, and in the cab Karl had unbuttoned the front of Natalye's dress. Now, as she walked down the avenue, her lacy pink chemise fluttered out of her bodice. "Where is Johann II?" She walked up to one of the statues, shook her head. "That's not him."

"I don't care about Johann II," Elsa said. Daniel pulled her closer to him as they walked.

"Look!" said Karl. "Even the bird shit here is made of marble."

They stood in front of Frederick I, his haughty face turned away, the sword against his thigh, a star of bird lime splashed on his hand. "He looks as if he could use some love from a good German woman," said Karl. "Natalye? Give him a blow." He took out a bill from his wallet and waved it in front of her face. She snatched it out of his hand, laughing.

"Why not? Easier than you."

She climbed up on the pedestal, writhing her body seductively against Frederick I's thigh, then caressed the armor at his crotch. Elsa let out a false laugh, but she felt small and ridiculous under the stars, the witness of so many trees, and she wanted to get away from the scene, pull Daniel to her and let him kiss her neck.

"Do you think he likes me?" Natalye asked.

"Definitely," said Karl.

Natalye put her mouth against the statue's crotch and moved up and down, giggling, while Karl lifted her skirts from below, making hog sounds.

"Come with me," Elsa said to Daniel, pulling him by the hand. "Let's find the one that looks like you."

They walked hand in hand some distance away from the other two, and Elsa took off her dress and spread it for them to lie upon in the grass. She had met Daniel only the night before, but the blood rushing to her center meant that she was in love with him. She cared less now for Arthur, the schoolteacher, with his big ears and easy laugh, although she'd been in love with him a few days earlier. Daniel's lips tasted salty. He stroked her arm, ran a finger over the strap of her chemise. She closed her eyes, aroused by the uncertainty of where his hand might land next on her. She'd at first mistaken the breeze on her neck for his thumb.

Later, when they had bid good night to the brothers, Natalye said, "Karl wasn't my favorite, but at least he wasn't stingy." She shivered. "He sucked on my fingers. I hate it when they do that."

"Why didn't you pull your hand away, then?"

She gave Elsa a pitying look. "That's why you're not getting more than a little pocket change, you know. You show your feelings too easily."

They drank schnapps at Café Bauer and then went back to Natalye's room.

"De Vris fired Margaret, did you hear?" Natalye said, unbuttoning her dress. "God, I don't want to get old."

"By the time we're as old as Margaret, we'll be long gone from the Wintergarten."

"Doing what?"

"I'm going to be the next Clothilde, and you're going to marry a wealthy man with false teeth." Elsa laughed.

"As long as he doesn't slobber."

In the morning Elsa stood in Natalye's nightdress splashing water on her face and under her arms. Natalye, yawning, tossed her a towel and then flinched. "Those aren't spider bites, are they?"

Elsa looked down where Natalye was pointing at her legs. Three red marks the size of pennies had suddenly appeared there. They looked unreal, as if someone had taken red ink to her skin in the middle of the night. She felt a small, despairing puncture in her chest.

Natalye held back her hair from her face. "You have to go to the doctor."

"It can't be that." Elsa tried to laugh but started to cough, as she bent to touch the marks, the skin roughing at their edges.

"Elsa—didn't you use the tonics?"

"Yes . . . usually." She thought of all the times she hadn't.

"Did you look at them all in the light?" Natalye pursed her lips.

"No—how could I do that?" She tried to laugh again. It seemed that if only she could laugh, the sores would turn out to be nothing.

"I do, I insist on it."

"Well, I just used the tonics." There was a blue bottle with a label that promised to make one immune for one hour, the liquid smelling like carrot peels.

Elsa looked down at the lesions again. They formed a triangle just under her knee, where yesterday the skin had been smooth and white, shaven. If only she could will her skin back to the way it was, the way it should be. Little hairs pricked up now around the redness.

"I bet it was that George—the one you thought was so sweet."

Elsa walked through the heavy door of the public hospital. The nurse led her to a room with forty cots and told Elsa to wait there until the doctor could see her. In the corner a woman was weeping, her sobs echoing through the ward. The other women were lying down or sitting up on their cots, gossiping, playing cards, their white gowns bright in the dimness. There was a tall window open in front of Elsa's cot, and she lay back, looking out at the patch of trees swaying through that rectangle.

She had seen the posters at the train stops, a picture of a man and woman kissing with an *X* drawn over their faces. She had heard the frightened talk in the dressing room. How could she have believed she would be immune? She had been with so many men—in bachelor rooms, hotel rooms, empty apartments, the backs of carriages, and in the park. Their members had been long and white, thick and pink, curved to the side, straight and smooth, and she had never seen a sore. Which time had she been infected? She had been so eager that she did not even bother half the time with giving her lover a prophylactic, not believing she was capable of getting pregnant either. Again she saw how she had been a rube, how the men must have chuckled to find a woman so blithe about spreading her legs—though she had called it love.

And there was no cure. The pox ate into your bones; people lost noses and toes. She prayed that she would not lose her nose.

In the corridor a man with no legs sat in a wheelchair, the empty trouser legs flat on the seat, and a woman with a bandage on her head, blisters all over her face like berries, walked in a circle, muttering to herself. The nurse took Elsa to a small room with an examining table. The doctor studied her sores, rubbing his thumb around the surrounding skin near her ankle.

"The signs suggest that you have syphilis." She'd known they were coming, but the words sounded hard. The doctor unhooked the stethoscope from his ears. "Have you ever noticed the sores before?"

"No."

"Do you get fevers, headaches?" His brow wrinkled into three parallel lines.

"No."

"And were you a sickly child?" The impassiveness of his face suggested he had never been afraid of the pox himself, and she resented him for it.

"Yes, I was prone to headaches and colds, and once I had the influenza."

He asked her to show him her teeth, and then he examined her feet, looking closely at each toe.

He nodded, wrote something down in his notebook. "We are going to treat you with mercury. A poultice first, and then tablets. That should alleviate the symptoms. You have the secondary syphilis." He adjusted his eyeglasses, blinking at her. "That means you were born with it."

"Tell me the truth, Doctor." It was just a false excuse people used, like saying one had picked up the pox in a public toilet.

He shook his head. "I don't have time for that. The truth is you were probably treated for it as an infant, and it didn't flare up again until now. Unfortunately, it's not that uncommon."

The clock on the wall seemed to stop, a painful hardness in her eyes. "You're saying my mother was infected? But my mother died of cancer of the womb."

The doctor raised his brow. "The infection can lead to cancer if untreated."

When she heard this, the pictures arranged themselves in a line: her mother's shame at bath time and her fear of the doctor, her father's whores, the gossip between her aunts. It was as if she had been told something she had read once, or heard her mother murmur when she was falling asleep.

"I've been with men, Doctor," Elsa said.

He cleared his throat. "I supposed you had." The Gothic letters on the vision chart looked suddenly sinister. "In the future I suggest you take precautions. After the treatment you will not be infectious, but there is a risk of reinfection, and I'm sure you're aware of the other dangers—gonorrhea, chancre." He left her to get dressed.

Blood of the dragon, they called it, the substance of monsters.

Elsa's mother lit the candelabra on the altar with the crucifix in her bedroom, knowing that it would keep Elsa's father out of the room. "We are just alike, Elsler. We are just alike."

When she was dying, there was a smell in the bed like candle wax and old honey. Her bones so sharp they seemed to click when she moved, her skin gray and opaque as old paper. Elsa could not stand to look at her beautiful mother's slop in the bedpan, at the blond hairs left on the pillow. Elsa sat at the bedside, reading Brentano aloud. *The world seemed to me to be frozen in itself. / In the wild roaring of the stream I heard / Only the wing beats of my own flight whirring!* When she glanced over at her mother's face, her eyes were closed, hands folded over her chest, and she was smiling.

For six weeks, every day, a nurse applied a mercury poultice to Elsa's skin, and she sat naked over a steam heater, so that the mercury could draw out the disease. She took blue pills that tasted of chalk. She vomited every morning, and at night her skin peeled.

In the ward a woman read her tarot cards and said she would become well known at a time when she was most unhappy.

"What does that mean?"

"I'm just telling you what the cards say."

She met a Swedish woman who had lost her foot, who smiled her rosy cheeks when Elsa told her she was going to take acting lessons after she got out of the hospital. Elsa knew that de Vris had surely replaced her by now, but she tried not to think of it. "Write to me when you're famous," the woman said. "I'll come see you at the Schteingart."

Elsa had been joyfully thoughtless, reckless in her affections, but that was all over now.

She read the cracked, torn books that had been donated to the hospital, horrible, maudlin stories about girls who came to the city, behaved recklessly, ignoring their parents, and ended up dead at the hands of a lover or else married to a bore who worked at a bank. She lay on her cot, thinking of all the places she wanted to go. If she joined an acting troupe, she could travel. Paris, Italy, Munich, Budapest. She might meet the famous Clothilde. She might cut off all her hair. She might learn to ride an elephant or play the accordion. She might go climbing the Alps with a blue-eyed dog as her guide.

5

Back at the boardinghouse, Elsa would wake up in the middle of the night and gaze at the still line of light beneath her door, listening to the wind blow laundry against the city houses. For weeks it seemed altogether possible that she could easily vanish—like soap bubbles or dusk or pieces of a dry brown leaf. She had lost her sense of taste and smell. Her body, lying beneath the sheet, felt inseparable from it, just a shape in the world, a lump. Except for the line beneath the door, the darkness around her extended infinitely, beyond the city, pulling her in.

She grew thin, hollow-eyed. Though the mercury treatments had alleviated the leg pains and headaches of the syphilis, she worried about what might happen if she were not lucky. Outside on the streets, she saw disease everywhere. There was a girl in the boardinghouse who, coughing constantly, left blood-flecked rags in the kitchen and lavatory, crumpled like carnations. Frau Hoffman developed a bumpy rash on her hands. On the trams she saw men whose noses had worn away, whores with stubs for arms, women with fevered faces and runny eyes. Jed, the juggler, caught something and lost all his hair, even his eyebrows.

Her own body seemed deceitful, as if the quiver and flame of her desire had only been a disguise for the disease. Her father, who, she was sure, had brought the syphilis home from a whore, was perfectly healthy now and married to Lottie, who was so strict and proper that Elsa imagined the brooch watch she wore was really her heart. She suspected that he'd gone for regular treatments and might even have been cured, but her mother had not gone to the doctor out of shame and instead let the disease worsen. She wondered if her mother's guilt at infecting her was the reason she'd been so lenient. She'd let Elsa run wild in the sea and snap crab claws to her stockings. She had let her eat chocolates for dinner and strudel for lunch, had not minded the way Elsa wore her hats crooked, her blouses stained, or the way she used the good china for a game like checkers and refused to bring her father his beer, even if he yelled for it.

De Vris had hired her back to the chorus, but only because another girl had just left, and he had fined her a week's wages for her long, unexplained absence. Natalye tried to cheer Elsa up. She bought her pastel-colored cakes and white chocolates. She took her to see *Tampa, the Warrior Princess*, with Clothilde, at the Lessing Playhouse. She began the habit of naming everyone who was rumored to have the syph.

"I heard that Sarah Bernhardt has a dose."

They sat in the theater balcony, where a woman was loudly eating peanuts and lovers crumpled together against the back wall. Elsa and Natalye leaned forward to see the stage. "Which play do you want to rehearse next?" asked Natalye.

"I don't know," said Elsa listlessly. "Maybe *The Quest of Simolina* again."

Clothilde wore a fur hat and fur corset with a short kilt. She carried a spear. Her hair was long and wild. In the play she saves her village by stabbing the warrior who had once tried to rape her, but then she is captured. The paper palm fronds and cardboard huts resembled objects from a child's playroom, and most of the actors moved as woodenly as dolls. But Clothilde was magnificent. Even as they were binding up her hands behind her back and she was forced to drop her glinting sword, she held herself like a woman who might survive purely on courage. Though she was captured, her face was proud, and she held it up in the light like a shield. Though the warriors who held her snickered, her voice was queenly: "You will not vanquish me." And in the next scene, there was the rustling fire made of paper, Clothilde burned at the stake, not saying a word.

When the curtain fell, Elsa was surprised to find she was weeping. Natalye handed her a handkerchief. "She looked beautiful in fur, didn't she?"

cஃSo

As the doctor had warned her, she often felt tired, and if she did not eat, her tongue tasted poisonous. She had fevers sometimes at night and stomachaches during the day. "It will pass," she told herself. "The doctor said it will pass."

She did not care to see the men who waited for her backstage, and she took to going home early after the shows. Even though she was not infectious, she might be reinfected, and sometimes, for no apparent reason, the symptoms could return, the doctor had warned. When love struck her again, if it ever did, she promised herself to be vigilant.

Elsa began taking acting lessons at the Dreslau Theater. The instructor was a plump, small man with a round face whose eyes were always opened wide. He spoke as if everything he mentioned—the tone of a woman's voice, the way she held her head, the time of the next lesson—filled him with inexhaustible wonder.

When he blocked out the scenes for them, he moved rapidly over the little stage like a child chasing a ball. He was always telling Elsa that her elocution was superb but her tone erratic. "Don't say that line loudly. You have to learn to whisper from the stage."

Since the outbreak of the syph, her vocal chords had been afflicted, and as much as she tried to modulate her voice, it squirmed all over at high and low pitches.

"Why do you sound so angry?" he would ask her.

He gave her voice exercises: gurgling sounds and repetitions of the same word at different registers. She practiced in front of the mirror, watching her lips and throat, and she screeched and hummed, her voice laddering up and down the scales.

She thought of how well her mother could recite Hölderlin or Heine, until the listener felt the top of his head shimmer and then levitate, until pictures formed in the air around her and she seemed not an unhappy woman, but something else. When Elsa auditioned, she would place her mother wearing a good wool dress and one of the new flat-brimmed hats in the center front seat. "Ask her," she imagined saying to the director. "Ask her what she thought."

Nearly every afternoon she went to auditions, but she had trouble getting past the man who sold trolley tickets at the station. "Why won't you smile? Smile and I'll give you your ticket." He was so smug in his shiny black cap and blue coat. "Where are you going? Tell me and I'll give you your ticket," he would say, holding it up behind the bars.

"Just give me the ticket, you slobbering dog," she would say, to the shock of the ladies behind her.

When he wouldn't, she walked from one end of Berlin to the other.

During the months after she left the hospital, she devoted herself to reading and practicing for auditions. She saved to buy books secondhand, stayed in the library as long as she was allowed. Between shows at the Wintergarten, she memorized parts, then rehearsed them in her room to the washstand and bedpost.

The directors stared up at her with blank, disinterested eyes and thanked her perfunctorily afterward. Many of the parts for young women were tragic, and she learned to make herself cry by holding her eyes open until they watered. She focused on what the instructor had told her. Keep your voice in its little box—it can move around in that box padded with silk—but it does not want to escape. Still, unpredictably, her voice would deepen and become suddenly loud, and when she had intended to say something in a delicate way, the line would crackle as if she were a street hawker selling sausage. The words "I will not be here in the spring" brought shocking guffaws. A speech that ended with "Lionel, do not go," incited annoying giggles from the audience of fellow auditionees.

On Tuesdays she practiced the lines for her parts with Natalye, who was getting more and more bored with the project. Natalye had begun to work at a bordello two nights a week. "Aren't you sick of boardinghouses?" she said to Elsa. "All those people watching you come and go, the dirty lavatories, no private baths. In six months I'll have enough money to get my own rooms." She wanted Elsa to come work with her at Madame Renault's.

"When I'm an actress, I'll get my own rooms," Elsa said.

Natalye examined her fingernails. "But why wait?"

One night Elsa went to a party near the cabaret district with a woman she had met at an audition. Looking disdainfully at Elsa's shoes, the woman snorted and walked away as soon as they arrived, leaving Elsa at the door. The large, dark room smelled of spices, and people clustered around the candles. There were only a few other women at the party, and the men were all talking earnestly to one another, smoking and drinking. Most wore shabby suits, but one man wore a cape and another a long black robe like a monk's.

The man in the monk's robe came over to her and introduced himself, offering her a glass of wine. His name was Melchior, but he told her to call him Mello.

"Already you don't look happy here," he said. "Did Rachel bring you from the theater? She is always bringing us actresses, and they always get bored and leave us."

"Why aren't you and your friends more charming, then?" Elsa replied. Against the black of his robe, his face appeared large and serious.

"Are you going to leave?"

"It's too early to tell," she said. He looked so unlike the men who appeared at the stage door, with their empty, jovial eyes. His face was pensive, as if he were remembering some wound he'd suffered.

When she told him that she was in the chorus at the Wintergarten, he grinned. "You must be joking."

"Not at all."

He took her hand and led her to the divan. His monk's robe was tied with a rope, and there were medallions at the ends that clanked together when he sat down. The effect of this vestment on a noncleric, both sacrilegious and flamboyantly earnest, made her wonder what he worshipped.

"I can see that you're very graceful," he said.

Another man was already sitting in the chair across from them. "Graceful is one word for it."

The man's animosity surprised her. Mello said, "Don't be a snob, Ernst."

Mello moved closer to Elsa. "Ignore him. He just lost a patron. Tell me, do you go to the theater often?"

Mello made his living forging stained glass. He said he had recently been commissioned to design the window work for the Romanische Haus, and the imperial court had also taken notice of him. "Everyone wants to be in a place that seems holy, because nothing is anymore," he said. "The churches are corrupt, the priests hypocrites, and the closest thing we have to a place of worship is the factory."

She liked his seriousness, the way he looked at her as if she might suddenly break into blossom. He led her to the window and showed her the pond behind the house, where ice-skaters moved in the orange light of torches arranged around the pond. A woman's skirt fluttered up in the darkness, then disappeared; a man glided across the pale yellow ice, his back rigidly straight.

The man who had laughed at her was holding out a drink for Mello.

"Go away, Ernst," he said.

One of the skaters blazed across the lighted space, the flame of a torch trailing behind him. Ernst jiggled the glass in front of Mello's face. "Are there any skates in the house?"

"Heavens no," said Mello. "I hate to exert myself. Do you like to skate?" he asked Elsa.

There was a pond in the forest in Swinemünde where she had gone at night, finding her way with a gas lamp, going around and around as fast as she could until she'd exhausted herself and forgotten her anger. "Never like that, arm in arm. One might as well walk. I like to feel the blade cut the ice, to work up enough speed to make sparks."

6

That spring the ticket seller at the station grew more and more meddlesome. He would not give her a ticket unless she told him her name. For once there was no one in line behind her, but she was in a hurry to get to Mello's, so she told him, "Marie. My name is Marie."

"Now, Marie," he said, leaning toward her, the pink mole on his cheek whiskered like a mouse snout. "When can I take you for a beer?"

"I hate beer."

"What about a kiss, then?" He dangled the ticket in front of the grate.

"I see why they have to keep you behind bars," she said.

He shrugged.

She walked all the way to Mello's. By the time she got there, Tomas, Joffrey, Christof, and Richard had arrived. A stick of incense pointed from the top of a skull that sat on the upright piano. Mello's latest stained-glass work, a flower blooming from the mouth of a dove, hung from the ceiling on ropes, the colors shot through with light from the gas lamp behind it. Books were strewn on the floor and on tables, and the men were already talking excitedly.

After most of the wine was drunk, they gathered around Elsa and studied her face as if it were a work of art that might instruct them.

"She's exactly like a pagan Madonna," said Mello. "Isn't she?"

"Maybe quattrocentro," said the man in the striped suit.

"You do not need to do a thing," said Tomas. "Don't even move."

"But I hate sitting still, even for the sake of flattery." She laughed at the way they all looked at her so piously. "I'm not any kind of Madonna."

Her education was spotty—after the gymnasium, only her mother's books, an English tutor who helped her read Shakespeare. It might have been shrewder to keep quiet, but she saw how Mello argued with his friends, how he smiled and leaned forward when they raised their voices.

These evenings at Mello's, the men so casually mentioned Hegel, Augustine, Apuleius, as if the authors had embarrassed themselves at the most recent party. Mello wore his monk's robe, he said, to show his devotion, and when his guests allowed it, he delivered homilies on the sacredness of art. Listening to them, Elsa wanted to educate herself, but not at the cost of pretending to know less than she did. All that time they'd been at the university, she'd been thinking and writing in her notebook, and who was to say her research was any less important? She had as much to say as any of them.

On the divan beside her, Tomas and Joffrey discussed Kant, and across the room Christof and Mello argued about whether or not colors corresponded with smells.

Mello said, "Art is the life behind the life—that is why there are all these correspondences between sound and color."

"There is no sound to a color, Mello. That's mystical flimflam," said Christof, who took an incense stick from the table and held it to his nose.

"I disagree. Absolutely. There are sounds attached to colors," Elsa said. The two men stopped talking and stared at her. "It's a matter of having the vision to penetrate to them."

There was a clinking of glasses and the scratch of a match being lit. She was the only woman, and she felt the men's eyes on her, their impatient fingers drumming, cigarette and pipe smoke fogging the room.

Marcus smirked at her. "You think it's a kind of intelligence, then, this vision."

Her face burned. She and her mother used to play a game in which they assigned each color a smell—pink was almonds; yellow, beer; red, cut grass—but she knew it would have sounded ridiculous to relate the pleasure of the game to outsiders.

There was a timidity she often felt in this company, and hated. "No."

Mello's eyes were on her as he leaned back against the sofa. She'd made love to him for the first time the night before. To these men it was only his interest in her that made her an exception among women, and they probably wouldn't listen. But that made her want to talk all the more loudly.

She felt her arms tremble and folded them tightly. "I don't think intelligence and intellect are the same. Intelligence is only brilliant common sense, a notion of the material—business, archaeology. Intellect is more of a spiritual property, an instinct developed until it comes to one's consciousness."

She lifted her chin, waiting for one of them to attack her theory, but none of them did.

Elsa and Natalye were soaking their feet in warm water before the last show, when they would have to stand again for a half hour on the stage. "It's amazing what this work does to one's feet," Elsa said. "I feel as if I'm growing a claw here." She reached down to touch the hard knob of her second toe.

"I earned enough last night to quit the Wintergarten," said Natalye, splashing the water a little with her foot.

"That's impossible. Who were you with—the Kaiser?"

Natalye shook her head. "It was two men, with me between them. They paid me so I wouldn't tell anyone."

"Obviously it wasn't enough."

"Oh, don't be a cow. I'm not telling anyone their names—they are important officials." She wore her hair piled up now in a way that made her head look heavy and proud.

"Well, are you going to quit?"

"I gave notice. I'm going over to Madame Renault's for another night. Why don't you come with me? It's so much better than this. Think of it, no more Deadly de Vris."

Elsa looked at Natalye's new dress with fluted sleeves. An admirer wanted to keep an apartment for Natalye, buy her satin petticoats and perfumes. She was saving to buy a Victrola and could go to sleep early now if she felt like it.

"I can't go to the bordello, Natalye." Elsa knew that as an actress she had a tendency for melodrama—but she could not help saying it. "I want to devote myself to art." Since she'd begun spending so much time with Mello and his friends, she felt purposeful, as if she'd finally discovered the tribe to which she belonged.

Natalye rolled her eyes. "You are getting so proper, you'd think you'd joined the church."

The night before, for the first time, Elsa had met another woman at Mello's salon. She was older, somewhere near fifty, an authoress who was about to leave for Paris, where she would write her next book. The men had gathered around her, leaning forward to listen to her hoarse voice, and the woman's intelligence seemed to emanate from her smooth, pale forehead like a lamp beneath the skin.

"Not the church at all," Elsa said now. "But my life doesn't seem quite as trivial anymore. Mello said it often happens when one reads Nietzsche."

"Oh, poo on Mello. How can you take a man seriously when he goes around in that dress?"

"It's not a dress. It's a monk's robe."

"Even worse."

Kaiser Wilhelm had put so many soldiers on the streets that on certain blocks they outnumbered ordinary men, and there were frequent military parades past the Reichstag—flanked by women throwing flowers.

Then one day Elsa realized that not all of these men in uniform were soldiers—some were train conductors, waiters, lumbermen. It made her nervous sometimes to see so many of them, as if they were all about to unholster pistols or swords. Everyone, it seemed, wanted to be a little Kaiser, the man who made the rules. Women stared after men in uniform. Men followed a military jacket with envious looks. An imperial militiaman got the best seat in a restaurant, credit at Wertheim's Department Store.

The trolley ticket seller's suit was blue, with useless stripes on the suit pocket. The more frequently she began to go to Mello's house, the more the ticket seller annoyed her. He winked at her and asked what she would give him for a ticket. "For a girl like you, a ride is expensive."

If there were men in line behind her, they would smirk when she looked their way. Incidents like this made Elsa feel as if the city had turned against her, only because some rotten man found her pretty. It made her want to wear a sack over her face.

"Just give me the ticket."

"Only if you smile. Why won't you smile?"

She bared her teeth, grunted insistently, and he pushed the ticket through the wire grate.

There was a pawnshop that Elsa liked to visit because it sold a collection of jade baubles that set off the red tones in her hair. One day she was browsing when she saw a Prussian officer's uniform displayed on the racks. Its style was out of date, but it still looked official, navy blue with brass buttons and a cap with a shiny black bill. She held the trousers against her, and they seemed about her size.

"Where did you get this?" she asked the proprietor, a fat man with a raspy voice.

He shrugged. "A widow."

"How much?"

"What do you want with that?"

"It's for a play."

"Two marks," he said.

She bought the uniform and took it home. She put it on, pulled back her hair in the cap, and rubbed some pencil dust over her upper lip and chin. An actress needed to practice all the possible parts. She saluted herself in the mirror and frowned, thinking she resembled her cousin, Hans, who was thin and arrogant.

She went out into the street and walked down Friedrichstrasse at a stiff gait. Women turned and stared after her longingly. As she passed a shop window, she caught the sharp envy of the clerk. The crowds parted on the street to give her more space. Two little boys followed her, calling, "Mister! Mister!" She had to press her lips together so as not to smile.

Thinking she would show Natalye, she went to the train. She stood at the end of the line, behind a plump woman wearing a bustle as big as her head, and saw the ticket seller's bland face as he called out prices and made change. The line moved rapidly, and when she reached the front, she spoke in her lowest-pitched voice. "You've been reported."

The clerk's face whitened, and he shook his head. "Sir, you must be mistaken. He pushed his badge through the grate. "Not me."

Elsa looked at the badge and said his name. "Adolf Swenzler, yes, that is
the name. You are trying to extract extra fare from ladies."

His face blanched behind the metal bars, and he began to fiddle with
some papers. "No. That's impossible. I've been at this job for five years, sir.
Not a single bad report."

Elsa stood her ground. Behind her she heard whispering, a man clearing
his throat.

The ticket seller leaned close to the bars, winked. "Please. I never did
that. I only joke a little sometimes."

"In inappropriate ways?"

"No, of course not." He scratched his ear.

"You know the regulations. There's the reputation of the city to uphold."

"Yes, sir." Elsa suppressed a smile as she took her ticket and went onto
the train. The men on the car snuck glances at her jacket. She knew they
were trying to gauge her status, confused by the uniform's lack of stripes.

When she arrived at the boardinghouse where Natalye lived, the land-
lady, taking her for a suitor, led her into the dank parlor with fringed uphol-
stery. Natalye approached Elsa slowly, her head cocked to one side, bottom
lip jutting out indecisively. When she was less than an arm's length away,
she grinned and reached up to knock off Elsa's cap. "My God, you almost
fooled me—what are you doing?"

Elsa told her how she'd finally got her revenge on the ticket seller, and
Natalye laughed so hard she weaved around the sofa and chairs, holding
her side.

7

There were times when Elsa was out walking, when the sun hit on
people's hats and gleamed on the horses' coats, and the trolley car
passed by, jangling and laughing, a woman's skirt trailing out the
back, and there was a smell of oranges from the fruit cart, and she felt all at
once how much world was missed in every second. She wanted to stretch
each of her senses, to hear what someone was saying across the street, to be
able to see the pupils of the horse racing by, to feel weather foretold on her
skin, taste air and water, note the happiness and gloom imprinted on faces in
a tramcar. She wanted to pay closer attention. When she looked up from her
book at the café, she felt this most acutely, seeing the soft waves in a
woman's hair, the shadow lace from a caned-back chair, hearing someone
outside whistling.

From Mello's bookshelves she took Flaubert, von Eichendorff, Novalis
Shaw, Rilke, and she read all day, in her little room, with the shades drawn,
until it was time for her to go to an audition or to the Wintergarten. *Only we
have reached the supreme goal: / First to pour ourselves out in a stream, / Then
to break up into small drops, / And also to sip at the same time.* Mello's books
seemed as much a part of him as his monk's robe and longish hair, and,
reading them, she felt her brain growing in circumference and intricacy, one
long ribbon reaching down her throat for her heart.

One day they were waiting to see his friend Richard's play, and Mello became enraged when he spotted Flaubert's *A Sentimental Education* in her bag.

"I have been searching for that all week! Who told you to take it?"

"You said I could take anything."

"Not anything!"

She was shocked at his snarling mouth, how he shook his fist at her. Out of instinct she fought back. "Take it, then! I didn't steal it."

Just then the dingy curtain opened, and his attention was drawn to the play. The theater was small, the seats rickety. Richard had complained loudly that, because of the Kaiser, who had taken it upon himself to define "true art," all of Richard's plays had been segregated to minor theaters like the Kammerspiele. Worse still, if an official saw one of his plays, it might be banned.

In the play that night, *Gustave and Lucinda*, one character died because he ate too many blueberries, and his best friend owned a blueberry factory. Someone was always dying in Richard Hauptman's plays, his exposure of hypocrisy a tonic. Afterward the world appeared muddier than ever, but it made one feel clearer inside oneself, the stomach muscles exhausted and sinuses cleaned from laughter.

At Mello's house the next night, they were discussing the barbaric cruelty of *Medea*. Richard said Medea wasn't any more hardhearted than some whores he knew, and Tomas argued that a wife abandoned for a younger woman would likely become suicidal, not murderous—it was a flaw in the play. "No woman would make that sacrifice," said Ernst.

Elsa inhaled the sweet smoke from Tomas's pipe, heard the fire popping in the grate. She could see which direction the discussion was bound to go— women are this, women are that. "There were sacrifices nearly every year in Swinemünde. Out in the countryside, gentlemen, don't fool yourselves— the *Volk* are barbarians."

"I've heard about the animal sacrifices—for the harvest, isn't it?" said Mello.

"Yes, my own father killed a goat every October. It was his only religion." Lying about her father almost satisfied her, though it was true that he liked to slaughter animals, feel the blood on his hands and touch the squirming organs.

When the conversation turned to music, Elsa, standing up to get a cigarette from the box on the mantel, said, "My mother was a concert pianist." She still felt a lack and a frenzy to fill it. "As a young woman, she toured Paris, Frank-furt, Prague. Her favorite artist was Chopin, and she went to Paris the most frequently because the French were mad for him. Once, just before she went on the stage, she received a note saying that her lover had died of influenza. She read the words just as the audience had assembled. Rather than weep, she told me, she played, banging on the keys until her fingers bled." She glanced at Mello, who lounged back with his feet up on the couch, his bare ankles visible between socks and black robe. "Afterward she ran off the stage. Her vision was clouded by tears, and she ran into the arms of my father, who was at the time a professor of zoology at the Sorbonne. He mistook her tears for passion and was smitten."

Mello smiled in a way not at all double-edged. Usually she could not guess what his expressions meant, but now she knew he was charmed. "And he gave up his post?"

"There was important research in Swinemünde—having to do with the Black Sea. He studied the fish there. And my mother never played the piano again."

"Where is she now?" Tomas said, lighting a match. She leaned forward, and he touched it to the end of her cigarette.

"My mother . . ." Elsa saw the corpse in the black coffin, the gray, sunken face, the dry, cracked lips. "My mother is remarried to an impoverished count—and they live in Sardinia. I rarely see her, and of course I've kept it from her, my career on the stage."

Richard chuckled.

She saw Natalye now only on those nights when she was not at Madame Renault's, and they took up reading Richard's play, *Spring Chariots*.

"I'm sure that eventually I will act one of Richard's parts," said Elsa.

"Oh, of course. He would insist."

Natalye's dresses were finely tailored, in expensive bright silks. She had taken to wearing a red wig, and she wore rouge on her lips and cheeks and, Elsa was sure, on her nipples now, too. She had moved to the bordello.

"*Man does not need only supper. He needs sustenance, the heat of a hearth,*" read Natalye. She looked up from the pages. "I know we are in different circles now, but that doesn't sound like anything I've ever heard a woman say."

"It's not supposed to be literal," said Elsa. "That woman is a joke. We're supposed to laugh at her."

"But it isn't funny either."

"Well." Elsa smiled. "If the actress fit the part?"

When Richard was at Mello's house, she practiced showing him her array of faces. She told him her insights about his characters, but he listened coldly, answering her with a curt phrase and averting his eyes.

Christof was the friend of Mello's who paid her the most attention. His miniatures, intricate paintings of love scenes, as tiny as insects, were the favorites of the Baroness von Schliegel, and he could live for a year on the sale of one miniature to her. Elsa and Christof often sat together in the corner gossiping about the baroness, whom Elsa admired for her ability to cultivate artists and for the witty things Christof reported her saying. She seemed like a woman who'd ride a bicycle through the Kaiser's palace, uninvited, and then ask for a glass of sherry.

"You make Richard nervous," Christof said to her one night. "He's attracted to you, but he doesn't know it."

Elsa watched the transparent wax drip from the candle onto the brass candelabra and caught a drop on her finger, let it harden to a petal. "Well, I only want to act in one of his plays."

Christof laughed so hard he spit out his drink. "Elsa—you! As one of his hausfraus?"

"Why not?"

"You'll have to start keeping quiet, then. I don't think you can do it."

She resented his jibe at her acting ability, but to imagine herself demure and silent gave her an itch as if she'd suddenly put on a tight wool jacket. "I hate to waste ideas."

"Exactly. That's why you frighten them. I've watched their faces when you stand up and deliver one of your little speeches. They look as if they might belch rabbits." Elsa had always thought she'd amused them, that they were only surprised that a chorus girl would care a whit for their ideas. "They like my speeches," she said.

"I suppose so." He pushed the cork back into the wine bottle. "But it's in the way they enjoy my stories about Franken seducing bellboys at the Hotel Bristol—they can only take it in small doses."

Elsa had made the mistake of letting her aunt Ida know she was in the city and where she lived, and Ida had written to her father. In October a letter came from him.

I understand that you are exposing yourself in some kind of burlesque. You must know how this pains me. For as long as you choose to live that life, the family charges you with Unsittlichkeit. *You do not belong to us. Your loving father.*

Loving. The word read like a profanity. The letter only proved that she was a zebra in a family of horses.

But she was surprised how his words could still cut her. *Some kind of burlesque.* She remembered riding with him in a carriage down to the shore, his large thigh on the seat next to her little-girl legs, how he kept saying, "There will be sweets—what kind do you want? Apricot? Chocolate?" She remembered the night years later, when they all stood in the neighbor's attic, where her mother had hidden, apples and nuts on the floor around the crate on which her mother perched, not recognizing anyone. For days he had driven the carriage around in the cold, asking if anyone had seen his wife. They were a family who almost never touched one another, but that night in the attic he put his arms around Elsa, and the warm weight of them had seemed to keep her from slipping through the floorboards.

But he was the one who'd poisoned her mother and her with his blood. She couldn't ignore it coursing through her veins—his stubbornness and temper, and the disease—so why should he be able to deny it with just a word? But he had. She imagined him refusing to say her name, the way he would turn his head and pretend not to hear it when some person who didn't know better asked after her.

One night, on Mello's desk, Elsa saw the framed photograph of a sweet-looking girl. She was blond and stood next to a flowering tree, coyly grasping one of the branches. Her wide eyes and parted lips were designed to be as enticing as a cake.

"Who is this, your sister?" Elsa held out the picture frame to him.

He grabbed it from her hand and put it back on the desk. "Don't touch that."

"Who is it?"

"My fiancée."

Her eyes stung as she looked again at the bosomy girl, skin like frosting. She imagined him licking it.

"When were you planning to tell me?"

"Why should I tell you? I haven't seen her in six months."

"But you're going to marry her."

"Yes." He pulled Elsa into the bedroom and pointed to the picture of her on the wall above his bed, the one he'd asked one of his friends to photograph, all angles and long arms like knives. "This is where you belong." He pulled her down onto the bed, unbuttoning her dress.

The next night, after the show, she put on the Prussian officer's uniform for Mello, but with her rouge and long earrings. When she arrived, he was writing something, drinking wine, and he did not look up for several minutes after she took off her coat.

When he finally blew out the candle and looked up, she said, "Would I fool you?"

He stared at her, walked closer.

She was sure he loved her better than the cake. "I fooled the train clerk."

He slapped her so hard she fell back onto the wall. "You are ridiculous," he said, the black robe swirling as he marched into the next room.

She touched her cheek, felt the pain starring her temple. There was a flick of memory, her father hitting her against a door, but she said to herself, "Mello has no sense of humor," and imagined how she would tell him this later. "I should have known it when you said you didn't like cabarets."

She went into the bedroom. He took his time, but eventually he joined her, smelling of wine. "I would like to hit you with this." In the lamplight he held a switch of branches. "You've embarrassed me."

Elsa turned onto her stomach, thinking that the little cake would never have the sex sense to indulge Mello in all the ways she had. "Yes, but don't hurt me."

"You would like me to, wouldn't you?" he said. This was one practice that she'd heard about but had not experienced, "the delights of the birch." The pain, she thought, would enliven the nerves to ecstasy. The branch came crashing down, and she lost her breath.

Where the stinging spread on her back, she felt his lips dabbing at her. Tears leaked from her shut eyes, and, turning to him, she wanted his exquisite kisses. When he collapsed over her, his forehead was wet, and he gripped her arms tightly, smiling down at her, grateful.

The note came for her at Frau Hoffman's on stationery bordered with hand-drawn red, blue, and yellow diamonds trimming the top and bottom of the page. *Dearest Elsa, I have much work to do. I am afraid there is no more time for wine, women, and song, and so I must say good-bye. Mello.*

She crumpled up the paper, opened the window in her room, and threw it out.

She paced between the washstand and her bed, rehearsing all the things she wanted to say to him: he was compromising his own ideals; he could not deny how his temperature rose when she pressed against him, how he relied on her for conversation. She searched her memory, uncovered the time she had forgotten to wipe her feet and tracked dirt onto his white rug, and another instance when he had looked at her sharply after she interrupted him to explain her definition of the hypocrites. Was the little cake so much better? Outside her door she heard the seamstresses talking about the dust on the banister, and she smelled Frau Hoffman's beef boiling downstairs.

Elsa had been planning to live with Mello, to be out of Frau Hoffman's sight—and away from the meek seamstresses and surly cooks, who watched her disapprovingly when she left the house just as they were arriving home from work. The propriety in that house—the stockings hung neatly on the banister and the ringing of alarm clocks—was limiting her thinking.

Days later Christof confirmed that Mello had been married. "Her father is very wealthy, and he won't have to worry anymore about selling his glass. He wants to keep all of it for his own house."

"I don't want to hear this," Elsa said. It was his fetish of purity, she thought, that had made him so feverish to marry—the little cake was probably a virgin, or pretended to be.

"I only tell you this because you should see how selfish he is—he always was selfish, but you didn't see it. Now you have no choice, and it's for your own good."

"Don't tell me that."

"It's true."

She thought of the way Mello drank wine, considering the color in the glass before he brought it to his lips, how he hummed when she got into the bed, pulling her beneath him. She thought of how he would get suddenly possessive of a book he hadn't read in years, how he always ate a particular peppered sausage at lunch. "Don't you see? I saw his selfishness—that was why I loved him."

Christof silently continued rolling his cigarette.

Natalye had not turned up for their usual meeting, and Elsa was so distraught she went to see her at Madame Renault's. It was a nondescript house with white shutters, not far from Welspricht's Department Store, and Elsa pounded the brass cherub knocker. The woman who answered the door wore a neat blue dress, and she had small brown eyes and wrinkles around her mouth from laughing. Elsa could hear the chatter of women inside, smelled the perfumes and cigarette smoke. "Natalye?" The woman sighed and flung out her hand. "Natalye left a week ago and took everything, even my pillows. And she still owes me money."

There was a fluttering in Elsa's chest. "Where did she go?"

The woman frowned. "If I knew that, I'd go find her myself, wouldn't I? Those pillows were silk." She slammed the door.

Elsa went home and put on the Prussian officer's uniform. She dabbed some pencil dust above her lip and more to darken her eyebrows. Already she did not feel like herself and moved woodenly, without thinking, as she wrapped a band of cloth over her small breasts. In the mirror she was a man with red, swollen eyes. She put on her monocle.

On the street two women smiled at her, and she nodded. Carriages passed, the horses trotting nobly. Occasionally one of the drivers, looking down from his perch, would salute her.

The women's skirts were bright as tulips, the shop windows silvered in the light. The electric streetcar whirred up the next block, and a crowd of schoolgirls chattered past her, staring. She felt her muscles hardening as she walked, her heartbeat strengthening in the air that smelled pleasantly of smoke.

She turned past the garden near Friedrichstrasse and walked down an empty street, full of houses with narrow, sharp roofs, like pointed wizard hats, the fences curled scripts of black metal. Ahead of her she spotted a soldier who walked with a slight unevenness that she at first thought might be a limp.

When he was a few feet away, about to pass her, his face distracted and blurred, he glanced at her coat and stopped. "Wait there."

She nodded to him and kept walking, not meeting his eyes.

He caught her by the sleeve. "Which militia?"

She turned her head and deepened her voice. "The seventh."

"Liar." He wrenched the sleeve so it knotted against her arm. "Where did you get that uniform? Don't you know it's illegal to impersonate an officer?"

He was shorter than she was and had a face like an angry squirrel's. She smelled the beer on his breath.

She wrenched away, but he caught her again, his arm around her neck. "Answer me, mister. Where did you get that?"

The tree branches twisted overhead. A bird twittered at the edge of one, cocked its tiny black head.

"Pfister's Pawnshop," she said.

He pushed her to the ground. As her face hit the cold stone, her teeth cut into her tongue. He kicked her in the side. Then he was yanking the jacket from her shoulders. "You idiot faker—I'll beat the beans out of you," he said. He kicked her again in the hip and seemed to be weeping as he harangued her. "A man must be special in order to serve, not just any man. Not a louse like you—are you a Jew? Is that it?" He turned Elsa over and spit in her face. She was sobbing, and the pencil dust had smeared, her cap fallen away from her head.

"My God!" His mouth fell open, and he pulled back, squinting. "A woman?"

When she saw the way his features scrambled, she was no longer afraid of him. She felt monstrously exposed, as if the pain in her mouth were newly grown fangs, as if scales formed through the blood on her shirt, and she wasn't sure what she was.

At first he extended his hand to help her up. Then he took it back and wiped it on his sleeve as if she'd soiled him. He turned and went running down the street.

8

Later in her life, Elsa would become fond of saying that each of her three husbands stole something from her. It made her past sound less maudlin. It made her husbands sound more devious and implied she had a passion for thieves, men who took what they wanted, graceful on their feet.

August, her first husband, stole her beauty.

Christof introduced her to August Lydell in the lobby of a playhouse, and for several months afterward, she would see him at artists' parties or at the cafés along Friedrichstrasse. Assuming he belonged to Christof's man-preferring crowd, she noticed the pleasant, weary tone in his voice, the intelligent spokes of lines around his eyes. She heard through Greta Schwartz, an actress, that August Lydell, though said to be too fond of hashish, was much in demand for his stage sets after he'd designed the houses for *Marshland* and the Oriental palace for *Dreams of the Siege*. "He has an eye," she said, "for the way a person crosses over a threshold, for the difference—to the audience's emotion—between walking under a low ceiling or a high one. But he won't be doing sets much longer."

"Why not?"

"Why design toy buildings when one can design the real thing?"

A few months later, there was August Lydell's name in the newspaper, citing the photography studio he'd designed—a plain white façade with a green stone dragon bulging out of it, a long spiked tail that swirled over the door. One reviewer called him "the vulgar August Lydell," and another called him the first visionary since Walpole.

Finally she'd been hired as part of the acting troupe of the Werschmidt Theater, on the outskirts of the city. When she received the note that she'd been chosen, she screamed so loudly that Frau Hoffman came banging into her room thinking she'd been hurt. When she told de Vris that she was leaving the Wintergarten for a place in an acting troupe, he said, "Sure, sure. Say hello to Natalye," and winked at her. She didn't care. She would send him the playbill, autographed.

The theater's other actors, three men and two women, were in their forties and fifties, and the director kept referring to her as "child." She finally corrected him one day. "I am twenty-three years old, Herr Proctor."

"Of course, yes. It's just your youth—It overwhelms me." He squinted behind his glasses. "It will do us so much good."

Since Mello, Elsa had taken many lovers—a curly-haired artist who taught her to look away from the center of a painting; a book critic who introduced her to Karla Scheine, whose city novels she came to admire; and Tristan, who used kohl and rouge and played the harp. All of the men had been disappointing in one way or another.

It wasn't until the party at the home of Gerhardt Schreiner that Elsa took a serious interest in August. Schreiner was a famous collector. Under a glass dome, a cigarette smoked by Sarah Bernhardt. On the wall, a birdcage that had once belonged to Martin Luther. Resting on a little black pillow, the bullet that had wounded the Baron Frierstag. The guests huddled around each display with their drinks before moving on to gaze at the next one, as if the man's house were a museum.

August was soft in the middle with broad, rounded shoulders and stocky legs. His hair was thinning at his forehead, and the folds in his cheeks made his face look like a pinched heart. There was a boyishness in him that kept up even though he was long past being a boy. He began talking about houses, the spaces where one was meant to be watched or to watch, the spaces meant for privacy. "In Japan," August said, "all the rooms are more open. They do not share our notions of privacy." He had traveled to Tokyo the year before and was designing a Japanese set for the Bulding Theater.

"How do they make love, then, out in the open?" She registered the shock in his face and grinned.

"Uh, there are screens." He had a soft, even voice, as if he carefully considered each word.

"I saw some of those screens at an exhibit, I think. I had no idea they were so erotic."

When they went back inside, he pointed out the bone in Schreiner's collection, said to be the finger of St. Jude, and the net that Lady Guinevere had supposedly used over her face to keep away the flies.

That night she was struck by his intensity, how he seemed to be looking through the eye of a telescope at the dream of his design. He was an artist, not someone lounging in saloons smoking cigars and making pronouncements.

She had the part of one of the sisters in *The Three Women of Frankfurt,* a not especially popular or well-received play, but somehow August had heard about it. When she came out from backstage the next night, she was surprised to see him standing there, and then she knew from the way his face opened up to her that she had been mistaken about his preference for men.

"Hello, August," she said. "Are you a Niederbeier fan?"

"To be honest, he's not one of my favorites," he said, and then invited her out to dinner.

She wasn't attracted to him at first, until he began to talk about his designs. All those currents washing through his face, whirlpools and coldness. He understood that a city was alive, that its streets and alleyways and buildings were not discrete pieces of concrete and mortar but interconnected organisms that grew out of the soil and grass. His buildings sprouted leaves around the borders of doors; ivy twisted up their walls, and birds stood permanently perched on eaves.

At the National Gallery, they stood in front of Adolph Menzel's *Das Balkonzimmer,* a painting of a room without people, the curtain blowing in the window, the mirror reflecting an easy chair, an empty wall with peeled paint. "It's a portrait of emptiness," Elsa said sadly. "I have no doubt that room is very cold and too bright."

"You see it with your entire body don't you? That's the way it should be. Look at the yellow there on the wall—"

They walked farther into the gallery, past the paintings by Karl Friedrich Schinkel.

"I know that he's considered a great painter," she said. "But I've never liked his subjects."

"That's because you don't have enough respect for landscapes. I've noticed you don't pay much attention to the spaces around you."

"What do you mean?"

"You get lost in the city often, don't you?" It surprised her he'd come to know this so soon after they met. "Then again, why should you care for Schinkel if you don't feel anything in your bones?"

His casual intelligence brought back the timidity she hadn't felt since she'd first gone to Mello's salon. But she was canny enough now to know how to suppress it, and it had to be done quickly. "My mother used to say something like that. She was a concert pianist. Mahler once gave her a necklace with diamonds from India, each one as large as your fingernail. She believed the diamonds emitted an energy that sweetened the timing of music."

"When was this?" August linked his arm in hers, and they wound their way toward the staircase.

"When we lived in Vienna after my father died. Mahler was very nice— though I was just a girl. He liked it when I made up words for his tunes."

Her lie felt genuine in a way that Swinemünde never had, as if she'd finally reclaimed for her mother what she had deserved all along.

August fought against the advent of the mechanized object—the cup, the button, the candle, once unique and imperfect, now factory-made and identical to one another, no longer reflected the artisan's soul. This, he believed, was why the bourgeois were so spiritless—they bought too many mass-produced goods.

"Aren't you overestimating the power of an ordinary object?" Elsa said. His intensity thrilled her, but she needed to test it.

"No, I don't think so. Why? Every day we have the opportunity to create, to make the ordinary beautiful."

"But, August, I don't really care which cup I use."

"Ah, but you should. It's a waste to use anything that's merely functional."

"What about a toothbrush?"

He would shake his head. "It should be hand-molded, with bristles made from real hair."

"What about a toilet?"

"Now you're being silly."

"Not if you mean what you say."

"Okay, it should be made from marble, with engraving."

"I challenge you to get yourself a toilet like that."

He was the first man she set out to make fall in love with her, and because she felt in awe of him, she teased him to calm her nerves.

"August is an unfortunate name, an awkward name to get past, like an ugly door. It's a name for an emperor or a king, not an architect," she told him. "So formal."

"Call me Tse, then," he said. "It's a Chinese word."

"Of course." Sometimes he called her Ti, which he said was the Chinese word for yellow, the royal color.

She heard him tell a friend at a party that he wanted his buildings to assault the eye, to make a person swoon or go mad for a few moments. Elsa goaded him. "That's an ambitious goal for a bank, say, isn't it? Or a shoe store?"

"No."

"Really?" Elsa went on. "Do you want money confettiing the streets? Shoes on people's heads?"

August laughed. "She takes everything I say so literally."

It was around this time that she decided to give up the corset. Someone always had to help her with it in order for it to be closed properly, and then, even with the ribs made of rubber and not whalebone, the pressure at her waist had sometimes made her nauseous and dizzy. The S of a woman's thrust-out breast and buttocks had come to seem sinister to her, like the shape of a snake about to strike. After the padding she had to wear at the Wintergarten, she wanted to assume her natural shape, small breasts, small waist, thin hips—more like a stalk or a tree than an S. August liked her this way—natural shapes, he believed, were progressive.

She was fascinated by his sex secrets. He confessed that he preferred to make love in closets, that he liked to hold a woman's feet. Once he asked her to apply her rouge to his lips and hers, and he kissed her all over her cheeks and neck until they were mottled red. He always undressed in the dark, and though he touched her everywhere, sighing, though he licked her face and nipples, he was reluctant to complete the act. He did not push her onto the bed or lift up her skirts. It puzzled her. He knew, after all, about her past. "Of course you know I'm not a virgin," she told him.

"Ah, but we have plenty of time," he said, caressing the fullness of her hip.

He often came to see her perform, though the audience was usually sparse. There were farces, the folk play *Der Millionenbauer*, Ibsen, Lessing's *Minna von Barnhelm*, Shakespeare, and Freytag's *The Journalists*. Elsa had small parts in each of them and was the understudy three times for more substantial parts. Each time she walked onstage in front of the audience space, which appeared fuzzy and amorphous like a huge piece of gray felt, she was momentarily horrified. No matter how small her part, her head felt huge, a pumpkin with garguntuan features, each subtle shift of mouth or eyes detectable under the lights. Then a kind of ecstatic wind entered her, as if she were spontaneously growing new strands of hair and thickening eyelashes, as if her body might at any moment thrillingly shrink or expand.

The newspaper *Berliner Anzeiger* took note of Elsa's performance in Schiller's *Don Carlos:* "Miss Plötz, as the Marquise de Montecar, acquitted herself well," and though her part was small, she was thrilled that the reviewer had noticed her. The company had plans to go on a tour to Cottbus, Munich, Frankfurt. August, though he said he was proud, did not want her to go. "Of course I'm going," Elsa said. "This is the beginning of the wheel turning in my career—don't you want to see it rolling and rolling?"

"Well, yes." He put his finger to his lips, pressing them closed for a moment before he spoke. "Maybe I will come see you in Munich."

Elsa was anxious to leave Berlin, where the audiences were so hard to please and the play got so little notice, whereas elsewhere it would be the showcase. She was happy with her performance for the first time, because she had learned to be aware of how long she waited before she said her lines and the way she flung her head back afterward.

The day before they were scheduled to leave for the tour, Herr Proctor came late to the rehearsal, dragging his feet slowly down the aisles of the theater. The strands of his gray hair were slicked back on his pink scalp, his dapper suit loose on his stooped frame.

They were rehearsing a funny play, *Edelweiss*, and Elsa played a shy girl who could not disobey her parents.

"I'm sorry, cast," said Herr Proctor. "I have some distressing news." Two of the actresses stepped to the edge of the stage.

Elsa jumped off the stage so she faced Herr Proctor.

"Our backer has withdrawn his investment, and we are now officially bankrupt. All of our engagements are canceled."

Hilda, who played one of the sisters, began to cry in humming, precarious sobs. Elsa looked out at the empty velvet seats. "What do you mean, he withdrew? He told you himself how much he admired the play!"

Herr Proctor shook his head. "He's disappointed in our audiences."

"But then find another backer! Why give up so easily?"

Herr Proctor extended his hands. His moist eyes made her impatient. "It's not a matter of resignation. One has to proudly accept one's fate. We cannot even afford train fare." He touched his throat and began to cough. "We have to make peace with life's disappointments."

All at once the paint-chipped walls, the pathetically small number of worn velvet chairs, the narrow center aisle, and Herr Proctor's pallid, kind face cast a furious red gloom over Elsa, as if her future were this empty theater.

She went back to standing in lines for auditions. No one wanted her.

During the day she lay on the couch or the floor, exhausted. When he came to visit her, August said, "I have not seen you smile in two weeks."

He still had not taken her to bed, and she believed now it was because her failure made her less attractive to him. "Find your smiles elsewhere."

He touched the basin on top of her dresser, drawing his thick finger over the floral design, then turned to her, his face sagging in a way that reminded her that he was older than she was. "You haven't given up, have you?" His optimism sounded halfhearted.

"You don't know a thing about it."

She wanted to throw a blanket over her head, but she didn't want him to know how desperate she was, how she felt herself gradually evaporating like a cup of water forgotten on the shelf. There seemed to be so little left.

"Elsa . . ."

She turned sharply from him. "Go away."

"All right," he said at the door. "Take a little solitude."

She stopped eating, and her ribs began to stand out palely, her shoulders jutting in angles. She woke in the middle of the night burning up with heat and went to the window to stare at the pocked moon.

This mysterious fever lasted for several weeks, and August sent cheery notes but did not come for her.

Then, one afternoon when she was alone in her bedroom, she took out her notebook. The page was there like an open field. She suddenly understood all of those conversations with August that, until now, had been abstract. One had to feel the kick and swoon of the thing one was making, the core of one's body in the form. That was how a line became animated, how a dead thing—pencil on paper—might move and come alive. That was the true theater. For the first time in years, she wrote two lines of a poem. *Into slate-vapor mist / That train clogs away*. Setting down this piece of herself, examining it, brought her breathing back to its normal state. She wrote to August and asked him to bring her pencils.

9

When she and August went to parties, Elsa would wear her big earrings shaped like oil barrels (given to her by a Moroccan friend who used only large, uncut jewels), which dangled almost to her shoulders. She liked the way they coarsely drew attention to her face. And she liked to go around the room with a bottle of cognac, filling the men's glasses, to argue her opinion about Oscar Wilde—"You know he said, 'All bad poetry springs from genuine feeling' "—or Adolph Menzel—"One can only trust the early paintings"—even if she knew that no one would agree with her. She told the landscape painter that she hated Blechen for his literalness, "as if afraid to make a mistake on the school assignment," and when she patiently explained to the professor her theory about how music was full of tentacles in the air, each one attached to a note that had the ability to fix itself to different parts of the body, each man looked at her as if she had sprouted a beak. Nathan Lindner, the client August was courting, could be especially dull. He would stand with his drink, pontificating about the nobility of women or the decline of Berlin, and she would refill his glass, smiling and disagreeing loudly.

"But you state yourself too baldly," August told her. "You have no tact."

"You have too much tact. That is why you have to get so drunk at parties—otherwise you bore yourself."

"Elsa, don't you see? You have to be patient with people, or they will never reveal themselves to you."

She commiserated with Christof about the rumors of those men in the higher posts of the Kaiser's circle, the general who liked to dress in a pink tutu, the military consul who arranged for beautiful tanned boys from Capri to be hired at the Restaurant Bleu, where he could call on them for orgies. The impassiveness of the Kaiser's face made her want to laugh. That mustache, which had become so fashionable now—one saw it on every other man in the street, the two slick segments of hair flying away from the mouth like birds' wings.

She tried to appease August sometimes. When she felt herself about to burst out with something, she would instead study people's noses and the way they moved as they spoke, or she would watch the shadows on the wall, how they mocked the party.

She at first believed that August's reluctance to penetrate her was part of his admiration of a woman's body—he did not want to rush. There was no reason to, he said. And didn't she enjoy his caresses and tongue? But then she realized these were just ruses.

He liked to paint her in the nude. He enjoyed watching her bathe. He liked to rub her back and the fleshy sides of her thighs. One afternoon she saw the truth: August loved her because she accepted this sexual hurdle as a challenge, whereas many women would have fled. Her experience was attractive to him—because she was the one who'd have to deflower him again. He wasn't a virgin, but she was certain it had been a very long time.

"You do not want a silly bourgeois wife," she told him. "If I can't be my true self, we'll both be bored."

"Of course—do I ever question what you say when we're alone?"

They lived on Karlstrasse, near the tourist gardens and shops, in a house detailed with borders of leaves and berries, the sunny rooms filled with handmade furniture and bright upholsteries. Elsa was so glad to leave Frau Hoffman's dusty rooms that she often wiped the wooden tables and chairs with dust cloths and each day arranged bowls of fresh flowers and fruit in the dining room and parlor.

Just as August strove to feel the lines and breaks of a blueprint in his own physical sensations, she began to notice how words corresponded with the body—the kick of an exclamation mark, the leap in certain rhythms, the embrace at the end of a sonnet. For a while she tried wearing her pencil tied to her garter, thinking that the warmth of her blood and muscle might fortify it.

August designed a two-story restaurant with a staircase like a twisted and vined tree, and a hotel with windows in the shape of human eyes. But the success made him nervous, and he smoked more hashish in order to concentrate and to get to sleep. He came home late and would sit at the table with a stupefied, tired smile on his face. If he smoked the right amount, he was articulate and excited. If he smoked too much, he was no good for conversation, because he believed that everything he said was important and allowed himself to meander into silly tangents of no interest to anyone who wasn't also intoxicated. Even the way he positioned his fork on the table seemed to fascinate him, or the transparency of beer in a glass.

Sometimes when Elsa tried to seduce him, he said he was too distracted by work. "This is my opportunity," he told her. "For some reason now is when they are all interested. You have to help me." She understood how he needed his vision to be untamed and let loose, why he had to be coaxed into admitting the extra vine around the staircase, the eyelashes over a window eave. He knew that she needed time alone at night in the Tiergarten, that she had to sleep occasionally with the dictionary open beside her.

In the winter she proposed marriage. August dropped his wineglass on the rug, then quickly sputtered his own proposal. They were married in March at a small church with a rosy statue of the Virgin. Elsa wore a white dress with bells sewn to the sleeves that jingled as she walked down the aisle.

For their wedding night, they stayed at an inn outside the city, with Moorish pilasters and a small dome. August slowly undressed Elsa, peeling the silk fabric from her shoulders, the tiny bells tinkling. He laid her down on the bed, kissed her toes, her ankles, then slowly moved his way up. Breathless, she waited for him. When the kisses reached her neck, she noticed that his eyes were red-rimmed, slackened from hashish, and she felt tender toward him for needing the crutch. After he kissed her hair, he smiled down at her, then lay down and turned away. When she reached for him, he caught her hand and said, "You're beautiful. Let's leave tonight like this."

They were getting ready for dinner with Nathan Lindner and his wife, and August was nervous. August inhaled hashish from his pipe and stared at the ceiling. "I want this commission." He tapped his foot nervously.

"Why would they be having dinner with us if they weren't going to give it to you?" Elsa powdered her arms and neck white. She wore the big jade earrings that looked like beetle shells and the ring with the blue ball on it, a ring that might blacken an attacker's eye or, if rubbed with butter, reflect visions of the future.

"To test me." He smoothed the sleeves over his arms. "They are a wealthy business. He could hire anyone. He's only speaking to me because Paul recommended me." Elsa did not like to see him lacking confidence in his designs only because they were soon to be judged by a man who had money.

"So you should tell him exactly what you want to do. Be bold and don't mumble. They won't engage your services if you're tepid."

August nodded and sucked again on the pipe, his eyes reddening. His fingers still nervously played against the patchwork panel on the bed. "Dear, don't mention that you were in the Wintergarten Revue. These people won't understand that."

She was suspicious of this. If August saw her lean in too closely or gesture too wildly, he would pull her away from the conversation, his face red and crumpled. She noticed that when there were no other women there, he did not mind, but if William brought his pretty young lover, or if Otto brought the older, married women with whom he was having an affair, August objected to her frankness. She hated that he was comparing her to others, women with wind-chime voices and blushing manners, women who hid their cigarettes in powder rooms or kitchens, women who were embarrassed to speak, women afraid to read philosophy.

There were mirrors on all the walls of the restaurant and, standing on pedestals, huge bouquets of flowers, lilies like grasping white hands and roses the color of tongues.

They sat talking across silver and crystal while the waiters hovered nearby. Elsa dined on duck liver wrapped in bright green cabbage leaves, rosy tenderloin of venison, a salad made of flower petals. Mr. Lindner wanted to talk about the scandal with the Kaiser. "It's shameful. It really is. The men in his cabinet are all honorable men." *Die Zukunft* had revealed that two of the Kaiser's advisers had homosexual leanings, "a tendency to sweetness," and had plotted the ousting of another.

His wife nodded and smiled and watched him. "Let's not talk about that."

"Sorry, I suppose it's not for the company of ladies." Lindner had hard, flinty eyes, which seemed to reflect back more than they apprehended. Elsa doubted if he had looked with lust at anyone for years—the sexspirit seemed to have been beaten out of him. She did not like the way he smiled at her when she spoke, as if he were only half listening, as if he were casting about for the joke he would tell about her later.

August wore his calm face, but beneath the table his leg was jiggling. She did not like to see him at the whim of this man. It went against all his principles about beauty that made her love him. He let Lindner go on and on about the new neighborhood near Potsdam, how there were gardens behind every home and wide boulevards, about the factory owners and entrepreneurs who had purchased the mansions.

In between his pontifications, there were several awkward silences before the waiters brought out their desserts. Over the pastries and sweet wines, Lindner talked about his father, who had lost so much in the 1874 stock-market crash. "All the Jews' fault," he said. "You know. They made such a profit off of it. That is why now, August, it is important that we remember the *Volk*, the ordinary German. Always. Never forget that. The ordinary. We can't be swayed to turn against our roots."

The *ordinary*, the very concept of it, was something she and August had raged against together—it was a false idea meant to give politicians and factory owners more control. She was astounded that August let Lindner sermonize without saying anything.

Elsa drank a fourth glass of wine, glanced up, and saw Frau Lindner staring at her, her mouth very still. Elsa knew that Frau Lindner disapproved of the kind of freedoms she had enjoyed, even if not one word had been spoken about her days at the Wintergarten. Elsa felt sorry for her, pent up by this jailer-husband, and she wanted to bring her out of her cell momentarily, make her laugh. "What do you think of the hobble skirt?" It was scandalously tight, so that women could take only tiny steps.

"A ridiculous fashion." Frau Lindner covered her mouth with her hand.

"A doctor once told me that the tighter the skirt, the more blood goes to the brain. That is why, though it's a little-known fact, Japanese women are very intelligent."

Frau Lindner smiled slightly, averting her eyes.

Lindner cleared his throat, demanding attention. "What I want for the company building is clean lines, pure forms. Something classical."

The architect has expressed power, power over gravity, Elsa had read somewhere, and the most eloquent expression of that power was in an architect's style. Elsa believed in August's work. No one could mistake his design for anyone else's. "What do you have against ornament? August's designs startle because of their original figures."

"Yes, but I am asking him to suppress that tendency."

"Why?"

"For the sake of purity."

"Purity is blankness. Why in the world would you want your place of business to be blank?"

August kicked her leg under the table. "I like clean shapes, too," he said. "When the speed of the line is eloquent. If there is any ornament, it has to be weighed in the balance of everything else. It could be extravagant or not, as you wish."

Lindner pushed away his plate. "I prefer clean shapes, nothing on the walls as decoration. Decoration is tawdry." Elsa hated his smugness, the way he dismissed a thing before even considering it.

"You aren't one of those men who worships virgins, are you?" Elsa said.

Frau Lindner gasped.

"Virginity . . ." Lindner's lips seemed to get stuck on his teeth. "It's a different category."

"No it's not. Virginity and purity are only the states before defilement, Herr Lindner."

Later she knew that August was angry, though he kept his voice low. As they got into the cab after dinner, he grabbed her. "You were rude tonight."

"I only said what you were thinking."

"Not that business about virgins. What did that have to do with it?"

"I think virginity should be surgically removed from every female at puberty—it would solve a multitude of problems."

"Elsa, that's ludicrous. You can't say every absurd thing that pops into your head! When are you going to learn? I need that commission. And don't say that I'm a hypocrite either, because if you think I can . . . I have always said that making a building is a collaboration between the client and the architect. Did you see how he changed the subject? Don't you see how this could hurt us?"

"You'll get another commission, August. You deserve to have a patron with more intelligence."

In the end August did not lose the Lindner commission, and Lindner said he trusted August to create something edifying. At the gathering to celebrate the building's construction, Lindner, in his formal suit and tails, avoided Elsa and would not even look her way when he spoke to August. He shook her hand limply at the beginning of the evening and acted as if he only vaguely remembered having met her before. "Oh, yes, a pleasure," he said. "Now, August." He clapped his hand on August's shoulder. "Let me introduce you to a colleague of mine." After the two men went off, Lindner's wife looked as if she were afraid Elsa might burst into flames.

10

Elsa straddled a saddle, the lilac curtains blowing in through the window.

August painted a nude woman riding a horse, her hair loose down her back, purple mountains in the distance.

She stood beside a floor lamp with a huge green shade, a rolled-up carpet curled beside her, a red ball in her hand.

In the painting, Eve listened to the serpent, plucking the apple from the tree.

Elsa posed lying back on the divan, one leg tucked behind her, her arm crooked behind her head like a broken wing.

The pillow became a little dog, the divan a throne carried by eight black arms, the triangle of her bent arm a gold crown.

She liked watching August's eyes as he studied her body, the concentration pressing in the corners of his mouth, the way he sat with his burly legs astride the stool. He was at once distant from her and almost unbearably intimate, as if he were finding a way under her skin. Though he still had not been able to make love to her, that would come soon. She saw how, when he was at rest, he would twist his arm and leg to a position vaguely approximating her own. "You have to feel the painting in your own muscles," he would say. "Or it will just sit there."

One afternoon as she posed, August said, "The Marlows want us for dinner on Thursday night. Peter finally found a publisher for his book." It was on the nature of color, how proper combinations could cure melancholia or inspire patriotism or lust. He had an elaborate theory, illustrated with diagrams of Vermeer paintings and test squares of reds and yellows for a person to gaze upon.

"And who else will be there?"

"Just the four of us. I know she is tedious, but try to be kind to Susanna—ask her about her garden."

"She's not tedious—she's actually quite knowledgeable about bullfrogs, their various colored spots and habits. Did you know there is a toad whose skin emits an intoxicant when licked and then turns blue?"

"She's good-natured enough."

"You've never actually had a conversation with her."

August sighed, leaned closer to the painting.

She liked Susanna because she had a full-throated laugh and an interest in biological things Elsa had never taken the time to learn about, but August never paid her any attention. Elsa's leg was falling asleep, and she was thirsty. She began to glance at the clock. Almost three.

There was a knocking on the window. A flash of a face, and then a black covering hid the sunlight. The room was suddenly dim.

"Damn! What happened to the light?" August dropped his brush on the floor and turned to the window, covered by a black cloth.

The hammering went on. He went to the window and opened it. "Who is banging?"

"You have neighbors, Mr. Lydell." A shrill woman's voice. "We have certain codes of decency. If you do not believe in curtains, then we will have to make our own."

It was that woman next door, Frau Weilspracht, who wore big felt hats like boats and turned her head away whenever they greeted her.

The woman continued to hammer. The black cloth covered the entire glass. August called through the window, "I need the natural light to paint!"

It was a side window—the woman had to have been spying in order to see Elsa in the first place.

"Then move to the country," said the woman. "With the other trash."

"So the neighborhood has gone downhill, has it?" August screamed out the window. "You're trespassing, Frau Weilspracht!" The way August held his brush against his breast as if he were pledging allegiance, the righteousness in his voice, made Elsa laugh.

"Your indecency knows no boundaries, Herr Lydell. Please, contact the police. It will make me glad."

They heard her footsteps across the alley.

"Well," said Elsa, recovering as she pulled on her robe. "She damned you to hell."

A couple of days later, Elsa watched August tear off the black cloth, fold it neatly, and then, from the window, saw him knock on the door of Frau Weilspracht's house. He handed the cloth to the sputtering, beet-faced woman and thanked her for the use of her curtains.

They moved to the attic. Upstairs, where it was warmer, the posing made Elsa more amorous. When the light started to go, she walked across the drop cloth, the wet paint squinching under her feet, her head dizzy with the smell. She slipped her fingers beneath August's belt and moved his brush over the skin rounding her breast, the blue smudging on her pale skin. His face lost focus, and when she kissed him, she felt the swelling of his trousers pressed against her.

A moment later he undressed, and they lay down together on the drop cloth. Then his erection vanished. He tried to pleasure her anyway, with a pained smile as he moved his paint-spattered hand over her body, but the dried pigment felt like scales.

One of August's portraits depicted Elsa stepping out of the bath, the muscles of her backside as round and blushed as a curve on a pear, her toes spread wide on the bath mat, reddish hair piled on her head. Wearing an expression both feral and maternal, she looked studiously down at her breasts and belly as she dried herself with a towel. The nudes were beginning to exasperate Elsa, and she thought it might be a liability to have a body with so many nerves, to be a woman so overcome by touch.

August displayed the nudes over the fireplace, the dining room table, the bedstead, the buffet, in the landing of the staircase, and in the entryway just above the bowl of keys. They were of numerous sizes, some as small as a book and others larger than the top of a desk. August was fond of saying to guests, "I only paint women these days—what can I say?" And the men would laugh heartily, studying one of the nudes, and then glance slyly at Elsa's bosom or haunch, as if the shapes could be discerned beneath her clothes.

That the architect Lydell displayed nude paintings of his wife was a source of rumors among that circle of Berlin bohemians. Elsa knew that her unrestrained talk and the way she moved so freely in her skirts only encouraged the stories. They were said to indulge in orgies including servant girls and acrobatic positions August had discovered at brothels on his trip to Japan. One man claimed to have slept with each of them, separately, on the same evening, while the other one watched.

Elsa was touched by August's seriousness, by how he needed to explain the lack between them, and it was true that she loved him in a way wholly different from all the other men. "It is in the spiritual realm that our union is important," August told her. "What do bodies mean to us? Your beauty does not lie only in your flesh—that's why I can't ever paint you as well as I should."

She thought now that it was his reverence for the sublime that inhibited him from penetrating her. Idealizing their love, he was afraid of disappointment. "But, August, dear. Bodies are what we have."

All her experiences—the men in cabs, the undressing in bachelor rooms, the furtive skirt hitching in the park—had been careening like a train to this challenge of curing August. Even the syph, now long in remission, had taught her the pain of the body, how pleasure was rarely free.

On Mühlenstrasse, she found the house of Peter Severlin, her mother's favorite living poet. He'd published only one book, poems that seemed to slowly unravel as they went along, and Elsa was fascinated by the sequence about a ghost who haunts her lover in a field. When Elsa had discovered the address through someone's offhand comment at a party, the back of her neck tingled. She remembered how her mother's hair fell around her face when she read for long periods, one blond lock running forehead to nose, how well rested she would appear when she finally looked up from the book.

Twice Elsa had gone to that house, with its green shutters and the marble tiara crowning the door. She'd loiter near the iron gate, barred with black swords, and wait for Severlin to appear. The first time a maid came out to empty a pail of dirty water in the bushes, and there was a rustling of wispy curtains in the upstairs window. The second time she saw a woman emerge, wearing a huge plumed hat, silver gray furs. She had a large bust that seemed to pull her forward. Severlin himself she never saw, though the solidity of his house, with its grand green door and the feather of smoke in the chimney, bolstered her ambition to write.

She told August many things, but she could not tell him about this ritual any more than she could tell him how she stood for long periods in front of von Carolsfeld's painting *The Annunciation* at the Nationalegalerie. The painting had a disarming immediacy, the angel waving, Mary wearing a secret, knowing smile, a book in her lap, her surprised hand reaching out to the air. Gold wires encircled both of their faces. Elsa liked to think about having a visitation from an angel, imagined touching the slick, muscled wings, the red-and-purple feathers, and the knobbed place where they met the shoulders. She had only occasionally attended church with her mother, and her notion of the spirit was as private as it was here, a riot of bright trees and mountains in the background, the surprise of a white dove. Piety didn't interest her, only the bright flash of inner sight, what she felt jumping from a trolley car or waking in the morning to snow, when a hole tore through the ordinary world.

She tried reading to August pornography she'd found on the back shelf of a bookstore. She tried showing him photographs of half-nude women peeking over their shoulders, rolling down their stockings. She tried approaching him with a ruler, slapping him on the knees like a schoolteacher. He blamed his inability to make love on his nerves, his business, the steak he had eaten, the old dress she was wearing, the gray winter weather.

She confided in Klara, the wife of Stephen, who composed operas. Klara's eyes, rowdy and blue, were always rimmed with black kohl. Since her sister had died in childbirth, Klara affected a slight mean-spiritedness toward men, which they tolerated, mistaking it for grief. Klara assessed the problem. "You're a virago to him. Anyone can see it when he looks at you. It must drive him mad not to have you. Some men require a certain punishment from their wives, but in August's case he can't conquer his fear of it. He's afraid of what you might take from him."

Elsa considered August's most recent nude. The figure of a woman stood next to a table, the bush at her groin like a swirl of smoke, the breasts sharp at the pink nipples, the shoulders square, the hands and feet long. The face was more beautiful than hers but also more predatory, a mass of hair wreathing the head and shoulders, one finger pointed down like a knife.

Perhaps she would have to curb her vanity and outbursts. Klara suggested that Elsa might pretend to be a slave girl for an evening or two.

That night when he was in bed with his book, she stripped slowly for him, laying each article of clothing on his lap. She did a dance of the veils, uncovering her breasts, slipping the scarf over her belly. She could see he was mesmerized. She thought it was not a physical problem but some locked door in August's head. Then she stood next to the bed beside him. He put his hand on her hip and pulled her over to kiss her. She felt him hard under the covers, and the hot damp between her legs.

It was so simple, really. That was what August needed to learn, that he had only to open the door, and the spell would be broken.

She made her way under the sheet next to him, the hairs of his arms and chest against her smoothness, his breath in her ear. She curled over him, thrust her hand into his pajama trousers. Then there was nothing in the space where there had just been firmness. It shocked her, and she pulled quickly away.

He kissed her on the nose. "I've spoken to Dr. Landau about . . . these sexual issues." Dr. Landau had commissioned him to design a sanitarium in the country outside Berlin.

She hated that he'd broken their privacy. "How could you do that?"

"He offered to treat you, as a favor to me."

"Treat *me*?" The blue books on the walls suddenly appeared red. The floor seemed to tilt. "That's ludicrous, August. What did you tell him?"

"It's not as outlandish as it sounds. Apparently it's quite common, our problem." He patted her stomach over the sheets.

"I have no problem, August."

His eyes were red from smoking. "You'll have a little rest, that's all. Massages and hearty soups. It's time we faced this scientifically, darling. The doctor says this condition can arise from a woman's anxiety; he says it's a dryness that repels tumescence." He looked away from her. "You'll simply have your womb massaged."

"*My* anxiety?" She wanted to slap him. She avoided doctors and certainly didn't want anyone tending to her womb except herself. All this time she'd been worrying, trying to help him, and now he blamed her?

"Dr. Landau has treated several cases like ours." She didn't believe there were more cases like theirs but stopped herself from arguing when she noticed the way his mouth trembled. He bowed his head, and she noticed the gray hairs at his temples. She saw how the situation pained him, that he was as desperate for a resolution as she was. She hated to think he might be afraid of something in her, but if he was, perhaps her submitting to this treatment would remove the fear. She'd seen his sketches of the sanatorium, a rustic building with copper cornices and pedestals covered with stars and moons.

She touched his hair. "My only anxiety is for you."

He kissed her on her forehead. "Shouldn't we try it?"

When Elsa was packing, at the bottom of her valise she found the beaded pot holder. The tweed of her father's old suit had begun to fray. The constellation pattern had lost several beads, and the whistle had cracked. It was too decorated to use under a pot—nothing would have sat evenly on top of it. Her mother had never had much of a practical nature.

There was the time her father went to Hamburg to buy tile, and while he was away, her mother brought in the workmen to paste up the new wallpaper, a panel of landscape alternating with a panel of flowers, all along the parlor wall, the workmen checking periodically, "Are you sure you wanted it this way, Frau Plötz?"

"Of course!" she'd say as she arranged and rearranged the new furniture, a pink velvet sofa with gold tasseled swags, a table with a crystal steeple poking up from the middle of it. She had the floors painted purple, the doors pale green, and Elsa's sister, Charlotte, was afraid to leave her room. Her mother had a lilt in her step all those days, a silliness that made Elsa imagine what she must have been like as a girl. The carnival colors and mismatchedness made Elsa feel as if her vision had been improved, as if she'd now be able to see into the insides of flowers, down to the stamen and pollen dust, that she could examine the tiny eye and maw of a butterfly.

But the day Elsa's father returned, the idyll ended. From upstairs in her room, she could hear his voice through the floorboards. Her mother had charged everything to an account at the most expensive firm, and if they didn't return the furniture, she'd have wasted half of his savings, which he had worked for, he said, "like a slave."

"I thought it would be nice," her mother said through her weeping.

"My God," he said. "It looks like a bordello." And that was when Elsa first guessed he went to whores.

What had her mother known about sexual relations? Elsa's father had been the only man ever to touch her, and in the end she would not even turn her head to look at his face.

Each morning the nurse came with a bud vase of daffodils and a glass of milk on a tray. Elsa was encouraged to sleep often and allowed to walk on the grounds only for an hour in the afternoon, if the doctor determined that her pulse was strong enough for exercise. He listened to her explanation of the history of her syphilis, then nodded judiciously. "Well, that's all behind you now, isn't it? They gave you mercury." She hoped he was right, but his brittle manner offended her.

The bed was wooden, with square designs in the footboard that she stared at for hours. On the wall there was a small picture of a goat in a pasture, green hills rolling around it like folds in a soft blanket. At first the scene had seemed comforting, but the more she looked at it, the more it upset her. The goat was about to be smothered by that wave of green coming up behind it, and there was a spot on its fur that looked like the beginning of a horrid disease. Out the window to the left, she saw a band of sky and a band of green grass. There was nothing to watch but the light and the weather, and she invented stories about these to occupy herself: The lightning cracked through the sky because the nurse came infuriatingly every morning at exactly 8 A.M., never a few minutes before or after. The sun streamed through the window like a plea to convince the doctor to allow her to go out for a walk that day. The white walls were sullen in the face of the nurse's chattering, the floor smelled of brandy, and she would have liked to get drunk every day she was there.

In the afternoon the nurse came with the oil and the irrigator, and Elsa lay with her legs strapped in stirrups while the nurse pushed the oil-soaked irrigator in and out of her vagina, sore with repetition. The oil was supposed to soften her, make her womb "more hospitable."

She was given teas with bitter leaves floating in the cup, milk baths in a cold tin tub until her skin smelled sour. Each day, while the doctor's wife took piano lessons or went shopping, the portly, bald doctor with his blond beard came into her room.

"Hello, Frau Lydell. And how are you feeling?"

He lifted the bedclothes first, glancing up at her face, and then put his hand up her nightgown.

"I must be cured by now."

"Not quite," he said, fumbling around her thighs. "Not quite."

And then his fingers were inside her, and she lay back. He smiled slightly as he did this, as if pretending he were doing something else, and she wondered if he enjoyed it. She felt alarmingly numb.

There were women there being treated after hysterectomies, miscarriages, and for various nervous conditions. Elsa talked with a few of them and realized that this was the doctor's treatment for everyone, no matter what her ailment.

The nurse always came into the room afterward. "This will make you more beautiful," she said. "Sleep for the complexion," she would say, closing the curtains in the afternoon.

But Elsa longed for conversation. "Did I ever tell you," she began, "about my aunt, the Countess von Schlegel, who was asleep for a whole year? When she finally awoke, all her family was dead, but she could speak French fluently—like a Parisian—though she'd never studied it before."

The nurse listened patiently. "How remarkable! Now you sleep."

Elsa began to distrust what August saw as her beauty—what was it worth? When she stood up and studied herself in the full-length mirror, she saw more flaws than ever—her skin pallid, a new kidney-shaped mole on her shoulder, thin spidery veins in her legs near her knees.

She began to suspect that their life was all tasteful artifice, all the leaves and stars and laurels bordering the rooms of their house disguises of the fact that they could not truly love one another. The sanatorium was luxurious compared to the public hospital where she'd had the treatments for the syph, but nonetheless, being imprisoned there—for *her* cure—because of *his* sex needs, reminded her of that desolate time when she'd felt as if her body did not belong to her anymore—it belonged to the mercury. And here whose was it? August's or the doctor's?

She watched herself submit to the orders of the nurse, to the doctor's hands. She would stare at her foot or her hand. They began to seem so strange to her, knuckles like hinges, toenails like buttons to press. This was how a person went mad. It began with not recognizing one's own limbs and ended with finding oneself neck deep in the sea, having no idea how one had got there, already drowning.

One morning she dressed, found a door where they brought in the food and linens, and walked out. She knew that if she went far enough, she would find a train station. There were hills and hills of rolling grass, and she imagined the carpet of green curling up and covering her, but she kept walking. She went through a wood, past a small lake, her legs gaining strength as she moved, until she finally found a road. At the end of it, there was a church, an alehouse, and a tiny train station.

She cajoled a clerk at the station to wire August and tell him she was coming back, promising to reimburse the clerk and leaving her pearl earrings with him. On the train ride home, the two women across from Elsa talked loudly about baking. Elsa gazed through the window at the landscape, but she couldn't block out their chatter. "You have to watch it until it just begins to brown and immediately . . ."

She thought of her sister, Charlotte, who had written that she had just given birth to a boy, her neat loopy handwriting imitating her timid, wanting-to-please voice. "Father is still very angry, but when I told him you were married, he seemed surprised and happy. He is a builder, too?" Her father would have found August's designs odd, like the other Berlin customs and styles he scoffed at after reading about them in the newspaper. As Elsa watched the sheaves of wheat running past, the hills cutting scallops against the sky, a white drift of melancholy settled over her.

As the train approached the station, Elsa searched for August's face and spotted him looking over the small crowd, hands in pockets in those pants that were too loose on him, his face concentrated on her imminent appearance. When she stepped onto the platform, he came toward her smiling. His hair was hanging down his forehead, and he had grown more portly, his suit's buttons straining in the front. She wanted at first to strike him. "Welcome back," he said.

In the weeks after her return, August would go into a frenzy, his body hot and perspiring as he kissed her everywhere, moaning, but he could not make himself hard anymore, and to Elsa it felt like an act. He was only pretending to love her because he knew she was a good wife—she understood his designs and would discuss his ideas all night. But he did not feel love in his bones, in his flesh.

She began to have a strange numbness in her fingers and toes. She had little appetite, and she often slept through meals. She had dreams about phalluses—huge male statues that came behind her and pressed their penises into her back. In the last week, at night, the imaginary sailors from her girlhood came through her window again, cooing, their talk bawdy and their muscles hard, and when she walked down the street, she would suddenly imagine all the men's trousers unfastened, their cocks hanging out or pointed directly at her.

One night she asked him, gently, if he preferred men to her.

His face turned purple, and the vein beat hard in his forehead. "Don't ever say that to me again. Of course not." That night his frenzy was wilder than ever, and the absurdity of his thrashing on the sheets made her sad. She would never be able to make herself small enough for him.

August had stolen her beauty and locked it up in his nudes. She hated them now. "He doesn't love you," the one with the apple sometimes said to her. "Isn't it obvious?"

One evening in the parlor, after he had drunk a lot of wine, he said, "Nothing can threaten us, Elsa. Our love is spiritual." He kissed her on the forehead. "It can't exist in mere flesh. We're two linked souls." He took her hand in his. The wooden clock ticked on the shelf. She studied the pattern of leaves, perfect as teardrops, ribboned around the top of the wall. "Though if you thought you might like a man to give you pleasure now and then, I couldn't deny it to you."

"Don't be ridiculous." Despite everything, she still loved him. Though there were one or two couples in the circle who openly conducted affairs like this, Elsa could not have pretended to love her husband while making love to one or two others—she could not cut her heart out of her body like that.

"All right." He drank more wine. "Let's dance, then."

She noticed the boy who brought the milk in the morning, with his fine, sharp shoulders and the sly way he looked away from her when she paid him. She smiled at the house painter when he came to work in the spare bedroom, and she passed the doorway several times a day trying to catch his eye. He had a broad body and merry, light blue eyes. She sketched the ripple of a man's bare back, the torso of a contortionist she had seen at the circus. When she closed her eyes, she saw the long members of every man she had been with, standing up and offering themselves to her like tall, wild mushrooms.

It overtook her like a fever, this desire for other men. She desired their salty, soapy smells, the slight roughness in the pads of their fingers, chin and cheek stubble, the muscle and warmth through wool trousers, the high handle of shoulders and firm arms around her waist. Her wanting did not discriminate. She leaned in toward men in chairs, whose paunches were suddenly secret pillows; she touched the arms of graybeards and met their mocking eyes; she followed stable and delivery boys, her gaze on their gangly, helpless gaits. She wanted all of them, one by one, and at once.

II

The Mauer Café was dim, and it took a moment for Elsa to spot August's round head, bent over his notebook at a table. The one hanging lamp lit the blond hair of the man sitting next to him. It was wavy and gleamed in the light.

When she came to the table, the blond man put down his coffee cup, and August rubbed his eyes. "I've told you about Franz." He had said Franz Trove might be able to introduce him to prospective clients. A poet and translator, he had recently written about August's designs in *Der Sturm*.

"Yes." She noticed Franz's long, slender hand against the wood of the table. His fingernails were smooth and pink and perfectly rounded.

"Elsa has just come from a painting lesson."

There was a coldness about Franz's face that surprised her. It was suave, but stony. "And what have you learned?" he said.

"Not much. I'm not convinced it can be taught." She was frustrated with the lessons, hated the way her canvases flattened after all this instruction, preferring the instinctive paintings she'd done as a girl, but she'd seemed to have lost whatever spark had moved her back then, and it annoyed her to be introduced as an amateur.

"Oh, come now, there are certain skills that are a matter of technique . . ."

August cleared his throat. The cakes on the table were frosted into white snowcaps, and the milk steaming from the silver pot smelled of almonds. "Franz was saying he saw a rat at this café the last time he came here."

"It was a huge one. It sat in that corner nibbling on something, but it didn't bother anyone. In fact, it was rather polite, sitting in the shadow with its tail curled around its feet. It must have been an aristocrat rat. He was very elegant."

Elsa took a lump of sugar from the bowl and put it in her mouth. "Maybe the Kaiser will appoint him to an office."

Franz smiled. He had very white, even teeth, but his smile was opaque.

"So I want Franz to understand this blueprint. You don't mind, do you, if I explain?"

"No, go ahead." While August conferred with Franz, Elsa took out her book and read, sipping her coffee, glancing up now and then at the other people in the café. There were two doughy women at a table near the window, giggling over their strudels. In the dark corner, a somber couple ate pastries together silently. Elsa imagined they'd just had a fight, the woman's face tight and small, the man looking over the room as if he had just purchased everything in it.

She would tell Franz Trove how she'd come to dislike the fussiness of most poetry—the stars and birds and flowers and their relentless prettiness. She did not like the smugness in so many poets, as if they had been given God's podium. She liked the sense that the poet had been collecting the words for years, and by chance they had finally grown together like vines on a wall.

"What do you think, Elsa?" said August. "Which night should Franz come to dinner?"

When she looked at Franz again, she was startled by the contrast between his blond hair and dark eyes, by his secretive mouth. August's eyes were bright, his posture proud, and she suspected that this Franz Trove had just paid his work another compliment.

"Any night he likes."

"On Wednesday I have to meet my publisher—I would be happy to come on Thursday, though."

"Thursday, then," said August, waving at a man at the bar. "Excuse me," he said, getting up. "That's one of my former clients." He went over to talk to the man, leaving Franz and Elsa at the table. Elsa spooned some jam onto a cake and took a bite of it.

Franz said, "Your husband is the talk at all the parties. People are either scandalized by him or in love with his designs."

Elsa swallowed the raspberry sweetness, licked it from her lips. "It's funny, he thinks no one is noticing what he's trying to do."

"Oh, but they are, they are. I love to see someone get foaming at the mouth about it. I find it funny, actually—August is such a gentle fellow, and they act as if he'd attacked them." Franz Trove's appearance made her think of the superficiality of beauty, how his blond hair and angles, the symmetry of his face, all harmony and light, hid anything that might have been unpleasant in him.

"That's what you wrote in your piece. I don't see that kind of thing, of course, being married to him."

"No, he protects you from it, as he should." It struck her as odd that he would say something so conventional, that he might really believe she had such a delicate nature.

"And do you shock people, too, Herr Trove?"

"No, poetry doesn't have enough fangs to bite anyone, and people expect a journalist will say anything just to get an assignment, so there's not much room for outrage there either." There were rumors about Franz Trove, some kind of unpleasant business behind his glamour, an abandoned lover left pregnant or money borrowed and never returned—Christof had told her, but she couldn't remember what it was.

"But you consider yourself a poet at heart."

His face froze, and he stared at her, fiddling with his lapel. "I wouldn't dare say that."

In the weeks that followed, she noticed he had an elegant way of moving through the room, as if each step were part of a thought. As she listened to him, Elsa would sometimes find herself wondering whether he had hair on his chest, whether the muscles in his thighs were round or long.

He had some kind of family fortune—he treated them at restaurants and dressed well, in the English style, tweed coats and narrow ties. He'd already published a collection with a Berlin publishing house, and his byline frequently appeared in the newspapers, under the art and theater reviews. Elsa found that the reviews had a showy arrogance, but his poems dazzled her. The phrases rose out of the paper, floated around her head in a dreamy nimbus. He had that mystical knowledge of the language, what Elsa's mother used to call *ein Wunder*, and Elsa envied it.

For one of Franz's visits, Elsa wore the necklace she had made with the large medallion in the shape of a bear's paw. She wore the green dress that flowed loosely over her thin frame, the front panel painted with a pattern of red cherries. She spied him looking at her rosy shoulders, her slim ankles, her white neck, but his politeness apparently barred him from flirting. His disinterest made her strain to shine up the conversation.

"I read one of your poems, Franz, 'Autumn Song.' August showed it to me. Why did you decide on the mountains at the end?"

"Franz, your tie is a little crooked. Should I straighten it for you?"

But he had a way of avoiding her bait, turning his head at just the right moment, or suddenly addressing some formal remark to August. She thought she detected a certain reluctant effort in this, but wasn't sure.

They were sitting in the parlor, and Elsa lit a cigarette. August liked it when she smoked—he said it drew attention to her lovely mouth and signaled that they were progressive.

"What I don't understand about Tillenhaus is why he's so fascinated by drabness," she said.

"He's melancholic. He is a genius at transmitting that, though, isn't he?" said August. "I feel despair looking at those gray clouds and timid hills."

Franz's face was cool and impassive. He seemed absolutely embarrassed by her smoking and would not look at her when he spoke. "I don't understand it either, Elsa."

Elsa lowered her cigarette to her knees. He did not like a woman to smoke? But that contradicted his elegance. "It seems to me that it's pretty easy to fake melancholy," she said, taking a last drag on her cigarette before putting it out in the star-shaped ashtray.

Elsa had just read a book by Hans Weber, a novelist they knew on the periphery of their circle. "Any intelligent woman who reads that book will know what he's up to when he tries to get up her skirt. She won't confuse the author with the hero, because his heroes don't marry fat widows for their money and titles." The story was about the incompatibility of art and life, but the end wasn't really tragic, because the hero was a nitwit who expected to find Truth in the middle of the forest.

She saw Franz smile at her vehemence as he leaned back in the chair. "But he prefers women who do not read—little tarts. Not all men like to see what goes on inside a woman's head. Most don't like to be distracted by it."

August nodded. "Hans likes frippery and whores. What do you like, Franz?" Franz's cheekbones sat high on his face, which gave him an expression of righteousness. What was it Christof had said about him—was it that he'd plagiarized something? But that was the rumor one heard often about writers. He brought the glass to his lips and swallowed. "Pride." He looked at Elsa but wouldn't meet her eye.

"Whatever happened to that minister's daughter?" said August, smirking.

Franz looked down at his shoes, shiny with polish and elegantly tapered at the toes. "I'm afraid our affections for one another were tested. Now her father has forbidden me to speak to her." She noticed that his fingernails were dirty and found this attractive next to the crispness of his shirt cuffs. She was sure there was more to him than she'd seen so far.

"There must be a way around that," said August.

Franz shrugged. "The time when we might have been together has passed."

The earnestness in his voice annoyed her. Elsa dumped the last of the wine into her glass and finished it with two swallows.

The painting instructor August had hired for Elsa, Jonathan Stetholtz, was a bearded man who had once taught at the academy. He held to the classical methods of composition and perspective—and so she began with painting still lifes—the feminine wine bottle and grimacing cut orange, the plucked chicken on a platter of wax grapes, and eventually, he said, they would move on to landscapes. But Elsa didn't like to calculate every brushstroke before she made it, and the painting had an odd, flat naïveté, like one of her sister's needlework projects.

She would have liked to ask Franz Trove to model for her, but of course he would refuse, and August would not model either—he would say he didn't have time to waste. When he smoked hashish, she might have been able to convince him to pose, but then his intoxicated, blank face seemed dead, and she would have had to paint a skull.

"You've lost the perspective there," Stetholtz told her in his studio, where a statue's dismembered parts—face, hand, leg, arm—hung on the wall.

"Whose perspective?"

"The properties."

"I never found them. It wasn't that I lost them."

He smiled at her in that grandfatherly way. She badly wanted to prove something to him, but she couldn't stay focused on his rules. "Discipline is not only for soldiers, Frau Lydell. It develops one's muscle as a painter. Weak painters believe imagination is all."

"But these pictures you show me are so lifeless," she said. They were hung on the wall, ten frames of master studies students were meant to copy.

He sighed, circled her easel. "It is difficult to scold you; you are so pretty. Oh, all right, let's go back to the landscapes, then. Why don't you spend a day painting in the Tiergarten?"

"I think I would do better with life drawing."

"Would you like to draw my hand?"

"A figure."

"Well, you see, figures are a problem without models." He looked away from her. "Perhaps you'd like to paint from one of the statues at the museum?"

One night Franz came to the house before August had arrived home. Elsa sat with him in the library, drinking wine. The day before, after seeing Franz in his golden tallness, with his bitten lips and spiked gaze, she went up to the study and, as she wrote, began to wonder if "masculine" and "feminine" were transcendent realities at work in the world, each with its own flora, fauna, and astronomy.

Franz sat with one leg crossed over the other, so his kneecap poked sharply through his pants. He told her about the time he'd got drunk with the painter Cézanne in Paris, how they'd argued about politics and, after the bar closed, walked the streets looking for another place but found only an old woman in a doorway with a deck of cards and a bottle of wine. "She told me I was going to be rich one day, which is a funny thing for a poet to hear, and she told Cézanne he would go broke. It was all I could do to keep him from flinging himself in the Seine."

"And she was wrong after all."

"For all we know." He shrugged. Stories like this interrupted his suave manner. His dark eyes lost their inwardness, and he suddenly made large, generous gestures with his hands. He had met Zola on the same trip, through a man he'd known in Hamburg, who spoke seven languages and kept rooms at the Regina Hotel. His name was Julius Frankel, and he'd taught Franz how to fence. "It's a difficult sport, because one's brain has to be as sharp as one's reflexes, sort of like chess, only one has to exert oneself." His charm sped him from adventure to adventure, and he never mentioned anything about having to answer to wealthy patrons for his writing. She envied his freedom.

When August came home, they all smoked hashish on the couch. August's face became puffy, his lips slow-moving. Franz's eyes turned languorous. But there was no more talk about Paris. Franz mentioned that he'd visited the studio of Max Slevogt, a painter he knew, whose work he'd reviewed positively in *Der Sturm*. "He's going to be very important   his work is French, really, not academic at all. One notices the scatter of shadow."

"I met him once." Elsa felt the pleasant prick of the lie.

August pulled the pipe out of his mouth. "You never told me that."

"He happened to be at one of the auditions, looking for models. We had a long talk about Iphigenia, because he wanted to paint a version of her. He finally asked me to be the model, but that was just before I was taken on with the acting troupe, and there wasn't time."

August cleared his throat. "She's had quite a lot of adventures before me."

Franz, after sucking on the pipe, stared up at the ceiling. She began to feel as if part of her scalp were peeling back and her brain was growing a variety of beautiful leafy plants.

Later on, after Franz had left and they were lying in bed, August had formed a plan. "I've figured it out." He lay with his arms crossed behind his head. "I'll hire a new boy for you each week, a university student. That way you'll never get bored, and I won't be jealous." He was only half serious, showing off his liberal notions about sex, which, now that it was hopeless between them, he did more than ever.

"It's not as if any replacement will do."

"Why not?" he said. "They aren't so special."

"Go to sleep," she told him.

"It's a perfect plan."

He seemed to think it was merely a bit of bodily housekeeping, a rub here, a spurt there, as simple as relieving oneself in the toilet. He talked about the soul, but where was it, then, if not the body? There was a line in one of Franz's poems: *Her shoulders sing of the heavens, her thighs scissor at the gods.*

One afternoon they were having aperitifs in the back garden, the sounds of the streetcars and the crowds eerily drifting across the fences and alleyways. Franz settled back on the wooden bench and said, "I'm going to Munich for a few months."

Elsa felt as if her body had become instantly elephantine and wrinkled. "What will you be doing there? I hear Munich is terrible this time of year—cold and raining."

August gave her a sharp look.

"I have business there—an investment."

"That ten thousand marks?" August said, raising his eyebrows. She and August tended to hear about Franz's past in small pieces like this, as if he were parceling it out, not wanting to bore them.

"What ten thousand marks?" said Elsa. She and August sat on the grass across from him, and she began pulling at the blades, ripping them up and letting the pieces drop into her lap.

"No, it's not about that."

"You can tell her," August said. "She's not easily shocked." August had said that Franz was overly careful about offending her, that he had mistaken ideas about her fragility.

"I was in love with a girl in Munich." Franz sighed, leaning back against the fence. "She was from a small town, a grocer's daughter, very innocent, and I met her through some friends of mine who were sculptors." Elsa heard the jingle of the electric streetcar.

"You've met her, Elsa," said August. "Geraldine. She was at the Bimler party."

Elsa remembered a very quiet girl with even features. Geraldine informed everyone of her undefiled state—and wore a white dress and a hair ribbon to advertise it.

"She came to me one day because her brother had got into some trouble—he had taken ten thousand marks from the man he worked for, intending to pay it back, but he lost it gambling. She was desperate, weeping, when she came to me, and I had the money, so I gave it to her. I was so fond of her." He looked down, rubbed the sole of his shoe in the grass. "I asked her to marry me, and she said she could not make that decision so hastily. And so we traveled together to Prague. We kept separate rooms, so that her honor would remain intact, but I could not convince her to marry me. When we returned, her brother threatened me with a sword— he said I had ruined her reputation by going away with her. 'But I want to marry her,' " I said.

"But you didn't," Elsa said, torn pieces of grass in her lap.

"Go on." August put his arm around her shoulders. Elsa looked up at the gray sky, which had the texture of coarse paper.

"She's had enough of you," the brother told me. So I was never returned my ten thousand marks, and last year she gave birth to some fellow's baby. I heard she was going to enter a nunnery." The story sounded incomplete— Elsa wondered if he was leaving something out to protect her, but he also seemed ashamed of his failure, unaware of his own sharp appeal.

"A neurasthenic, obviously," said August.

Elsa studied Franz's somber face. Why did men adore virginity? Everything, even a goat, was a virgin at some point, so why adore it?

"I hope you get your money back," Elsa said. She picked a weed, sucked on the sour stem.

"Oh, I don't expect to," said Franz.

August chuckled. "You *will* look in the galleries for Benter and me, won't you? He has his mind fixed on a Slevogt, but I prefer Stolle myself."

"Of course."

Franz had offered to help August fill his client Benter's new house with art. He was a horrible little man with no aesthetic sense of his own. Though he didn't need it, he walked with a cane and told anyone who would listen how he had hurt his leg chasing a thief.

Franz said, "And if I do find some things in Munich, how much can I be free to offer?"

"Whatever you think is fair. Benter wants to give you a fund. He's been reading your reviews so devotedly, I don't see how you could disappoint him."

Franz was going to leave. In the gray light, his hair lost its gold sheen, and already his face seemed to have faded.

12

A month after Franz left, Elsa began to get letters from him, very proper ones, in small, even handwriting and straight lines. He wrote about how an editor had enraged him. "Have you ever noticed that when one is angry, there is always something else there, too? Disgust, pain, even amusement? It is not a very pure emotion. In this case it was despair." He wrote to her about the French translation he was doing and about the cafés and bookstores in Munich. He wrote about the poems he was trying to compose, what he wanted them to be and how they were falling short. His newspaper reviews reminded her of doors slamming and drawers thrown shut, but one day she'd have the nerve to show him something she'd written.

In her letter she discussed the recent death of Griselda Weiss, the writer she admired for her female characters, always forced to compromise but clinging to their tumultuous thoughts. Because their struggles were so unbearable, reading the episodes of capitulation always came as a relief. Weiss had fallen in love with a married man, so the rumors went. After he ended the affair, she had jumped off a bridge in the middle of the night. "Don't you wonder what we've missed? What the next book might have been?"

The letters continued to arrive during those three months, and he signed each of them "fondly." Then one day she was reading one of the posts in the bedroom, the light dappled by the flowering tree outside the window, a cool breeze on her fingertips, and she came across this line: "Between sense lust and mind peace, man has but one anxious choice." She thought it was a quote from Schiller, and suspected this was his way of telling her he understood the friction between them. She felt perspiration at her temples, her heart banging in her chest. Then she reread the paragraph and realized it could have just as easily been a joke referencing that piece he was writing on Chopin.

She often thought of Franz's hands, long and slender and more full of expression than anything he said. She tried to paint them from memory, but their shapes came out stiff as gloves. She could not paint their scintillating movement, the way they angled and curled around his ideas, how even at rest one finger nuzzled another, the thumb circling the air.

"We're a modern couple," August said. "There's no reason you can't take lovers. We'll look for them together." He'd just completed a design for a theater, which would have a vine of bananas wrapped around the grand entrance, and there had been invitations into a new circle of wealthy friends. The men he wanted her to go home with were paunchy libertines, or married men with obese wives. "It's better than it was, isn't it? I told you, you should sleep with Heinz. He's asked me outright if you're available, by the way."

His sly grin annoyed her. She was becoming like one of his designs, miming the natural but denied any sensation. "You offered?"

"Of course not. But I couldn't blame him for asking."

Heinz was a pudgy man with a penchant for Chinese checkers who edited a cultural review of the arts called *Maniseris*. He had thick, dark eyebrows that hovered like a singular caterpillar over his eyes, and when he saw Elsa, this caterpillar roused itself.

"I don't want Heinz."

August sighed. "Oh, come on, Elsler. You can tell me about it afterward." His eyes were opaque. Part of her still wanted to have every sex experience that offered itself, but she was repulsed by this one.

"He does not attract me. Did you think it would be so easy?"

"Sex confuses things between us. Isn't there enough mess in the world already? Let's keep things clear and not argue anymore. We'll find someone for you to have a dalliance with."

She looked at the small nude over the dresser, a pale figure walking

blithely through a dark wood. She folded over the bedsheet in four even sec-
tions. She said it at first as a joke, in the same tone in which they always
talked about finding lovers for her. "Okay, if not you, then I want Franz."

August sat up. "Not Franz, darling. He's my friend."

"So is Heinz."

"Heinz isn't anyone's friend." He patted her hand. "You understand how
awkward it would be. Besides," he chuckled, "I don't think you're his type."

"How do you know?"

He propped himself up with the pillow behind him. "Well, I'm pretty
sure he prefers men. At least that's what I've heard. That minister's daughter
was only an infatuation—he never even touched her." August's eyes were
cracked with strands of red, the corners of his mouth turned down. "Look,
when I was working all that time on the Schroeder building, I asked him to
visit you, to keep you entertained." His boyishness was fading, and he was
beginning to resemble the man who'd sold lumber to her father, who'd had
the infuriating habit of patting her on the head, even after she was grown.

"You did what?" There was a sharpness in her eyes like pinpricks. "Don't
ever ask anyone to entertain me. It's an insult to my inner resources."

"I'm only telling you what I know, darling."

She turned over, pulled the pillow on top of her head, the sound of her
eardrums marching furiously against the mattress.

They went to a party on Christmas Eve. August smoked so much hashish
that he did not speak at all but only smiled at everyone beatifically.

The women wore tight, narrow skirts, their buttocks gleaming beneath
silk and satin. Elsa wore a Grecian-style dress with full sleeves and a hand-
ful of huge rings one of their friends had made for her out of seashells.
There was a biting scent of cinnamon from the hot grog. A man played the
piano with one hand, a punch glass in the other.

She was trapped in the corner with the Schmidts, a couple who for some
reason always sought her out, Albert Schmidt telling her about his most
recent article of language study in boring detail and Berenice Schmidt winc-
ing at Elsa as if she were a strong sunbeam.

Elsa was getting ready to disagree with something Albert had said about
French when, above the gatherings of dull and brown heads, she saw the

blond hair like spun yellow glass, and as the crowd parted, she saw Franz's broad shoulders where he stood pouring himself a drink.

"Excuse me," she said. "I see someone I know." She went over to him, smoothing her hair. "I didn't know you were back!"

He looked at her, then away quickly. "You were right. Munich *was* miserable this time of year."

They walked to the window, and he told her about the bug-infested hotel and the publisher who sucked on his teeth. They drank eggnog and ate cakes, and a couple of guests got so inebriated that they had to lean out the window to vomit. Someone played the piano, and she and Franz danced, while August sat in a chair, intoxicated, turning a box over and over in his hand.

Afterward Franz, August, and Elsa went home and sat on the blue couch in the parlor, and Elsa opened another bottle of champagne. There were carolers outside their window whose voices sounded hysterical, as if they might break the windows and rush inside. August had hung garlands of mistletoe over the doorways, and strings of popcorn and cranberries hung in scallops on the tree.

Elsa wrapped the blanket over her shoulders. "Where my mother was from in Poland, after the midnight mass, there was always a party at the castle, with stewed wine and plums and a diamond ring hidden in a cake." She turned to Franz. "Her father was a nobleman who lost all of his money— and then one day hanged himself." It was true that he'd killed himself, but the family's claim to nobility might have been a legend. Elsa's father had certainly never believed it, which was partly why she so badly wanted it to be true. "My grandfather supposedly had fine pianist hands like my mother's, but after he was ruined, they became arthritic. The diamond ring was his, and whoever found it on their plate or in their mouth was the one who wore it that year. It was the family's only treasure. And my mother, miraculously, had the ring three years in a row. For her, Christmas Eve was the night fortunes were restored. She was always so happy. But since she died, I feel this holiday mocking me."

August's eyes were closed, his head leaned back on the couch. "Don't pay any attention to it. It's a pagan holiday anyway." She imagined his tongue, limp and ashy in his mouth.

Franz's long fingers rubbed at the velvet of the armrest; then he smoothed it with the back of his hand. She wanted to offer him the velvet on her sleeve. "What's wrong with paganism?" he said. "It's a celebration of the winter. The primitives knew it was the best way to obliterate the cold and despair bound to come anyway."

August began to snore. His chest rose, and then came the plaintive honking.

Elsa looked over at him and then at Franz. "Try not to listen to him. He's had too much."

Franz sighed. "He's been working hard, hasn't he? Sometimes the only thing to do is to get drunk."

He was too formal with her, and she wanted to continue the conversation that she'd begun in their letters, to convince him to forget himself for a few moments, relax into their easy rapport. "Tell me about this novelist you met, the one who never removes his hat, whose wife is deaf. Did he ever become interesting?"

"Yes, in a way . . . but then our conversation was interrupted."

He looked as if he were about to say something else but then shook his head. He had a strong, perfectly formed nose, a worried, listening expression, and when she looked at him now, her arms began to tingle.

"Between sense lust and mind peace, man has but one anxious choice," she said. "What is your choice?"

Franz gazed at her. She wanted to touch his hair, and dug her fingers into the sofa's upholstery.

"I don't know yet."

August honked and sighed again.

"Should we put him to bed?" Elsa said, leaning over to touch August's arm.

August started. "What?"

"Why don't you go to sleep, dear?"

He rubbed his eyes. "All right," he groaned. He got himself up and walked up the staircase.

Franz and Elsa sat alone. The carolers had moved down the street, and now their voices sounded prettier, softened by the wind.

She poured them both more champagne. She could not stop looking at the shapely bend of his knee in his well-creased trousers. She wanted to cover it with her hand.

"I loved reading your letters," she said.

"Well, yes." Franz kept looking out the window, his voice flat and cool.

"Thank you for writing to me." She suddenly thought he must have written to many women. He was that type, handsome and remote, so that one leaned in closer and closer to make sure he heard what you were saying, never certain that he wasn't looking at the woman behind you. She was near enough now to see his skin's exquisite roughness, a faint pink scar beneath the beard shadow. She wondered if many women fell in love with him. She didn't believe what August had said about his preferring men.

The floor began to spin a little, as if it were the edge of a dangling ball. She moved closer to him on the couch. He seemed to be looking at the apples embroidered on the blanket.

It had been a year since August had tried to make love to her, and all that time seemed to be trembling in her now, the frustration heating up her blood, the longing awash on her skin.

She touched her hair, ran her finger along the smooth band of ribbon at her temple.

She watched as his thumb rubbed at a spot of powdered sugar on his trousers. She heard the clock hands click together, a rickety carriage outside on the street. They sat silently for a moment, Elsa's hand trailing closer to him across the sofa.

When she finally turned and fell against him, she briefly saw August's face. Even as Franz leaned away, his arm encircled her, and they kissed. She tugged away his fine tweed jacket and loosened his tie. He murmured something that sounded like "Hurry."

She shrugged off her dress, gathered up the lace of her chemise, and he rolled on top of her, warm and smelling of Christmas punch. His wide, muscled shoulders and strong, lean legs gave her the sensation that she was miraculously moving through a wall.

13

August raked his fingers through his thinning hair and held his head. "You chose Franz, of all the men in Berlin?"

"You wouldn't touch me, Tse." They were in the bedroom, where, within the leaf-squared frame, the nude nymph peeked out from behind a tree.

"I thought we were beyond the lines of the body."

She hated his metaphysics now. "God, you are such a gnostic. The world is not divided into spirit and matter." She sat down on the bed. "You wanted me to sleep with Heinz!"

He was pacing in front of her, throwing his arms around as if wiping away cobwebs from the air that obstructed his way. "And don't you see how much better that would have been?"

"No, I would have resented you. What do you think it would have meant to throw away my body like that?"

"Franz will leave, you know. He's not the type to keep a mistress for long."

"No, August," she said. "We're going away. To Italy." There in Berlin, the familiar buildings and friends pinned down her life in a way that made her feel old and exhausted, and she felt she had to leave, or else her affair with Franz might dissipate. For now it was tenuous and changing, like silver water running in a stream to a sea she couldn't visualize yet. In an unfamiliar place, her future with him might not seem so unlikely.

August sat down beside her on the bed and covered his mouth with his hands.

The slump of his body irritated her. But a moment later she felt overwhelmingly tender, as if all along they had only been brother and sister, and their marriage had been a sad mistake because no one had warned them.

She put her arms around him. "Stop, dear," she said. "Stop."

During this time she felt cut in half; one half hated the other, and the fight between the two confused her so much she had trouble remembering simple things like where she had left her key and whether or not she had washed her stockings. Franz did not seem to notice that only half of her was with him. He kept saying to her, "I feel terrible about August," just as he drew her to him by the belt of her skirt.

All that week they spent together, but August could not be left entirely alone. Elsa went back to him at the dinner hour, finding him sitting in a chair smoking his pipe, his eyes red, his words slurred as if his mouth had become too cumbersome for his face. He seemed so weak. "Don't leave, Elsa."

She warned him not to smoke too much hashish, she bought him a distracting novel, she took him to the café to make sure he ate. She was afraid that he might let his aesthetic sense of the pain get the best of him, that he might become fascinated by the red of his own blood or by the sensation of leaping from a bridge, convinced he was throwing himself into the sublime.

Franz bought three passages to Naples because he did not want to leave August alone, though she objected. She wanted to wait in Berlin until August seemed sturdier, but Franz was anxious to leave. The rumors had already begun, and Franz did not like the insinuation of his editor that he'd had designs on Elsa all along, or the way August's architect friends turned away when he saw them at the bar of a café.

"By the time we get to Italy, he'll be used to the idea," Franz said.

"What if he's not?"

"Let's not think of that."

The ship's rocking over the sea mimicked her own unsteadiness. When she was with August, she looked at his plump face and thought, "He's my husband. He knows me." Despite everything, she was comfortable with him. He had seen her drunk, puffy-faced, and weeping, her face covered in the red bumps of a rash; he had seen her ill-tempered and impatient. And then the boat would rock when she saw Franz. She thought of his square hands on her breasts and his wide shoulders lying over hers, the urgent way he pulled her to him, and the smell of soap on his arms. He didn't even seem to notice his effect on her. Her thighs would be burning, and he would calmly turn to her at the table and say, "Would you like a coffee?"

It was a five-day voyage. The three of them ate meals together as they always had and played pinochle when it rained. Elsa felt herself pulled painfully in two directions, while, oddly, Franz and August didn't even argue. She often felt as if one of them had died and, when they sat at the dining table, as if one were really a ghost.

There were musicians on board the ship, and every evening after dinner, passengers danced in the small ballroom. She was surprised to find that Franz was a somewhat awkward dancer, his body heavy and his sense of rhythm too regular to detect nuance. She gently guided him to the shadowed part of the dance floor, away from the couples under the yellow light.

"I want to go to bed." She pressed her breasts against him, felt the reassurance of his hard chest.

"Our exit would be too obvious. We don't want to be cruel." She agreed, though August had seemed to want the pain of watching her leave him, to draw it out in excruciating detail, as if his study of it would increase his understanding of doorways and exits, as if it would expunge some confusion in himself. She'd hoped he would be stronger by now, perhaps distracted by his commissioned design for the new museum. All of her sexual efforts seemed piled up like blocks she had to balance on her head. They pressed down, threatened migraines, but she couldn't let them collapse. She had to be strong because August couldn't be. "We'll say good-bye to him in Naples, then."

Franz looked past her, his mouth tight. "Of course."

At the end of the dance, Elsa found August at the edge of the dance floor. He was bleary-eyed from smoking but moved gracefully as he took her in his arms. She was furious at his helplessness. He needed to leave her in order to find his pleasure. How could he not know this yet?

"This music is awful," he said. "Did you hear the strings?" The dozen musicians sat on a raised platform, each one wearing a red tie, the bows of the strings speared above their heads, the horns gleaming.

"Well, what do you expect? They aren't real musicians." They danced, August squeezing her hand so hard it hurt her fingers, his other hand lightly pressed to her back.

"This ship, though, is much better than the one I took to Greece years ago. At least the cabins are clean."

Since they had boarded, he studiously avoided the subject of her leaving him. They talked about nonsense—the eggs at breakfast, the captain's cap, the ladies who played checkers on the deck eating licorice. "Franz is still looking for some art pieces for Benter's home. I would think Italy would be an excellent place to collect. Benter would like to have an antiquity or two. A fragment for the mantel or a small statue for the foyer, and Franz knows a dealer in Rome."

This contradicted what Franz had said about severing himself from the entire project. It saddened her that August would choose to ignore this, too, as another way to cling to them.

Being at sea erased one's past and future—only water in every direction. It was pleasant, that feeling of suspension, when she did not get dizzy. She would have liked to be allowed to swim, but that was impossible. One day they saw a shark fin razor up to the surface, and she had heard there were man-eating fish and giant octopi in those waters. Octopi fascinated her— blind and wiggling tentacles that grasped in all directions, a creature made entirely of need.

The women wouldn't look at Elsa, in her corsetless dress and barbaric jewelry. While some men might have surreptitiously watched her, others swung their heads away as soon as she came into view, so their wives wouldn't accuse them of anything untoward. The other passengers, affluent Germans and Austrians, avoided them, Elsa could tell, because they sensed something that was improper. She overheard one of the waiters saying that a complaint had traveled all the way to the captain, that these artists were conducting an unsavory perversity, right there on the sea, and wasn't it in his purview to arrest them? But he apparently had bigger worries, having to navigate the ship through two storms.

During the days on board the ship, her life could almost feel as it had before, Franz tall and aloof in the sunlight on deck, August silent or loquacious, his voice muddy from smoking.

One night the three of them stood at the railing on the deck, looking out at the sea. August had smoked so much hashish that his speech was slow and halting. Franz had drunk so much bourbon that he was slurring his words, and Elsa had a headache from the wine. She stood between them, watching the lights from the ship on the water like bright confetti ribbons.

"It's hard to believe there is anything out there," said Franz. "Except water. Now I feel as if the whole world is made of it."

"They call it sea blindness. It drives sailors mad," said Elsa. "Haven't you heard this? They start to believe the sea is solid like a vast, flat, blue desert, and they step over the railings of the ship because they are so desperate to touch it."

"The ocean is terrifying," said August. "Mad or not, I would never willingly go into it."

The music from the ballroom was faint behind them, and they could hear the water lapping below them against the sides of the boat.

"I would," said Elsa. "It would be so easy to climb over the rails."

Franz gazed at her, and she was conscious of how her silk shawl blew back over her shoulders in the wind. She imagined lifting her skirt, planting one foot on the bottom rung, and hoisting herself over. She wondered what it would be like to swim in her skirts and how far she would get before she exhausted herself. At the moment she felt as if she could swim for hours, water rushing in her ears, the sky dropping to the sea in a single endless horizon.

August put his hand on her shoulder, and she felt the familiar weave of his suit against her. "You wouldn't do it, dear. Your sense of self-preservation is too well developed for that."

Despite his barb, she felt a knotted love for him. "But I *can* see it."

"She daydreams," said Franz, sighing.

"I know." August's voice was bitter as he moved away from her. They stood quietly for a few minutes. Elsa felt the breeze against her bare arms. In that moment, annoyed at the ways they pretended to know her, she wanted to be rid of both of them.

"Do me a favor." August walked over to Franz. "Make sure you keep an eye on her when she is crossing the street."

Late in the voyage, Franz was in their cabin writing when Elsa and August lay reading on folding chairs on the deck. Elsa had drunk too much champagne the night before, and she felt as if hot taffy had been wrapped around her head. She tried to lose herself in the Knut Hamsun novel she had brought, which was strange and vivid like certain bold dreams.

"It's about time you finished with that book," said August.

"I thought we were on a holiday. I didn't know you were giving me reading assignments."

"This is my tenth book," he said.

"Congratulations."

"I'm thinking again about stage sets, how the structure interprets the drama it shelters, how certain sets are protective and others more open and libertarian." His mouth looked slack, and she wondered if he'd been smoking. "Because I can't sleep at all," he said. "I lie there thinking I can't believe that my friend is in bed with my wife. You think he will get your poems published, don't you?"

"Don't insult me."

"He won't, though. He only cares about his own fame. He wants to be *remembered*—how many times have you heard him say that? You're really in love with his poems, aren't you?"

She was afraid she might slap him in front of all these people pretending not to eavesdrop as they lounged on their deck chairs. "August, stop talking now."

"You made promises to me."

"Dear, you made promises, too. You couldn't keep them."

He laid his book down and touched her arm. "Let me try again. Now."

She looked at his drawn face, the green shadows beneath his eyes. Yesterday he had spent the day vomiting, and so had Elsa, watching the luggage roll out from under the bed and back, like giant, shy cockroaches. Franz had been fine—he had stood outside in the wind.

"No, August."

"Elsa, you don't have to leave me. I had a lot of time to think yesterday. I believe I could tolerate your affair. I've tolerated it all this time, haven't I? I only want us to be together when we go back. I understand that Franz—"

"Do you want everyone in Berlin to know? I'm not good at pretending. You know that." The ship's horn blew, muffled in the wind.

"We'll just avoid the gossips. The three of us could live together quite happily." The woman next to them, in a large straw hat, had put down her needlework, obviously listening.

"It would destroy your career."

A stiffness came to August's face. "I don't care anymore about that."

"But you will. You will soon."

He could not admit that he didn't want her, and his dishonesty about this fact infuriated her. And why couldn't he defend himself? She was afraid he would begin to weep.

"I don't know what I will do. I don't know. He doesn't love you, Elsa. No one loves you except me. No one has ever really loved you except me."

"I don't believe that."

"Franz doesn't—he can't—he's had too many women."

She had hardened herself against him—it was the only way. "I thought you said he preferred men."

He didn't answer but bowed his head. She couldn't help it if she'd hurt him. "If you love me, then why did you send me to that goddamn hellish sanatorium to have my womb twiddled?"

His face reddened. "I regret that now."

"August, dear, you can't make your cock hard for me—maybe you can for someone else."

She heard the woman in the hat gasp. He tapped his foot and balled his fist, finally angry. "You'll realize it too late, Elsa. You think he can give you everything, but he can't." He stood and walked away, his pants sadly baggy and loose around his thighs.

That evening, though, when he joined them for dinner, it was as if he had not said these things to her. He joked with Franz, smiled at Elsa. His dishonesty made her want to avoid him, but every day at breakfast, lunch, and dinner, there he was, her husband, sitting in a chair next to her lover.

14

Elsa had just bathed in the women's dressing area. She powdered herself, combed her hair, put on her gown, and went back to the cabin. August was sitting in the dimness.

"Where is Franz?"

"He's smoking on deck," she said.

"When he comes back, I want to watch you—" His eyes were haunted and desperate. "I want to see what you look like, the pleasure on your face." For a while she'd known this, without telling herself she knew, and for a moment she considered what it would be like to have both of them, each attending to different parts of her.

His eyes looked wild, but their hazel color had dulled. He bit his lip salaciously. "Please. It would give me something to think about." He must have known that Franz would never agree to it. Franz was already embarrassed when a man he was playing cards with told him the rumor going around the ship about the three of them.

Franz's books were laid out on the bed, his newly polished dress shoes neatly lined up in front of the closet. "You saw the way he looked at me all along, didn't you? You knew about the letters—you must have seen them on the table. And you never said a thing. You kept inviting him to our house. You wanted this to happen." Her hands were shaking. "You wanted him to be your surrogate."

"No."

"What did you want, then?"

August shrugged. "I thought he might love me. . . ." He hid his face in his hands.

Looking at the sunburned top of his head, she thought at least it would be easier to leave him now.

"How could I not?" he said.

From the deck of the ship, Elsa and Franz watched the approach of Naples. Out of the sapphire water loomed a green hill checkered with neat red-tiled roofs, cliffs of majestic rock spilling into the sea. To the right sat the ugly, square Castel del'Ovo, where (she'd read) Virgil had buried an egg, predicting that when it broke there would be some disaster. In the blond southern light, the landscape looked just as she'd seen it in paintings—lushly green and gold-misted—except for that monstrous castle like a block of gray set down to erase some part of the picture.

August had suggested that he would stay in the same hotel as Elsa and Franz, but Franz flatly refused, and she was relieved that she would soon not have to explain herself to August anymore.

"He's almost as in love with you as I am," Elsa said, stretching her bare arms in the sun.

Franz shifted his feet as if they had begun to hurt him. "Don't be silly. We had a friendship, and it was only grief that made him say that to you. Grief muddles things." He turned his head to the shore and pointed out the busy port.

When they landed, August planned to rent a bicycle and ride it around the Amalfi coast. "I need to clear my mind," he kept saying, resentfully.

They parted after a drunken lunch of spaghetti. At the restaurant, crowded with square tables and men with sunburned faces, the proprietress mingled among the tables and sang in an operatic voice, flinging her arms in the air with a furious look on her face.

Franz said, "He's not going to make it easy for us. I think you should wait until he calms down before you ask him for a divorce. You have grounds, of course, but it would be humiliating to use them. And he could always blame the problem on you."

"He already did that, Franz. Did you see the pathetic way he looked at us when we left him there? He's smoking so much I don't know how he's going to ride a bicycle."

Franz set his lips and nodded. "He'll be all right in a little while."

In Naples they stayed at the Hotel Medici, with its plush carpets, paintings of pudgy, creamy girls with dark hair, and chandelier light, so at odds with the twisting, crowded streets. They visited a chapel where the remains of a nobleman's servants had been preserved behind glass, for the study of their anatomy; they went to a performance of *Tosca* at the opera house with its balconies of gilded cherubs. After a week they went on to Sorrento, where they lived for a month in the Cocumella, a former monastery with great sweeping archways and stained-glass windows, a garden of lemon trees behind it. Every morning Elsa climbed down the cliff to the shore, where she swam in the clear water, and when she came back, Franz was waiting for her, naked, in the bed.

She could tell he was disappointed in her responses to their lovemaking—she tended to be silent, concentrating on the nerve-buzzing fervor in her breasts and between her thighs. Afterward he would sigh and glumly watch her face, and she tried to reassure him with kisses and laughter. She was so happy she did not understand how he could not see it. Finally, on the third day he told her, "I cannot seem to satisfy you." Daylight glowed beyond the pale curtains.

"What do you mean? Of course you do." He shook his head and asked why she never felt "complete."

"That's a silly myth, Franz. Women don't complete the act the way men do. The whole business is in their nerves, the fingertips, the toes, the tongue." She licked his cheek.

He moved slightly away. "Of course a woman can come to climax." She saw the surprise in his face and briefly recalled how Natalye had said something like this. But men were so easily deluded about women and what they wanted, and this was how the rumors started. "You've been fooled by some lovely who knew how to perform."

"I don't think so." He shook his head, inching his hand beneath her chemise.

All of that week, he tried to prove her wrong. Lying beside her, he teased her with his finger and tongue. Her challenge to him had made him patient and intent, and more than once she laughed at his seriousness. But then he put his warm hand somewhere else on her body and her breath caught, or his lips on her thigh suddenly made her feel as if she had an excess of blood pressing against her skin. When she finally felt the tense, hot unspiraling, she was astonished. As if her spirit had bucked out of her in those few seconds.

They followed the usual European tour: Capri, where they sailed through the eerie blue grotto; Positano, where they climbed down hundreds of stairs and ate sea breams from salty plates; Amalfi, where they sat in gardens, gazing across the water at Mount Vesuvius in the distance, guessing when it would next erupt, though calamity seemed distant in that sea air smelling of lemons. They spent as much time in their hotel rooms as they did sightseeing in little boats guided by tanned, shirtless sailors, or in carriages driven by wizened men in big hats.

When she was with Franz, the occasional recurring symptoms of the syph—the headaches, the vague stiffness in her knees, and the stomachaches—disappeared. The doctor had predicted time would cure her, but she believed the real antidote was her newfound pleasure.

They had planned to spend just one evening in Ravello, a stone city at the tip of a tall hill full of gardens and chapels, where the air smelled of violets. They stayed at the inn where Wagner had supposedly once spent the night composing the second act of *Parsifal* on an out-of-tune piano, while outside the villa a thunderstorm raged.

That night two officials climbed the steep hill and visited their inn to arrest Franz Trove. They accused him of embezzling seven thousand marks entrusted to him by August Lydell and Marc Benter.

15

On the carriage ride to the jail, she looked out at the sea below them, the moonlight sifting in the water. It was all a mistake, but neither of them would be able to explain to these officials, who knew so little English. "Of course he invented this to get back at you—I knew that any arrangement with that troll Benter was bound to be a disaster," she said.

"Men do terrible things when they're desperate."

In the dank police quarters, they sat marooned among the restless Italian conversations, the police at the table, the bystanders near the door, the sputtering man in handcuffs in the hallway.

"Why don't you just return the money?"

"I haven't got it, Elsa."

"What do you mean?"

"I don't have the money."

She had never considered the exact nature of Franz's wealth, only knew there was something there because he was always so handsomely dressed, so free at restaurants. "Really? But you didn't steal the money." Her stomach clenched. She thought of waking up in a hotel bed without him, the empty room, the empty drawers.

He stared down at his folded hands. "No—Benter never sent me his share, and he's claiming that he never received the Slevogt paintings that were shipped to him months ago, when I've seen the receipts that he signed after they arrived."

Where was August? He should have been there, accusing Franz to his face, demanding his money. Instead he'd cowardly sent his surrogates, who barely spoke German and knew only to hand him over at the border. How could Franz defend himself? The matter was too complicated.

She put her arms around him. "The truth will come out soon enough."

He gave her the money he had in his wallet and in a little pouch he kept hidden at the garter for his sock, and he said, "The judge will be apprised of the situation, and I'll be back before too long."

Franz received a sentence of six months in a Munich prison.

Franz insisted that she stay in Italy, in the healthy sea air and light, even if she would not be able to visit him, and the money he gave her was enough for her to live on if she was careful. She went back to Sorrento and stayed for two months in the Cocumella, where she liked to sit among the lemon trees with her notebook. Some days she lingered around the statue of Tasso in the park that looked out at the sea. Tasso, the great Italian poet whose words she could not understand, kept his eyes on her. She held imaginary conversations with him in her head about the names of a certain spindly tree, the hard-shelled beetle she'd found in her bed, and the little white fish she'd seen eddying in a pool among the rocks. If only she could name certain things she had seen, it seemed she could stop the trembling in her hands, the twitch in her eyelid, the way she shivered each night in bed.

She'd seen the pained surprise on Franz's face when, in Naples, she showed him the poem she considered the best in her notebook. As he looked down at the pages, she thought he'd be shocked that she didn't write "lady verse," treacly lines with insipid rhymes, but he only said, "I think perhaps you should continue with this," and then, very formally, handed her back the notebook.

Of course she would continue with it. That had never been a question. "But what do you think of it?"

"It's promising," he said, clearing his throat. Then he pulled her to him and kissed her.

Soon her fingernails and eyelashes and saliva would all be in the service of a poem. She wanted to devote herself but did not yet have the patience. At night, enervated and high, she would write long poems, and then the next day, loathing herself, tear up the pages. Only a few verses that she didn't hate accumulated in her notebook, scrawled down the page in her blocky handwriting like outlines of crumbling buildings.

Your face lightning-thunder
A drunken flower

In September, August had the gall to find out through the prison officials where she was and came to see her at the old monastery in Sorrento. She was standing in the gardens, on a cliff that overlooked the blue sea. There was a tree nearby with leaves that smelled oddly like semen. Looking at the boats gliding evenly in the distance, she wondered what Franz was doing at that moment in jail, how he was occupying his mind.

August suddenly walked up through the lemon trees. He'd grown a beard and looked thinner, his pants clipped around the hem for pedaling the bicycle. Seeing his exhaustion, she felt a rush of guilt before she remembered what he'd done. She ran to him and slapped his face. "Liar!"

"Elsa, it wasn't me, believe me. Benter filed the charges."

"Why should I believe you?"

"I swear. Don't you think I know how that would seem? But look, Franz is a fake—he took all of our money. He kept promising that the paintings had been shipped, but they never arrived."

"Then why did he want you to sail to Italy with us, if he'd just cheated you? I argued against it."

August's face swerved away. "That's simple. He wanted me out of Berlin so that by the time I realized the shipment had never arrived, it would be too late."

The gardener approached through the grove, plucking lemons from the trees and laying them in a basket. He smiled at them, his wrinkled brown skin like the shell of a walnut.

"You're lying—Franz told me he'd seen the receipts. Benter's the crook here. He's a ridiculous man—how could you even trust him?" She remembered how he waved his cane at pretty girls as if it were a gun he'd wanted to shoot them with. "You'll take any man with money, won't you? Even the stupid ones."

"Benter isn't lying, and I did try to stop him—I'd prefer not to have the scandal."

The gardener, humming, came closer, inspected the fruit on the tree nearest them.

"Oh, of course! A scandal! Don't even think of a man wasting six months of his life in prison, and you didn't even have the decency to accuse him to his face." The blue sea beneath them was calm, a fishing boat in the distance, the rocky cliffs on either side of the bay grand and severe. It was possible that she might be alone for a long time now.

"That doesn't matter," August said. "Come back with me to Berlin. I'll take care of you. Don't be foolish."

Looking at August, she panicked. She'd rather struggle alone in a foreign place, penniless and homeless, than return to that house, with its sneering, celibate nudes. "Will you please go away? Nothing you say will keep me from waiting for him here."

"Oh, and then what will you do? We're not even divorced yet."

He put his arms around her and tried to kiss her, but she turned her head. He pulled away from her. "I won't grant you a divorce," August said.

The gardener said, *"Bella, bella,"* holding out the basket to them and gesturing for them to take one. Elsa took a lemon and held it to her nose, but August shook his head, and the gardener scowled at him before walking away.

"Dear August," she said coolly. "Our marriage isn't even consummated."

"You'll change your mind." He wanted to stay with her in the hotel that night, but she insisted that he leave, and he went pedaling off on his bicycle in the night.

She traveled back to Naples, the city born out of the grave site of Parthenope, the mermaid who, as her tour guide had put it, had made her own grave on the Neapolitan shore. All over there were portraits of the mermaid, her bare round breasts, her thighs hidden in the fishtail, her face mournful, as she'd died because of her doomed love for that man, Ulysses, who'd gone off without her on another adventure. Elsa, tired of seeing that sad lady's face everywhere, wished she had swum off and had underwater adventures of her own. Couldn't she have fallen in love with a seahorse or a whale?

One day an Englishwoman she met in the hotel dining room, apparently wanting to practice her German, told Elsa in scandalized terms about the school there in Naples for artists' models. "I saw it near the square—clearly marked. These Italians have so little shame. It's all the beach air and light."

Elsa, eating her pasta, said, "Isn't that what you came here for?"

She had not meant to be unfriendly, but the woman's mouth went ajar as she stared down at her plate, and she seemed relieved when a fat Irishman joined them at their table.

Elsa was bored, and the idea of posing for Italian painters intrigued her. The memory of August's nudes still taunted her, but she thought maybe posing for others would allow her to take her beauty back for herself. Already she liked the way Italian men's eyes lingered on her form, the brash and inept way they flirted. Their eyes on her suggested they envied her privacy, wanted to peer inside it, to the hidden poems still unwritten within her.

She enrolled in one of the classes. Even though she understood only a small amount of the woman's Italian, she understood the basic instruction. There were classic poses that enhanced the beauty of the female form—arms caught behind the back to bring out the breasts, a hip turned to one side to exaggerate its curve, sitting with a leg extended to show the muscles of the calves.

Now that she knew her own climax, how spirit and flesh collided, celibacy made her feel barren and heartsick. She could not sleep, and when she did, her dreams were strange and disturbing, full of antlered deer chasing her and instances of putting her hand to her mouth and finding that her teeth had started to crumble. During the day she could not eat more than a small amount, and she was always shivering in the bright, humid sea air. She sat on a bench in the square, while the coal-eyed men and women, spoke their liquid Italian to one another.

On the way back from the school one day, she stopped at the museum where she liked to study the ancient statues and artifacts from Pompei. There was a room where women were not allowed, cordoned by a blue velvet rope and blocked by a stern guard. Elsa marched up to him with his prim mustache. "I am not Italian, see?"

He shook his head and held his arm out across the doorway to block her.

"You don't have to worry about protecting my honor." She didn't know the words in Italian. He obviously did not understand.

He glared at her as if she were a schoolgirl.

"What are you afraid of? Riots?" A storm rushed up in her and wanted to blow all over the museum. She was alone in the world. Why shouldn't she do whatever she wanted? Why shouldn't she see everything?

She pushed past him and ducked under the velvet rope. *"Signora!"* he roared, but there were tourists standing behind her, and he did not go after her.

Inside the room the light was pale and milky around the statues of beautiful nude men, standing on pedestals as if they had just stepped out of the bath, oblivious to all the others. Each singular body was muscled and graceful, his member curled or cupped, his eyes stony, staring into the distant future.

Along the back wall, there were cabinets with glass doors, which, remarkably, while the guards fretted about what to do, she had time to examine. They were filled with ancient phalluses, unearthed and brushed off. There were some as large as thighs and others as small as fingers. Several had wheels attached, ready to speed like chariots; others had grown wings or feet; others pushed greedy faces from their tips. This ancient culture had understood it, what she'd felt with Franz—contact with the spirit—direct. The manifestation of a life force. But one never saw a phallus in the galleries in Berlin, only an occasional hidden or disguised limp penis. For some reason, in this era, it was left to the nude woman to draw out that life, as if there were some lack in the world now that the hole inside a woman mirrored. But once there had been a male power equally potent, and wouldn't it have been better to have both? She checked the cool glass door of the cabinet, wondering if she could successfully smuggle out one of the artifacts. Then she heard the footsteps and shouting of the guards.

She turned around to find them rushing into the room, their black hair gleaming, as they raced around the statues calling, *"Signora!"* When one spotted her, he clapped his damp hand over her eyes and grabbed her elbow, muttering in Italian. The other one followed, shouting angry, incomprehensible words at her back.

When she was in her hotel again, she opened her notebook, her neck tingling, and wrote into the night:—*Octopus love pillow's / recuperating capacity / suck disks / to sharp arm within / ecstatic elastic / feminine.*

She worried about Franz, so elegant and charming, imprisoned in a cell without light or conversation, forced to eat stale food and sleep on a wormy cot. They let him keep his books and papers, thank God. She wrote letters to him about his ability to "make her star explode"; how, when he returned, she wanted him to put his hands on her breasts while she looked out the window, and perhaps she would bend over the sill, and then she wanted him to take her into a closet while a dinner party went on in another room, their love-making sweet and furtive, how she wanted to eat grapes from his hot skin, how there was a tree with a leaf that smelled of semen, how the warm salt water made her ache for him, and she wanted him back between her thighs.

A letter came from Franz: *Darling, please do not be so forward. The guards are cutting out pieces and reading them. They say they are censoring, but I hate to think of them amusing themselves with your words.*

Standing knee-deep in the seawater one cloudy day, as Elsa looked out at the roiling waves, she was afraid. She kicked up the cold water, smooth stones hard under her foot as she walked. She could not help thinking of her mother's penchant for sad stories about people unsuited for the world, the beautiful woman who had no legs or arms, the man who hid in an attic, drawing intricate landscapes no one would ever see. She knew that her mother believed it was her own doom to have chosen the wrong man, but perhaps she simply hadn't known how to be happy, and it would not have mattered who she married.

For now the only way Elsa could reach Franz was her correspondence, but it consoled her to tell him everything. She resolved to be surgically precise in her dealings with him, to get rid of every duplicity that she'd harbored in herself.

That day my mother put on her velvet dress, with a heavy train and embroi-dery on the bodice and sleeves, a vine of yellow roses from the shoulder to the wrist. There was snow and ice on the ground, but she did not wear a coat or hat when she went out. Until now Elsa had kept the story to herself. That day her mother had walked down the street and turned through the market square, avoiding the sidewalk, dragging through the mud and horse shit, and then, near the marina, she took the path through the spear weeds down to the sea.

Elsa wondered about those people on the street—the shopkeepers and women buying vegetables, the tobacconist and the hatmaker—they must have seen her and known that something was wrong. But in her middle age, her mother had become frightening to those timid provincials. *And they must have been afraid to stop her.*

She walked through the sand, hard with ice, her footsteps making chewing sounds, until she reached the water, which would have been so cold it shocked her, though the act was deliberate. She kept wading in, her steps slowed only when the water reached her thighs and her skirts tangled around her. Still she glided forward, her eye on that expanse of gray-green, until she lost her footing. Her head dipped underwater. *She wanted to die. But at the last moment, she was too afraid to drown.* That was the moment Elsa always thought of, the cold black water, the smell of salt, and the sudden fatigue in her legs.

No one saw her. No one came to her rescue.

Later she walked through the market, her blond hair plastered to her head so she looked bald, her drenched dress sparkling with sand and ice. Then the gossip began to burn through the rotten wood of all those dull lives. *Why didn't anyone try to help her?*

Franz wrote to her that when he was released, if August would grant them a divorce, he wanted to marry her. She wrote to him about the time her father had burned her paintings, how she had seen him in the streets with the woman who kept a room above the tavern, how he was never sick because he drank boar's blood on Sundays.

I am hearty like my father, but not dishonest.

Elsa blamed her mother's despair on her acute shame and did her best to annihilate this tendency in herself, which was why she struggled to write everything for Franz, even about the modeling school, where she earned "at least as much as the cows and goats they bring in," and even about how after dinner the other night at the hotel, she had passed wind, "just a little ball."

She wrote twenty poems during those months in Italy, though she didn't feel she'd focused enough on any of them. She was distracted by the orange flowers and dark-eyed men; she drank too much red wine and sat in the shade with her pencil, just watching people pass by. The things she wrote were like private little mirrors, phrases only she would recognize, rhythms she'd heard one day but could not recall later.

On the day Franz was released from prison, she took the train to

Munich to meet him. Riding in the carriage on the way over, she noticed several women wearing hats so wide they would not easily fit through a doorway, the new fashion. She was nervous about seeing him again. He had said he would marry her, but maybe when he saw her, in her straw boater hat and Italian cotton shirtwaist, he would change his mind. She couldn't help taking his absence as a slight, though it wasn't his fault. She knew that it was irrational, but it had felt as if he were practicing to leave her.

When she walked into the waiting room where he was sitting, his kneecaps so sharp against his neat black trousers, his saucy nose turned to her, she rushed over to him. Before she could touch him, he said, "Let's get out of here," taking her by the elbow and quickly escorting her outside.

After he closed the door of the carriage, he pulled down the driver's window shade and kissed her, and she forgave him for his long absence. Back in their room, she forgave him again.

16

Y ou're thinner," she told him. "They did not feed you well."
He brushed the lint off his new herringbone. "Actually, a cell makes a good office."

"You cannot mean that."

"No—I do. I missed you, of course, but the austerity was good for poetry."

She soon found out that he had not completed a poem in over a year.

They went to Paris, where Franz could meet the French writer André Gide, whose novels he had been contracted to translate, and they lived in a small hotel in the Marais, near the Jewish district.

Franz was no longer so easy with money, because he understood now that it might cost him his freedom. He'd even slightly curbed his manner, to a more straightforward, less flamboyant style. He'd lost his easiness, and without the cover of glamour, a cruelty leaked out. Even her mildest flirtations at a party sent him spinning in rage. "Your rouge and powders only make you look older," he told her. She helped him with his translations, wrote out the tedious passages, and listened to him read the finished chapters, but if she made a mistake, he scolded her. "You can't just stack up the words like kindling, dear. You have to make the fire."

Still, he was lovely with his blond hair and eyes intent on her as if they were always seeing through the fabric of the clothes. And, though she endured his snips and tirades, each night she was drugged with pleasure.

Elsa and Franz traveled, following the work of his translations, avoiding Berlin because of August and all the unpleasantness that would surround them when they returned. After Germany declared war on France and Russia, they continued to avoid Berlin, where Franz risked being called into military service.

They spent a year in Paris, where they saw almost no one except Gide; a year and seven months in London, where there were frequent drunken parties; another ten months in Switzerland, where Elsa rode horseback and learned to cook meats. Elsa wrote in hotel rooms, train cars, and cafés, collecting the poems in cloth-covered notebooks that she kept hidden in drawers because they weren't ready yet to be read by anyone except herself. She was still learning how to listen and see. She wanted to find out how to include the silence in a poem, how to wrap words in their essences so they hung organically on the page like fruit, but she was impatient with her progress, and she ruined several attempts by hurrying.

August finally agreed to an annulment of their marriage when he realized Elsa was not coming back, and as soon as she signed the papers, she and Franz were married by a jolly judge in a Paris government building. Then they got drunk on Pernod in the middle of the afternoon, and Franz sang to her.

A few weeks later, she grew tired of wearing her long hair pulled up into a knot under her hat. Why grow one's tresses long if they were always hidden? On a whim one day, she asked the beautician for a bob and henna.

The shampooers came over to examine her, shaking their heads. "It's good for a woman to look feminine, no?"

Feminine, Elsa knew, was a power so pervasive it didn't need landmarks or signs. "Cut it," she said.

The scissors trembled in the beautician's hands, and afterward Elsa looked like an Irish Cleopatra.

When she arrived home, Franz gasped. "What happened? Why is it so red?" He acted as if her head were a wound.

"It's only hair," she said testily. Men didn't understand how a fashion, repeated so many times, became like a punishment.

"Dear, you look low-class."

"Why are you so concerned about low-class?" She knew it was because he'd been in prison, but this nonetheless hurt her.

"We'll buy you a wig."

He did not like her oilcan earrings or the dress with the painted panel, so he bought two dresses in the high style, both "proper for a married lady," one with a tall collar and a wide belt, and a velvet one with a less modest neckline. He was so pleased with himself when he presented them to her in their boxes that she did not have the heart to say that they looked drab to her. Resentfully, she wore them.

In bed he petted her, called her his cat. She took him in her mouth, in her fingers, in her ass. He held his hand over her mouth so she would not cry out. He expertly ran his fingers along her hip bones, her belly, her breasts. He let his lips graze her thighs and put his hand on either side of her body as if to hold her in, or to lift her. When he was inside her, he didn't notice anything, not even the wind howling through the open window, not even the boisterous singing in the next room.

Franz wrote his poems on stiff paper and tacked different versions of them on the bedroom wall. Elsa saw pieces of herself appearing in them—a phrase she had said, a pink scarf she had worn, the story she had told about the hairdresser in Swinemünde. It flattered her to know he'd listened so intently. But he couldn't finish anything, and that only darkened his moods. His poetic fragments were so polished perfect, she thought, each one like a jewel somehow missing the rest of its necklace.

At one party Franz insisted to a group of friends that he would make his mark somehow, that he wasn't at all satisfied with his meager output so far, stunted as it was by all the hackwork he had to do. Later in the evening, among the tweedy London men and their wives, she overheard him saying, "A woman writing poetry is absurd." At first she delayed her reaction, as if it had been someone else who said it. Most men thought this of women poets (flowers, emotions like sticky candies, lacy rhymed verse), like that woman, Danae

Meyer: *Alas he died that winter / Snow falling like powder.* Later Elsa internally defended herself with the notion that he considered her the exception.

She dreaded showing him her poems, but she wanted to know if they could be absorbed by anyone other than herself. She bided her time, waiting for the lines to arrange themselves in a way that held. Too often, reading a poem later, she'd want to change everything, and this weakened her confidence. Finally, one evening in their hotel room, she read to him the poem about the marina in Swinemünde. He knew the landscape, and she thought he would appreciate its intention. It was called "Thunder."

Until she had finished the last line, his expression was that of a captured animal. "It's pretty," he said afterward. "It resembles that Müller poem about the garden."

Her breath caught, as if the table where they sat had suddenly crushed into her. "It's pretty? The burned ships and sawing shadows are sweet?"

He shrugged at her and closed the notebook. "What do you want me to say? I think it's a good diversion for you. It takes years to develop a genuine ear." She did not know what he meant by "genuine." She wanted to hear fiercely, like a hunting dog.

"Tell me, then, you don't like it. Don't patronize me."

"I like it because you wrote it." She'd heard him criticize himself and had read those reviews of his that seemed to wrap barbed wire around the work, and it annoyed her that he didn't seem to believe she was strong enough to hear his true opinion.

"You think it's amateur work."

"Yes, it's amateur work. So what?"

She would make it better.

In London, Franz worked on translating Oscar Wilde for his German publisher, and Elsa, still stung by his last critique, ripped up some of her poems and wrote new ones that one would never call "pretty." If a woman writing poetry was ridiculous, then she was going to swim in her own absurdity, let the least likely words crawl out from her pencil, hunched and bloody, unrestrained.

> *Let me taste the perspiration of*
> *Your windtangled skin.*

Your Octopus charms
In the tournament of sheets.

Franz's temper flared more often as the war wheeled forward, as if he felt some personal stake in it. He didn't like to go out anymore, and he began to complain that he was sick of eating in restaurants and wanted to move to a farmhouse. In Switzerland they had begun to meet on Wednesday nights with a group of Austrians, among whom there was a novelist who said he wanted to read her poems. Franz did not care for him. They spent most of their time alone in the small villa, borrowed from friends, whom Franz resented because they hadn't told them where to find the things they'd need—candles, blankets, wine. And because Franz wasn't writing, he had tantrums ending in long, solitary walks in the middle of the night, and he wouldn't eat the Stroganoff she'd taught herself to cook for him.

When he came home with the mail one day in June, shouting that he'd won the Schwendeman Prize for Verse, she was relieved. He was always happiest when he won prizes, and it had been a long time since one had come along.

"Were they new poems?"

His blond hair gleamed in the lamplight, his eyes tired-looking from reading. "Yes, of course. And it's an American magazine, *LETTERS*, that's publishing them." He suddenly cooled his voice and manner, as if embarrassed by his joy. "The prize is three hundred dollars."

Along with the money he'd just been paid for a Shaw translation, they had enough money for boat fare to New York. "I want to get out of Europe, away from all this hack work and all the newspapers," he said. Now that the war continued, whenever they saw a German newspaper, there were slogans: EVERY SHOT WILL HIT A RUSSIAN. EVERY STAB WILL DOWN A FRENCHMAN. There were rumors about soldiers raping women and shooting small children. Two of Franz's friends from Berlin had enlisted, and then he'd lost touch with them. Europe seemed to be fragmenting, just as the publishers began to ignore Franz's poems, so America held promise of unknown success and escape.

Elsa had never been interested in visiting a wilderness like America—she preferred old cities—but it was the first time in a long while that Franz was hopeful. He believed that his English was good enough to translate his poems from German, and said he'd heard that Manhattanites loved Europeans. After some time away and the prize of this publication, she thought he might regain his confidence, and things would not be so strained between them.

On the boat there were two beds in their cabin. On one, Franz irritably finished the translation of another novel by André Gide, and on the other, Elsa studied her English dictionary, reading Lawrence's *Sons and Lovers* and the guidebook. The voyage was so different from that first trip to Italy, when the uncertainty of their future had been dazzling. What would she have to say to these Americans, with their cowboys and Pilgrims, their somber presidents' faces carved out of rock, and their Model T Fords zooming the streets like mobile monsters?

17

She had to push her way through crowds on the Manhattan streets, a man's hot breath on her cheek, the brief scent of female powdery sweat, someone stepping on her toe, a man crying out, "Lucinda! Come back!" and a woman turning to another: "Have you been in the shop with the lamps next to the hats?" And just as she pulled herself out of the fray, a wall assaulted her: BEECHUM'S FORMULA FOR STRONGER BLOOD.

She walked and walked and still did not see all of the city. The buildings, so tall they shaded the streets, dimmed some spots so that it was almost impossible to know the weather. Mirrors and chrome zigzagged down Fifth Avenue; electric lights in Times Square replaced the constellations with SHOW and CODY'S. There were hundreds of banks, dressed up to look like Greek temples, and department stores that looked like palaces, and gilded figures of Venus or heroes in armor perched atop an ordinary hat store or tile factory.

Franz tried to hide it, but he was frightened of Manhattan—the loud trains and crowded sidewalks. He preferred to stay inside the rooms they rented on Thirty-second Street, writing and sleeping off hangovers as if they were in the country during a storm. She hated the old-woman furnishings, the lightless rooms. She needed to go out and walk the brash, frenetic streets, and when she did, he always found a reason to be angry with her.

Franz had met with the editor of *LETTERS*, who had given him a note of introduction to three publishing houses, but Franz kept muttering, "No sense in going until the poems come out. Until the issue is published and I have something to show the bastards." Franz was disappointed in *LET-TERS* once he saw an issue in the bookstore on the shelf among many others—the *Masses, Poetry*, the *Glebe*. "It wasn't even displayed prominently." And when he went to visit the office, he said it was shoddy—"one room and a hundred piles of papers"—and the editor, who was as tiny as a twelve-year-old boy, announced apologetically that the issue in which Franz's poems were to appear would be delayed by two months. Mrs. Schwendeman, a German widow who had donated the prize money, wanted Franz to give a public reading, but, for a reason Elsa didn't understand, he was reluctant, said his English wasn't good enough. The invitation only seemed to depress him. He sat next to a window, his body hunched like a crab around his notebook.

Elsa walked alone through the green of Central Park, through the overly lit shops on Ladies' Mile, to the monumentally tall Woolworth Building, where she nervously rode the elevator all the way to the observation deck on the fifty-eighth floor and looked through the window down at the shrunken people and automobiles.

New York had no history, only a future. Things changed so quickly one could never be certain what one saw. On the street there were beautiful women with long scarves and large red mouths, who, as they came closer, were changed into hags in shawls, screaming. There were tall, elegant men in tailored suits, carrying canes, who were transformed by proximity into men in work suits with pipes clutched in their hands.

One day she would walk down Twenty-sixth Street and spot a hat she liked in a store window, and the next time she went down that street, the hat shop would have become a butcher's, the mannequin heads metamorphosed into sausage rings. Her favorite café was changed overnight, it seemed, into a barbershop, and she almost burst in on a man getting a shave. There was construction everywhere—half-finished buildings opened up to show the guts of plumbing, just-poured curbs fenced by sawhorses, with boot prints in the soft gray mud.

One day near Times Square, she got caught in the rain without an umbrella and ran through the crowds, across the shiny streets, the car lights bright beads in the silver downpour, the street signs blurred. She ran up the stairs of their building, her dress dripping wet—and found that Franz had left. The empty room—as the lightning flashed—seemed to lift up and slam down again.

Her shoes sloshed wet across the floor, and she went into the kitchen, found the note pinned to a dish towel.

Dearest Elsa,

I have gone away. Our fighting and our unhappiness would destroy us both. I have left a hundred dollars in the envelope on my desk, and the names of people you should write to, for passage back to Germany. This was all a mistake, but it's too late to be undone.

Franz

After she read the note, it was as if she had known what it would say all along, even before she'd seen it, even before she'd walked into the apartment, even before they'd landed in New York. Shivering, she peeled off her wet clothes and lay down on the floor, the hard boards beneath her cradling her bones. She closed her eyes, felt her nakedness in the dark room, and when she started to weep, realized that she'd been tightly holding her breath for a long time.

The bath in the building where Franz and Elsa had been living was a shared one, and the pipes had frozen and burst, so she was forced to go to the Kleinfeld Baths, where one could wash for a fee. Elsa sat in the dressing room waiting for her hair to dry before going out into the cold. The rooms had a stale, yeasty smell, and there were patches of emerald fungus in the corners of the tiled stalls.

A ruddy-faced woman sat at the mirror combing her black hair. "I didn't know you had to bring your own soap," she said. "Did you?" Her hair hung in streaks on either side of her face like paint.

Elsa was very cold, with her coat wrapped over her dress. At the front entrance, they'd charged her for a soap sliver like a shaving of cheese. "I did not know there would be so little heat."

"I'm going to get a room with a private bath as soon as I can. My fiancé is looking."

Elsa ran the towel over her head again. Without Franz she didn't know how much longer the landlord would let her stay, but she tried not to think about it.

"I've had a lot of admirers"—said the woman, wiping pomade over her scalp—"about twenty—but this is the first one to propose. Are you married?"

"I was."

The woman turned around. "I'm sorry. You lost him?"

Things did not change so quickly in Germany, where the resonance of centuries, palaces, and kings sounded behind even the slightest everyday activity—a walk to the store, a kiss in the park. She didn't belong in this place with its cheerful coarseness, its banks dressed up as cathedrals, and the shininess and speed of streets built for millionaires. She wanted to go home.

"He didn't die."

"Oh."

The woman turned back around and began twisting her hair into a knot. "This is the first one who proposed—I think because I let him, you know, I wanted him to do it, so he did. All the others, I didn't want to do much with them, you know? I didn't want to give them anything. A man has to feel as if he can ask his wife to do anything for him. Don't you agree?"

Elsa's hair was still wet, but she could not stand to sit in the smelly room any longer. "Some men don't feel things at all. That's what they need us for." She stood up.

"You're not from here. Where are you from?" She had a way of talking as if her mouth were full.

"Me?" Elsa saw her face in one of the mirrors, watery around her lips, as if her mouth were dissolving, her eyes pink and shrinking, not quite a human face. "The moon."

Elsa pushed the door of the baths open and went outside into the freezing air, feeling icicles form in the roots of her hair. She would be ill, but she was cheered slightly by the brightness of the snow on the sidewalk, glittering around the hard patches of footprints.

She had wanted to be scrupulously honest with Franz, but he punished her for it, and eventually she'd given up. The gluey wigs and proper dresses were lies, no different from the ways she'd learned to obscure an innocent flirtation at a party or her disagreement with his praise of that English writer Trollope.

She took account of her lies: she had given up on the notion that Franz would one day write a great sonnet; she'd told the Austrian novelist that she would meet him in secret to discuss her poems; she had lately been feeling stale and flabby; and yet, regarding each of these matters, she had told Franz that the opposite was true. Like many women, she massaged facts until they pleased her husband, but she'd done it badly.

In the last two years, she'd been drawn by the gloom caused by his unfinished poems. She realized that the gloom itself had even begun to arouse her, as if despair were an exalted state and it was noble to sit with the shades drawn, to forget to eat, to smile reluctantly. Now that she felt the raw cold inching up her sleeves and under the hem of her coat, she saw how frivolous they'd been with plain creature comforts. No decent art ever came out of self-pity.

After she returned to the apartment, she began to go through the last of Franz's things, thinking again of how he shrugged away when she took his arm in public, how he snapped at her on days when he could not work. She'd felt that she'd owed him—because he'd brought her alive again after that dead time with August. But his cold demeanor wore away at her gratitude. He'd seemed almost numb, and she'd begun to start fights, just to get his attention. The last time they'd argued, when he'd threatened to hit her, she'd felt a thrill at being able to evince this much passion from him. And what kind of marriage was that? One of them might have killed the other. He'd reduced her to needing so goddamn little from him that she missed even the familiarity of his turning his head away.

She told herself that she was throwing out his things, but she was also looking for clues, for some sign at least of where he had gone. In a box he'd left behind, full of old buttons and pen nubs, she found the letter from Benter:

Dear Franz Trove,

Now that it has been agreed upon by a judge that you owe August and me 7,000 marks, I would think that you'd have the decency to pay us. If you don't, I will be forced to contact the publisher of your transla-

tions in Berlin, where, as I understand it, you are making quite a decent living. . . .

This was why Franz had made such a fuss about avoiding Berlin even long after the gossip had died down, and why he'd been anxious to leave for America so quickly, without even notifying his publisher. The revelation sent her reeling out into the streets.

She walked down Broadway, past crowds of people in coats and hats, mufflers, the nut vendors with smoking carts and the men standing outside, hawking in loud voices, "Hats!" "Gloves!" "Linens!" "Pots!"

She stopped in a tobacconist and said to the clerk, "A packet of cigarettes."

He had a pointed bald head and smirked at her as he slid a packet across the counter. "What brand does your husband smoke?"

There was a sudden dampness in her chest. She flung the packet at the man's face and went out the door.

An automobile sped by, spraying a fan of gray water over her skirt. Three years she'd stayed with Franz. Three years wasted on a life that hadn't even been hers, hitching herself to him as if he were a carriage that might take her somewhere, if only he had enough energy, enough goodwill.

She and her mother had often been castigated for being absentminded, forgetting people's names, leaving the fire burning in an empty room, losing hats and gloves. They told one another it was because of the higher state of daydream that descended on persons of their temperament. Maybe it wasn't a higher state at all, though, but a mental defect that prevented one from taking note of the obvious.

She went down to the Village to Washington Square Books. She scanned the shelves of magazines: *Poetry,* "a magazine of Verse," with its winged horse galloping through the Gothic type, its laurel and quill pen; *Others,* "a magazine of the NEW verse," stark type against yellow; *Rogue,* with its checkerboard cover; the *Glebe,* advertising "songs, sighs, and curses." Just as she reached for it, *The Little Review,* elegant and blue, was snapped up by a man with a feather in his lapel.

The tall clerk wearing round glasses smiled at her, sad lines around her mouth, though she looked young, as if she were wearing stage makeup to play a middle-aged part.

"I'm looking for *LETTERS*," Elsa said.

"Yes, here," the clerk said, pulling it from the shelf and handing it to her. "Here's one with the pages cut."

The clerk stood there a moment watching until Elsa stared back at her, and she turned and busied herself at another rack.

There was a murmuring and then a bell at the cash register. Elsa opened the magazine, scanning for Franz's name, as she had so many other times. There were three clever cartoons, fashionable ladies with bare stick arms and legs, a couple of angry articles about America's angle on the war, poems by a Michael Moralis, an advertisement for Crane's Mary Garden Chocolates: *Your chocolates are the finest I have tasted anywhere in the world*. Finally she found the pages where the poems were and began to read "Solitude": *I go. / Sycamore pike / Sibilant wind whistles*. She dropped the book on the floor, and the pages splayed open at her feet. "Miss?" said the clerk.

He must have copied them from her notebook. He'd changed the titles and one or two lines, but the poems were hers.

18

The picture house on Forty-first Street resembled a Greek temple, white pilasters framing the bright posters for *Carmen* and *The Lamb*. Each afternoon she went there wearing her best dress, black with a white panel hidden in the front pleat that gaped when she walked. After every picture she sat in the lobbies of hotels, where theater people were said to be staying.

She wanted to get a job acting again, or as the manager of a chorus, to get to work as soon as possible so that she could earn enough money to go back to Berlin. She did not want to ask favors from Franz's friends, whom she hoped to never speak to again. Obviously, even a forged success had meant more to him than she ever had. She imagined how he'd rationalized it, telling himself that she hadn't known what she was writing, that his small, expert changes had transformed what were mere words into poetry. She could hear him making the argument and, in her mind, rehearsed her replies: *It was ink from my pen, you bastard, my idea, my phrasing.* Unfortunately, everything she had learned about Franz, she learned too late.

It was her third evening at the Hotel Ritz. She noticed this man because he was tall and wore a long-tailed gray suit and because he passed by her in the lobby so many times, glancing at her ankles. The last time, as she asked the waiter for tea, he paused and stared at the marble floor as if he had lost something there.

After the waiter brought her the tea, he came to where she was sitting. "You're German, aren't you?" he said in Deutsch.

She answered in English. "So are you." The round disks of his eyeglass lenses turned opaque as coins. He nodded, said his name was Josef von Freytag-Loringhoven, and sat down across from her, his long legs moving restlessly under the little table. Seeing such a tall man squeezed into that skimpy space made her smile.

"How did you know?"

"Your book." He nodded to the Goethe in her lap. He wore a purple tie, his hair oiled but mussed in the front, and his small teeth were sharp in his smile.

"It's a good lobby for reading, isn't it?" He felt familiar to her in a way she was trying to fathom, as if he were a cousin she had forgotten about or someone she had seen a hundred times on the street. "It's a good lobby for sleeping, too. Honestly, I saw a man snoozing in these very chairs yesterday afternoon. He sounded like a bassoon."

She laughed and moved her knees to the other side of the chair so that he would see them. He had a small red birthmark on his cheek, the size of a thumbprint or a rose petal, and there was a nervousness about him that was appealing.

"Someone sent the bellboy over to wake him, and the boy stood there clearing his throat, and when that didn't work, he bent over to scream in his ear, 'Sir! Sir!' The man finally opened his eyes and pretended as if he'd been awake all along. 'Why are you raising your voice?' he said. The bellboy told him he was sleeping, and he threatened to have the bellboy fired." He was watching her laugh.

"Don't worry," she said. "I'm not tired."

"So long as you don't snore, I'm sure no one would mind." At the New York Palace, she actually had fallen asleep with her head in her hand, but apparently no one had noticed. She had woken up, a thin line of drool leaking from her mouth, brutal lights and idle chatter around her, and because she didn't know where the hell she was, she had stood up and said, "*Scheisse*." The businessmen and waiters had stared.

First Josef offered to buy her something to drink, another cup of tea and maybe a sweet? She said she would rather have champagne. They went into the Red Room, where he bought a bottle of the best in the house, and the waiter came over with a bucket of ice and two fluted glasses. Their table was in front of the dance floor, and on the other side of that gleaming parquet, a band was beginning to play. The singer stood on a pedestal, a man with a long nose like a knife. He held his arms outstretched as he crooned, *Since she left I'm a fool. Nobody listens to fools.*

The room's darkness was tinted red, and the candlelight glowed into their faces, Josef's paled as if he were in a film.

"Bobby has lots of friends, though you wouldn't know it when he sings that way," Josef said.

"How do you know him?"

"I come here almost every night," he said, pouring more champagne into her glass. "I like to meet my business partners here."

When he spoke, she liked the way his lips so definitively formed the words. "What kind of business is it?"

"Investments," he said, shrugging. She was disappointed to hear this, but he had a sense of humor, which always made the difference between a dull man and a sparkling one.

"You're a banker?"

"Not exactly." Josef turned toward the band, tapping his foot. "Would you like to dance?"

She was entranced by the way he moved, as if he were even taller than he was, and he was an expert dancer, pulling her into the fox-trot as if it were the most natural motion in the world. She liked the tall nervousness of him, the smell of shaving soap on his smooth cheek. After they danced, they went back to their table and drank champagne. He wanted to know why she had come to America, and she told him the truth: "I came with a man." She watched his face to see if he would flinch.

"The bastard left and stole my poems." She told him the story of Franz's theft, how it had brought them to New York in the first place, how she'd written to the editor of *LETTERS,* a Mr. Caldwell, insisting that the poems were really hers (minus the titles and one or two lines), and he had responded by sending a note that he would contact Franz Trove—where could he reach him?

"It must be strange, having someone take your words like that."

"It is."

"But there's more where those came from, isn't there? And luckily you're here now, in Manhattan—skyscrapers! The Brooklyn Bridge!" He poured them each more champagne. "Everything new, and that war is far away—it's not ever coming here, no matter what they say."

They talked about Swinemünde and his home in Berlin, and the lack of decent black bread in America, and then the conversation turned back to the war. She hated the way it buzzed behind things even now, like a machine that wouldn't be turned off.

"I came here just as it was starting," he said. "My brothers are officers, and my father is a general. They think I must have some deformity of the nerves, because I don't want to fight."

"Are your brothers in the trenches?"

"No, it's worse. They order men into the trenches." His mouth flattened, and he took another drink.

"They're bullies, then. Kaiser lovers?"

"I suppose they are," he said. "Have you lost anyone?"

"I wouldn't know." She stared at his long hands around the silver stem of the glass. They were beautiful hands.

They danced for hours and drank another bottle of champagne. When most of the couples at the other tables had left and the dance floor cleared, Josef gave Bobby some money and asked the band to play longer. He took off his jacket and danced with her in his shirtsleeves, his cheek rough against hers.

It had been a long time since she had drunk champagne, the first two glasses like aphrodisiac soda water, spraying dewdrops into her nose, making her prettier, happier. After the third glass, she forgot all about her need for a job and her scheme to make her living again on the stage. And Josef, so tall, seemed like a man she had known for a very long time, and the way he held her and laughed, his sure footing during the tango, carried her into a kind of blurry bliss, dark and pink and red, the music raining down around them. The last thing she remembered was a pause in the dance when Josef rested his hand at the nape of her neck and slowly kissed her. When he drew back, he said, "I have a feeling you'll make me lucky."

The next morning she woke up beside him in his bed, her good dress crumpled on the floor, her chemise pulled up around her waist. He was sleeping with his back to her, thick hair spiked up at the top of his head. She put her hand on the side of his arm, felt his warmth, his deep slow breaths, and his leg stirred as he turned toward her, his face swollen and boyish.

He said, "I couldn't let you sleep outside in the lobby."

She hardly even resisted falling in love with him, he came at her so quickly with dinner invitations and places to dance, reasons why she should live with him in the Hotel Ritz, and his jokes and his hands on her face. Josef had been with her for weeks before he told her he was a baron, and then she laughed.

"You don't believe me." His name was one of the old names in Berlin, but he was always teasing her or telling her fibs because she was so gullible.

"Why didn't you tell me before?"

"Because it doesn't matter in America anyway. And you would have thought I was only trying to impress you."

"Then why are you telling me now?"

He grinned, lifting her skirt to put his hand on her knee. "Because I want to impress you."

He asked more questions than most men did. At dinner: Did you like that sauce? At the picture house: What did you think of the girl jumping from the train at the end? In the room: Do you henna your hair?

When she tried to tell him about Franz or about August, her first mistake husband, he would turn away or tell her not to talk about it.

"But you should know," she would say.

"I know now," he would answer.

He did not want to hear about the past because he was impatient to live in the future. "Those new motorcars with chrome like wings? I must learn how to drive soon." "Have you been inside the Woolworth Building, up on the top floor? You can see all the way to New Jersey." He never wanted to take a carriage or the train but wanted to take the new white taxicabs everywhere. He teased her about the way she tensely peered out the front windscreen—automobiles made her fearful; she held her shoulders tightly, clenched his hand, yelped when the driver stopped suddenly.

He wanted to try every gadget and read the newspaper less for the news than for the new inventions. "No one pays attention now, but when the war is over," he said, "people will look around and see that the world is improved." He wanted to invest in one of the new machines before anyone else discovered it but hadn't yet found the right situation.

He knew how to pleasure her, and she felt drawn to his body, the tuft of hair on his smooth chest, the slight softness in his belly, the fine skin of his penis like the skin on her wrist or eyelid, its pinkish brown color, and the way it curved slightly to the side when erect.

Josef's tall frame was narrow, with sharp shoulders and long, thin legs and arms, long feet, long hands. She loved the sense of his height against her body. To put her hands on each of his shoulders, only a little wider than her own, excited her. To feel her feet against his shins, the stretch of his legs after that, the spread of his big hand on her back. He would lift up her skirt at the most unlikely times, excited by her surprise or her feigned resistance—because a man enjoyed having to convince a woman now and then. He made her feel as if the whole world were infused with the erotic—the shaving cream in the sink, the water left in the tub, the worn clam of soap, the folds in the curtains and the light peeking through them, the veil of smoke from the chimneys across the street.

She tried to write about the pleasure she had with him, about the time they left the alarm clock singing, unwilling to pause in their lovemaking even long enough to reach the button, how he gave her one of his good-luck charms, a blue stone worn completely smooth, and the way he hummed tunes to her in the morning while he dressed. But nothing came to her. German began to sound singsong and silly, and English words didn't seem to have enough fuel—they sputtered out quickly. Josef kept saying, "If you write poems, I don't see why you can't write me a love poem." But she couldn't now. Franz had written love poems, unsentimental, exquisite—and as dishonest as a butcher.

Josef came home one night with his face cut just over his eye, his nose bleeding—it was very late, and she had not known where he had been. "It was a card game," he said. "There was a cheat there, and I hit him."

"And he hit you," she said, wetting a washcloth in the sink. "What did you care if he cheated?" She patted his cut.

"There was money involved," he said, whiskey on his breath. And that was how she found out about the gambling. She realized that the lists of names she occasionally found in his suit pockets were not perfumes or prostitutes or plays but horses.

She began to be as superstitious as he was, wearing red for luck, turning the bracelet on her wrist twice each afternoon after she kissed him good-bye, wearing only black and red underthings. She began to recognize the approach of a certain tinselly luck. She wrote more confidently now that Franz had left, but she began to see how much of what came from her pen was pure fate, come to her through some disembodied voice not exactly her own. One day it was there, and the next day it was not. She couldn't help but feel it was encouraged by a particular blue pencil, the proper angle of her notebook to the window.

When Josef won, they were giddy. They danced the tango, the monkey slip, the chicken scratch, the fox-trot, Josef singing into her ear, *If I could offer you the Taj Mahal, if I could talk to you for just one hour*, her skirts moving to the shape of her legs. They went out three nights a week to the Gold Room, where the dance floor lifted and slowly revolved, to Murray's Gardens, where Egyptian mummy cases lined the saloon, and to the Metropol, where the dance floor was surrounded by trees. They ate at Bergdon's on Thirty-fourth Street, where the German opera singers ate; at the Rainbow Restaurant, where the shrimp was served on ice carved into a swan.

After a big win at Central Park Casino, Josef had come home one day with a bottle of French perfume for her, "Chez Amour" because she loved everything French, especially now that France was Germany's enemy and the prospect of bombs falling on Paris made its artifacts all the more precious.

He went immediately to the bathroom and turned on the tap. "I'm drawing you a bath," he said. "We're going out."

While she lay soaking in the warm water, he sat on the edge of the tub, telling her how he had won at the game of blackjack by bluffing a cardsharp who assumed he was an immigrant yokel. "I wrote your name with my finger on the tablecloth for luck, but he must have thought he'd caught me doing the arithmetic."

Josef, more than anyone else she had ever met, knew how to hope. When he went off to the casino, his face held an expression of infinite possibility. If he won, they might live in China for a year, Elsa might become a film star, and his father might tell him that he admired him. If he won, then Germany might make amends with France, the Kaiser might dance through the streets in a dress.

In her new life, Franz came to seem like a self-absorbed, foolish man, and those days were like rust that threatened to mar her new shininess. She tried not to think of them.

That night she wore a blue velvet evening dress that had a hem made of long feathers, and earrings crafted from pretty thimbles.

In the cab to the restaurant, he sang, and he gave the driver a three-dollar tip. They ate oysters and steak, each dish served like a small, exquisite present, and they drank a bottle of champagne. The slick-haired waiters came over to the table whenever a piece of silverware was dirty or a glass empty. One of them, staring at her thimble earrings, accidentally spilled soup on the tablecloth and profusely apologized. At the next table, a gray-haired matron stared disapprovingly at the feathers curled now around Elsa's high-heeled slippers.

Josef would not order the frogs' legs, though the maître d' recommended them, and he told Elsa the story about when he was a boy and he and his brother Stefan had caught two frogs in the pond near their house. "Stefan said that if you cut off their legs, they would still move for a while afterward, and even hop. We wanted to see what would happen, so we began working at them with our pocketknives, but it was harder than I thought it would be, and my frog screeched, and when I saw its blood, I couldn't do it. I tore up my shirt and bandaged the frog's leg back to his body, and I was weeping the whole time. Stefan kept on with the experiment, and it turned out that the legs gave only little disappointing twitches, and my frog died anyway."

"That's a sad story," she said. It was this delicateness that made her tender toward him.

"It's a good thing I never heard an oyster scream," he said, taking another one on his fork.

Josef's father was a general who wrote books about the strategies of soldiers at battle. "Of course, now he's a friend of the Kaiser's," Josef said. "I was brought up to learn how to solve military questions: What should a regiment do if it's surrounded on all sides? How is combat on horseback different from combat on foot? It was understood that my brothers and I would become officers."

She knew the street where his parents lived, and must have passed by their house many times on the way to the Wintergarten. "But you didn't become an officer—"

He shook his head just before taking a long drink of champagne. "I couldn't stand the military. Being around men all the time isn't good for a man." Franz had been tormented by his own reluctance to nobly sacrifice himself to the cause, and she loved the way Josef had shirked the military without guilt.

"When I left the military, my brothers assumed I was a fairy," Josef said. "That was when I came here."

"That explains why you want so badly to win at your games."

He shrugged. "Maybe. But doesn't everybody like to win?"

"Not as recklessly as you do." He'd bought her a fur coat, a diamond bracelet, but when he lost, he brought her a funereal face, as if the corpses on the Belgian battlefield were there because of him.

After dinner they went dancing at the Metropol, where there were orchids in the flower boxes, and she drank a sweet cocktail that seemed to make her taller. When they took a break, Josef leaned in across the table to listen as she shouted over the music, and after a few minutes, they were up again, twirling among the other dancers.

They stayed until the waiters began stacking the chairs on the tables, and it was almost dawn by the time they were in a cab again on their way home. "Wait a minute!" Josef called up to the driver. "Drive over to City Hall, will you?"

"They're not open yet, sir."

"I know. There's something else I want to do."

She closed her eyes and rested her face against Josef's jacket, which smelled of cigars. He paid the driver to wait for them, and when they got out of the cab, they were standing at the foot of the Brooklyn Bridge. "Let's walk to the middle," he said.

They were both still a little drunk on champagne, and her satin shoes were already wobbly and torn from the dance floor. She laughed. "Why, want to go for a morning swim?"

The bridge felt ancient and new at the same time, a dragon's bones made of steel and wire. As the sky lightened, they stood at the crest, while a boat moved slowly beneath them, and Elsa could just make out the top of a man's head.

It was the first time in a long while that she was awake for the sunrise, and it felt as if they had suddenly landed on another planet, with its own weather and time. Josef pointed to the skyline of buildings, barely visible through the mist. The tall buildings, like man-made mountains, looked as light as rain or air, as if they were about to rise up and dissolve into clouds.

"Look, I wanted to show you this. The city is floating now."

Her body felt light, too, a tingling in her fingers and toes, as if any minute she might begin to ascend.

19

She wrote back to Mr. Caldwell and explained again that the poems that had won the prize were hers, and if he did not believe her, here were three more poems by her, so he could see for himself. She didn't know where Franz had gone, but maybe by now *LETTERS* did?

A few days later, a messenger brought her a reply—it was an invitation to the *LETTERS* offices.

The address was down in Greenwich Village, on Christopher Street, which was connected to the city by the new Seventh Avenue, but with its tangled streets and squares, still a village itself, flanked by noisy piers and el trains, and the maidenish, gray-brick homes of the wealthy.

Wayne Caldwell had founded *LETTERS* three years earlier, with an inheritance from his uncle. In his Editor's Notes, he'd set out the vision: a magazine for intelligent people without agendas—not Socialist or Anarchist, but Humanist, the poetry avoiding all -isms, and the stories without morals.

When Elsa arrived, a boy was stacking books and manuscripts in boxes, and Wayne Caldwell sat writing behind his desk, a tiny, slender man with wiry black hair and a high, nasal voice.

"Come in, come in," he said, clearing off a chair for her. There was a strenuous elegance about him in his red tie and narrow suit, but, seeing the disarray of the office, she suspected she would never get paid for those poems. Maybe she could at least convince him to print a correction.

Smoothing her new herringbone tweed skirt, she sat in the leather chair, anxious to reclaim ownership of her work. "Mr. Caldwell, do you believe me now that the poems were forgeries?"

He stared at her, one finger pressed against his cheek. The electric light above them flickered, and she smelled cigar smoke and pencil dust.

"I believe you, yes, though I don't know what can be done. That was such an unfortunate circumstance, though I suppose things might easily get muddled when two literary persons are married."

"It wasn't muddling—he stole the poems." She should have known that he only wanted to see her about Franz. Had he won another prize, or had he swindled this man out of money, too?

Caldwell sat up taller in his chair, the wings so large they exaggerated the narrowness of his shoulders, the thinness of his neck. Something in his voice suggested he liked gossip. "I'm afraid I don't have any way to reach him except through you—I'm sorry, Mrs. Trove." Caldwell tapped his pen on the desk.

"I've remarried. I am now Baroness Elsa von Freytag-Loringhoven." It had been only a month, and she enjoyed how long it took to pronounce her new name. She'd decided to ignore the Paris marriage, and neither Josef nor the clerk objected when she claimed she'd lost her birth certificate. In the application for the marriage license, she said she had not been married before and claimed she was three years younger, because she wanted to take those years back from Franz.

"Actually, I didn't invite you here to discuss 'Solitude' and 'Early Light.'" Wayne Caldwell's slightness seemed to free his body to have more energy than most men—his finger tapped out a rhythm now on the blotter, and she sensed his leg noodling around under the desk.

"He changed the titles."

"But these new poems, the ones you sent—" He started to cough and pulled a handkerchief from his breast pocket, which he pressed over his mouth. The cough rattled his shoulders. After he finished, he pulled the handkerchief away and cleared his throat. "—which are much better. Did you know that when you wrote them? You must have." She studied the serious pucker in his mouth, the straightness of his gaze.

Behind her the boy slammed a pile of books into a wooden crate, and she jumped.

Caldwell said, "I would like to get these into print immediately." He tilted his head as if to see her from another angle. "Would that be possible?"

A warmth bloomed in her chest, and the outlines of the inkpot and pencils on the shelf seemed suddenly sharper and more clear, as if a brightness pulsed behind them. "I certainly sent them with that purpose in mind." She must have. But until now she hadn't allowed herself to hope. She watched his face, waiting for its goodwill to absorb into her, only it was taking a moment. "Of course—yes."

"Unfortunately, *LETTERS* is temporarily bankrupt," he said. "As you can see, I'm being forced to move the office to my residence, but I have plans to raise money, and when the magazine resumes publication, I want to lead with these."

She was happy, but out of breath and exhausted from the effort of hiding her surprise. "An odd question maybe," she said. "But was it Franz Trove who put you out of business?"

He averted his eyes and tapped his finger more rapidly against the blotter. "No, no, of course not. There's no money in this. All of us—the *Masses*, *OTHERS*—we run by the skin of our teeth. We had a backer. . . ." His voice trailed off. "But my doctor has required me to spend time in the dry air because of my lung ailment. I will be in New Mexico until next summer."

"The desert," she said, remembering what she'd read in the guidebook, sand and cacti and donkeys.

"Yes." He held up her manuscript, the papers trembling in his hands. "It's as if you're writing from some deep pocket inside English that no one else has thought to open."

The poems had that effect because she'd pushed her absurdities into phrases and sentences, because the other English words hadn't come to her yet, and it hadn't occurred to her that her newness to the language might be an advantage. But she didn't want Caldwell to know this. Editors could be fickle, particularly in the face of bankruptcy, and she wanted to solidify her presence to him. "Of course, if you were ever to go to Berlin, people would know my name." She felt she deserved this white lie. The poems were there for their own sake anyway, but she had waited so long for them to be read, and now she'd have to wait again.

Caldwell nodded several times. "I had a feeling . . . but then you must have used Elsa Trove?"

Her ears winced at hearing the name again. "No, a pseudonym." She hurried past this point. "I would gladly allow *LETTERS* to publish any number of my poems, so long as the plagiarist's work doesn't also appear there."

Caldwell's face tilted curiously, a faint tiny smile, thick eyebrows digging toward his nose. "Yes, well. I found that incident very embarrassing, but it matters less now that I have these poems in my possession."

When she left, she felt herself glide through the building hallway and into the gilt-framed opening for the elevator, buzzing as it brought her down to the street. Her poems were going to appear in print, set down safely apart from her and the ramblings of her life. She was still too elated by this news to remember exactly what Mr. Caldwell had said about them.

One day Elsa took out the dress she'd worn for her wedding to August, the fabric covered with tiny bells. She cut off the sleeves and attached linked safety pins until they made a kind of chain mail, and she put on the dress while they were getting ready to go dancing at the Metropol.

Josef knotted his tie in the mirror and turned to her. "You're going out in that?"

"Why not?"

"Actually, I like the bells, but the armory around your shoulders—isn't it a little strange?"

She'd been thinking about prettiness, silk flowers, intricate lace, all those fabrics that looked like rain—fragile material that quickly ruined or ripped. A modern woman had to fashion herself to be tougher than that, and more enterprising. Now that she was thirty-two years old, she wanted to look different—not mature, exactly, but maybe not so easily taken for granted. "This is my own self-apparel. It's too easy for a woman to wear what's sold to her." She turned so the pins gleamed in the lamplight.

Josef grinned, took her wrists in his hands. "What's wrong with easy?"

Sometimes her moods seemed to worry him. "Calm down," he often told her. When she saw the old woman vomit on the streetcar and began to weep, he said, "She's just drunk. Calm down." And he put his arm around her. When she laughed at the squirrel eyeing the foliage in a woman's hat, at an advertisement for the new candy with the hole, she laughed so hard that she could not breathe unless she ran or danced, moved the hilarity out of her bones somehow. "Calm down," he said with a puzzled smile. "It isn't that funny." After they saw a play she hated because the ending was so falsely sentimental, he said, "You just didn't understand it," and when her fury made her uncharacteristically silent, shrugging away his hand, he said, "Calm down." When she saw him flirting with that cow at the roof garden, she threw a cocktail in his face. "Calm down!" he screamed. "Calm down. Calm down." If she and Josef were out and she was angry or happy, her voice would go low and loud. "People are staring," he would say.

"*Arschloch,* " she would answer, shaking off his arm. She did not want to calm down.

If she calmed down, there would be no more poems.

Wayne Caldwell wrote to her from New Mexico. *Of these, "Blast" is the best because it is the most untamed—that voice out of the netherworld. But all of them are good. "Metaphysical Speculations" goes on too long, I think. Cut the last four lines. We could say in the magazine that you are the new American, that voice. We don't need rhymes anymore or images in circles—we need voices. Send more.*

She stood on the Ritz balcony holding Caldwell's letter, while the sun caught the wind glass and glitter below, and it seemed that for a long time she had been moving toward this moment, hovering above the city in the sooty breeze. Among all the poets her mother had taught her to adore, none were women, but this had never seemed like a law of nature, only a matter of circumstance. She felt lucky not to have been overlooked, even if some men would find her efforts ridiculous, no matter what. Hölderlin, Goethe, and Heine had written in homes not yet veined with plumbing, under gaslights, not electric ones. Of course it followed that her poems would be absolutely different. She was modern. What the dismissive men didn't know yet was that Femaleness was its own wily force. Looking out at the india-ink outline of water towers and telephone lines, the dusky side of the nearest tall building, she thought that if it were ridiculous for a woman to write, then she would perfect the folly, croak out its lyrics and learn its absurd measure, write a thousand ludicrous songs.

Josef saw the green bills the way he saw leaves and flowers. They came and they went. When money was gone, he was certain it would come back, and when it was there, he did not worry about when it would be gone. His father sent him a periodic allowance, but he placed wild bets—two hundred dollars on a single hand of blackjack, five hundred dollars on a horse with terrible odds. "Money loves you only if you don't care a thing about it," he said.

It wasn't logical to believe that Josef would win more than he lost, but she had never cared much for logic. Logic told her father that if his daughter misbehaved, it was proper to punish her. It was according to the logic of symmetry that August found beauty in abstraction more than flesh and blood. Franz used logic to rationalize that if he possessed her body, then he possessed her work, and logic to justify his abandoning her. Logic said that a German woman with a past like hers would never be a poet, but logic was a liar.

When Josef came back to her all smoky late at night, he kissed her, found her bare shoulder with his thumb, and said he had missed her. Gambling transported him to a fast-talking country with its own customs and natives, and when he returned, though he had only been up to the club on Fifty-seventh Street or to the casino in Murray Hill, he acted as if he had been traveling a long distance.

"I wish you had been with me."

"Take me with you."

"I can't."

It infuriated her that she could not go into those clubs, casinos, or restaurants, only because she was female. Even the Abercrombie and Fitch store, with the stuffed bear in the window that fascinated her, would not allow her admittance. She'd often heard men say that the rules were there only to protect delicate sensibilities from coarseness, but Elsa knew better—the rules protected men and their secrets. "I'll find a way in one day," she told Josef. "I'll surprise you."

English words were like beautiful objects that sometimes slipped through her fingers and crashed into fragments. She was beginning to love the crashing sounds they made, like the clattering and clanking of the city.

She sent Caldwell "Spring in the Middle," "Moving Picture and Prayer," "Once Upon a Time There Was an Ernst," and a letter she wrote on Hotel Ritz stationery, with its tiny swan printed in blue ink at the top. She told him she was inventing her own system of punctuation marks. What most women meant by a period after all, she joked, was a semicolon, meaning more to come. She preferred dashes—"joy marks"—like little shouts at the end of a line.

Though she had not noticed it at first, the Ritz was an excellent place for a poet. One night she and Josef had been seated at the hotel restaurant next to the ballerina Anna Pavlova, who ate nothing except oysters and water, but spoke to her male companion in a rapid-fire Russian like bullets sent across the candlelight. Another night Elsa had a conversation with Enrico Caruso, the opera singer, in the Palm Room, and though he was very drunk on wine, he asked her to recite for him the same lines from Goethe over and over again: *Selig, wer sich vor der Welt / Ohne Hass verschliesst, / Einen Freund am Busen hält Und mit dem geniesst.* . . .

Mary Pickford, the blond actress, lived at the Ritz for a week, and when Elsa loaned her face powder in the ladies lounge, she offered to recite one of her poems, but when Pickford turned away from the mirror, she was crying and shook her head. It might have comforted Mary Pickford to hear "She" perhaps, or even "Blast," but Elsa understood that it was difficult to concentrate when one was distraught. She thought of scribbling down "She" on a candy wrapper and tucking it into Pickford's purse. Elsa handed the actress her silk handkerchief, with which Pickford wiped her eyes, and then she took it with her out the door.

Elsa wore a tight-fitting red dress with a little fur collar that accentuated her slim arms and waist. She and Josef sat in the crowded tram car, eyeing the crowd.

"That one," said Josef, nodding to the portly man with a perfect purple handkerchief folded in his pocket. At the next stop, Elsa moved toward the man in a way that would appear as if she'd just boarded. His smiling mouth and lively eyes made him look brash, so she winked.

He perked up next to the silver pole and grinned at her. "Would it be rude of me to say that you're the prettiest woman I've seen today?"

She lowered her eyes and tried to flatten her accent. "Only if the next thing you say is impolite."

He looked around at the faces in the crowd as if to make sure no one was watching him. "What if I asked you to get off with me on Fifth Avenue?"

Then Josef was behind him, but helping an old woman steady herself.

"And why would I want to do that?" Elsa said, stroking her fur collar.

"You'd make me very happy if you allowed me to buy you a lunch."

Josef slipped his hand into the man's pocket, took the wallet, and suddenly swerved around to stand next to Elsa.

"Oh, there's my brother!" Elsa said. Josef cleared his throat, eyes mocking outrage.

Perspiration beaded on the man's forehead. "Well, I was just saying . . . hello."

Josef pushed in front of Elsa. "Mind your manners, sir," he said in his best American accent, which he could affect quite well, and just then the tram stopped and Elsa and Josef hopped off.

When they were all the way down the block, Josef took out the wallet and counted the bills. Money, when they were out of it, needed to be brought back insulted and debased. Otherwise it took too much power from them.

"How much did we get?" Elsa said.

"Not bad." He wrapped his arm around her shoulders. "Thirty dollars!" Enough for Josef to gamble for the next week until he won back his "egg."

Josef often took trips out of the city to pursue his business ventures. Three times he went down to Florida with the intent to buy property, twice to Chicago for a scheme to sell fire insurance, and four times up to Hornell, New York, where he was investigating the viability of scenting train cars with lavender. If he had not gambled, the allowance from his father might have sustained them, but Josef needed to win or he sank into depression, and the schemes were only another form of gambling.

While he was gone, she hated the way Mr. Collins, the manager, would not allow her to sit smoking alone in the Palm Room or the Saloon. "Madam," he would say, taking the cigarette from between her fingers and stubbing it out in a napkin. "Please. Wouldn't you be more comfortable waiting for the baron in your room?"

She would fill her notebooks with poems, leaving the newest ones tacked to the wall. She had begun to think that all poetry was a foreign language, and hearing English every day confirmed it, the skipping trills and hard "ays," which she heard as pure music. It was better that she learned the intricacies of English grammar as she went along, because this way the difficulty of poetry wasn't hindered. American language often sounded shallow to her, but she wanted to break through the syntax, twist its rhythms until it had the depths she wanted. But sometimes she gave up and had to write in German, because it was the only way to get the thing said in the right cadence. Words came to her in fits and starts, and when there wasn't any voice she went out. She walked the streets, all the way down to Chinatown and the Bowery and up to Central Park, and when she got back, her head would be full of what she'd read on billboards or overheard—Irish, Italian, German, French, Chinese. There were ink stains on almost every one of her dresses.

She'd been married enough times now to know that each marriage had a distinct profile and coloring, and the particular stamp of this one first became clear one night when they went out with Barney Fitch.

Josef liked to tell his friends that she was going to be famous, and Barney Fitch was the one who always said, "Sure, sure. And I'm going to be as rich as J.P." He was a drunk with a big red beard who teased Elsa and pestered Josef about his title, but he gave Josef confidence and sometimes money for his schemes.

They were eating steaks and drinking wine one night in a dark restaurant in Greenwich Village. "Ah, a little red meat," said Barney. "I need it to strengthen my blood. I've been lackluster lately."

"It's the women," said Josef.

Barney raised his eyebrows at Elsa and smiled. "If only."

She felt something touching her knee under the table and moved her leg away from it. She wanted to steer the conversation from investments and gambling strategies, boring subjects they tended to dwell on. "Let's discuss Mata Hari. I've been wondering if she knew all along she would be caught."

"Eventually," said Josef.

"But was it an act of nationalism or an adventure?" Elsa speared a stem of asparagus with her fork. Elsa imagined her a woman constantly aware that she worked on borrowed time, someone loyal only to risk.

"I don't think she was a woman at all," said Barney. "A woman could never be so ruthless. Mata Hari was a man who knew how to do a good imitation of a woman."

"Barney, you don't actually believe that?" She felt something warm on her knee again and realized it was his hand. She moved her leg away and glared at him.

He winked at her, then turned to Josef. "All right." Barney threw up his hands. "She got away with it because she was beautiful. Beautiful women can commit murder and go scot-free. For all we know"——he fixed his eyes on Elsa——"we have a spy right here."

She remembered how her father would flirt with the big-busted woman who rented beach chairs at the resort, how he'd probably slept with her, too. She turned to Josef and said to him in German, "Your friend is groping me."

Josef smiled as if he hadn't heard her.

"Hands to yourself, Barney," she said.

"I don't know what you're talking about—if I accidentally touched you, I apologize."

Josef grinned at Barney. "Accidents happen," and he reached under the table to push his hand up under her skirt. "It's a beautiful knee."

The waiter came and took their plates, and the men went back to talking about a machine for washing dishes. "That's where the money is," Barney said.

"What about a machine that brushes your teeth? I hate brushing my teeth," said Josef. She was annoyed and wanted to go home, but Josef wanted to see the club Barney had been harping on.

They took a cab through the tangled streets of the Village, and it was half an hour before Barney found the place. "It's not where I thought it was," he kept saying, as they circled the block.

Finally they got out and walked across Bleecker toward Christopher Street. "Ah, yes," Barney said, leading them down a set of brick stairs into a dark basement room with red-checkered tablecloths on tiny tables littered with ashes and glasses and empty bottles. They sat in the corner, at a table with a battered-looking elephant figurine in the center.

The speakeasy smelled of onions and tomato sauce, and there were pictures of actors and actresses cut out from newspapers and pasted to the walls. There was one painting, a large nude. A very bad painting, Elsa thought, amateurish. The woman's head was set at an impossible angle to her body, her breasts bluish and arrowed downward.

Paper lanterns hung from the ceiling. In the corner, pillows of smoke ascended from behind a purple silk curtain. The smell of the place shifted slightly, the scent somewhere between burned sausage and a harsh detergent.

There were several men there. A woman, who was very fat and wore a red dress that exposed the plump tops of her enormous breasts, seemed to be sleeping in a chair, her head leaned back against the wall.

Barney and Josef were telling jokes, and Elsa glanced over at the women at the next table, then saw they were not female after all. In the lantern light, Elsa saw the dark lather of their beards spread around their red rouged lips.

Barney grinned. "Did you have a childhood pet?" He was so drunk now that he was slurring his words. "I never recovered from the death of my shepherd. That's why I've never married, I'm sure."

Josef raised his eyebrows and shook his head. "Well, there may be a few other reasons, having to do with a certain Bard House, don't you think?"

"Not in front of your wife, please."

Elsa rolled her eyes. "Everything in front of your wife, please." She resented being patronized, and besides, it was vital for a woman to have as much worldly information as possible—and maybe she needed it even more than a man did.

"Okay." Barney lifted his index finger. "I have a story for you from Skip Drake. There was a man who had a beautiful wife—blond hair, a figure one took notice of, red lips, the kind of beauty a man wonders about because it gets him right in the groin each time he looks. Not a respectable kind of beauty, but the wild kind. He was sure that she was sneaking off while he was at work to go to the dance hall, and when they went out, he noticed that several men's eyes were overly familiar with her, as if they'd seen her before and knew what to expect."

"Just another ogle-y man who wants to grow eyes in the back of his head," said Elsa. "It's not very attractive, the eyes bulging out through the hairs." She was hoping to tease him away from this stupid story.

Barney shook his finger at her. "A woman like that leaves in the middle of the night with no warning—she gives herself like candy to your worst enemy. But for this woman things turned out differently. Her husband got her pregnant. And she stopped going to the dance hall—he could tell because he checked the bottoms of her shoes. And when the baby was born, a son, he was colicky and feverish, so she was forced to stay home nursing him. He screamed when she spoke to men who weren't his father. It was as if God had sent the little bugger to make sure his mother behaved herself."

Elsa felt a pressure in her head. She wanted to like Barney, and she knew that the tale satisfied him only because he believed that this beautiful woman would never have danced with him, but it bothered her that Josef spent so much time with him at the club. "That's a goddamn awful story," said Elsa. "I don't believe a word of it. That woman is still cuckolding her husband, dancing the tango all over New York."

Barney shook his head. "A dishonest woman always gets what's coming to her, and, you know, that kind of fast beauty—it doesn't last long."

Elsa stared at Barney's narrow blue eyes, his blob of a nose and red beard, the black tie carelessly knotted. He really did believe his own stupid axioms. This was why there had to be poetry—to break apart these easy slogans that fitted so neatly on the tongue that people couldn't see the lies in them.

Just then the fat woman was standing next to their table, frowning. She had a gorgeous full face, with plummy lips. "No girls allowed," she said in a New York accent so thick Elsa barely understood her.

"What?" She thought it was funny to be called a girl.

"But, madame, I don't see any signs," said Barney, suppressing a giggle.

"And *you* are here, after all," said Josef, leaning back in his chair to look up and smile at her.

"I'm not a friggin' girl, I'm a woman," she said, leaning with her hands on the table. "Get out," she said, glaring at Elsa.

Elsa glared back. The pressure in her head made her giddy.

A small man in a plaid coat came over to the table and put his hand on the woman's back. "What's the matter, Iris?" He turned to them. "You understand, folks, don't you? This is a man's place."

Elsa was lying on the bed in their room, which she loved—the long velvet curtains that hid the light so well one could sleep easily until five o'clock in the afternoon, the octagonal mirror over her dressing table in which her complexion was smoother and of better color than in most reflections, the bathtub with working hot water and a special radiator for heating the towels afterward. She even loved the little drawer in the nightstand by the bed where she kept her pencils, the picture on the wall of a girl stiffly holding flowers.

She opened her book in her lap, then remembered to tell Josef about another letter she'd received from Mr. Caldwell. "He's been writing to me every week." She giggled only because she almost couldn't believe it.

Josef, on the chair by the window, put down his newspaper. "It would be arrogant of me, wouldn't it, to assume that I would always be the one you were in love with."

This was the jealousy that was bound to come sooner or later. "Don't be silly. I'm not in love with Wayne Caldwell—he's an editor, remember? The one who liked my poems."

The oil had blown out of Josef's hair, and a lock stuck up near his forehead. "Not him." He shook his head. "It doesn't really matter. Why not see love like travel? One goes away for a while, but one is always happy to return home."

She propped herself on the silk pillow. Now she thought he was flirting with her, testing her reaction. "Or one moves to Tahiti and never comes back."

"I would never do that," he said, smiling slyly. There was a stubborn optimism in his eyes. "It's the idea of freedom more than the practice," he said. "Just because we get married doesn't mean we have to live in a box. If you felt you had to have an affair in order to be happy, then I wouldn't want to stop you. How could I, if I said I loved you?"

She worried that this might be some kind of ruse and thought of the night he'd come home at 4:00 A.M., the way he'd smiled at the blond hatcheck girl. "There's another woman, isn't there?"

"Of course not." He leaned forward, rested his elbows on his knees. "But people have more than one friendship. If you think about it, why should it be any different with love?" So that was it—he wanted to talk about the future again, how one day babies would be born without pregnancy, and there would be no difference between the sexes, and marriage would be obsolete. Everywhere he went, he eyed people and their gadgets, trying to forecast what people were beginning to want or need. In the city, wires wound through objects like veins with a new kind of blood, lighting up and moving things and blowing air. There was the electric dishwasher, the electric iron, the electric clothes washer. Soon there would be an electric baby rocker, an electric table setter, an electric woman for those nights when the wife had a headache.

"Intellectually, I agree with you," she said. "But in my heart it would be difficult." Even with August, it was impossible for her to accept such a casual arrangement of infidelity—like having one down-filled, satin-covered bed and slicing it into pieces so there could be places for more people to lie down. She didn't see the point.

"What do the poets say, after all?" Josef said. "You told me you've had many affairs."

"But always only one at a time."

He smiled at her as if he'd seen her with these men, knew how fickle she'd sometimes been. "I would just have to hope that you'd eventually come back to me."

"I wouldn't leave you in the first place," she said.

His lips were moist, and the lamp lit his eyes, naked and unguarded now that he'd put aside his spectacles. "Who knows? There hasn't been enough research on the matter." He lifted up the newspaper, leaned back, and put up his feet. A moment later he said, "Want to go to the Gold Room tonight?"

The conversation haunted her. The truth was, she was not sure anymore that any kind of love could last. Time was against it, as were the variety and press of the world. She thought perhaps Josef sensed this doubt in her—he saw the glint of her desire, though maybe not the blade. But to speak of this directly would have ruined their easy closeness.

She received another note from Caldwell, this one written on odd brown paper that smelled of ether. It praised the poems again, though he asked her to drop the last line of "Moonstone," which undermined the rest. *LETTERS* had a new backer, and already there were poems from Mina Loy, a story by Djuna Barnes, an advertisement promised by Lorimer's Music, and a letter from Gertrude Stein for the next issue, which he hoped would come out in May. He wanted to print a thousand copies and see if he could convince Mrs. Schwendeman to offer a prize to a German again. It would be several weeks before he was able to write another letter, as he was having a small operation and would be in recovery, for which he was required to lie flat on his back without any exertion at all. He didn't say what the operation was supposed to correct.

She imagined his small, perfectly proportioned limbs lying under the sheets, attended by two nurses, a cloth on his forehead. She was eager for him to return—there were sixteen new poems she wanted to show him.

In an art gallery on Fifth Avenue, Elsa studied paintings that reminded her of the houses near Swinemünde, the landscapes crushing in, the women all sweet-faced with beefy arms. Moving slowly past the row of frames, each one more flat-colored and homely, she murmured, "These are hideous."

"I agree." The man next to her smiled, his black hair pushed away from his face in glossy waves. "These could have been my grandmother's paintings. They are that exhausted." He was Russian, and they began talking about a play they'd both seen at the Athenaeum, and he invited her to have a drink with him at the café down the street, where he was supposed to meet some friends, but the friends never came.

She was taken with his dark eyes and the way he leaned in toward her when she spoke. She found herself lightly touching his arm. His conversation was voluble and funny, and he sat up very straight in his chair, like a schoolboy. She told him she thought art had to account for people's blind spots—there was no such thing as a true whole picture.

He seemed to listen intently, blinking several times when her voice veered up in volume. "But so much of the world is blind now," he said.

She thought she only wanted to kiss him. She only wanted to feel his hand, even larger than Josef's, against her breast. Wasn't this what Josef wanted to include in their lives, if she took him at his word, what he called "traveling"? Considering the Russian's angular smile, and the way he laughed at himself, she thought maybe Josef had been wise in his proposal. It was as if she had entered a book that she could close at will, and then go back to Josef.

The Russian seemed startled when she proposed to him that they go somewhere private, but, taking her arm, he stood up immediately and paid the check.

His room was cluttered with canvases and jars of paint, and they wove around them as they made their way toward his bed.

As he undressed her, she felt as if she were in a dream, as if he were one of the sailors from her girlhood or Josef in disguise, and he took her lightly on top of his large body, when she'd imagined he would be rougher, more urgent with her, and as he was kissing her neck, she glanced over at a canvas leaned against the wall. "What's that?" she said.

"My painting."

It was a landscape made of false, dead trees like green lollipops and a stream that looked like a road. "Oh," she said, his hands and mouth suddenly rubber against her skin, her arm pinched between the bed and the wall. "I have to go now," she said, pulling on her dress.

She went home and confessed everything to Josef.

"You little slut," he said. He was smiling, but in a pained way.

"I thought I would try out our arrangement." She tried to sound casual, to show him she was modern, but her voice careened into a shout. In a panic she remembered Franz's rages, the sad awfulness of the Russian's painting, the faint sourness on his breath.

"You had to be the first, didn't you?" Josef grabbed her and began to unbutton her blouse. "Understandable. But you didn't have to tell me. Why brag?"

He kissed her hard on the mouth. "And will you see him again?" She didn't know if this was jealousy or if he was aroused.

"No."

"Why not?" He slipped off her blouse, pulled the straps of her chemise over each shoulder.

"It was just an experiment."

He had her jacket off and pinched at her breasts. "Don't tell me about it next time."

He hiked up her skirts, pushed her down on the table.

One night in the Village, there was a tall blond man with an elongated, pink face, who scooted his chair close to hers while Josef was at the bar buying drinks for them. The narrow angles of the stranger's face fascinated her, and she began talking to him about the book he had in his pocket by Henri Bergson. "He's the one with the crazy ideas about time," she said. She had read Bergson and liked the idea that time could not be measured by an objective

standard or divided into discrete compartments, but rather had to be appre-
hended by one's intuition. Her time was different from this stranger's time. She
glanced at Josef, and when he turned around, he smiled and nodded to her.

When she looked back at the blond, his mouth was suddenly on hers, and
she tasted the whiskey in it.

She pulled away and saw Josef grinning at her. When she put her hand
on the blond man's chest and rubbed the cotton up to the collar, it was for
Josef. She felt as if her mouth were suddenly full of honey.

"I like your honesty," the stranger said, his head weaving a little on his
neck. "I think you would tell me just about anything." He was very drunk.

Josef was watching intently, but something was odd about his stance.
Then she realized what it was. He had his hand at the hip of a busty woman
talking drunkenly into his ear.

He nodded to the door, and then she excused herself and met Josef outside.

Under the streetlamp, Josef pressed himself against her, kissing her ear
and neck, and she felt as if the parabola of light around them were shining
from her skirt.

In the cab on the way home, Josef had his hand all the way up her dress,
and that night, when she took him inside her on the elevator, her skirt tore.

20

Six weeks after the last letter from Caldwell, thinking he'd be recovered, she sent him another group of poems. But there was no reply. Worried, she wrote him again, and when there was still no reply, she sent another letter. It was returned to her with a note scrawled over the address in accusing red letters: *No such patient.* Had he died? She wrote to the sanatorium to inquire, but there was no response.

When she thought of Caldwell's thin chest, ratcheting with a cough, and how cagey he'd been about the operation he was supposed to have, she realized that he might not have survived it, whatever it was. Tuberculosis, probably. And when she told Josef, he said, "I don't blame him for not telling you the seriousness of the situation. He didn't want you to pity him."

"But I would have thanked him." She felt a dragging weight in her chest. "He didn't want that."

She'd just bought H.D.'s *Sea Garden* and had written to Caldwell that she admired the tightness of the poems—like bright word globes—but she was tired of poems about flowers. More than ever, she wanted to write about the mixed-up landscape of the city, the way streets ran into parks and chrome glinted in clouds, the way buildings cast long shadows that made an afternoon look like dusk. She wanted to know if it were possible to write a poem that resembled walking in a crowd across Forty-second

Street. But maybe the city was already a poem and didn't need her—what did he think?

Now that Caldwell was gone, the letter seemed momentous, and she hoped he'd read it, only because he must have been so lonely out there in the desert, and more ill than he'd let on, and she'd hoped he'd understood what his letters had meant to her.

Around this time Josef ended up losing a thousand dollars on a horse—Fool's Luck. It had been slated to win by a man Barney knew on the inside of the operation, but the jockey who rode Senator, the favored pick, who was supposed to be drugged, ended up riding anyway and winning the race. Josef hit a losing streak after that, one quick loss after another. He lost three hundred dollars at a game of cards that got "heated," as he put it. He lost another two hundred dollars to the roulette wheel.

"I will not go back to being a busboy."

"You were a waiter, not a busboy." This was before he had met Elsa, when he'd gone through several months of what was to him pure humiliation.

"But I can't. It's torture to rely on the charity of tips. I'll have to go back to Berlin to get the money my father put in a trust for me. When I left the military, he said I'd forfeited it, but my mother just told me he never took it out of my account. With her help and Stefan's, I'll convince him that I've got legitimate investments."

"But if we go back now, we'll have to stay there." There were travel restrictions with the war, and it would have been difficult to travel at all. Hell's Hinges and War Brides played on and on at the picture houses. Rumors spread that there were German submarines circling New York, just off Long Island. Men had begun to challenge Josef at the club, pulling him aside and saying, "Tell me, where do you stand?" The war no longer seemed so far away, and Elsa noticed how, at the sound of her accent, certain shopkeepers would snub her. She was beginning to wonder if it were true that the Germans would invade New York.

"Stefan will help me convince him. And then I'll come back and be in business again." It annoyed her that he spoke in that clipped, cheerful way he usually reserved for money talk with friends.

She thought how strange it would be to return to Berlin, wondered if they would bother taking the train to Swinemünde, and if Josef would want to meet her father. "Do we have money for boat fare?"

"Elsa, you can't go."

Something tore in her, and she felt herself spilling out, the emptiness splashing over the bed, leaving big ugly stains on the Oriental rug. She couldn't let him leave without her. "Of course I can."

"Darling. Calm down." His expression was so serene.

"Don't tell me that. You gambled badly—so what? Make a little more and we'll be fine." There were many arguments against his leaving. At least a hundred, and she'd pile them up in a blockade, keep talking until he changed his mind.

"If I don't get that money now, who knows what will happen to it?"

She gave reasons why he should stay. She didn't care if they moved out of the Ritz—they could live more cheaply, get rooms downtown, he could pawn his coat-of-arms ring, but Josef only tried to joke with her, said his luck was going to turn.

She began to weep and threw a bottle of perfume at him, which crashed on the floor near his feet. "I won't let you go without me!" The floral smell of Amour Paris filled the room.

"Calm down. It's just a run of bad luck that I have to break."

Even when one traveled as a civilian, there was the danger of the boat ride (from German torpedoes), the danger of crossing borders, and the risk Josef continually denied, that as soon as he arrived in Berlin, his professor-of-war father and military brothers would try to turn him back into a soldier. "You may be the black sheep, but they'll try to bleach you."

"Don't be silly," he told her. "I hate marching."

He had a plan. The safest way for him to travel was to go to France first and from there hire a car to Germany, posing as a textiles merchant. "Look, it will be easier for me once I get past Paris."

They talked into the night. Little by little, his seductions and his jokes convinced her that maybe it was not so dangerous to travel. And because she realized she could not convince him to stay, she felt herself wanting to agree with him, finally, to consider this trip as incidental as all the others, the dangers only nuisances.

Days later, even after they'd agreed he would go, he gave her pitying looks, which annoyed her. "Solitude," she finally told him. "It improves my thinking."

On the cab out to the piers, Josef's wide smile seemed to separate his chin from the rest of his face. She caught him rubbing the birthmark on his cheek.

She did not want him to tell her to calm down, but on Fifth Avenue she felt the sting of tears. She gave him back the blue stone he'd given her for luck.

"Thanks, I'll keep it in my pocket." He lifted his hip to push it in his trousers. "I'll be back by February," he said, kissing her forehead. "Mid-March at the latest. It's not so long."

He dipped his fingers under the collar of her blouse and stroked the top of her breast. "What shall I bring you?"

She didn't answer. She would find handsome men to entertain her while he was away, men with hot hands and pillowy lips, lots of money. She would make him jealous, despite himself.

"Of course myself," he said, squeezing her hand.

"And something red," she said.

"All right then, something red." He put his arm around her and kneaded her shoulder.

The cab dropped them off at the pier, and she went on to the *Caledonia* with him. He could not get into his cabin yet, so they went into a little space between the dining area and an engine. He opened a door, and they went inside a tiny closet, though the door would not close with both of them inside it. He bent down to grab the hem of her skirt and pulled it up, unbuckled the garters of her stockings, pushed her underthings aside. There were people spilling about on the deck all around them, but they would not have seen the couple unless they were searching for them in the dark of that small passageway. He unbuttoned his trousers, wrapped the ends of her skirt around his waist.

"Look, when I come back, we'll be flush."

"Let me go with you. I'll just stay here on the boat."

"No. That's all we need, to be arrested for you stowing away."

"Let them arrest me."

"They'd throw you off the ship, sweetheart."

He rocked into her, gazing down at her face the whole time. She closed her eyes. Outside the dimness where they were, she heard, in the roar of the crowd around them, the horn signaling that guests were to leave the ship. He shuddered and fell against her, his breath on her neck. She gripped his arms just below his elbows, squeezed them hard enough to leave bruises. A man shouted, "Good-bye, New York, and good riddance!"

Later, standing on the pier, she watched the ship pull away from the dock. Around her there were a French couple, three Belgian men holding up beers to the water, a well-dressed Fifth Avenue society woman weeping into her handkerchief. A girl in a green dress stood at the edge of the pier, constantly waving. Counting the portholes, Elsa tried to find Josef's cabin. There was a pleasant soreness between her legs, his smell on her shoulders, and though there was noise and talking all around her, the world seemed weirdly silent. The boat glided out to the water, and she felt a painful pull in her chest. After a moment she turned away and walked through the crowd, past a band of sailors singing in a language she didn't know.

PART TWO

21

APRIL *1917*

When she first opened her eyes, she saw the drop of blood. She felt for the cut before she realized what it was, her eyes following the ladybug as it meandered in leaf shade over the small mound of her breast and through a fold of lavender silk and disappeared under her arm in the grass.

It was an early spring day, and Bryant Park was filled with people. Near the pavilion a man tried to persuade passersby that the war was unjust, a conspiracy planned by the executives at Standard Oil. Behind him a small boy beat a drum, and next to the library, a man sold bags of peanuts. Women strolled in hats heavy with silk flowers and wax grapes. Children chased balls and squirrels, weaving between the regiments of trees.

Elsa did not know how long she had napped, a few minutes or an hour. She had spent the night before on a bench in the train station, and her cheekbone was bruised where it had pressed against the hard wood. In the morning she had managed to clean herself up in the lavatory, splashing water from the sink onto her chest and under her arms, wetting her hair and combing it straight. Afterward she had painted her fingernails blue with the oils in her box and made an epaulet for her shoulder out of horse-blanket pins.

She stood up and dusted herself off. Past the fence a horse clomped down the street, morosely nodding its head and dragging a wagon, while an automobile honked behind it. She took the case from her bag and opened up the clasp, where the heads of ten cigarettes peeked out. She slid one free, flicked the lighter at the tip, and inhaled. With three more puffs, her shoulders were scarved in airy white feathers.

Two men standing at the lamppost glared at her. The shorter one wore a hat too big for his head. She sucked at the cigarette, leaned back, and blew out a gorgeous geyser of white. The shorter man scowled and turned away.

She sat down on the bench and studied the city roses on the bush, red and turning in the wind like little wheels, then peered through the bramble at the automobile on the street outside the park. She thought she had recognized Skip Drake's car, but the man who stepped out from behind the chrome was not Josef. His hair was too dark, his shoulders too thin.

There had been a string of afternoons Elsa lay in bed smoking, staring out the window at the crowds on the street, willing him to appear. Then her longing for him grew barbed. How could he allow her to worry like this? How could he leave her with so little cash? She had begun to worry only when she saw the buds on the trees. Since then sightings of him teased her wherever she went. Going down the stairs of the train platform, the back of his head; in a café window, his profile; in the mirror just behind her reflection, his face. Weeks ago she'd almost kissed a man because he wore a gray, creased hat like one Josef liked to wear, and she followed a tall man with dark hair all the way to the river, past the chophouses and saloons, pretending it was him. She knew it was unlikely, but she couldn't help the sightings—some physical reflex jarred by hope.

She stood up and lit another cigarette, holding the smoke for a moment in her mouth and nose. Two women on the pebbled walkway turned their heads away from her, their wide-brimmed hats tilting into plates.

The shorter man suddenly stood in front of her. "You know, that's not pretty." He nodded to the cigarette.

"Why should it be?" She blew smoke into his face.

He eyed her blue fingernails, then hit her hand so the cigarette fell in the grass. The smoke curled up through the green blades.

"*Scheissebreck, verdammter!*" she yelled. Since Josef had left, it seemed strangers felt they'd been given orders to torment her, as if her solitariness were writ large on her forehead, some kind of bull's-eye for men who liked to throw darts.

The man smiled and nodded to his friend, then marched down the gravel path.

She tried to calm herself, sat down, and opened her notebook. She pressed the pencil into the paper, the weight of her hat falling low on her forehead. She wanted to write, to put a lid on the loneliness that she felt, while the city carouseled around her, but the words weren't coming anymore.

On the library's gray-white walls, she could just see the outlines of sculpted leaves and flowers, as if they had flown out from the park and arranged themselves there in garlands before turning into stone. Nature was frozen that way in the city, captured, but then the city had its own wildness, the wind in crowds, the rush and clatter of trains, engines growling at every corner.

It was just yesterday that the Hotel Ritz had evicted her because the bill had not been paid. She had ended up at the train station because she could not drag her trunk of clothes more than a few blocks, and she did not know where else to go. There the man at the cigar stand had told her she could leave her trunk in one of the lockers behind the ticket counters, and she had hidden her money in the hem of her skirt.

She smoked as she walked, glared back at disapproving stares, blowing the smoke to the side, so it didn't catch under the brim of her hat. People expected a war bride to wilt into herself or hide, and this made her want to climb up lampposts, screaming.

From the sides of buildings, flags hung over the sidewalk like colorful laundry on the line. Now that America had entered the war, there were so many of them—little ones in toothpicks stuck in ice cream sundaes and large navy blue ones displayed on the doors of houses, one star for each man conscripted from that household. The bands played patriotic music, and the soldiers walked through the streets grinning and tipping their hats.

Josef had sent a single wire from the ship: ELSA VOYAGE SMOOTH BUT DELAYED TWO DAYS ALL MY LOVE.

On Broadway she walked through a stream of people, their faces bleached pale in the sunlight. Scraps of strangers' conversation trailed her as she went. "She wouldn't forget . . ." "This darling little shop . . ." She was pulled along in the crowd. She swerved her hips to avoid hitting a woman's hatboxes and lifted her arm so as not to hit a man's elbow.

Elsa stood in front of the Wanamaker's window. The mannequin wore an evening dress whipped with silver stitching. One of her slender hands touched the slick surface of an electric stove, and in the crook of her elbow hung the nozzle to an electric vacuum. Elsa studied the mannequin's tilted head, her perfect, curious smile. Electricity made even cooking and cleaning appear glamorous, the shiny chrome of each appliance like a giant piece of jewelry. Elsa remembered how Josef would shake his head at windows like this, wondering about the gadgets of the future, staring at the machines as if they would tell him something important.

She went through the gold-rimmed doors, into a room full of mirrors and white. Garlands of ivy wrapped around palatial Greek pillars, and glass chandeliers gleamed expensive electric light. She closed her eyes for a moment and touched her temples, then walked slowly toward the glove counter.

The clerk smiled at her. "May I help you, miss?"

"No, I won't be buying any gloves," said Elsa. She saw the woman's mouth tighten at the sound of her accent.

"We just got these kid leather pairs . . ." She was staring at the horse-blanket pins on Elsa's shoulder as if she could not decide whether she had seen them in the *Sun*'s fashion pages. Elsa looked past her—the gloves were gray and delicately tooled.

"How did you hurt your hand?"

Elsa glanced at her blue nails. "Oh, that's oil paint."

"I see. Funny, it doesn't look like you spilled it."

"I didn't."

"Oh." The clerk gave her a curious look, as if she were trying to decide whether Elsa had any money.

At the next counter, hairpieces and ivory combs hung against a satin-covered board. She fingered a curled chignon of auburn hair that hung by a piece of ribbon, the silky strands stiff with starch, perfect as an artificial flower, some poor woman's tresses.

Beneath the sign that said FOR SPRING, a woman in a lace dress stood with her finger over her mouth, staring down at a table of stockings as if it were a textbook.

Elsa had called the shipping company, and each time a thin-voiced operator told her that the *Caledonia* had not sunk, that it had arrived at its port and no one had fallen overboard. She wrote letters to Josef's parents and brothers, but they did not write back to her. She visited the German consulate, but they were overwhelmed with queries about combat fatalities, and after she sat there in the sweaty waiting room for five hours, the man who finally saw her told her that she was not the only wife waiting for her husband to come home. She had no idea where Josef was. He might be singing, drunk, in some Berlin nightclub, riding on a train, wounded, or ill with influenza. Her false sightings were a comfort only in the shallowest sense.

Elsa lifted her skirt to go up the stairs, then walked into a pink room. On the hangers there were pretty underpants, chemises, and slips. The mannequin torsos wore corsets laced around plaster waists and those ridiculous new cupped covers for breasts, called brassieres, which reminded her of muzzles.

There were two women in front of a rack. "I never wear a corset anymore."

"But how do you keep your shape, then? Without a corset I have no shape."

"That's ridiculous, Edna. Of course you have a shape."

Elsa caressed the silk of a pair of ruffled underpants. They made her smile. She liked something funny in an undergarment—a ruffle, a pompom, a fringe. Josef liked ruffles, but not pink. Already she missed their lost bed at the Ritz, the silk pillow he turned over once before laying down his head, the pineapple-shaped knob on the headboard that she gripped when they made love with her on top, sailing over him.

She went to the elevator and asked the operator to take her to the appliances floor. They landed with a lurch, and Elsa walked out.

"Think of your hands," said the salesman to the woman. They stood near a silver box on a raised pedestal. She nodded solemnly, stepping away as if to better examine the machine's shape.

The husband paced behind her in a half circle. "So the soap spreads how?" he asked the clerk. Elsa saw the sign—DISHWASHER—imagined ten mechanical spongy hands scrubbing at plates and cups inside.

She walked along the wall, watched the vacuum whir back and forth along a slip of red carpet like an anxious pet.

Down the aisle a couple stood watching the electric clothes washer, colorful pieces of clothes swirling behind a soapy round window. "I just can't believe that machine could really get things clean," said the woman.

"Better than that woman you hire out," said the man. "Go ahead and touch it—you can feel the strength of the engine."

"I'm afraid to touch it," said the woman. "That's just the problem. It looks like it might swallow my hand." She backed away, shaking her head.

Elsa stepped closer and laid her hand on the hot metal lid of the machine, feeling it vibrate violently, as if the clothes inside wanted to escape.

The couple stared at her. The clerk, quickly approaching, cleared his throat. "I can guarantee you, it will get out the stains, and it won't complain about them either."

Soon there would be an electric pain reducer, an electric stomach filler, an electric sex organ, an electric heart.

"You were interested in an electric vacuum?" the clerk said to the couple, and the three walked away. The overhead lights made the room enervatingly white, and hot. Elsa watched the clothes washer, hypnotized by the tilt and swirl of bright cloth and soap behind the window.

She sat down on the floor, took off her jacket, noticed that the clerk at the register was staring at her. She concentrated on this block of black metal with the glass-topped hole. The machine gyrated, one side bouncing against the floor, and there was a groaning, panting sound. When she glanced back at the window, a disembodied hand tumbled in the clothes, then a foot. A chill hit the small of her back. She touched the window. The machine sprung a bell sound, then stopped shaking.

"Madame?" The clerk stood behind her. "Please do not touch that."

She stared again at the porthole on this miniature soapy sea, but the hand and foot were gone.

There were riverbeds of red lines on either side of the clerk's nose. "Can I assist you?" he said.

Shaken by what she'd seen, she stood up and said, "No thank you." The vision made her feel as if she were coming apart, as if Josef had taken something from her that she badly needed. She took the elevator down one floor.

A display of umbrellas. There was one with a barber's-pole stripe, one plaid, one dotted, one with a pink ruffle. The ruffle reminded her of a skirt of her mother's she'd liked to stand underneath when she was still small enough to fit there, her face against the netting, her hand on her mother's knee, which smelled of talc and sweat. She had loved hiding there, the grown-up voices muffled through the fabric. The quick pleasure of the

memory transformed the umbrella into her personal souvenir, as if it had
been lifted out of her childhood and was mistakenly for sale in this store. At
the register the clerk was wrapping something for a man who judiciously
studied a black case, and, glancing over at Elsa, the clerk said something in a
confidential voice that made the man laugh.

To anyone else the umbrella would have remained something to carry on
cloudy days and keep hidden in the closet the rest of the time, but for her
this umbrella had transcended its obligation to keep one dry. It was a mater-
nal ruffle, a tent for eavesdropping. She heard the clerk laugh again, mali-
ciously. She grabbed the umbrella, stuffed it under her jacket, and headed for
the elevator.

A family came to stand next to her, also waiting for the elevator.
"Tomorrow we'll go to Coney Island," the husband said. The children
cheered.

"Don't promise them that," said the wife.

The fabric was cool and smooth against her chest, the rubber ribs fortify-
ing her. Even if it was secreted there under her coat, soon enough she would
open it, and just like that her life would bloom. Josef would return. She
would fill a book with poems.

There was no need to rush to the stairs. She walked regally, stopping on
her way to admire the belts arranged like snakes around a large wooden block.
She descended the stairs deliberately, saw that no one was watching her.

When Elsa got to the exit, a man's voice called from behind her, but he
could have been calling anyone. "Miss!" She stepped inside one of those
revolving doors that made her feel as if she would never get out, but then, in
a turn, she was released into sun and air.

A crowd came toward her, and she found a path that maneuvered
through it, between the ladies in their pigeon-breasted voiles, past a large
man with an ice cream.

"Miss? I'm sure you didn't mean to run off with that umbrella." A hand
gently squeezed her elbow, and she turned.

The ends of the clerk's mustache trembled. "Now, please give it to me,"
he said, holding out his hand. "Unless you'd like to pay for it, and then we
can check on the price, miss."

"Baroness."

"Pardon me?"

A crowd formed a small hushed circle around them. "Look at her hair," one woman said to another.

"I said I'm not miss, I am a baroness."

"Oh." The clerk seemed to stare at the horse-blanket pins. "Baroness, then."

She sighed and unbuttoned her jacket, yanked out the umbrella, and handed it to him. The ribs and pink fabric looked forlorn and faded in the sunlight.

The clerk pursed his lips as he took it away from her. His mustache hung complacently over his lips in a way that made her want to tear off the ends of it. "Now, madame, should we call your husband?"

"I will make sure that you are *paid well* for this customer abuse." She tried to sound rich and bored, but her voice escaped in a screech.

The clerk, caressing the umbrella's ruffle in a proprietary way, began to laugh. "Abuse? Madame, I'll have you arrested."

She kicked him in the knees, and he fell forward, gripping his leg. She started to run, heard him yell from behind her. She got as far as the corner before a policeman, chasing her into the street, caught her arm as an automobile careened to avoid them, its horn blaring.

22

The warden forced the baroness to empty her pockets and snickered at the pack of cigarettes. "Ah, a smoker, too, are you?"

"Aren't you?"

"Only cigars," he said, winking one of his tiny eyes.

They'd taken her to the jail for women at Jefferson Market in Greenwich Village. She felt as if the fabric of her life had just been wadded into a dirty ball that this warden was sitting on. She tried to explain that her husband would be looking for her, but the warden simply smiled and said, "Tell us the truth—there is no husband, is there?"

She didn't see the point in arguing. She could already hear women weeping and talking down the hallway of cells beyond the doorway, and it seemed as if anything she said would only add to that pathetic chorale.

On the desk he shuffled through the contents of her bag—a compact, rouge, some coins and a small roll of bills, a pencil, her book of Novalis poems, a rubber disk she'd found on the street, her notebook.

"We have to hold them," he said, picking up her notebook. He flipped through the pages, idly pausing somewhere in the middle to read. She did not want his tiny eyes shitting on her poems and was going to spit in his face when he abruptly put the notebook down, looking bored.

"We have to keep you here until you can see the judge."

She heard the slam of metal against metal and became aware of a faint smell of urine. "When will I see him?"

"Don't know, Reddie." A smile puckered into his cheeks. "That's a pretty dress. Too bad you tore it." She hadn't noticed until now how her dress had ripped, then remembered how the thin fabric belt had caught on the door of the police wagon. At her midriff now was a web of lace and pale skin.

"You tore it for me, didn't you?" he said, and she was struck by the waxiness of his face as if there were a layer over it. He laughed at her.

She would kick him in the groin. He would buckle over. He would cup his crotch and groan, and she would grab the key from the desk and find the door beyond all the shelves of papers and the cluttered tables. It would give her just enough time to run.

Another guard walked into the office and took her by the arm. The guard and warden led her down a greenish hallway. Through the bars shuttering past, she saw a woman sitting on a bench, knees pressed together, back perfectly straight; a girl lying on the cement floor, who sobbed through the long matted hair; an Irishwoman cackling and talking to herself over a lapful of crumbs.

When the warden opened the cell door, the bars swung back quickly.

The cot smelled of vomit. Elsa sat on it and looked at the smear of something pink—it looked like rouge—against the cement wall.

If only she had been a better liar, she might still be at the Hotel Ritz, signing for her meals and slipping into the Red Room now and then for a dance. Sadly, she thought of the red glass lamp that had tinted her skin rosy in bed, the shell-shaped sink where fine black hairs would settle in a circle near the drain after Josef had shaved, leaving a bit of white foam on the fish-shaped faucet.

If she had tried, she might have been able to hold off Mr. Collins a while longer with promises. She could have said that Josef had written that he would be sailing home in May. Or she might have said that her in-laws were making arrangements to send money for the bill, only there was some confusion about the gold standard. When Mr. Collins came to her room that day, she could have wept or pleaded with him not to throw her out, but she'd been too stupid and proud.

"Yes?" She'd opened the door as if she did not know why he had come. He avoided her eyes. Why was it that his fuzzy hair always made her expect something more congenial from him? "Have you heard from your husband? I have to ask, because the bill, you must realize, has not been paid."

"You know he is abroad."

"Yes, well." He scratched his nose. "I'm afraid we can't offer you credit any longer."

"Of course you can, Mr. Collins. In two weeks you will have your god-damn money," she said.

He looked at the wall, knitting his brow. "There's a women's home on Twenty-fourth Street."

She slammed the door in his face and spit at the peephole. He knocked again, but she didn't answer.

When the two policemen finally came, in their beetle helmets, she was wearing her best lavender dress and she had fixed her hair and powdered her face, dabbed perfume at her wrists.

Collins stood at the door with the two policemen while she packed the last of her things. "The bill must be paid," said Mr. Collins, his voice full of fake sorrow. "There isn't a thing I can do about that, is there?"

The woman in the cell across from hers was round, her flesh pressed up against the bars as she muttered in a guttural Polish voice, a dark patch of hair over her sensuous, red lips, a lace collar hung askew on her dress.

"Calm down," Elsa told herself. She needed to think about the judge. He would sit high above her in a black robe, his face impassive like a sphinx waiting for the answer to a riddle. She only had to think of the right thing to say to him, and he would let her go. "My husband is abroad, you see." Though she hated to do it, she would make herself weep. "The war."

She had written nine letters addressed to the von Freytag-Loringhovens in Berlin—the address Josef had given to her, a house with a lion's-mouth brass knocker and giant mahogany doors. They'd disapproved of his mar-rying a woman whose surname they didn't know, a master mason's daugh-ter, but Josef had been estranged from them for so long it didn't seem to matter until now.

She watched a line of roaches crawl along a seam in the wall, the fine hairs of their antennae wiggling forward. On the dirty floor, there were tiny wads of paper, a butterscotch stuck to the cement like a worn jewel. The hollowness deepened inside of her. It seemed she could take objects into it—the bar rusted to a bright orange, the brass buckle on her shoe, the padlock, the butterscotch.

From the next cell, she heard the woman's voice. It moved up and down inside its pitch. "They scratch out your eyes. They skitter through these bars and bite off your fingers." Lying back on the rough mattress, Elsa felt her hands begin to tremble, and she pressed them over her ears.

She had had nightmares about being imprisoned, but the cell always turned into a collapsing tunnel that shot her down through the earth and up again into some unrecognizable place. Or the walls expanded like chests breathing heavily, hot and moist, and just before suffocating, she woke up. But there was a hard stillness to this cell. The drab gray walls and floor, no matter how long she stared at them, would not sink or stir. When she tried to banish them to background, they didn't flinch.

To distract herself she tried to compose—

> City stirs on eardrums
> Lake—palegreen—shrouded—
> Skylake—clouded—shrouded.

The words jumbled and rearranged themselves in her head, and then she put them away.

The warden was talking to someone down the hall about the beautiful peaches he'd bought the day before. "They're as big as my fist and so juicy and sweet you wouldn't believe it." She couldn't hear what the other person said, she could hear only mumbling. Then he said, "No, honestly, talk to Mr. Strummond at the market, and he'll give you the best."

At that moment the pain attacked her legs, an infinite small slicing from a hundred razors, up and down her thighs, a sensation she had not felt since her time with Mello. She lifted up her skirt, pushed down her stockings, but there was nothing there—the skin sallow and unmarked. No blood—like a hex from a warlock.

A little later the warden brought her a tin cup of water and thrust it through the bars. "You're probably thirsty," he said. "After all this."

She got up, took the water, and glared at him. "When will I see the judge?" Her legs wobbled. She would touch her throat as she made her case, make her eyes start to tear.

The warden sucked on his teeth. "In an hour he leaves for dinner. If there's no time before then, you'll have to see him in the morning."

When she handed the cup back to him, his fingers held hers a beat longer than they should have. "But we might make an arrangement, if you were smart, a little nice."

Across the way in another cell, she saw a flash of shiny fur skitter across the floor. She knew that if he was even offering, there was a chance she might be released anyway.

"On this stinking mattress?"

"Anywhere."

"And then what will you give me?"

He laughed as he walked away, his footsteps echoing against the cement. "Calm down," she told herself, taking deep breaths because her heart was flaring up in her chest. "Calm down."

She heard footsteps in the hall, the whores laughing and cursing at the guard. "You can't keep us here for walking down the street. We were just walking."

"You weren't just walking."

"We were just walking, you ass."

The guards barked at one another. "What happened to that key?"

"It's in the drawer."

"It's not in the drawer."

And another voice: "If you were just walking, why don't you show me that, then? Show me how—"

Elsa stared at the gray pockmarked walls, feeling the pains in her thighs fade and throb.

She heard clapping footsteps, the clank of keys in a lock. Somewhere down the hall, a door whined open. "I was only asking for a loan, Officers. You understand, he was in love with me." The woman sounded drunk, and Elsa didn't hear the guard's reply before the cell door slammed shut.

She saw the warden's beefy face striped by the bars of her cell. "All right, Baroness von Freytag-Loringhoven." He said it as if he didn't believe her title. "The store has agreed to let you go with only a warning—luckily they got the stolen property out of you." He made a tsking sound. "Otherwise . . ."

He unlocked the door and opened it. She began to walk past him, and he blocked her way. Through the silk of her skirt, he grabbed the top of her thigh, where it was sore. She moved to hit him, but he caught her by the wrist. "Now," he said. "You want to leave, don't you?" She wrenched her arm away from him, and they walked down the hall to the front desk.

There another guard handed her her bag, her novel, her notebook, but not her cigarettes. At the bottom of the trash can, she saw the crumpled packet. She stooped over and picked up the packet, but it was empty.

When she went out the door into the open air, she walked furiously for several blocks, the houses and stores around her a blur, the wind in her eyes so they teared at the corners. "Calm down," she told herself. But she had no idea where she would go.

23

For five nights she slept at the train station, her dress smelling of her unwashed skin, her hair gradually matting in odd shapes against her head. She was looking for a room to rent in the Village. One stubble-faced landlord had said, "I don't rent to dirty Huns," and slammed the door in her face, and another tried to rent her a windowless stable. She met a man named Guido Bruno, who offered "First Aid to Struggling Artists," but she soon recognized from the teary-eyed way he talked about artists as if they were animals in his zoo that he was an opportunist coasting on the money a woman was willing to pay in order to call herself bohemian.

And he wasn't the only one selling Greenwich Village—there was a gift shop on Charles Street where a woman peddled batik dresses, other "Village garb," soaps, postcards with stage scenes from the Provincetown Playhouse, Mexican sandals, and wine-bottle candlesticks. There was a sign on the door that said GREENWICH VILLAGE TOURS: EVERY DAY AT 2:00. Elsa overheard someone call the tourists who came downtown on the train "Uptown Swillage." Sonja the cigarette girl carried through the streets her box that advertised "no criticism or hard looks" for women who wanted to buy them. And there was a boy waif who roamed the teahouses selling "soul candy," and a man who stood on MacDougal Street with a pencil and paper, offering to write "free verse" for a quarter.

The local Italian and Irish kept their tenements closed to people like

Elsa—even if she could have withstood the noise and odors of cooking, and
all the laundry, so much laundry hanging everywhere like limp ghosts.

Even here she had phantom sightings of Josef. Turning a corner, she'd
spot the figure in her peripheral vision, quicken her pace, her heartbeat fast
though she had already prepared herself for disappointment: *How could you
say it would only be a month?* When she got closer and saw how the man's
weight had settled around his middle, she'd slow down her pace, continuing
to rehearse her harangue: *Did you expect me to sit by the window and cry? Did
you think the Ritz would open a charity?*

She finally found a room on Fourteenth Street, near Eleventh Avenue, in a
tenement building—brick and fire escape, exactly like the one next to it. The
hallways were black and green with mold, the stairwell littered with papers and
bits of food. Her room was small and dim, with one cracked window. There
was a rust-stained sink near the door, where some kind of blue substance had
been ground into the wood of the floor, a closet without a door. The striped
wallpaper had been ripped from the wall in a jagged coastline. That was the
only part of the room she liked, a diagonal break in the design, those frayed
edges of yellow and blue bars and the curl of paper left behind in the corner, the
remnant of some fit of passion. The landlord, leading her to the basement, had
let her choose from the furniture that former renters had abandoned. She'd
found a deal wood dressing table and mirror and a bed that would have been
pretty if it didn't tilt to the side. The mattress was stained purple and brown,
and she covered it with a silk sheet she'd stolen from the Ritz.

She would have to look for work, though she knew by now that no the-
ater director would hire an actress with a German accent—all of the
actresses in the plays she'd seen sounded British—and at thirty-four she was
certainly too old for the chorus. She could have looked for work in a shop,
but her accent would have again been an obstacle, as certain customers
would not trust her, and there was also her sheer inability to accurately
count American money. She saw the wax-faced women who came out of the
factories, and she supposed a boss might overlook her Germanness to hire
her for a low wage, but she was afraid of those places, where hours were
packed into neat squares; the angry, repetitive tasks; the large, airless rooms
that locked into firetraps. That kind of work would suffocate her poems and
make her invisible.

Across the hallway a cardboard sign read PHONE CALLS 5 CENTS, INSIDE 2D. A pimply faced illustrator rented his telephone. The wires rattled and crackled as if the voice were coming through a tunnel of wind. Every afternoon she heard the telephone ringing. He collected the nickels in a little cup and sat facing the callers as they spoke, pretending to sketch but presumably guarding his loot. If she was desperate, she'd telephone Barney Fitch for help, or one of Josef's other friends, but she hoped it wouldn't come to that. She hated to beg. Besides, she'd always saved herself before in the nick of time. Though this time it might be in the nick of nick.

One day she walked up to the Art Students League on Fifty-seventh Street to see if there was any work for models. She'd kept the certificate from the Naples modeling school all this time, folded up in the pocket on the inside of her trunk, and she took it with her, hoping that the European imprimatur would impress.

The instructor, Gilbert Dixon, a painter who had a bearded baby face and slow, indecisive eyes, looked down at the certificate, sighed, then looked at her and said, "We have so few models trained in the classical tradition." She soon became his regular model. Every Tuesday and Thursday afternoon, for one dollar an hour, she stood nude on a dais covered with an old Oriental rug. Dixon arranged her in awkward poses, which left her muscles hard and sore afterward. She stood with one leg dipped low behind her, her front knee bent, or with her arms raised above her, her torso twisted to the left. "It brings out the muscle," he was fond of saying, and then he would turn to the classroom of easels and students, close his eyes, and scratch his head, as if deep in thought.

During the breaks Elsa, in her kimono, smoked cigarettes in the foyer, looking out through the glass at the street. Nearly always Gilbert Dixon appeared beside her, feigning interest in the window view, and lit up his pipe. It was made of ivory and curved suggestively, with a wide, round pot, like a pipe for smoking opium, and he kept the bag of loose tobacco in his pocket. He didn't say much, but his eyes fell on the gap between the folds in her robe, or drifted down to her ankles in a way that amused her. He began to send roses to her building with notes begging her to meet him, but she ignored them, suspecting he was the kind of man excited by coolness, and because she knew that the more he desired her, the better chance she had of keeping the work.

She missed Josef most in the evenings, when she ate her tiny suppers of tinned meat and bread, or when she got into bed, covering herself with a blanket, the open window blowing with street noise and ships' horns. There were no false sightings of him at night, only fantasies of his returning to her. Maybe because she imagined Josef there, she missed Berlin, too: the baroque busyness of Brandenburg Gate; the formal manners of people, which did not make one feel assaulted by friendliness; Christof, Natalye, and other old friends who might be dead by now; her old cafés; the stately buildings with courtyards; the green meadow of the Tiergarten, the parties where people in shabby clothes discussed philosophy; the sausages and a certain apple sweet.

She'd given the Ritz her address, and when the concierge sent word that a letter had arrived from Josef, she took the train uptown to pick it up. Inside the lobby there was the chandelier like an overturned crystal birthday cake. There was the painting of the wood nymph running through the forest, the wind god puffing out his cheeks. There were the chintz-covered sofas and the velvet-covered chairs; the small, round wooden tables; and the pinkish marble of the fireplace. The only thing that had changed was a hideous brass thing shaped like an acorn between the elevators.

She closed her eyes, walked past the Tiffany-shaded lamps and straight to the concierge's desk, and spotted Mr. Collins, busy with a notebook. When he looked up, he smiled and then frowned. He gave her the letter, the envelope marked *Hold for two weeks only—RC*. Bastard. "I am waiting for your apology," she said.

"Mrs. Loringhoven, I have certain duties."

She tore open the envelope and saw Josef's cheerful small scrawl.

Dear Elsa,

There were only bores on the ship, though sunning on the deck was pleasant, despite people's fears. Still, you would not have enjoyed the trip, believe me.

In Calais I won a game of mah-jongg that I played with a Chinaman at a café. There are soldiers everywhere, and at night people hide. There are no eggs and very little milk or butter. I have hired a car to drive through Alsace and into Dresden.

I finished that book you gave me about the student, and now I've lain awake with insomnia ever since—why did he end up murdering the woman? I keep trying to puzzle it out.

I'll write to you from Berlin and wire money from there. Josef.

The letter had been posted two months earlier—in March.

The handwriting broke off. The curved lines brought back his voice, and she heard him murmuring the kinds of things he liked to say to her in bed. "Put your hand here." "Let me see your breasts." She folded up the letter and slipped it into her chemise against her bosom.

By the time she had walked all the way back to Fourteenth Street, there was a pain in her fingers. It pricked into the bones, through the blood vessels and tiny muscles. She knew the syph was probably creeping back, and who knew for how long? But she tried to fight it off, telling herself that she was strong, that she couldn't afford to wilt now.

Hatted, blank faces passed by her, the honking chrome of traffic. The train rattled efficiently overhead.

At home she opened a cheap bottle of gin and sipped it to blunt the stinging. She skipped dinner, sat in bed with the bottle, turning the pages of O. Henry stories. The words wobbled and ran back and forth on the page, so she read in both directions, the language strange and withholding, smiling darkly. More than ever, since Josef had left, English made her feel as if she'd been reincarnated, as if her German self existed in some other realm, with the dead and the past. But tonight she longed for the familiar words—*Weide, Wein, wollen*—for that café in the Berlin theater district she'd asked Josef to visit, to see if Peter was still the owner and if they still served grog, where she'd gone to read alone or to stare out the window at the snow, knowing that no one would bother her, because Peter said he liked having her at her usual table. Later in the evening, she held the half-drunk bottle again to the light, to see what was left. The floor seesawed under her, and the coastline of torn wallpaper began to shift back and forth. Even her feet were imbalanced, and she tripped when she got up to get her notebook. She couldn't find a pencil anywhere. And without a way to write them down, her thoughts felt temporary and imbalanced. The sink was dripping, ghostly thin plops. The scatter of clothes and books on the floor looked unreal, as if there had been some violent scene she didn't remember. The pain pushed through her drunkenness, nagging her. She fell back on the bed, grabbed the bottle, and took another sip. The throbbing became familiar in a way that lessened the impact, and she wondered if there was a good way to phrase this, or if pain was always beyond words. She got up again to look for her pencil—she thought she'd left one stuck between the pages of a book, but which one was it? She opened the pages of a tattered *Sons and Lovers*, the words swimming up at her, and no goddamn pencil.

She threw the bottle against the wall. It shattered, the gin dripped against the striped paper and gray wall. The antiseptic smell filled the room, and she went over to collect the broken glass. As she laid the pieces in her palm, it bled, red streaming down her wrist, and the blue shards began to fascinate her, like something she'd read in a fairy tale, sapphires plucked from roses.

Crouched there, she held her hurt hand, staring at the broken glass. Then she briefly glanced out the window. Just beyond the crack in the glass, she saw the shine of two eyes.

She stood up, dropped the shards of glass, and, holding her wrist, went to the window. With her good hand, she pushed up the sash. The eyes belonged to a little dog, standing on the fire escape. Its fur was light brown, almost pink, its face all eyes and ears. She let the dog smell her knuckles so he would know she was friendly. He pushed his wet nose against her fingers, licked at the blood. There were purplish raw patches where his fur brushed in the wrong direction. She was about to reach out to pet him when the dog leaped in past her arm, hit the floor with his legs splayed, and skidded to the dressing table. He jumped up, grabbed the last of a sardine sandwich in his teeth, dropped it, and began to gobble it up. His head bobbed over the crinkled waxed paper. His triangular ears quivered as he chewed.

The room was turning, and the dog seemed to multiply and disappear, multiply again and disappear. As he licked the floor for crumbs, the legs of the dressing table seemed to wobble and splinter. "Pinky," she said, "you'll eat the glass next, and then what will you do? All scraped up inside." Her eyelids felt suddenly leaden, and she lay down on the floor and fell asleep.

24

The dog Pinky stayed with her. She fed him fish heads that had been left out in the trash behind the grocery and an occasional bone from the butcher. He slept at the foot of her bed, his huge ears pricked up and turned to her. When she looked inside one of them, the whorl of pink seemed to spin down all the way through his little head, down his body, to his twisted tail.

After Josef had left, the pages in her notebook sat there like white empty fields, complete in their silence. Whenever she wrote in German, she thought of him; it had been their secret language, what they'd spoken in bed (*Möchtest du?*), at the high pitches of arguments (*Warum? Was bedeutet das?*). And it was the language of her past, which sometimes washed up against her, threatened to spill into everything new. So she wrote instead in English. The words were broken and jagged, but the serrated edges glittered, and she arranged the pieces until the rhythm matched one of the very faint voices she was beginning to hear in her head, either rushed so she missed most of it before she could write it down or so slow she had to strain to hear the end of the word.

It was hard to work in such a noisy building. There were twenty-five rooms on five floors, and from the second-floor room, where Elsa lived, she heard constant footsteps, doors slamming, music, and shouting. All day she heard people come and go from the toilet, a room covered with black mold

and stench. Someone was either banging on the door down the hall—
"Hurry up and tinkle, Laura! I've got to go to work!"—or calling down
from upstairs—"Mike, you can use the hot water now!"

Elsa sharpened her pencil, sat cross-legged on the bed next to Pinky, the
lead smell clearing the stale odor of her studio. The important thing was not
to pity herself, to keep going, to follow the crazy veer of hope.

Next door a bed banged against the wall, the mattress squealing.

"Affectionate," she wrote. It was for Josef, but less ambitious than a love
poem. She went back to the lines she had begun that day in the park.

> *Wheels are growing on rosebushes—*
> *Gray and affectionate*

She wondered if the listener would get her disdain for the word "affection-
ate," which had been cheapened and rusted by sentimental hacks. She
wanted to get down the motion of the roses she'd seen that day.

> *Did some swallow Prendergast's silverheels—*

She put down the pencil and paper, stood up to study the magazine pictures
she had pinned to the wall: a photograph of a horse on a barren city street,
an advertisement for Pears' soap, which had a pretty jingle, and a drawing of
a zeppelin, an invention that fascinated her, for its huge and awful lightness,
like a sinister mechanical cloud.

She went back to the bed, licked the tip of her pencil, and began to write:
be drunk forever and more.

That was not fancy—that was what affection felt like.

Then she needed a thin sound, a thinness and a little surprising trot.

> *—with a lemon appendicitis?*

While she was writing, the deliveryman came with the roses from Gilbert
Dixon. *Meet me at the Brevoort Hotel at 5. You are beautiful—please send
word.* Elsa took them upstairs to the old woman she'd seen in the hallway
one day carrying a burlap sack. Elsa held out the bouquet to her and looked
into her wrinkled face. Through the doorway she glimpsed the shadowy

rooms—furniture piled with crocheted doilies, tables crowded with bud vases and ceramic figures of horses. "I don't want these," said Elsa. "Do you?" The roses were still dewy and fragrant.

"I could never be bribed with flowers either," the old woman said, taking the vase. Her eyes were the color of irises, her smile disarming and lovely.

"I don't know why men think it's so easy," Elsa said.

Later she looked out the window and spotted the old woman on the corner, wearing an extravagant, wide hat that made her figure resemble a mushroom. The roses sat in a bucket beside her, and she held a stem out to the passersby. One man stopped, dug his hand into his pocket, and handed her a coin. She gave him the rose.

Elsa hoped she made a good profit.

She'd heard an art student say that Gilbert Dixon was married to a wealthy woman, and this explained the roses all the more. Men like him idealized a woman until she was everything the wife was not. She'd noticed how Dixon gazed at the mole on her shoulder, how he smiled when she was rude to him, how he seemed to listen intently to whatever she said, even if it was nonsense, and shook his head at the students' attempts, looking up again at her nudity. He ignored her gooseflesh and her scowling. His desire wasn't for her but for his own seriousness or ambition or something else he'd lost. She continued to ignore Gilbert Dixon's notes, and at the school he never made mention of either the notes or the roses, as if it had been some other man signing his name.

The next day, after another bouquet arrived, she was taking it upstairs when she recognized a man she had seen weeks earlier. He had been carrying a large piece of glass, almost the size of a store window, one hand on either side of it, his body pressed against the glare as he walked gingerly up the stairs. She had wondered what the glass was for and could not help noticing his patrician profile. Now he came down the stairs empty-handed, his black pants perfectly pressed and angular, kneecaps popping up against the fabric, and she saw he had laughing eyes. He seemed to want to tell her something. She stopped on the landing. His lips were pursed as if to hum,

but no sound came from him. He looked down at her and said, "Ah, roses."
He was French—that mellifluous, perfumed voice, a passionate throatiness.

She held the vase out to him. "I don't want them. Do you?"

"You don't like them?"

"I don't like the one who sent them."

His eyes crinkled, and he laughed. "*Merci,* then." He took the roses
from her and held the vase out in front of him. "I will give them to the train
conductor."

She turned to watch him go down the last flight, his dark hair forming a
V above the back of his shirt collar. He had a light step—she could barely
hear it on the creaking stairs.

In the classroom at the Art Students League, Gilbert Dixon leaned over a
student's canvas, sketching with his finger in the air. He looked down at the
canvas, then up again at her. She thought most of the figures in the paintings
were rounder and pinker than they should have been, bland versions of the
female form that had little to do with her own. She couldn't decide whether
she was grateful or insulted by this anonymity. She doubted that they had
not noticed the particulars. Now that she was older, the skin had lost its
sheen, the blue and red veins like ink marks on her thighs, the new softness
just over her knees. It seemed there should have been some signs of her past
in the paintings—August's flaccid hand on her shoulder, Franz's cold stare
on her cheek, her mother's tears, places that had been kissed and spots that
had been cut and healed over—but the students' nudes were imprecise and
unblemished.

One night, when the other students had left the room to drink coffee in
the lounge, a young woman stayed behind, still painting.

She had extravagant eyebrows and held the end of her paintbrush near
her nose.

When Elsa walked over to her easel, the woman said, without looking up,
"It must be so odd for you." She was small and plump and had a face like a
kitten's—slanted green eyes, a pink mouth.

She applied the paint thickly, and there was a black line around Elsa's fig-
ure, like a kind of armor or shadow. "The line suggests something, doesn't
it?" the woman said.

Elsa examined the painting. "Breath."

"Maybe."

"But you should put more yellow there in the corner." Elsa pointed to the top of the canvas, where the paint ended.

The woman twirled the brush between her fingers, glancing sideways at Elsa. "I see what you mean."

"Something to turn the eye away." That was the problem, often, with paintings; the eye was drawn only to the center—and the center was always dead. In a poem one's eye was drawn to the beginning or the end, depending on one's attitude—the poet had the opposite problem of making sure the middle held some interest.

"That green there." The woman pointed. "You have a bruise on the back of your thigh, did you know that? It's the size of a potato."

Elsa touched her thigh in the spot and remembered how on the train she'd fallen against a metal box in a man's lap. "I didn't see it in any of the other paintings."

The woman shrugged. "That doesn't surprise me."

The next day Elsa stood barefoot in the lamplight of the young painter's bedroom. Her name was Sara Albright. "I got this idea in the bathtub," she said. "Womanly feet without heels or buckles—just toes and ankles and soles. I'd paint my own feet, but they're hideous, and it would be too hard to work, looking down the whole time." Elsa's dress was held up with clothespins at her thighs.

The room was large, with a fireplace against one wall, a window on the other, canvases stacked in each corner. Sara's ukulele lay on the rumpled bed, the top of her dresser cluttered with paint tubes and brushes and books. Her canvases were painted in broad and aggressive strokes, the colors layered but not muddy. Sara's paintings made Elsa think of the way a thing could vibrate in one's memory, both brighter and less distinct than it had been in life—how one feature could magnify to blur the rest of the face, how the arm or hand might be frozen into a single gesture. There was an intensity in their composition that made one take note, as if the thing in her focus literally required more eyesight.

Sara sat on a chair in front of her easel and would now and then get down on her knees to examine Elsa's feet more closely. "Can you bend your right knee so the ankle comes forward?" When Elsa got tired of looking down, she looked up at the thick, battered wooden beam down the center of the ceiling, which sometimes steadied her and sometimes reminded her of the slat holding the strings to a marionette's skinny arms and legs.

Sara got down on her knees and seemed to be staring at Elsa's toenails. "Your second toe is larger than the first," Sara said. "That's supposed to be a sign of intelligence."

In her head Elsa was counting the little money she had left. Enough for rent until the end of the month. Enough for food if she ate only bread and milk. She'd seen a cigarette factory that advertised for help near West Street, men and women coming out all at once in the early evening with brown-stained hands.

"Move your left foot toward the other one more. It's true—it's freak-ishly longer, but sort of beautiful. Do me a favor," Sara said, her face calm with concentration. "Move your ankle there just slightly." She stirred her brush in the old jam jar. "There's something about the way you stand. . . ."

The longer Elsa posed, the more fitting for a portrait her feet seemed. They were narrow, a crow's claw of blue veins over the top of each, the ankles thin and pink. Over the hours as she stared down at them, they began to transform themselves variously into pale stones, loaves of bread, holders of dull, dusty light.

"You're the first woman who's ever asked to paint me."

"Your feet, dear."

"Nonetheless."

"Is it any different?"

Rain came down outside the open window in dirty silks. Elsa breathed the wet scent of it, thinking how odd it was that she felt comfortable in this room, sheltered and relaxed, with this girl she barely knew. "I was wonder-ing that. I do have my clothes on." She remembered standing for August in an ocher light, nipples pressed out like nails, the down on her arm tinseled. "Yes, it is. With a man there is a little bit of exaltation—as if one is an icon. With you I could be paring my nails, soaping my armpits, it wouldn't matter."

"I'm looking at that vein now." She pointed the brush at Elsa's left foot. "So what is it that you really do?"

"I write poems."

"In German?"

"In English since last year."

"That's good. It's not as if people are reading much German poetry these days." She scratched her cheek. "It's a shame, though. It's not as if it was the poets who started torpedoing ships, is it?" She dabbed some blue paint into her palm and studied the color. "Poetry is important—it helps me see the underside of things. I like the free-versers."

Afterward Elsa and Sara sat in a café with gingham curtains and a tiny fireplace.

Elsa was aware of her arms flailing, how her voice flitted up in volume. She still didn't quite trust most Americans, and it confused her how easily some of them would call you their friend, but she liked this girl with her tentative smile and her austere, frayed dress worn with those large beads around her neck like bubbles.

She told Elsa how she'd come to Manhattan from a place in Ohio, where her mother was a schoolteacher, her father a lawyer, and the girls in her class called her "Sorry" because she kept to herself and her parents had money. No one knew she was painting—her brother was the artist in the family—but she'd told her parents that she was teaching at a progressive school, and she survived on the amount of money they sent for her clothing allowance. "My dresses are so shabby. But at least I'm free." Sara leaned earnestly over the table, her bright eyes flashing. "Tell me, what have you admired in the galleries?"

Elsa said that the only place where she ever saw anything interesting was 291, where the owner, Mr. Stieglitz, talked to visitors about the art, not the selling. One day not long after Josef had left, Elsa went to see a group of new paintings, and she had discussed with him for an hour the difference between painting fragments and painting motion. The fragments didn't move, unless aligned by a feeling of rapidity. That kind of motion was elusive, hard to paint.

"I once saw these opaque little riddles there," Sara said. "Someone named Picabia."

Sara had a touching way of clearing her throat and leaning back in her chair as if preparing to say something. Elsa was aware that women often shied away from her, afraid of her brashness, and she snubbed them, too, out of a fear that their dullness or frivolity might confirm some doubt she carried around in herself. It had been years since she'd talked intimately with another woman, and she'd forgotten how much she loved the endless twine of it, the patient braid that made her see the design of herself more clearly.

For some reason she didn't want to say Josef's name. "The one thing I don't have to worry about is that he'd ever fight," she said. "The baron doesn't care a crap about honor. He certainly wouldn't get himself killed for it." She liked the slap of her lips around American slang.

"That's lucky," Sara said. "My brother, Jim, patriot that he is, just enlisted."

"I'm sorry."

Sara avoided her eyes. "He'd never been to Europe before. He's been writing to me about the paintings he's seen on his leave. He said there are masterpieces that literally glow, though they're peeling with age. That's why American painting is so crass—most of us haven't seen anything really old, mystically old."

Sara was so young her complexion, unpowdered, still had that unreal purity, like clear water.

"If you could see it, then you would see why it's dead. It would release you from feeling as if you had to honor it," said Elsa.

Sara shook her head. "I don't think it's that easy."

"Your paintings aren't crass." Elsa sipped her tea, milky and not sweet enough.

Sara shrugged. "I don't think they matter much, considering everything else."

Except for the fact that she was plainspoken, like a farmer, and didn't seem to be man-crazy up to her ear tips, Sara reminded Elsa of the way she had been in her youth. She needed a tougher shell.

Sara said, "Jim has these ideas about honor; we had huge arguments before he left. Don't you find it strange that my brother might be shooting at someone you know, that your friend or relative might be shooting at him? But look, I don't feel any animosity toward you—why should I? Where is this defense of humanity he was always talking about?"

"I wouldn't lift my leg to pee for humanity right now," Elsa said, scooping more sugar into her teacup.

Sara narrowed her eyes, then abruptly laughed. "Well, these days I read the newspaper with one hand over my eyes."

❧

Later Elsa opened the little box that she pulled out of the bottom of her trunk and looked down at the things Josef had left behind: a pair of black serge pants with the hem gone out of one leg, a cuff link with the letters *FL* embossed in the gold, a worn deck of cards in a silver case, a book of inspirational sayings from a yogi. He said if his mind were thinking positively just before a game, then he would win, and if he lost, it was largely because he had allowed the negative energy to somehow secrete itself inside of him. She picked up the book, turned the page. "The mind should be open like . . ." A thin piece of paper, folded in two, fell at her feet. She reached down to pick it up and read the note: *Cassandra at Pops*. A good-luck spell? The name of a play?

She smoothed out his monogrammed handkerchief, examining the yellowish stain in the corner, shaped oddly, like a beetle. She took out the starched collar, punched its stiffness back and forth, clacked the cuff links together, and smoked one of his cigars, which tasted like mud.

25

The seventh of the month came and went, and Elsa couldn't pay the landlord. He banged on her door on the eighth, but she didn't answer. On the ninth he was waiting, skinny and bird-eyed, posted outside her building when she came back after walking Pinky in the park.

"I don't care if you're Shakespeare," he said, shaking his finger at her. "If you don't give me forty dollars by Friday, I'll empty out your apartment and give it to someone who pays their bills."

Pinky, with his high-pitched bark, loudly protested. At her desperation, his tiny bones shivered and the slick strands of his fur pricked up.

A cart rickety with barrels trundled past, the rounded metal beating against the wooden slats. She had to shout over the noise. "Mr. Bruno, of course I will pay you!"

He shook his head, threw up his arms, and turned away, running into an Indian man carrying an armful of purple silks.

She had waited for as long as she could. Though immediately after Josef left, Barney Fitch had come for her with invitations to dinner and plays, all this time she had not relented, and she avoided calling him. She had stopped trying to find the charm in him long ago, and somehow asking him for help would seem to confirm Josef's absence as long term. The thought of seeing Barney's face when she appeared at his door appalled her, but nonetheless, she couldn't make herself work a machine in some airless loft. She couldn't write with the landlord banging on the door every day, and she didn't want to be thrown out again on the street, and she had Pinky to think of now, too.

Barney Fitch lived in the West Thirties, in a building with haughty green statues of lions perched on either side of the entranceway steps.

The apartment was very small—one room, a sink, and a stove cluttered with dirty forks. On the windows hung bright polka-dot curtains that brought on a headache if one stared at them too long, and the bed was covered in papers—magazines and torn scraps with scrawled numbers.

He quickly tidied up, hid the shaving brush and cream behind a cabinet, tugged down the undershirt drying over the bathroom door and stuffed it in a drawer. He sat on the bed and offered her a chair. "What would you like to drink? How about a gin?" He opened a small cabinet over the stove and pulled out a bottle and poured her a glass. When he handed it to her, he caressed her hand.

Outside the window there was the relentless slam of a sledgehammer, and Barney spoke loudly over the noise. "They're doing so much construction on this block I can hardly think. My God, you'd think they'd stop, take a break now and then. But if they're not building something, they're tearing someplace down." She thought of a line in a poem she'd read recently in *Others*, one of the magazines they sold at the bookstore on Washington Square. It was by someone named Mina Loy: *Constellations in an ocean / Whose rivers run no fresher / Than a trickle of saliva / These are suspect places.*

They sat until the hammering finally stopped. The silence felt cool and clean.

"There's usually a break at this point. I've learned to time it." He looked at her hungrily.

"Barney, I need money."

He grinned and nodded gratefully, as if she had been the one to offer him something. "Of course. Of course." He reached into his pants pocket.

His eagerness annoyed her. She imagined his fantasy of this transaction: she, bowed before him, a slave girl, he the benevolent king. And it irked her that she'd taken part in the drama. "The bastards threw me out of the Ritz. I had to get a room on Fourteenth Street."

"Aw, is that right?" He drew out his wallet, thumbed through the bills and chose several, rolled them up in a tube, took Elsa's hand and wrapped her fingers around it. "Think of it as a gift." His mouth, when he closed it, always looked full, as if there were something he still had to swallow. As he patted her hand holding the money, she studied the way his eyebrows curved away from his watery eyes. Was it the usual arrogance she saw in his face, or pity?

"You know where he is, don't you?" she said.

"Haven't you heard anything?" Barney got off the bed and walked over to the window, opened the curtains so a slant of light fell across the room.

"Don't protect me. I hate that. If it has to do with why he lost all his money, I want to know."

"You always want to know." He looked down at her paternally, his bright red beard obscuring his smug smile.

"Tell me." There was something he held back from her, something he would not give her. His friendship with Josef had always been a gate that locked her out.

"You won't understand it, honey, and it doesn't matter anyway. But in the simplest terms, we had a certain arrangement that Josef was planning to work out in Belgium. All was going as planned, and then I stopped hearing about it."

"What kind of arrangement? Not a bet?"

"Look, it's complicated—he was bringing some things into the country."

"What?"

Barney tilted his beard to her as if she'd said something amusing, but he didn't answer. "You wrote to the in-laws, didn't you?" There was a drilling and crashing sound out on the street, and the walls and floors shook. "Didn't they tell you where he was? They should have." She wondered again why Josef had ever liked him.

He sat next to her, put his arm around her. "Look how he left you alone. A lady like you, alone in Manhattan."

She wanted to pull away but couldn't afford to have him take back the money, so she satisfied herself with a little speech. "You know, Nietzsche has a lot to say about solitude, how it purifies the mind and feeds the artist his visions—there's no reason to think of it as a degrading state at all. Who is better company for me than myself?"

He rubbed her shoulder more forcefully. "Josef had a roving eye. You know that, don't you?"

She adjusted her stockings through her skirt. "All men with any sex sense have a roving eye."

"Did you really think he could be married? Men don't take to it easily, Elsa. Most women ignore it, but you're not the type to ignore anything."

Barney did not understand how a person's *sexurge* was like a plant—it had to be watered, it had to flower, or it died. Josef had been true to her, even if his eye wandered. God, even if he had a woman or two. She had been true to him, too, despite the episode with the Russian painter and a few other temptations. There wasn't any reason to quantify love, to put a price on passion.

There was a sound like banging thunder, something metal crashing against stone. He took her hand and rubbed it between his palms. "Remember that trip he took to Philadelphia? He stayed there a long time, too." He winked.

"What are you saying?" The polka dots vibrated against the red of the curtains with each blow of the hammer outside.

"Oh, nothing. Let's think about lunch. Where would you like to go? Let's have lunch and then go see *Anabelle's Party* at the Driscoll."

She'd seen the way Josef touched her face each time before he gambled, how he turned to her in his sleep, how he said her name as if it were part of a song. "Who was there in Philadelphia?" She remembered he had gone to see about a scheme of his to sell shatterproof windows for trolley cars. "Who, Barney?"

"I don't know her name. She was a dancer."

She resisted being hurt by this, put her jealousy off to the side. She had told Josef all along that she did not want to know about the other women who might tempt him. Maybe her antics had worn him out or he'd become impatient with her moods. But as Barney leaned over and brushed his beard and lips across her cheek, she didn't trust him. She yanked her hand away from his moist palm.

His face was shiny. "All right, look. I'm not saying it is someone else, but there always is, right? That's how love ends up. If he really wanted to get back here, don't you think he would?" He sat beside her and kissed her on the cheek. He smelled of pepper. "In the meantime let's get lunch." He kissed her ear, grabbed the buttons at her neck.

He must have thought he'd bought her gratitude, that she'd finally revealed her true weakness to him, and now he could take what she owed him. He would enjoy thinking about it later, how the woman who always fought him had finally resigned herself, laying herself down for him, how he'd finally had her. She grabbed his hand, pulled it away from the buttons, and stood up.

His stomach pouched over his trousers, his eyes flat and satisfied.

She smiled, coyly turned her head. Hating both Josef and Barney at that moment, she slowly unbuttoned the front of her dress, softened her voice. "First, mister." Her red silk chemise shrieked between the opened gray fabric. She lifted her skirt, revealed her heels and black stockings, one garter coming loose. "You have to do some work."

He grinned, his hand pawing her leg.

She stepped back. "On your knees."

She heard him hit the floor. She lifted her skirt, pushed down her drawers. He put his hands on each of her thighs, brought his mouth closer, and she felt his breath before his lips and tongue. She covered his head with her skirt, felt his beard scratch against her.

She looked at the track roster laid out on the bed: Seventh Seal and Fool's Luck. That was the horse Barney had caused Josef to lose so much money on. She noticed how part of the dust on the lampshade dimmed the light on one side, and that the bottom window was coated with dirt. Barney's head moved under the serge fabric. She noted a newspaper picture of a society girl, innocent in her bonnet, pinned to the wall—*Eliza Banganet*—the packet of cigarettes on the bureau, next to the presumptuous little notebook and arrogant beer stein.

She looked away again, at the bureau knobs, square and polished, then caught the gleam of something gold—a pocketwatch partly hidden under the cigarette packet, the long chain slinking past the notebook.

She moved her hand stealthily to the right, swiped up the watch. The cool roundness smooth against her palm like a woman's compact. Goddamn him, she deserved it. She gently pushed Barney's head away. "That's enough, thank you."

He looked up at her, sheepishly grinning.

"Go wash yourself and come back," she said, arranging herself on the bed. She winked.

"Oh, I've got something for you all right," he said.

She heard the water begin to run as she pushed the watch and money into her bodice. She buttoned her dress and grabbed her bag. She tiptoed past the bureau to the door, opened it, and quietly went out. At the stairs she ran.

She pushed headlong into the street, past a band playing that American song about spangled stars, past a moving-picture house with a line out front of people hugging their arms from the cold, past a grocery where chickens dangled in the window like mangled fists. The asinine thing was, money gave a woman permission to live alone in this world, and she didn't have any. If she'd had a head for finances, or if she'd followed Natalye to Madame Renault's, she'd be a wealthy courtesan by now, but instead her head was all heart. Men said money was a gift, but it was really a price—and Barney had wanted her to know it.

She walked in the direction of home, the money from him rolled up and slipped inside her bodice, the watch hung on the strap of her chemise. Hope slithered beside her all the way, like a snake that did not raise its beautiful head.

Passing the doorway of a store with a sign that said MEN ONLY, she fumed. She lit a cigarette and smoked it as she walked. The sky clouded up, and people's faces on the street began to appear dull and unwashed. She walked slowly, in a daze, until she fixed on the sign. NO WOMEN. The paint so neat on the plaque.

Though she'd passed by Joe's on the corner a hundred times, she'd never seen the sign. She pulled it off the hook, threw it on the ground, and pushed open the door.

It was a moment before her eyes could adjust to the dimness. She coughed at the cloistered smell of the gas lamps burning against the walls. The cramped tables were cluttered with ashes, broken glass, and empty bottles, where the men sat, laughing, leaning forward or reared back, arguing in loud ragged voices. As she moved toward the long, pockmarked bar that stretched before several empty wooden stools, heads turned to watch her. The racket fell to a hush. She felt them eyeing her femaleness, sizing it up.

The bartender had a twisted ear and grunted, "I shouldn't serve you."

"Give me a whiskey anyway," she said.

He threw up his hands. "All right, honey."

She wanted to get drunk, to kill the hope snake, coiled now around the legs of her stool. Behind her she felt them watching her narrow back. She felt the sharpness of her bones, the thin warmth of her skin.

The bartender put a full glass down before her, and she put some coins on the bar. Suddenly there was a man on the stool beside her, his blue pants covered in some kind of orange dust. "Hello there," he said, putting down his beer. "What are you doing with a bunch of dogs like us?"

She looked at his grin, one tooth chipped, a pink worm scar crawling across his cheek. "Drinking," she said, gulping down the whiskey. "Do you have a cigarette?"

He gave her one and lit it for her, then said in a lowered voice, "I like your totties."

She looked at the bartender, wiping glasses with a rag. *"Nein, danke,"* she said. "We're not going anywhere."

"Like another drink, then?" said the man with the dirty pants.

Suddenly there was another man on the other side of her. He had a wild beard and dirty-looking hair. "Aw, I wouldn't trust him, miss." He sounded Irish. "He'll get you drunk and have your skirts off in a minute." Behind her a clattering sound, loud male laughter, the clinking of glasses.

"I can get myself drunk," she said.

"Shut up, you fucking Init," said the man with the scar.

Elsa finished her whiskey and signaled to the bartender for another one. She wanted to stay and drink several more. She turned away from them, swiveling around on her stool. Here and there they looked up from their tables: a man licked his lips, a man narrowed his eyes, a man rubbed the end of his nose. They were a jury, judging what had brought her there alone, whether she was a prostitute or a slattern.

She finished the whiskey, smoky in her throat, and asked the bartender for another one. He shook his head, and she tapped her glass on the bar several times.

"Come on, give her another," said a man, shooing away the wild bearded one. "Are you one of those social workers?" he asked her. "Because there are some men here, they need reforming." He had huge, almond-shaped eyes and a handsome, triangular face.

"All men need reforming, mister."

When he laughed, she noticed his very pink tongue, like a child's.

"I thought you might be on duty, though you don't look like one of them—you're much prettier."

The other men, edging away, looked over at them with furtive glances.

"I am a baroness." She drank down more of her whiskey and felt the edges of herself beginning to fray. "I don't work at anything, though I sometimes pose for portraits."

"Oh, a baroness, huh? Fancy!"

His arm rested in the small of her back. She was beginning to feel more precise and fluid, as if she could make sense of how she might want this man. He was wearing a work shirt and pants, and his skin would smell of dried sweat and cigarette smoke. She was trying not to want Josef so much, and she missed being touched. If he was kind and worshipful of her charms, she could make herself fall in love with him for an hour or so. Travel, travel. That was what she should do. China, India, Singapore. She should travel with the sailors.

"I used to be on the stage," she went on. "In Berlin. The Wintergarten Cabaret. Have you heard of it?"

"Were you a singer or a dancer?"

"I was a living statue, a living picture."

"I'll bet you were, a living picture, just like that." A hundred drawers appeared in her head, each one opening to fascinating contents: a paisley silk slip she'd worn, a love letter she'd written to Franz, August's idea about muscle in painting, lines from Fontane—*The Queen held the King's hand. / The candles went out*—a jade necklace a man she'd forgotten had given her, lost in a park's grass. When she put her hand to her cheek, it felt smooth, and this simple fact meant she would be okay. She felt an intensity that she wished she could preserve.

"And then I was an actress. I went everywhere—Paris, London, Switzerland. I cast spells on the men. Juliet or Cassandra or Penelope—tall, short, plump, it didn't matter."

He looked confused. "And are you in a play now?"

"Now," she said, her eyes stinging from all the smoke, "I don't need the stage anymore to cast spells. I write poems." The words made her giddy, as if she'd suddenly discovered she could fly around the room. She would hover overhead, looking down at the gleam of bottles and balding heads. She would sweep the hem of her skirt over the edges of the gas lamps.

He chuckled nervously and finished his drink. "Roses are red, violets are blue?"

His hands looked suddenly freakishly small and raw. She began to change her mind about him. "Of course not."

A man thumped to the floor, his eyes closed, worn boots tipped to the ceiling. Two men stood over him, shaking their heads. Then one bent down and started slapping his face.

Her sailor ignored the commotion. "Well, now, I just enlisted. It won't be long before I'm sent overseas. I only have two nights as a free man. Where are you from, anyway? Belgium?" Hadn't he been listening? It amused her that he could not tell the difference. "I'm German, but not a Nationalist."

He pulled back and made a mocking, pop-eyed face.

"I love the French, I live in America," she went on. "A man like you should know when a lady isn't his enemy."

"Oh, I can see that."

She put her hand on his thigh, looked at his crotch, and said, "I can see what you see. There isn't any reason you should resist."

He slammed his mouth against hers and violently pinched her waist. "Who's resisting? Let's go."

His hand was still in a grip on her waist when she jumped coquettishly off her stool, which pulled him forward and caused him to spill his drink in a dribble down his pant leg. "Hun bitch," he slurred, still smiling.

The hotness she had felt for him was doused—she suddenly realized that a toilet would have served him just as well as a woman. "I don't tolerate insults," she said. "I think I'll stay here."

"Leave her alone," said a sailor at the end of the bar. "Honey, do yourself a favor and get out of here."

"Come on, sweetheart." A man with a pipe was at her side, taking her elbow as if she were an invalid, his hand creeping up toward her breast. She jerked herself away from him. "Bastard—get off me," she said.

A fat man grabbed her arms and pulled her to him as if to dance. "You're a drunk little hussy, aren't you?" he said, his breath sour with onions, and someone laughed. His hand was near the neckline of her bodice, and she was afraid he'd reach in and take the watch or the money she'd had to beg. She pulled away from him and headed to the door, but a group of men stood around her, blocked her path, their eyes predatory. She kicked the man who had pulled her into a dance and said, "I don't dance with assholes."

His face purpled, and he lunged for her. She spit at his eyes. As he lurched back, she kicked him in the stomach. He fell away from her, and she stood up, pushed between two men in work shirts, and ran.

A muscular man grabbed her arms from behind. She felt her shoulders crack out of their sockets as the room spun, the man's hands squeezing her. Men were yelling, glasses crashed to the floor. She was fighting down nausea when she saw the soldier who had been flirting with her cheering on a man who had unzipped his pants. "Get her! Go on!" Someone tore off the shoulder of her dress.

The sweaty faces pressed toward her, gaping mouths with gold teeth, sour tongues, eyes like nails. Fifty hands grasping at her, something metal scraping her cheek, someone pulling her hair, beer dropped over her, stinging her eyes.

The bartender, with a rag slung over his shoulder, glumly came around the bar and gripped her arm. He pulled her between the groping men, muttering, "I should have never served you," and pushed her out the door. "Now, get out of here before you bring in the cops."

The sidewalk was stunningly quiet, though she could hear a pounding on the door behind her and the roar of the men's voices inside. One man burst out after her, his beard tangled with bits of food. "Where are you going?" He staggered toward her, his arm extended.

"If you follow me," she said, "I'll tear your balls off."

His arm went limp, and he waved at the air as if wiping off dirt. "Oh, go away, you slutty Hun."

She wove along for two blocks, feeling the sidewalk slip beneath her, brick walls turning half spins on either side. She stumbled up the stairs of her building, her toes catching on their corners, opened the door, and threw up a pinkish soup on the floor. She lay there, head pounding where it rested against her arm.

26

In the morning in her lopsided bed she listened to the pipes whine, a parade of hurried footsteps on the stairs, the first heavy, the second light, the third syncopated. She heard the Russians upstairs arguing, though it was still so early the weak light had just begun to waver through the curtains. Because her head felt as if it had been pounded against a rock, she closed her eyes and tried to sleep again but could not. The memory of the men's hands on her contaminated the warm silk sheet, and she wanted to bathe but would have to wait for the tub to be free.

She felt a heaviness in her hips and back muscles, touched the angry bruises on her arms. If only she'd had a gun or a knife in her bag last night. Now it seemed her head was turning into metal, and there was a sore sourness on her tongue. Barney would be after her for an explanation and his watch, and she'd have to hide from him. She squinted at the light. She had nothing to eat, nothing to do today. There didn't seem to be any good reason to move. She was sure Barney had not told her the truth, though she also knew there were things Josef had hidden from her, places and people he'd never mentioned. She was furious again at his leaving, furious at herself for letting him go. She rubbed her feet together under the sheet, hugged the pillow over her ears to block out the Russians upstairs. Pinky came to the edge of her bed, his eyes huge as he waited for her to take him out. His need was comforting, and, seeing the insistent wag of his tail, she roused herself.

On her way back from walking Pinky, she saw the Frenchman, just as he was leaving, handsome in his black suit, whistling as he came out of the building. "Hello," he said, tipping his gray hat, then stopped a moment. "*Mon Dieu*—your earrings, madame, are miraculous!" She'd made them by attaching teaspoons to wires that strung through her earlobes. He grinned at her and crossed the sidewalk to get into the automobile that was waiting there for him. She didn't understand why a man so elegant would want to live in this building, where it was difficult to get hot water, and wondered how he stayed so clean-looking, his black suit spotless and pressed. When he got into the car, she noticed his pale face behind the window, as he turned to watch the Salvation Army band coming up ragtag and bleating on the sidewalk. He pressed his hand against the glass, the reflection of a lamppost over his profile. And then he sped away.

Absently she reached into the mailbox and felt the envelope. The Ritz had sent it on. It was postmarked from Berlin, and beneath the large red *X* and the new Fourteenth Street address, the handwriting wasn't Josef's.

She tore open the envelope, the paper trembling in her hands.

> *As you must know, we have not always known the whereabouts of our son Josef. Since you have gone to the trouble to contact us, we feel it our duty to inform you that as we did not recognize the marriage as legitimate in the first place, we do not intend to provide you with any financial remuneration. I have spoken to my legal counsel and understand that no legal action will be necessary.*

The signature at the bottom was spiked at the capital letters—Gustave von Freytag-Loringhoven. The writing looked like pieces of squashed flies.

Why couldn't his father say simply that Josef was fine? It seemed so unkind that he had not. And she hadn't even asked for their money—that was the insult. They thought she was only a gold digger. The precise and official-looking seal on the envelope seemed to define Josef's absence like some cruel court order. Did no one know where he was?

Gustave von Freytag-Loringhoven, general of the Prussian army's Third Division, friend of the Kaiser. Her father, loving the Kaiser as he did, would have been ashamed of the way he'd treated her and proud to know she'd become a von Freytag-Loringhoven, however covertly. And she was tempted

to write to him and tell him but didn't want to give him the satisfaction of
having something to brag about to his friends.

Elsa was afraid her poetry would shrivel away without the carnal pleasures
that Josef had been so careful to satisfy. Already there were so many days
she could not concentrate long enough to write a single phrase—she sus-
pected her writerly fertility depended on finding some spark in her genitalia.
Other women bore children; she bore poems. She would have to find a place
to bury her love for Josef, so it might grow something new. She would have
to sharpen her eye.

In a newspaper Elsa saw crumpled on the ground in front of her building,
there was this notice:

WHAT CAN I DO? HOW THE CIVILIAN MAY HELP IN THIS CRISIS
BE CHEERFUL
WRITE TO SOLDIERS OVERSEAS
DON'T LISTEN TO IDLE RUMORS

The war would never end. Its tank machines and bombs dropped from
airplanes were part of the future, like the telephone and automobile. She
barely noticed the flags hanging everywhere now. In front of the bank, two
women stood at a table with a red, white, and blue banner that said FIGHT
THE GERMAN MENACE. The government had shrewdly convinced pretty
women to recruit soldiers—they were all over the city at tables like this one,
or marching in the streets in their neat shirtwaists carrying posters to hang
in the shop windows.

When she saw a tall, long-limbed young man, with his rosebud mouth
and neatly trimmed hair, leaning over to sign at the table, she thought of
Sara's brother, Jim, and the photograph Sara had shown her. He was stand-
ing with one foot resting on a rock, in puttees and boots, hills in the back-
ground. He looked like Sara in the mouth and pointed chin. His hands were
large and awkwardly placed on the tops of his thighs, his face turned
slightly away, as if distracted by the birds.

She met Sara at the Samovar for drinks. The brick walls were covered with crinkled paper flowers and streamers. "There's a party tomorrow," Sara said.

"Where?"

"Cornelia Street."

Sara took Elsa with her to every party, where they mingled among the capes and hats, the drunken stumblers and gropers, and to gallery openings, where they stood in front of bad and good paintings, listening to jealous gossip. They went to a reading by the red-haired Edna St. Vincent Millay, who'd just published *Renascence and Other Poems,* one hundred people with their ears tilted toward this woman as she loudly declaimed verse with her eyes closed. Elsa found the poems too pretty but admired the glitter of the performance. Everywhere they went, Sara managed to somehow mention that Elsa was a baroness from Europe, and Elsa was surprised to find herself feeling maternal toward Sara, who, despite her verve, seemed to have lost her way. Sara would redden and raise her voice in outrage at the posers, those men and women who dressed in Village peasant garb, smoked and drank in the cafés, and never wrote or painted a thing. She shrank in front of artists she admired, too shy to speak or move. But she was a good painter herself, a serious painter who had a superior eye. Elsa tried to convince her that nothing but the work mattered, even if she had to spit on her detractors, sneer at the ones who intimidated her. It was the only way for an artist to make her way in this world—only other women had the luxury of acting demure.

"I'm sure that there will be lots of posers, but Susan's all right," Sara said. "And we could get our dinner there. You look as if you could use a ham sandwich."

"Does my face look wan?" Elsa touched her cheeks. "Alas, the cure might require more than a sandwich." The waitress brought a steaming bowl of soup to a woman in an effusively feathered hat, who sat in the corner smiling and watching the customers, clearly a tourist from uptown.

"I have a little money—let's share something," said Sara.

They ordered cheese on bread and wine. Sara was telling her about the painting she'd just finished, a portrait of Richard Borne, a hunched man who wrote about politics and was a notorious flirt. It was difficult, she said, to incorporate the way his hands moved as he talked. "He's one of those men who probably couldn't speak if you tied up his hands." He'd stopped posing for her because he had a deadline, and now she was stuck.

There were people sitting at the other tables, drinking, talking boister-
ously. At the table under the picture of the Japanese geisha, Elsa noticed the
black curls on the head of a man sitting alone. "Maybe it's better to complete
a painting without the model. This way you won't be distracted by him,"
Elsa said. Glancing over again, she noticed the tiny shoulders in a blue suit
that looked to be cut for a boy and felt the little jolts of recognition. At first
she thought it was another false sighting.

"But I just can't seem to do it," said Sara. "And I hate myself. When are
you going back to the League? Maybe I should return for another class."

Then Elsa saw his face. It was Wayne Caldwell, miraculously returned.
She stood up and went over to him. Dull-eyed, he looked up from his news-
paper but didn't seem to recognize her.

"I thought you were dead!" she said.

His features seemed to register her then, and he ran a hand through his
curls. "Well, that's a lovely greeting."

"What happened to you? The sanatorium said you were 'no such
patient.'"

She thought she saw him wince. "Baroness, it's good to see you. I did try
to reach you at the Ritz when I got back, but they said you'd left. I apolo-
gize." He folded his newspaper. "After the operation there was some
unpleasantness that I'd rather not go into. But time got away from me, and
when I finally got around to— I still think about your poems. 'Cosmic
Chemistry' has haunted me all this time. Do you want to sit down?"

She was trying to assess whether or not he'd been purposefully avoiding
her. Maybe she'd offended him in one of her letters without meaning to.
"Come sit with my friend and me."

When he stood up, he looked even tinier than he'd been before, wearing
a dandyish yellow tie with a silver, star-shaped pin, his black curls neatened
with hair oil.

Elsa introduced Sara to Wayne, saying, "This is the editor of *LETTERS*."

Caldwell shook his head as he sat down with them and poured himself a
glass of wine. "Not anymore. There's no money." He tapped his fingertips
on the table, but his nervousness only slightly distracted from the wanness
in his face.

"What about your patrons? That woman—Schwendeman?"

"They're all buying Liberty Bonds, I guess." Even now that she had none, Elsa found the brutal power of money difficult to accept. "But I haven't forgotten your poems. God, no. We'll find another place for them." He turned to Sara. "Have you read them?"

"Not yet." Sara pursed her lips thoughtfully. Elsa suspected that if Sara didn't like the poems, she wouldn't say so, but she'd gradually end the friendship, quietly, without explanation.

"You should. Five years ago I wouldn't have known what to make of them. But now they seem part of the future. Do you know what I mean?"

His praise sounded tepid, but it made Elsa want to tread the waters of the conversation. He was the first serious person to ever read her poems, and she wanted to honor that. She talked about the poem she was writing now, which she hoped would be a funnel of sound, and then about the Wallace Stevens she had read, this American poet whose rhymes flew off the page like doves, how when she'd met him in his brown suit at an opening, he would not look her in the eye.

Sara laughed. "He never looks any woman in the eye. He's from Connecticut. What do you expect?"

Caldwell raised his eyebrows. He sat up straighter and drummed on the table. She felt his foot tapping against the floor near her own. "Any word from Franz Trove?"

"I never received an apology," said Elsa.

"An editor doesn't like to be played the fool like that. Of course, if I ever see him again, he'll deny it. I've noticed this in some married men I've known. After a number of years, they can't tell the difference between themselves and their wives—it's a kind of blind spot."

"He knew the difference, believe me," Elsa said. "I just happened to marry a thief."

"You say that about all of them," said Sara.

"Does she?" said Caldwell.

Elsa felt herself begin to relax. She liked this line, *All of my husbands were thieves,* which arranged the events of her life in a way that seemed adventurous, not unlucky. "I suppose I like them. Men who take what they want, who are graceful on their feet." Seeing Wayne Caldwell, she felt lucky again. She had so many things to write, so many ideas, and the absence of love seemed less pertinent now. Already, she was silently going over the new poem: *afleet / across chimneys—/and a tinfoil river / to meet another's dark heart! / Bless mine feet!*

"Thieves. Hmm," said Caldwell. "They can be noble if they're stealing for an adequate reason. I once knew someone who refused to pay for booze. He said it was like mother's milk and should be free."

They sat talking for hours that night, and though Elsa didn't believe that Caldwell would find a way to get her poems published any more than he would revive *LETTERS*, she was glad to have another friend in the Village. Sara said she liked the way Caldwell talked, as if Shakespeare were a clown no one could control—Caldwell recited some of *The Tempest*, weaving his arms in the air. Later, very drunk, he told a story about how when he first rode in an elevator, he lay down on the floor, closed his eyes, and pretended that it was a spiritual levitation. Sara, also drunk, described how her brother, Jim, had a way of teasing girls that made only the stupid ones like him, how he whistled Mozart through his teeth, and as she described how he'd taught her to clean a fish, she began to weep.

Elsa pinned the beaded pot holder to the dressing-table mirror. The beads looked down at her like twenty bird eyes, twenty round seeds. The silver braid curled off at the corner like a noodle, the lace stained with a bit of rouge. The gift hung up there, above Elsa's reflection, as she sat writing at the dressing table, among her cosmetics and powders, the single bottle of perfume. Elsa was thirty-four years old, nearing the age her mother had been when she died. Her mother's face had a vagrant beauty, as if she'd just escaped from hunters, as if she'd forgotten something. Whatever she'd lost kept her in a perpetual state of incompleteness. She let her sentences trail off into murmurs, left her dress half buttoned, started to touch someone's cheek and then stopped herself. In a different form, Elsa realized, she'd inherited this state of unfinish.

The voice came lately only in the middle of the night. She'd get out of bed, waiting for it, look through the cracked window, the drunken men in coveralls and whores in gaudy hats, the late-night truck deliveries and policemen twirling sticks, a lost wheel in the gutter, white paper fanning up from the trash. When she finally put down a word and followed it to the end of the line, it was like starting down a road and crashing into a tree. It frustrated her how she'd lose her way, write until she hit a brick wall or found herself wading through a puddle of the same word rippling in repetition. But she had to continue, even if lately she rarely finished before the voice, so similar to the silence it arose from, went completely quiet.

She walked uptown toward the Art Students League. The pains shot up from her ankles, as if her bones had sprouted thorns. The war was causing Americans to change the names of things. In a store window she saw the sign for "liberty sausages," twenty-five cents—the new word for sauerbraten. Dachshunds were "liberty hounds," stollen was "liberty cake." Everything German was outlawed. The German opera had played its last performance at the Lyceum, the German Orchestra its last show at the Biltmore. Foreign-language schools had been ordered to excise German from the curriculum. Elsa's mind rebelled. That was why, even when she tried to write in English, the German words invaded:

> *Anuyata, Delores, Carmen,*
> *Da mi li morose,*
> *Die Gosse—barmen.*
> *Nothing is in itself*

She turned onto Broadway near Forty-third Street when she heard someone calling her name. She looked back but didn't see anyone, so she kept walking. Next to a church, a building was being torn down, its circuitry of pipes exposed to the street. Then she heard it again—a man's voice. When she turned around, there was Josef's friend Skip Drake, waving his hat, running through the crowd, and his freckled wife, Betty, trailing behind him.

"Elsa!" He was grinning, out of breath. She wished she had not stopped. "I haven't seen you since—heck, I don't know when." He tipped his derby to her. "Where have you been?"

Betty arrived then, her face flushed, wearing her hat with its red, white, and blue ribbons, a miniature stuffed eagle perched precariously on the brim. "Hello, Elsa." She held her head back in an accusatory way.

"I live on Fourteenth Street now—the Ritz was too much for me after a while. I'm writing my poems," she added quickly, not wanting pity, but maybe money.

Skip's smile faded. "Joe didn't come back?"

"Josef had some deal with Barney—but he hasn't heard anything."

Skip's nose worked its way up and down several times like a rapid series of sniffles. Josef had told her he did this whenever he was getting ready to bluff. She thought of the time he came to the hotel wearing his new raccoon coat, calling her "sweetie" until she told him to stop.

"One of their schemes, you know. And Josef hadn't got to Berlin yet, according to his pinched-face father anyway. He might be lying."

She found her voice growing steelier. "I don't know where the hell he went, do you? Russia? China? What do you think?" She thought of Skip and Josef together at the Jockey Club, where the men played cards and checkers, chuckling to themselves as if everything in their lives had the neat triviality of a game. Her head was pounding. "What did he tell you?"

"I know about as much as you do, Elsa." Skip scratched at his forehead. "But you should keep the title anyway—you deserve it."

He pulled Elsa and Betty out of the cold and into the doorway of a laundry, steamy and warm. A group of chattering men passed by on the sidewalk.

"Goddamn it, what do you know?" His placid face made her even angrier.

"Hey, Elsa, calm down." He reached for his wallet, but now she didn't even care about the money. Money made women pawns, and she wanted to rise above it, at least for the moment.

"What do you know?"

He took out his wallet and counted some bills, took her hand and slapped them there. "This is what I know—he was a cad, all right? He wasn't cut out for married life."

Betty shook her finger at Elsa. "No wife deserves that kind of treatment. Have you contacted the authorities?"

Skip turned and gave his wife a stern look. "See, it may be for the best. I just hope he's all right. You okay, Elsa?"

Elsa watched his thin lips moving, not taking in what he said. The words chased around in her head. One saw how much satisfaction Skip took in his "gifts," how he'd say to someone later, "He left her—the poor thing has nothing."

She felt a cup of dizziness over her eyes, and the sidewalk seemed to slant beneath her. She moved out of the doorway into the crowd. "If there's anything we can do . . ." Skip said, taking Betty's arm, but Elsa was already walking with the horde. *Go to hell!* she shouted into the wind.

⤲⚭⤷

That evening last year, she had been watching the clock, waiting for Josef to come back, wearing that ridiculous harem girl's costume that he had bought for her at Wanamaker's, the billowy silk pants, the brocade jacket, nothing underneath. She had been sitting on the bed, waiting for him, thinking of how she would seduce him and how pleased he would be to find her there like that, awake and ready for him. After midnight she could not keep her eyes open, and the book kept falling against her chest, but then she would rouse herself, shaking herself awake. The streetlight shone in through the curtains, and she listened to the voices outside of people coming home late.

She was so tired that by the time he came in, she felt shaky and blurry. It was as if she had drunk wine but could feel only the fog of it, not the light.

As soon as he came in, his tie gone, his collar crooked, he went furtively into the washroom and closed the door. When he came out, he kissed her quickly and began to get undressed.

"Where were you?"

"At the club with Barney and Skip."

He had received a letter from his father the day before, which always set him off to drink more. He paused before he pulled his belt from the loops of his trousers. His laugh sounded tight and forced. He unfastened his trousers and lay down in the bed with his shirt still on, and in a few moments she heard the labored breaths that meant he was asleep.

She tried to wake him up, but she couldn't. She put her mouth to his ear. "I smell perfume!" But he only turned over and scooped his arm around her as if she were his pillow.

She walked, though she hardly felt her legs beneath her. On the corner a newspaper boy in torn pants held a stack of papers, calling out "Seventy-eight dead! Seventy-eight dead!" An automobile screeched to a stop, and an old woman shook her cane at the windscreen.

Elsa glanced into a window filled with fine china, cups with gold rims as if they'd been licked by gilded tongues. She walked past the dress shops, past Knox's Millinery. She dragged herself from shop window to shop window, trying to distract herself. The light stuttered against the glass of the one where a cloth-covered dress form wore a black collar and the absent arms wore sleeves with velvet handcuffs.

If only she could have marched into the shop and bought something new for herself—a hat, a jacket, beads, anything. She needed transformation, disguise. She missed the way it felt, how a new fashion could make one feel knowing, how a new dress could present a new future.

She'd been avoiding the question, banging it out of her head as soon as it arrived. All these months she'd scavenged for food, hiding from the landlord as he came down the hallway, yelling and pounding on doors. She couldn't understand how Josef could leave her without any means. She envisioned the silver mesh purse, the brass clasp, the delicate chain, the silk lining the empty pouch. Then she thought of how quickly Barney had come to her with invitations to dinner, how easily he gave her money, all the notes he had written, and that satisfied glint in his eye that she had not been able to place until now—she had seen it in the eyes of a man admiring the stuffed head of a moose he had killed. The suspicion knifed her. It could be that Josef had handed her over to him, if not purposefully, then with the casual confidence of knowing that Barney would step in if necessary, with the kind of unspoken understanding between men that left women out of their logic. A heavy wink. *Take care of my wife, will you? Who knows when I'll be back?*

Elsa walked faster. The alignment of buildings where Fifth Avenue met Broadway in a *V* caused the formation of a wind tunnel that on blustery days sent trash bins rolling, carts overturned, skirts and capes flapping. A few men usually lingered on that corner waiting for the breeze to catch under a woman's skirt.

When she crossed the street and approached the Flat Iron Building, the wind tunnel suddenly shivered and blew up her skirt around her thighs. There was a man perched on the pedestal of a streetlight staring at her. He rose up on his toes so he could see better, his mouth open, eyes wide. All morning, she thought, he had been waiting for this, for the infamous windy corner to lift a woman's skirt, for a glimpse at anonymous female legs.

Elsa stared silently at the man's leering face, his eyes at her knees as the wind whipped the fabric and she gathered it in her hand. What was she now?

She was the space between the sole of a shoe and the pavement, the air rattling in a loose windowpane, the sound no one listened to, like trouser legs rubbing together. Gray and loose and unnoticed.

27

There was a Chinese barber on Christopher Street who sold hashish and prophylactics. Elsa passed the swirling pole whenever she went to the butcher for Pinky's bones. Once, through the film of glass, she spotted the handsome Frenchman getting a shave, his head thrown back as if in a fit of rapture, while the barber worked the blade over his chin. Another day she met Caldwell, just coming out, smoothing his face with his hand. They met often these days, as Caldwell had taken an apartment not far from hers on Jane Street, and sometimes he would come over to her room with Sara, and the three of them would drink gin and talk until the candles melted into the floor and Pinky was sleeping in one of their laps.

He kissed her on the cheek and said, "What's that on your face?"

She was wearing a British postage stamp as a beauty mark. One day, watching the postman fill the boxes, she'd realized that the stamp was the perfect signal for movement—it sailed paper from one place to another with beautiful precision. And it was more original than a mole.

"Queen Elizabeth," she said.

He grinned at her, nodding. He reached into his orange bag and pulled out a paper packet. "This is for you. It's peyote—Mabel Dodge swears that it opens up the mind."

Elsa had heard about Dodge's parties, how patrons were charmed, fame dispersed like a fine spray.

"You have to smoke it. Do you have a pipe?"

"The baron had one, I think."

His eyes danced back to the postage stamp on her cheek, but this time with discernment. "I'll demonstrate. Why don't I come over? Do you have anything to show me?"

"I have one." It was a poem made almost entirely from phrases she'd ripped out of advertisements she'd seen while walking in Times Square, words she'd liked and others she simply couldn't get out of her head. She wanted to find melody in the jumble of them, the pattern in why she'd chosen one and not another, to know how this might reflect a certain state of mind. Because the mind was imprinted by the city, its buying and selling, its noise and insistence, and she wanted to explore this idea.

But if he walked home with her, she didn't want him to detect that she was having pains in her legs. She wanted to stimulate people in her company, not burden them. That was why she'd trained herself to act as if her time with Josef had been a lark. She'd devised several jokes, in fact, for moments when the subject of the baron came up. "Men come too fast and go too fast," she said. "The engine that drives them to me also drives them away." Sara would look puzzled when she put things this way, but Caldwell would nod. "I can't be a good wife because I can never bow before men; I can only fling myself."

She'd given up on Josef's return, and though she tried to doubt that he'd ever loved her, she still felt the loss of him as a kind of splintering in her chest.

When Caldwell offered her his arm, she took it, thinking they would have to walk slowly, arm in arm like this, and so she'd be able to manage.

While Caldwell showed her how to smoke the peyote, holding the smoke in her lungs as if she were underwater, Pinky, nervous whenever Elsa had a guest, paced back and forth in front of the door, claws clicking against the floor. The smoking relaxed her. It made her feel focused and clearheaded, though her lips felt huge and heavy as she read.

> *Hands off the better bologna's beauty—*
> *Nothing so pepsodent-soothing*
> *Dear Mary—the mint with*
> *The Hole—Oh life buoy!*
> *Adheres well—delights your taste—*

Continuous germicidal action—
Postum Lister World War—
A wealth of family Vicks!

She'd been trying to capture these little songs, advertisements shouting at her from brick walls—the letters cartwheeling, the dots of *i*'s bobbing up and down. Rhyme after rhyme. This was America's real art—selling—but done with such fanfare it made her smile. She called the poem "Subjoyride" and wanted to write more like this, lines with little jokes that sucked the music out of everyday words.

"That reminds me," Caldwell said, inhaling from the pipe. "Mabel Dodge introduced me to Jane Heap."

"Who is she?"

"Oh, one of the editors of *The Little Review*. I told her about your poems. You should send them something, Elsa. These days it's the only magazine of art that publishes art. The rest are imitators." She noticed his dark curls sculpted over his ear like a coif on Greek statuary.

"What about *Rogue* or *The Glebe*?"

He winced and shook his head. "*The Glebe* spews sewer material into free verse, *Rogue* claims to be more *American*, whatever that means."

"Give me the address," she said, handing him a pencil. "This smoke makes my mouth taste like bark."

"Isn't it lovely?" He scribbled on the paper.

She'd bought a copy of *The Little Review* at Washington Square Books—there was a story by Djuna Barnes with a plot that flew as impossibly as a magic carpet, and a poem by Mina Loy that she'd liked for its use of the phrase "ludicrous halo." The cover was blue paper with thick red lettering, and there were slick papers in the middle printed with reproductions of paintings by Picabia. She had wanted to submit poems somewhere, but had been waiting for an introduction like this. She knew that fortunes accrued in the Village because one happened to be standing near the window next to someone who remarked on the heat, or because one's good friend had offered a cigarette to some painter, or because one friend was angry at another for not showing up. Everything was an accident.

The happiest accident occurred later that week, when Sara announced that Marcel Duchamp had bought the painting of Elsa's feet—Duchamp, whose own painting Elsa had admired for years.

Duchamp had invited Sara to the Arensberg salon on Wednesday night, and she wanted Elsa to go with her, but only if she kept her insults quiet. Elsa had been trying to teach Sara how she might use a witty but pointed remark to protect herself from the posers and braggarts, but Sara had not yet learned the art. It was a way of testing people, Elsa told her, to see whether their interests were genuine, and also a way of protecting one's pride. Elsa thought it might keep Sara from wilting the way she tended to in public, but when Elsa demonstrated for her, Sara shrank back into her seat or covered her face.

"An invitation to the Arensbergs' is an invitation to the center of New York—I want to be invited back," Sara said. It was a coup to have been invited, and the prospect of going to that art-packed apartment on Sixty-seventh Street was even better than the time she and Franz had been invited to a party in honor of Bernard Shaw, because this time Franz wouldn't be there to complain about her.

Elsa blew smoke out through her nostrils, two delicate curled strands. "Sara, dear. A woman has got to defend herself."

She had so much to teach Sara, but Sara was still resisting. She still believed in *politeness*, that sham set of rules that prevented honesty or any real forward motion. It was the old way—corseted matrons in drawing rooms pouring tea, men bowing and spewing meaningless niceties. The new way was genuine contact, *direct*.

She imagined herself talking to the poet Wallace Stevens, ice clinking elegantly in their glasses as they discussed the invalid's passion in Keats, or to Mina Loy, who would agree with her that there was a place for ugliness in verse, then moving to the wall, where there would be a table of cheeses and caviar, and she'd attract the notice of Francis Picabia and then Marcel Duchamp, who, if he admired her feet, would be even more pleased with the rest of her.

She wanted to wear something witty, something extravagant to this Arensberg salon. But she was exhausted with mere prettiness, weighed down by knowing that it would only become more and more difficult to achieve, and she hated feeling the effort in herself. Besides, prettiness at these salons was trite, and she wanted to put her femaleness to more potent ends. She wanted to inspire questions, to entertain, challenge. She spent a few days creating the ensemble. Out of the black silk evening dress she had ripped that night last year in the elevator with Josef, she had sewn a skirt, but she needed something electrical. She found the taillight on the curb, and it took her only a few hours to figure out the mechanics of it—she had learned something about wiring from Josef's doomed inventions. At the top of the high bustle, she attached the taillight, which flashed when she squeezed the lever in her pocket—like a visual insight.

On the night of the party, she wore the skirt with a petticoat underneath made from pieces of old lampshades. She tied the wide red ribbons over her breasts, midriff, and shoulders, winding them into a tight mummy bodice. Around her neck she wore a silver tea capsule filled with pieces of Pinky's shed fur, which peeked elegantly through the silver holes. By the time Sara arrived to pick her up, she had stuck a postage-stamp beauty mark on her cheek for extra spunk.

"Where do you expect to be mailed to?" said Sara.

"Heaven."

When they arrived at the Arensbergs' lushly antique apartment, with its Oriental rugs and high ceilings, Sara was greeted by Walter Arensberg, who wore a pince-nez and a mocking thin smile. "Quite an ensemble," he said, glancing at Elsa.

"She's the model for the painting Marcel just purchased," Sara said. "He'll want to meet her."

"Everyone wants to meet Marcel, don't they? Sara, I want to show you what I discovered in the latest manuscript." Sara had said he studied cryptography, especially the various folios of Shakespeare's plays for clues about whether or not he was really the one who'd written them. He led Sara over to a desk.

Elsa went immediately to look at the paintings, a dozen hung floor to ceiling. She first glanced quickly at the ones resembling crude road maps and inventors' sketches, the one by that man Picasso, until she spotted the painting she had been looking for above the couch, *Nude Descending the Staircase*, which she had admired in reproductions all these years but had never actually seen.

It was a nude of the mind, a body with angles, arms and legs whose movement traced shapes in the air—the swivel of hips a bustle, the bent knees and shins forming the flare at the bottom of a tight skirt. The nude of the mind, graceful as a violin or lamplight, even in her disregard and naked-ness, rushed goldly downstairs to the one she hoped to seduce.

The Baroness felt a heat, like a candle held to her forehead.

Sara came up behind her. "I'll never paint anything like that."

Sara was too easily crumpled by genius, and what was the good of genius if it didn't inspire? "Why should you? You have your own paintings."

The room was dim. Men's faces faded, their voices clattering French and English. Earrings and pendants jangled and glinted as women laughed through red, bowed lips. Perfumes mingled in a cloud of female incense. Sara pointed out to her the poets in the crowd—Mina Loy, a beautiful woman with dark hair and delicate clinking bracelets, and John Rodgers, who had a shy face and wore a brightly embroidered vest.

As she wove through the crowd, Elsa could feel people staring, and it pleased her to garner their attention, to know that her existence this evening in this particular place would be registered. She stood up straighter, lifted her shoulder delicately to pass the fat man, rubbed the lever in her pocket, and followed Sara's slender back through the tunnel of evening clothes. She wanted there to be no trace of bitterness on her face; she wanted to amuse every single person in the room.

Two dowdy-looking women in white lacy dresses gossiped in the corner. Grasping the stem of a wineglass from the tray the maid offered her, Elsa noticed on the mantel two jade statuettes, which seemed to wince at her, and she was tempted to take down the African mask on the wall and put it over her face. Sara introduced her to Louise Arensberg, one of the dowdy women, her hair loosely piled in a way that drooped onto her forehead. She was rich, yet she was plain—her frumpiness a kind of shyness that some men found attractive.

"You are the model for Sara's painting. I've heard all about you," she said, but Elsa could tell she was lying, and it made her nervous to have the hostess looking at her like that. Women said they'd heard about you just in case you were ashamed of yourself.

"You have heard about the length of it, then, and how it curved to the side."

Louise widened her eyes, cocked her head curiously. "What?"

"My husband's member."

Louise laughed, looking up at the ceiling and smoothing her hair. Then she nodded at Elsa's ribbon bodice. "What a lovely shade of red."

The other woman returned to whisper something to Louise, who excused herself, and Sara pulled Elsa over to a group standing near the piano. "Did you have to say that? I'm looking for patronage. I'd like to be invited back."

"What? She doesn't like jokes?"

"That wasn't a joke. That was nasty."

Elsa felt momentarily regretful but worried, as always, that if she held back her thoughts, they'd tarnish, and these guests expected sparkling conversation.

A woman wearing a large collar stood with one finger plinking idly at the piano keys. "Men are hounds, and women are cats," she announced to the man next to her. "Think about it—men are loyal to the thing they are hunting, and women are sly about where and how they hide."

Elsa felt her bustle slipping lower and adjusted it, so the taillight sat high again. A dizziness of colors and smoke swirled over her. She sipped her wine and stepped toward the empty part of the room, where a man stood looking out the window, hands in his trouser pockets, the back of his neck lovely against his dark suit.

"Frying Pan," Sara whispered. It was her new nickname for Elsa because drunkenly one night she'd been unable to pronounce Freytag-Loringhoven. "That's Marcel."

When they came to the window, he turned slowly toward them. "Hello." He smiled. "Oh, yes." Elsa had that sudden jolt, the feeling of her toes and fingers momentarily flying about the room without her. It was the elegant Frenchman she had met in the hallway of her building, the one who had taken the roses; the one she had been watching for without knowing it.

He held a lit pipe in his palm, but with some disinterest, as if it were an object he'd idly picked up to admire, just to feel the shape in his hand. "We have actually met before, haven't we? The teaspoons!"

When he turned to the tray of drinks and chose a glass of champagne, he bent forward slightly, spotting Elsa's taillight. "What a spectacular dress! Where did you find it?"

Elsa felt her face heat up again. "I didn't find it. I made it. A car and a bicycle have taillights. Why not me? This way people won't bump into me in the dark."

"Of course," said Marcel, gently turning her around to admire the back of her. "For a woman of your speed and grace, it might even be considered a necessity." His chiseled, smooth white face balanced a secretive smile that made her sweat against the tight ribbons.

She pressed the lever in her skirt pocket, so that the taillight flashed red against the paintings on the wall. People turned from their circles to stare.

"*Ravissant!*" he said. "Is there an engine, too?"

"Of course—inside me!"

When he laughed, a warmth spread in her breast that she had not felt for some time. She looked into his dark blue eyes, just barely marked with wrinkles.

Sara moved between them. "Have you ever had so many people staring at your behind?"

"Certainly," said Elsa. "You forget I was in the chorus at the Wintergarten Cabaret."

"We should all have lights there," said Marcel. "May I work the lever?" He was the first man who seemed to fathom what her self-apparel intended, how the light was meant to express an idea.

"You *may.*" She took his hand and pulled it inside her pocket. She felt his finger press down first near her hip bone, then at the lever, and the entire room was tinted red. Around them pink-faced people stopped talking. The walls of paintings blushed. A woman said "Oh, my!" and a glass slipped from a table and shattered.

"*Merci.*" He pulled his hand away, and the light went out.

"You must come upstairs and visit me one day," he said, and his blue eyes appeared oddly distant and sharp at the same time. There was something remote in his expression, as if he were counting or praying under his breath.

A man came over grinning and began to speak to Marcel in French. He shrugged and replied.

Sara pulled her aside and whispered, "Don't monopolize him. It's bad form."

"His studio must be in my building—it would be so convenient for me to be his model."

"But I've never seen him there."

"Sara!" Her friend Sam called to her and came over with two other men. Elsa wanted to go back to Marcel, but he had walked away. While the men were talking to Sara, Elsa pictured each of them as a different animal, one a pony, one a rat, and one a rhinoceros.

"How was I supposed to remember you couldn't buy meat on Tuesday? Half the time I don't even know what day it is anyway," said one of the men, shaking the long handful of hair at his forehead.

The rat hunched forward. "For your country you're supposed to develop a better memory, kid."

The rhinoceros lifted his plump legs in a mock march, singing softly, *"We're going to take the germ out of Germany."*

She thought now it was best to make the war into a joke, because the alternative was too bleak. Besides, she was no more "the enemy" than a chair or a hatbox. She leaned into the circle, feeling her accent weighty on her tongue. "I think I will become a black-market German-language schoolmistress. Would you like to be my pupils?" She laughed, but the men only gaped at her.

She felt something tickle at her stomach and saw that the ribbons tying her bodice together had come undone, and her nipples poked out between the bars of red satin. They'd hardened in the air, brown and shriveled to points. A tall woman opened her mouth, then covered it with her hand. A couple of men turned their backs, but the others froze. Elsa had become so accustomed to standing nude before people, she'd forgotten its pure shock effect. In the sunbeam of all that attention, she felt wholly herself for the first time in years. "Oh, well!" she said, fiddling with the ribbons. "The present's come unwrapped."

She caught sight of Marcel across the room. He lifted his champagne glass to her. Out of the bubbles sprouted something like a bird-plant, chirping and blossoming, a thing only the two of them possessed the insight to see.

Sara moved in front of Elsa and tried to cover her, but she still felt glittery. "Don't worry, Sara." She pointed to the paintings. "There's at least six other bosoms right there on the wall."

28

Barney Fitch had been coming around her building, trying to get his watch back, and whenever she saw him standing there in the foyer, she told him the truth: "I do not have it!" She'd pawned it as soon as she could and used part of the money to buy Fred, the canary, and a wooden cage.

When she'd seen the bird in the window of the pet store on Patchin Place, the yellow feathers like loud singing in the morning, the sassy little beak, full of bird obscenities, she decided she needed him, a light to flutter in the corner of her room, a tiny beaming heartbeat.

She moved around her studio with the canary chirping its dirty limericks and curses, Pinky at the window barking at the horses out on the street, which he must have thought were giant dogs. (He barked at everything that was larger than he was, except Elsa.) She watched them display their superior senses of hearing—Pinky could detect a thunderstorm approaching, a siren from blocks away. Fred heard the landlord's demands hours before he'd come clomping up the stairs, as if his tiny bird ears picked up waves of the near future. She fed Pinky meat scraps and Fred bread crumbs and seeds, and they appeared grateful—it was comforting to be reminded of her own animal nature, its necessities and pleasures. Pinky happily scratched his testicles; Fred spread his white poop like paint where he pleased.

But Barney Fitch wouldn't give up. He waited for her under the fire escape to her building, which zigzagged over his head like a joking diagram of his thoughts. "Elsa, you're behaving like a loon. Now, give me the watch. If it's money you need, I'll give it to you." She walked right past him, pretending she didn't see him.

Once someone let him into the building, and he waited outside the door, leaning against the wall with his arms folded. "It's about time you got back. Where have you been?"

"I don't want another husband," she said, turning the key in the lock.

He tried to follow her inside, but she slammed the door in his face.

She heard him say, "There are other things I can tell you about—the plan Josef and I had, why it probably fell through, and how you can get from him what you deserve."

His persistence angered her. It implied how certain he was of her neediness, his confidence in her eventual capitulation. But she didn't need him. She would get more modeling work, she would publish a book of poems. She had her own friends.

And this was why she invented a story about Josef. Once upon a time, she was married to a baron, who was fond of automobiles, was handsome in his suits, carefully folded the pants over a chair back each night after he'd taken her dancing. The Ritz kept a special table for them at dinnertime, and they'd dined with that rodent man Charlie Chaplin, dashing William Farnum, and the opera singer Genevieve Vix. He was a gambler, unfortunately bad with money. The more she talked about him in cafés or at parties, the less often she mistakenly sighted him and the less often something he'd said came whispering back to her when she was trying to go to sleep.

The last afternoon Barney tried to talk to her, he forced himself inside the room. "Be reasonable, Elsa. Let me help you." He moved toward her, smiling, burly arms outstretched. She kneed him in the groin, and Pinky bit his ankles, tearing his trousers. "Get the hell out!" she screamed, throwing a bowl that just missed his head.

After two weeks, when she hadn't heard anything from *The Little Review*, she decided to visit the office in person. Either they wanted the poems or they didn't, but since she'd found out what Josef had been up to, she'd promised herself not to wait anymore for anything. Sheep waited for things to happen. Lizards waited, drying out on a rock. Pinky and Fred, like her, were impatient.

To show that she was modern and to distract herself from nervousness, she dressed for her introduction, clothing herself in city objects—a kilt she'd found in someone's garbage, a bolero jacket that had once belonged to her Spanish dress, earrings she'd made from clothespins, and a necklace made with electrical wires and Wrigley's wrappers.

The office was on Eighth Street, above Capelli's Funeral Parlor, in a building with giddy angels peering out over the window eaves.

Caldwell had told her about Jane Heap and Margaret Anderson, who were lovers. They'd founded *The Little Review* in Chicago, using Margaret's inheritance, which was mostly spent by the time they arrived in New York. They now depended on sales and subscriptions to keep the magazine going. "But it's good," Caldwell said. "Most of these magazines are too timid— they don't expect to be read. But Margaret and Jane really believe they can help along a revolution, God bless them." Margaret was a little frivolous, he said, but she knew how to use her beauty with men, despite the fact that she didn't care for them.

When Elsa came to the door, Jane and Margaret immediately knew who she was, which surprised her.

Margaret, her bowed red lips pressed impishly together, said, "We don't get many poems written by German baronesses."

Jane Heap, a large woman with a tiny, elegant head of cropped hair slicked behind her ears, came up behind her. She was wearing a man's suit. "Your reputation precedes you."

Elsa was conscious of her accent, like a dark velvet drape that fell across bubbly American conversation, but she hadn't thought it was so immediately detectable—there were a hundred accents in Manhattan, each one strange and distinct.

"Wayne Caldwell was right—the poems are small explosions," said Jane. Her accent was plain and low, as if she were flattening the words so that she could speak more rapidly.

"They're the lingerie of English," said Margaret. She spoke as if she were mocking bells, her high voice ringing out and then lingering. "Hidden close to the body. One would have to know how to unbutton in order to read them properly."

The walls were painted black and the floor magenta, which gave the effect of standing inside a night with a levitating bottom. A large desk and a small desk sat side by side, and there was a smell of soap and tea. So much of her was entrusted for the moment to these strangers—Elsa imagined her luck dangling by a string. She could not read their faces. "Are you going to publish the poems?"

Jane fingered the strands of beads she wore around her neck. "We were just drafting the letter."

LETTERS had gone bankrupt after all, even with Caldwell's promises, and why should it be that these women would find her poems more worthy than others? There was that shiny, tambourine feeling, but she did not trust it yet.

"Sit down," said Jane, motioning to a red velvet sofa hung by two chains from the ceiling like a porch swing. There were velvet pillows there and on the floor, needlepointed ones on the chairs and the desktops—circles, squares, and petite loaves to place under one's neck.

"We've heard about your ensembles," said Margaret. "But it's quite a different thing to see for yourself." She turned to Jane. "It makes Theresa's lampshade hats look pretty tame, doesn't it?" Her dark brown hair gleamed against her pale, plump cheeks.

Jane laughed, leaned back into an easy chair in front of a desk. "Ezra's going to be pleased with these poems, but I don't care if he isn't, frankly."

Margaret crossed her legs daintily in a hard-backed chair. "He got us the patronage—don't forget that."

"That was six months ago."

Elsa envied the easiness between them, a way they had of seeming to wink at one another when they spoke. Their conversation was like the harmonious patter of couples who have been together for a long time, and the lush coziness of the office seemed to reflect their attachment to one another. Elsa imagined one bringing the other warm milk in bed, how they would draw a hot bath in the tub she'd noticed just outside the kitchen.

Jane turned to Elsa. "We're discussing our European correspondent. Have you read Ezra Pound's poetry?"

Elsa was startled to be addressed so directly on the issue. She had read *Lustra*—the poems were oracular and otherworldly, and she admired the circular music that practically had the smell of hot candle wax and cathedrals. "He writes through masks, doesn't he?" she said. "I can't imagine what he looks like—he's like a ghost with a ventriloquist's talents."

"The poems are marvelous," said Margaret. She was a woman, Elsa suspected, who used this word often.

"I've always thought they seem written outside of time," said Jane. "He's a genius poet, but a bit of a bully with us."

"Jane!" said Margaret, shaking her head.

"I'm afraid it's true, Margaret. The man thinks we don't know how to read for ourselves the manuscripts he sends us—don't you see how he explains? But he's brilliant, and he understands how imperative great poetry is, and I'm grateful to him, and I don't care if he goes on believing we're fools."

Margaret sighed. "Rosalind, who gave you that information, is not the most reliable source."

"Anyway," said Jane, slapping her knees. "When will we have the pleasure of reading more of *your* poems?"

There was a voraciousness in her that Elsa trusted, but she wanted to be cool with them, not too eager. She hid her private, silvery elation in her haughtiest voice. "Well, I *could* send more," Elsa said. "There is one called 'Moonstone' you will particularly like."

"Marvelous!" said Margaret, her movements languid in a way that seemed to hide overly anxious nerves.

Jane nodded to Elsa in a proprietary way. "We'll give you five dollars for each of them." She had ravenous eyes, talking as if she might starve if she stopped.

Margaret served tea on a daffodil-spattered tray, and Elsa sat with them most of the afternoon. As she became more comfortable, Elsa told a story about Pinky, how he'd once grabbed a lost glove in his teeth and refused to let it go, apparently thinking it was edible, and the man who'd lost it followed them all around the park, until Pinky finally dropped it when he spotted a yellow card, which he must have assumed was a piece of cheese, and gobbled it up. "Eating is his art, you see."

Jane and Margaret laughed, both of them sitting at the large oak desk, crowded with teacups and papers. Jane explained her theories about poetry, how rhymes sounded too much like advertisements now, and if there were stars, then they'd better be electric ones. Elsa said she admired the "loud-mouthed lines" in the "Love Songs" Mina Loy published in *Others,* and Margaret winced. "She's promised to give us the next ones." They mentioned that they kept the magazine afloat by being frugal in other ways—they cut one another's hair, they sewed their own clothes. Margaret cooked on most nights, though Jane could not resist one or two nights out. Elsa noticed the door open in the back, where she glimpsed a bed and saw the stove and sink against the back wall. "We live our work, as you can see," said Margaret. "I'm the buzz, and Jane's the sting."

Margaret took down several recent issues and showed them to Elsa, each cover bearing the motto MAKING NO COMPROMISE WITH THE PUBLIC TASTE.

"Margaret loves Crotti, so we have reproductions in the next issue," said Jane. "We'll have your poems in the middle, 'Blast' and 'Deathwail,' and another chapter from this Irishman's peculiarly intricate and live novel, *Ulysses.*"

"They wouldn't publish it in France," said Margaret. "We've beaten them on that."

"We are sometimes accused of internationalism," said Jane. "But in my opinion, that's not an insult."

Elsa pushed the poems under Marcel Duchamp's door with a note that said, *Soon to appear in* The Little Review.

They were friendly now. He'd invited her up to his studio, where she'd noticed the outline of the Murphy bed in the wall and a carpet of gray fur in the corner. Sara's painting hung over the table. When Elsa looked at the figures of her feet, they reminded her of a mountainscape, shot through with blue streams, callused, wrinkled rocks covered with pink cloths. She'd told him about her theory that art was like a staircase and souls the balls that rolled up or down it, which sometimes produced pain. This was why so many artists died at an early age. She told him about the pawnshop on Orchard Street, where she'd seen an elephant made entirely of matchsticks, and they discussed trains, how each one screeched in a different tone and, if someone were to line up the sounds, there could be a new form of music. "The city works on you, doesn't it?" he said.

It wasn't the way she would have put it to herself, but she was flattered.

All of the artists she had known before had considered their work soberly, pensively, but when Marcel mentioned his own, he laughed. He didn't seem to have any of the usual arrogance, as if he considered his work no more valuable than hers or anyone else's. She was attracted to the way he read aloud from her poem "Blast": *Take spoon—scalpel— / Scrape brains clear from you /—how it hurts to be void!*

"Mon Dieu! I'll go around brainless for hours now," he said, and then laughed the way he did after half his sentences.

He fished a pair of dice from his pocket and handed them to her. "Let me ask you something—will you let me have a look at your chance?"

She smiled and unbuttoned her collar. She rolled the dice across the table. A one and a two. She rolled them again. Two fours.

"Fantastic!" he said, scooping up the dice. She watched his bright eyes. He rolled. A six and a five. "Do you see that? My chance is completely different from yours."

"Mine isn't as lucky."

"Who knows? No one can know their chance—that's the beauty." He had a smile the exact shape of a half-moon on its side and intense eyes with glamorous, lazy lids. He leaned over the table and studied the dice. One of them was chipped in the corner. "When the Romans didn't have enough money for food, they would eat one day, starve and gamble the next. It was the unseen plane that helped them fast and dulled the pain." What he saw in the dice was not luck or unluck (as Josef would have seen), not money potential, but a metaphysics.

"It sounds like a religion."

"My God, not religion." Marcel was suddenly serious. "In scientific terms the realm beyond the retinal—what can't be seen."

As they talked, ideas flew around the studio like sparks, while the light went gold, and then a watery blue-gray. She admired the way there were no borders between how he poured a glass of wine and how he sketched for his art or discussed the beauty of the Woolworth Building. Talking to him, she felt luminously intelligent, as if events in her past had happened in ways that automatically amused him. He made her feel as if her marriages had not been failures, but only adventures, as if finally, she were beginning something important.

When he turned on a lamp, she noticed the perfect cleft in his chin, like a tiny woman's décolletage. "Have you ever really looked at the Hudson River? That oily, black movement?" she said. "Don't you think all emotion is expressed in motion?"

"Everything is expressed in motion now—haven't you been to the picture houses lately?"

29

Each time she visited Marcel, she wore one of her self-apparel pieces—
a dress covered with bits of newspaper ("I could read you," he said),
tights and a bodice with little bells sewn all over it ("Every woman
should walk in music like that"), necklaces she made of fruit that she gilded
with gold paint and a bracelet she made from chewing-gum wrappers. She
made him laugh, but in his laughter was a kind of concentration, an inten-
sity. His gaze made her feel as if her blood were filled with tiny lights and
whistles.

She met him in the stairwell one afternoon. He was carrying a brown paper
bag, his lips set frown-straight, his descent heavy and periodic. She had not
gone up to see him all week and had recently learned that most nights he
spent back at another apartment uptown.

"What's in the bag?"

"Just an ink pot. I wanted to give it to Walter Arensberg because the
name of the company is Mark."

"Mark Ink. It's like a kiss from God, a coincidence like that."

He opened the bag and peeked inside. "I'm convinced it's proof of a sys-
tem we don't know about yet."

His hands, crinkling the bag, seemed to have an intelligence of their own, insight in the curl of each finger. Whenever they met, she did not want him to leave. She wanted, even now, to stand on the staircase talking with him into the night about chance and her self-apparel, her thief husbands and the possible virtue in having so much taken away from one. Exquisitely weightless, Marcel had mainly ascetic habits, and it was impossible to imagine him rich. That was why he kept a studio in this shabby building; he wanted to live on as little money as possible so he wouldn't be made impure by work.

"I'm invited to a party next Wednesday evening," he said. "The hostess, Mabel Dodge, asked me to invite two interesting people. Would you like to go? I have an engagement beforehand, so I can't accompany you there, but I will put the address in your mailbox if you like."

"I would," she said. "I hear that her apartment is entirely white."

When he smiled, there were two dimples in each cheek, one lower and one higher, and his teeth dazzled.

"It's a psyching party—a theme I'm not much fond of. But the scotch will be good."

She'd heard about these psyching parties. People in the Village were reading Sigmund Freud the way people in Berlin had read Nietzsche. "My neurosis," a person would say protectively, as if he were naming his treasure. A few people had ebulliently rehearsed their dreams to her at parties, oblivious to how tedious they were. But if Marcel were going to this fête, she would not be bored.

"Meet me there, then," she said.

Later, smoking peyote in the pipe Josef had left behind, she thought about Marcel, how he made her garrulous, how he would speak to her in perfectly polite English and suddenly utter a French phrase that she realized a moment later referred to her underpants. Her scalp tingled as it stretched, the strands of her hair heating up. There were no words for Marcel yet, though seeing him, with his neat, gleaming hair, she wanted to write, to find names for him, terms. This was what happened when one became infatuated with a sensibility like his; it made the motor of one's own brain spin faster. When the intoxication completely cleared her mind, the words sped out from her pencil. *Spread on thickly / Massage briskly with Vicks / Until skin is red— / Then repeat if necessary / Caution / Don't rush please! / Life's best work an ambition realized / Against jars.*

She liked his ideas about the fourth dimension and the beauty in thumbtacks and cracker packages. The other day he'd given her a mock timeline of her life that made her laugh: "1919: The Baroness publishes her first book of poems, *Blast*, 1921: The Baroness publishes *Tail Light*, a romance between a lady and her automobile, 1924: The Baroness poses nude for the *Saturday Evening Post*." He wrote a parallel timeline for himself. "1920: Marcel Duchamp at work on the *Glass*, 1922: Marcel Duchamp at work on the *Glass*, 1924: Marcel Duchamp still at work on the *Glass*." She admired his indifference to his own fame, the way he pretended not to need anything at all, not even food or sleep, but didn't like to think he might be resisting her, too.

White everywhere: the silken upholstery, the polar-bear rug, the walls, the lamps, the light birch table. Entering the apartment was like walking into a warm snow. A woman wearing a long white caftan and dangling pearl earrings came over to Elsa, her face alight, looking not at her but at the space above her head, as if a question mark hovered there. This was Mabel Dodge.

Elsa introduced herself as a friend of Marcel Duchamp's.

"We *like* friends," said Mabel. "I'm thrilled," she said, taking Elsa's hand. "I am absolutely certain we can make some progress here tonight, too." Her turban made her face appear young but slightly deranged.

"There is so much white," said Elsa. "I'm afraid to dirty it with my neuroses."

"Well . . ." Mabel said, staring at Elsa's blue dress, to which she had sewn ten kewpie dolls, their round faces looking out from the folds of her skirt like hidden children. "I have always hoped that the purity might clear people's minds, make room for ideas and inspirations. Your dress, for instance, is much more visible against this background—how did you ever think of the design?"

"Sigmund Freud, of course."

Mabel Dodge flitted off to greet someone new at the door, and, out of a slew of men in black suits, Jane Heap appeared, wearing strands of beads like green algae against her blue blouse. "I didn't know you knew

Mabel, but I should have guessed. She tends to find the people with talent." She moved like a senator, her shoulders held stiffly as she approached.

"I just met her, to tell the truth. It was Marcel Duchamp who invited me—is he here yet?"

Jane smoothed the lapels of her suit. "I haven't seen him. What would it take, do you think, to convince him to let us reproduce this mysterious artifact he's working on now? Is it really something glass?"

"It's not finished."

Jane nodded. "That's what I thought, but I wondered if he actually had finished it and was keeping it a secret from us—it's only increased everyone's interest in him, this long fallow period. You haven't seen it, have you?"

"Yes, but only because his studio is in my building."

He had explained to her that time moved in more than one direction, and he wanted the *Glass* to demonstrate that. "Lately though, it just feels like transcription," he said. "And it's beginning to bore me." The black marks were carefully drawn there, but only he could discern what they were becoming. He was trying to get away from the notion of the artist's hand and the thick matter of materials. Hence, the *Glass*'s transparency. He said he was trying to be scientific on the matter of perspective, but Marcel had his own private science, theorems and hypotheses he'd invented out of thin air, as far as she could tell.

"You must be a close friend of his," said Jane.

"Marcel and I share an interest in looking at chance. I became intimate with the subject because my husband was a gambler, and Marcel has invented theories about what might be made from it."

This idea seemed to delight Jane, who, as she piled chocolates onto her plate, analyzed the difference between an organized God and a disorganized one, then determined she preferred the latter.

Elsa felt the pains pricking in her legs, a soreness around her abdomen. She followed Jane to the bar to ask for a strong drink.

Sharply carved sculptures loitered next to the couches against the wall. There was a woman pouring water from a bucket, a man chopping wood, a girl leading a donkey, all of them wearing the same angry and surprised face. In the center of the room, large pillows were arranged into three distinct circles.

Caldwell joined Elsa and Jane at the bar. His suit was neatly pressed, and the fabric gleamed, but he appeared even smaller next to the bulk of Jane Heap, and his bright purple tie was crooked. He had been doing interviews for the *New York News,* going around the city with his notebook asking politicians and stage stars questions.

"How are the hunger strikers?" Jane asked. The suffragettes had been jailed and refused to eat—they were being force-fed, and this was a source of horror and jokes.

Caldwell shuddered. "I wouldn't be fed through the nose by a tube for five thousand dollars. Look, the vote just isn't worth starving for at this point. But I suppose better to have vomit on your hands than blood. It makes them vomit, you know." He and Jane talked more about the vote, Jane saying, "I shudder to think whom the masses favor," and when Jane turned to someone else, he lightly touched Elsa on the shoulder. "Don't you ever get tired of them staring at you?"

Two women sharply turned their heads away when she looked in their direction. The man sitting on the couch nodded to her. Caldwell assumed that somehow the gazes of others took something away that she might one day need. But she felt that the one forum a woman always had was her dress—so why not use it? There were ideas she wanted to test, questions, and people were either attracted or repelled, as they should be   it was a way of winnowing the crowd.

"I suppose you think a plain black shirtwaist would be better?"

"I'm only suggesting you might want to give yourself a rest now and then."

"You've heard of wearing one's heart on one's sleeve? I'm wearing my neuroses on my skirt. It will save people time analyzing me."

Caldwell bent down to examine the dolls. "I know that redheaded one— I've got that one, too, I think."

Among the guests were a novelist who was said to only rarely leave his Brooklyn apartment; a dancer who'd studied with Isadora Duncan; and a follower of Emma Goldman, a woman with bright red cheeks who smoked cigars.

The room was loud with talk. Somewhere a Victrola played, but the music was muted by laughter. Caldwell and Elsa stood next to a group who eagerly anticipated having the chance to psych Marcel.

There was a woman who had a lazy eye and hair bobbed like Prince Valiant's. "Men that handsome have a mystery," she said.

"Perhaps we'll gain an insight into his genius," said the woman with her, who wore a tiny hat the size and shape of a teacup.

"He hasn't done anything in a long while," said the skinny man who stooped over them. "But it doesn't matter, does it? He must talk a good talk." There was a little white dog sniffing around their feet.

Elsa and Caldwell took their drinks to the other side of the apartment, near the polar-bear rug, and Elsa stared down at the spread paws and legs, the stuffed head with its curled ears. "I don't think Marcel will let himself be psyched by these people."

Caldwell tugged at the ends of his tie. "It's that French aloofness. Dazzling, isn't it? I wish I had some of it myself, but I can't help it. I talk too much. And I'm not sure I want to be psyched either. I give people too much information—who knows what they'll find?"

"Caldwell, dear, then why did you come?" She realized how much she enjoyed being taller than him, how it made her want to touch his curls, hug his slender shoulders.

"The same reason you came, I'd guess—I didn't know if I'd ever get another invitation."

"Who invited you?"

Caldwell nodded to a bald man who was studying a sculpture in the corner. "That's Hugh Senner. I wrote pieces for him at the *Call* before they stopped paying me and asked me to work voluntarily."

Of course Marcel had not arrived yet. Elsa realized then what he'd probably planned—to arrive just after the psyching festivities, so he wouldn't have to expose himself or say something off guard. But it annoyed her that he hadn't advised her to do the same.

Sara, wearing a peony in her hair, suddenly walked in the room like an electric sign that had just been turned on and brightly made her way over to Elsa. "I didn't know you were coming tonight. I tried to send you a note, in fact, but my invitation came at the last minute."

Sara was lighting a cigarette when Jane Heap joined them, towering over Sara's small frame, as Elsa introduced them.

"I heard about you—you sold a painting to Marcel Duchamp, isn't that right?" Jane said.

Sara nodded. "That's right."

Jane quickly began talking about the paintings they tried to reprint in her magazine, how difficult it was to get good reproductions because there was never any texture to them, and then said that she believed that certain paintings actually were anarchist—she hadn't believed it before, but someone had recently convinced her.

Sara listened with a rapt expression, her lush eyebrows angled inward, as they did when she was thinking. "Maybe I'd like you to have a look at my paintings sometime," she said, and Elsa was glad to see her acting so brashly. She thought it must have been the expansiveness of Jane that had drawn her out.

Mabel Dodge, adjusting her turban, lifted a silver triangle and wand and began to bang the wand against the triangle. "Time for the psyche," she called.

Elsa, Sara, Jane, and Caldwell ended up in a circle with Floyd Dell and Hugh Senner, who tended to preface his sentences with "As a political philosopher . . ."

Elsa liked the notion that one could get important information from dreams, but she had a feeling the unconscious was more likely to be swirling in the punch or wafting in the cigarette smoke, not likely to be revealed in this overly serious parlor game. The rule was this: In one's turn one had to say the first thing that came to mind.

The words went around their circle.

"Fire."

"Match."

"Strike."

"Mother," Sara said.

"Your mother hit you? Is that where your women problem stems from?" said Hugh, puffing out his lips.

"What women problem?" said Sara, rolling her eyes. "I was thinking of work. Women's work and workers and strikes."

"Are you rationalizing?" said Floyd. "We're just not adept at this yet. Let's go on."

The game continued, the words spit out like accusations. "Zoo."

"Bars."

"Gin."

They finished several rounds, discovering that Floyd, with his nervous, limpid eyes, was furious with the managing editor at the *Masses* but had been afraid to admit it because the man reminded him of his brother. And later, "Oh, dear!" Hugh said, his voice suddenly booming out at the discovery. "I must be afraid of water!"

Elsa stood up and quit the circle, and Sara and Jane followed.

They went over to the table. Exquisite squares of sandwiches sat next to a plate of elaborately sliced pears. Jane lifted up the crusts with her knife, examining the sandwich fillings, and Sara reached down and chose one. Elsa drank another glass of punch. It was made with some kind of alcohol, but she could not taste it. The room was beginning to fold in and out, like a wobbly piece of origami, and her feet felt unsure of themselves taking steps on the rug.

When she turned back to Sara and Jane, they were leaning close to one another in the dark corner, and Jane grabbed Sara's elbow just as she seemed to be making a point. Sara laughed, looking down at her foot, which she kicked languidly back and forth. Elsa felt oddly isolated, as if their conversation were a veil she couldn't penetrate.

The floor levitated and fell sharply. Voices, laughter, and music twisted around her like airy bandages tightening and loosening. Where was Marcel? Elsa decided to get more punch.

She picked up the silver ladle and poured more from the bucket into her glass. The punch filled her with sweet air, a forgetfulness that tasted of cherries, and she thought that if she drank enough, she might simply belch and float away.

She looked around again for Marcel. There were two young women wearing billowy silk harem pants and eager, upturned smiles, as they moved from the bar to the wall. A filigreed mirror reflected their rosy faces. Two potbellied men stood smoking at the window, grunting to one another past their pipes, lamplight in patches on their suits. A woman wearing sandals and a sacklike dress lay down on the couch, touching the back of her hand to her forehead, and then a bluish man came and knelt beside her. It was nearly ten o'clock, and it annoyed her that Marcel might have been so impolite as to invite her and not make an appearance himself.

Jane and Sara joined her again, followed by a pretty woman with sharp features in a chic, dotted skirt. She had an unhappy way of talking, as if she were leaning away from the conversation. Sara introduced the woman, Mary

Dryar, to Elsa, and as she spoke, Elsa surmised she was a patron, the heir to the Dryar fortune. Elsa didn't like the way she dropped names like bouquets, or the way she wrinkled her nose while she listened.

Just then Floyd and Hugh joined their circle, already in the middle of a debate. "The way I see it," said Floyd, "is that artists are workers like workers in a factory. We're one of them, and just by recognizing that, we help them."

"I don't see how we can know what the workers want," said Hugh. "The only true art for anarchists is destruction."

Elsa was bored with the earnestness of Floyd's argument, the way it consoled guilty writers and painters. She was more interested in the anarchists, their elusive plots for explosions and disruptions of government. But for her, all the questions were beside the real ones, which had to do with how far one could go and whether one woke up to find light on the black paint of the fire escape or not, or whether there were scratches in the silence where something might emerge.

"Just don't give me any politics in poems," Jane said. "I want peace and silence from the masses." She reminded Elsa of a traveling salesman, but one who carried around ideas and names in her suitcase, and when she took one of them out, it was nearly impossible to resist the sales pitch.

Floyd turned to Sara. "I heard about your sale. Maybe you can teach Duchamp a thing or two."

Mary Dryar, leaning back so her hips jutted under her narrow skirt, said, "You *must* be drunk. Where is he, by the way? He's supposed to be my escort tonight." Elsa searched Mary Dryar's pointed chin and narrow blue eyes for a sign of disingenuousness.

"He *is so* mercurial—it's part of his original nature, I think."

Floyd's laugh spurted between his teeth. "Why defend him?"

Mary Dryar smoothed the front of her blouse, a diamond ring sparkling. She seemed confident in her attachment to Marcel, her knowledge of his habits. "Floyd, of all the men you know, that man deserves your respect. Marcel Duchamp has given his life to making art for humanity."

Humanity? Mary Dryar, Elsa thought, couldn't have known him well at all. Just yesterday when he and Elsa had walked to Union Square, he'd remarked, "Why does art have to leave messages when we have telephones?" It was one of the reasons he'd given up painting, he said, because people confused the form with "beauty" and all the other edifying words that had "lost their salt"—like "humanity."

Elsa shook her head and walked away. She didn't know how much longer she could wait for him to arrive, Marcel with his joker eyes and smile, who would glide through the door as if he had come at precisely the right hour, as if it were only a coincidence that Elsa was there in that room so white she suspected Mabel Dodge even washed the soap before she used it. Caldwell, very drunk now, sat by himself in a chair, staring at a Chinese-checker board.

Sara followed her to the table, where two wooden sculptures stared balefully at the crowd. "Mary Dryar could get a book of your poems published."

"I'd rather gnaw off a finger," said Elsa.

Mabel came over to them, shaking her head. "You've given up already? You have to give time to the unconscious."

While Sara and Mabel gossiped about an actress they knew, Elsa finished her punch, got up, filled another glass, and carried it with her as she followed a tall girl in a cape who was exiting the party.

Elsa was wobbly on her feet and took the stairs slowly, following the swoosh and bounce of the blue velvet cape. Out on Fifth Avenue, she headed toward the square. If Marcel was not going to show up until midnight, then he would not find her waiting for him. She was done with waiting. And she certainly didn't want to be caught in another conversation with his other guest. What possessed him to invite a woman like that—so prickly and sentimental, like a porcupine protecting a ball of sugar? The street was an oily black, no one on the sidewalk except a man slumped against a building, the soles of his shoes worn away.

There was another party somewhere on MacDougal Street, and she hoped she might be able to remember the address by the time she got close to it. Somewhere on the next block, she heard wheels screeching, the rumble of a motor. She did not want to go home yet to her apartment, where she'd hear the drunken longshoremen cavorting off the piers, jazz music from the illustrator's Victrola across the hall, the giggles of women being groped in the vestibule.

She felt restless, as if she might run all the way uptown or jump off the piers for a bracing swim. When she looked ahead, the sidewalk tipped sharply up and down. Then there was a man beside her. A sailor.

"Hello, miss." He grinned at her, gently brushed his hand against her back. He had black eyes and a generous smile. His clothes smelled of gasoline.

"Hello, sailor. You shouldn't talk to a German that way."

"Hey, that's not how it is. You're American now, aren't you?"

"I'm not anything."

His teeth caught the streetlight. "Want to have some fun with me, then? I know a good place."

"Sure, I need some fun," she said, throwing her glass in the street. The glass shattered against the cobblestone, red punch splashing up.

They went to a saloon on Union Square, where the drinks were expensive, but he seemed to have money and did not mind paying.

He told her about the show he had seen the night before, with dancing girls dressed as cats and a forest they had wheeled onto the stage, with a half naked woman bursting out of a tree. "I've been a lot of places," he said. "But, gee, I see things in New York that I'd never seen anywhere else. The other day I saw a man in a dress directing traffic. I saw a Chinaman selling cats' ears. I see you here, wearing dolls on your skirt."

"Stay with me," she said. She heard herself slurring her words. "I'd like to show you strange things." She put her hand on his thigh, which was hard and warm. "You know, I can read people's minds. A medium showed me how to do it once—one only needs a gas lamp. And I can put people into trance."

"Hypnotize me, then," he said, holding her hand now, pressing it further up his thigh. It had been so long since she'd had a man, and she wondered if, when he touched her under her skirt, she would think of Josef.

She took him to Union Square, to the darkest part of the park, where a bench was surrounded by hedges. He sat down heavily, as if he were exhausted. It aroused her the way he tilted his head, how he draped one arm across the back of the bench, let the other hand fall to his lap, where he worked at undoing his trousers. He was younger than her, she noticed now, his face flushed and unmarked. She sat on his lap, facing him, her knees on either side of his thighs, and lifted her skirt. He ran his hand up her leg, kissed her softly on the mouth. She pulled herself closer until their stomachs were touching. His damp cheek stubbled against her neck.

An empty cookie tin rattled against the slats of the bench. Mosquitoes tingled in the air. Not far away, a screech of tires.

Afterward she got off his lap and lay down on the bench with her head resting on his thigh. She looked up at the tree, which seemed to be full of furry frogs, where just below, his face wavered, a crooked smile. He rested his hand on her breast. She closed her eyes and fell asleep.

She dreamed of frogs with fur like rabbits, and long, pink tongues that smelled of whiskey, and she chased them into the park, corralled them with a black ribbon, until the ground beneath them cracked, and then she was reciting to Josef all the poems she had ever written, while he sat tied to a chair with ropes of pearls.

When she woke up, her mouth tasted like rags, streetlight slashing at her eyes. She stumbled home in the dark and fell into her bed. It would not be until the next morning that she found the two dollars the sailor had stuffed into her chemise.

30

Where the sailor had stuffed the money against her breast, a rash of red bumps had formed, symptoms of her distress. She'd had to pretend to love him, and he'd misunderstood. She was telling herself it was not an awful solution, finding a lover who just walked out of the night, and afterward, letting him walk back into it.

Elsa went up to Marcel's studio, pounded on the door, and he let her in, holding a chocolate bar, the foil peeled back. "Why did you invite me to that party if you weren't intending to go yourself?" she said. She was wearing a brassiere beneath her bolero jacket, and she saw him pretending not to notice her bare skin.

"You like parties. I was under the impression you wanted to meet artists for your modeling prospects." There was a glass of water on the table, a pencil.

It was their talk that she thought about in bed at night, how he teased her about her capers, the debate they'd had about ladies' hats—whether silk flowers were more prevalent because of the war or feathers more common because of the way they looked bobbing in the air—her explanation that dogs listened better than humans, and his idea that all women should ride bicycles. How was it that bubbles of air survived in soda, and why was it that people craved constant happiness, an obvious impossibility? He loved things he did not understand, things that were *abstract*.

"I wanted to meet you."

He opened his mouth to speak, then closed it.

"I met your friend, this Mary Dryar."

Marcel smiled, touched his ear with his forefinger, a habit she'd noticed before. "She's one of my French pupils."

On several afternoons she'd seen the women holding French dictionaries coming down the stairs—a schoolgirl in braids, a buxom matron, a woman with round, white cheeks—all of them drugged, apparently, by his charms.

"I thought Arensberg was supposed to save you from employment."

"Not entirely, unfortunately." He went over to the window, tapped lightly on the glass. "I'm not a very good teacher. I only try to engage my students in French conversation, and they pay me a few dollars. It's the best I can do, but frankly, I find having to work for a living mildly embarrassing—like having to eat standing up. I'm convinced, in fact, that as the world progresses, we'll find a way to get rid of the whole notion. I'm very lazy. Last night I wanted to stay home and concentrate on my breathing—isn't that enough?"

The light from the window illuminated the blond strands in his hair, made his skin appear paler. "Not when you've invited me to be your escort." Somehow Josef's absence had seemed to create an opening the exact size and shape of Marcel.

"Baroness, I apologize. I thought I made it clear."

She didn't regret going to the party, but she didn't like not being able to trust him, as she wanted to believe she knew when he was joking and when he was not. She stepped closer to the gray fur carpet, wondering why it had been cut so precisely, then saw the sign: DUST BREEDING. TO BE RESPECTED.

He smiled at her when he saw she'd noticed. "It's remarkably easy to breed, as it turns out."

The carpet of dust was beautiful in a way, a strangely uniform gray, and what had at first seemed like fur now resembled a tiny, low fog. She'd noticed how he cultivated a love of relativity through his passiveness. He liked anything that at first seemed to be one thing, then became another—puns and optical illusions and jokes. But this love of doubleness might have made him untrustworthy.

The glass gleamed ceremoniously on two sawhorses. There was a diagram pinned up on the wall above it, a few black marks that he'd painted on

the surface; he said that he'd chosen glass rather than canvas because he
didn't want to have to be bothered filling in the background, and he liked the
way the paint didn't oxidize but retained its true color. She admired how he
made minute emendations and precise notes, though it was difficult to see
any change in the whole.

She considered the carpet of dust. "It doesn't look easy," she said. "It
seems as if you took care with it."

"What do you mean? Only with the sign," he said. "Don't you take care
with your poems so the result looks effortless? I admire that apparent ease."

A nimbus of pleasure hovered over her ears.

He opened a tin full of cookies and offered her one. There was an odd
picture painted on the lid—a mother, her mouth wide, apparently scream-
ing, holding a rolling pin, and two grinning boys, running off with a plate
of pink circles.

"That's strange, isn't it?" Elsa said, examining the lid. "My mother never
baked, but she wouldn't have refused me a sweet, ever. She never would
have screamed like that—would yours?"

He shrugged, munching. "My mother was deaf. Not having to hear us,
she didn't pay much attention to what we did—that was the au pair's job. My
mother lived in a world of her own—and she was quite happy there."

He swallowed, and she noticed bits of sugar glistening on his mouth, his
face already beginning to turn away from her.

"She didn't speak to you?"

"She could read lips when she wanted to, but she wasn't often interested
in what people were saying. She could speak if necessary, but it embarrassed
her. Usually she wrote things down."

Elsa pictured an elegant woman with a small notebook hung from her belt.

He smiled. "I envied her, the way she could so easily escape all of us. It
was as if she was allowed to live in two worlds at once."

Elsa watched his long fingers playing with crumbs on the table. "Look
at that," he said, the top of his finger sparkling. "It could be little bits of
diamonds."

She couldn't resist his sensibility, trustworthy or not, open-eyed and
playful, with a streak of meanness. She envied the way he seemed not to
worry about anything, and thought she might learn from this. "My mother
spoiled me," she said. "I had anything I wanted—dresses, sweets."

He licked the sugar from his finger. "I can tell."

Sometimes it seemed that he would not touch her out of kindness because he was afraid he would hurt her, but other times it seemed his reluctance was malicious, as if he were holding his hand out to her and then at the last minute, when she was about to reach for it, he pulled it back.

She took off the bolero jacket, felt the air on her shoulders and midriff. He leaned his head to the side. She stepped closer, touched his cheek, smelled the sandalwood of his soap. As she leaned forward to kiss him, he turned his head slightly, so her lips met his cheek.

"Your husband," he said, gently pulling her hand from his face.

"The baron is gone now." It was the first time she'd admitted it out loud.

He blew a sigh through his delicate lips. "How can I explain it? With certain women it can be a sport. With you it would have to be a religion."

That night she would write, *Thou now lives motionless in a mirror! / Everything is a mirage in thee—thine world is glass—glassy! / Glassy are thine ears—thine hands—thine feet and thine face. / Of glass are the poplars and the sun.*

He picked up the cookie tin and studied the scene again. "Actually, the mother could be screaming at them, but she also might be singing."

31

Elsa did not write to her father—he'd become a hazy thing to her, a dark space she'd escaped, like the fruit pantry where she used to hide from him. Her sister, Charlotte, occasionally still sent letters, but Elsa sometimes wanted to know more than her sister would say, whether his temper had softened, or if he'd only gone from bullying one wife to bullying another. Charlotte wrote that their stepmother, Lottie, had broken her ankle and their father moved slowly now with arthritis, that the roof of their house had to be reshingled and Lottie had bought pretty curtains, that their father had shot a wild boar that had been stalking the new puppy. Elsa sent Charlotte two of the poems that had been published in *The Little Review*, but her sister only wrote back saying she couldn't read English. Her letters never made mention of anything Elsa had said about her own life, so they had an efficient, impersonal tone, like certain newsreels. Charlotte considered herself an expert on the war and wanted to make sure that Elsa wasn't being brainwashed against the Germans, now that America was no longer neutral. *I have not heard any stories about the French,* she wrote. *But the Brits are apparently barbarians. They rape women and force children to march until they collapse. I heard the worst story last week from Louisa's brother. There's a no-man's-land, you must know, between the trenches, where, now and then one side or the other captures a soldier. What did the Brits do when they captured a German? They crucified him, as an example.*

Elsa, Jane, and Sara met at Polly's Restaurant, sitting at a square table next to four women wearing batik dresses and smoking clove cigarettes. Hippolyte, the mustached waiter, had just set down steaming plates of Stroganoff that smelled of sour milk, and they were drinking cups of the tannic wine Jane had bought from the Italian grocer down the street.

Sara cleared her throat and flung herself back in the chair. "I got a letter from Jimmy. He's bored, he said. One would think they'd be marching or practicing marksmanship every day, that his nerves would be on edge, but he said that most of what they do is wait. They tell one another stories and play cards. He was in the infirmary. With dysentery, he claimed, but it must have been something worse. The poor thing only had a single marble to amuse himself with—a friend had given it to him. He said he stared at it and studied it as if it were a globe."

"God, we should send him some reading material," said Jane. "What can we send him? Socks? What about Pound's new book? Does he read poetry?"

Sara shook her head, daintily pricking the meat with her fork. "He's got everything he can carry. He's doing better than my mother, I think. My father says she has pulled out almost all of her eyebrows. 'It makes her look surprised,' he said, which I guess is appropriate. I know what she's doing. She's getting up in the middle of the night and wandering the house. She's baking so much my father can't possibly eat it all. She's filling up her liberty books and writing to Jim about all the errands she's done for the war effort. My father reads the newspaper, gets distracted in the courthouse, and forgets what he's saying because he's thinking of my brother and how he wishes he was out there in Belgium with him." She picked up the wine bottle, started to pour, then stopped, plunked it back on the table. "And Sara stays here painting her stupid little paintings." The insecurity that Sara hid beneath her serious faces and sober dresses felt familiar to Elsa, that self-deprecation with a hint of laziness that prevented her from really working. Sara still expected someone to come to her with a blessing, because she felt her art had to measure up to her family's pain.

Elsa swallowed the hot, sour meat. "Oh, Sara, that's *scheisse!*" The last time Elsa went to see her, she'd found one of Sara's paintings in the alley with the garbage. Of course one had to throw away mistaken attempts, but this was a streetscape of Fourteenth that Jane had admired, and Elsa had pulled it out of the potato peels and hauled it up to Sara's room, saying she ought to save it, even if she hated it. "Why?" Sara had said, turning the canvas to the wall.

"Because your eyes may be all wrong at this moment."

"Don't you see? That's exactly the problem," Sara said.

A group of men stumbled through the door, two carrying papers and one with a stack of posters under his arm. Another held a megaphone. Elsa had seen them around the corner, one of the men yelling through the megaphone that everyone should stop going to work. "If you people stop going to work, then the war will end in one day, my friends!" The other two men had constellated around him, handing out flyers and yelling at hecklers.

Jane fitted her cigarette into its holder. "Your paintings are not stupid, dear." She put her hand on Sara's, and Sara gazed at her as if Jane might be able to save the paintings, even if she herself couldn't. Sara had not admitted anything, but Elsa suspected from the way they touched one another that there had been a recent tryst.

"If Jim dies, I'll just be his fraud," Sara said. "He's a much better painter—you should have seen the portraits he did of our mother. They were like early Cézannes, and he had no idea—he just did them. I got everything from him."

"Not everything," said Elsa. No one could make you want to drive into the clouds and mud, to risk loathing yourself. "That's your hand holding the brush, isn't it?"

Elsa was surprised at the urgency she felt—she didn't want Sara to make this mistake, and she could see how she might. Sara painted to escape that place Ohio, and maybe the escape was even more important than the paintings. She was so young. Who knew what she still might do? Elsa felt her voice going up a register. "You think that if you make a sacrifice and go back home, your brother will return. But miserableness is only miserableness—not penance. It won't change anything."

"What was it that I heard Marcus say the other day?" Jane said, holding up her hand as if to wave. "One thinks one's life is made from sacrifices, but it's really made from defeats." With her large, kingly gestures, Jane had a way of making things definitive, so that one felt protected, as if she knew better than anyone else. "Anyway, that portrait of Beatrice—it's going somewhere."

"Did you think so?" said Sara. "I was afraid to show it to you."

Jane flung up her hand in the air. "Afraid? There's no reason for that. I may not like something, but I believe people ought to be able to make mistakes, or else they never get anywhere."

It was up to Jane and her to save Sara from her fears. "Hell," Elsa said. "My poems are made of accidents. Maybe I knew they would happen, maybe I didn't." Jane laughed, but she wasn't kidding. The best lines came when she didn't exactly know where they'd been or where'd they'd go— they crashed into the poems, perfect and whole. Or a phrase suddenly appeared after a hundred bad, crossed-out attempts. A real poem had violent twists and forward surges like a life, and, in fact, more and more she wanted to be surprised, to allow the subterranean to surface.

Sara watched Jane, her eyes half lowered, her face flushed. "Well, I'm not about to give up painting yet. I have another idea. Where's Margaret tonight?"

Jane shrugged. "She went to a play, *In the Zone*, which she thinks is marvelous, but I'd already seen it with her once and didn't think it was sturdy enough to withstand a second viewing."

"Oh." Her eyes were intent, as if the subject were serious. "But don't the two of you usually agree?"

Jane leaned away and sighed, pushing her short hair behind her ear. "Not lately."

Jane began talking about Madame Cluette, who promised to show the "Soul Light Shine" of "Hindoo Origin" from her Bleecker Street parlor. But Elsa still felt the pull of Sara's worry and wanted to cheer her out of it. "I have an idea about what we should do to counteract the recruitment campaign."

"What's that?" said Jane. "Do you know, I watched, aghast, while this well-dressed matron wrote a ticket for the poor hat cleaner who didn't have a poster in his window. It was terrible." Jane shook her head. Every shop window was required to display a recruitment poster now, or else be fined. Elsa hated this cheerful goading of young men to war.

"Whenever a man is about to sign the papers at some recruitment booth, we should have a whore there to distract him. Do you know what the bordellos on West Street are called? Faith, Hope, and Charity."

Sara laughed. "It might have worked with Jimmy."

Jane blew out a fan of smoke. The men at the next table stared. "Oh, that's John!" said Jane, waving to a big-toothed man. He nodded back to her. Hippolyte came to take the plates, and they all signed slips of credit except Jane, who put some coins on the table next to her glass. While they'd been eating, the place had filled up.

Jane and Sara were discussing a woman who'd gone with Mary Dryar to Mexico to study the indigenous peoples, and because Elsa had never met the woman, she soon lost interest. Her eyes began to sting from all the smoke, and she blinked several times to keep them from watering.

The kitchen door opened and closed, smoke pouring out with the cook's curses, and in the grayness there was a swath of velvet. It was a moment that almost dissolved but then didn't. Her mother's dress materialized and then her face, wet hair streaming down the edges. She stood next to the piano, reached over, and with one finger touched the keys.

"Elsa would not have liked what she said about H.D."

"She's not even listening to us."

The sleeve of her mother's dress draped over the keys. It was ribbon-trimmed and red. No sound came from the piano. Then the face gently crushed back into itself.

"Elsa!" Sara shook her arm. "Are you soused?"

Sara crumpled her forehead, but Jane only smiled slightly, looking curious. "Behind you, over there," Elsa murmured.

Sara turned to look behind her. "There's no one there."

Elsa's hand trembled as she reached for the candle and pulled it closer. "Well, isn't it true that when one is really working, one's eyes play tricks?"

Ever since the vision at Polly's Restaurant, she constantly had the sense that there was a task she needed to do. It caused her to compulsively stare out the window, counting the automobiles that passed, or the horses, measuring how the day's shadow moved across the street and how slowly or quickly pedestrians walked. The feeling made her unable to sit comfortably anywhere. She moved from the bed to the stool to the floor, the restlessness exaggerated by the futile rattling of her radiator, which emitted so little heat that she had to sleep with her socks on, Pinky warm next to her.

One day in a gallery, Marcel showed her a photograph of an eggbeater, called *Man*, by Man Ray. "It's a little simple," Elsa said. Why was the woman always at the center of these picture jokes, even when the title said otherwise? Marcel was afraid of what an honest woman like her might do to him, and when he was fearful or sad, Marcel looked for a way to laugh—he flailed awkwardly like a drowning person until he found the raft.

"It's not, actually," he said. "Women can't see this, that sex is just a mechanical act. They prefer to attach some manufactured emotion to it." Was this a seduction, some way of his testing her? He waited for her to blush and laughed when she stared him down.

"There are such things as souls—machines don't have them."

"Souls? 'Soul' is just another word that is losing its salt." He finished the sentence with a delicate smack of his lips, almost a kiss.

"I don't mean souls as in goddamned saving them."

"Anyway, tell me, why do women prefer to attach something to sex? It's only society's judgment in you making itself manifest. Why not just admit that the sex act is no less understandable than a kind of lever?"

"You don't mean that."

"I do. We could never be lovers, for instance, because our levers don't match." Elsa swallowed her disappointment, then argued for passion and heart, hating the way she sounded like a sentimentalist. Marcel went through all her marriages and explained each of them according to his theory. August's equipment was malfunctional, so she had to leave. Franz's was fine but would have become tedious to her in another year or so, and the same was true for Josef. Her life was actually better now, as it was more honest to be *dégagée* and responsible to no one. But, she said, she could not unchain her heart, and Marcel said that this was precisely the problem with women: their emotions kept them from the necessary freedoms.

She argued against him, but it didn't matter, because she saw in the tense way he held himself that this was how he protected himself. He wanted to be detached, like some lithe, handsome Buddha, so that his mind would not be distracted from his *Glass*. His *Glass* was made entirely of the mathematics and glide of brain—he kept his heart apart from it. This was why he made so little progress.

She considered that she might have wanted him only because he refused her, but she decided it was not his resistance that made him rare to her. It was the way, when she was with him, that her body magnetically swayed in his direction, the way her head hummed with intelligence, as if the antics of her heart released energy into her brain. She thought of mind pictures, the phenomena there were no words for, like the space where lips touched cigarette smoke or the sound of corduroy pieces rubbed together, and the hearty resonance of jokes masked as tragedies and vice versa. He brought all of this out of her, as no one ever had, and when, in his low French voice, he read one of her poems aloud, she thought she would faint. And as much as she wanted him, he made her want to transcend her own passion, to go beyond the bumps of physical desire that had knocked her off course in her life. Marcel made her want to enter his *Glass*, to become translucent and light, everything stripped away except art.

At Jud's Chophouse down the street, longshoremen, sailors, butchers, and deliverymen went to drink and eat steaks from the nearby slaughterhouses, the men's bodies warm with whiskey and cow's blood, the longshoremen waiting for the bosses to call them to jobs at the docks. The men she saw going into Jud's intrigued her because of their broad shoulders and burly arms, their loud voices and ruddy faces. Jud's was only mildly more refined than Joe's, the bar she'd been tossed out of all those months ago, but now she thought she could match the men's strength. Marcel, whom she'd nicknamed Mars for his celestial beauty, had been tickled by the idea when she'd told him, though she knew he thought of it as a prank. But it wasn't entirely. She felt there was something wrong having her poems solely in the hands of aesthetes—they needed the sweat and belch of the city, the clink of beer glasses. She would test herself against Jud's. She would barge into the place, drink with the men, and then perform.

The first time she went, the hecklers paused at the sight of the taillight on her dress, the coal scuttle she wore for a hat. She stood under a red gas lamp, and the room hushed at the oddness of a woman imposing herself, and, in her dark German voice, she recited:

Thought about holy skirts—to the tune of "Wheels are growing on rosebushes." Beneath immovable—carved skirt of forbidding sexlessness—over pavement shoving—gliding—nuns have wheels.

The men began to call out to her. "What are you doing there? Are you cursing us?"

"Look at those totties."

"Lift up your skirt, sweetie."

Her voice went loud over the din, and by the end of the poem she was screaming. She felt huge and untouchable.

Kept carefully empty cars—running over religious track—local—express— according to the velocity of holiness through pious steam—

After she'd performed at Jud's a few times, she would sometimes stay for a drink, pleased with how most of the men seemed afraid of her and left her alone. Sometimes, though, there was one brave enough to pick her up. She knew she wasn't mechanical, as Marcel argued, because she couldn't always make herself fall in love with one, even for an hour. There was Robert, an Irishman, who gasped poetry into her ear as she wrapped her legs around his slim hips. He had come to her three more times, in the middle of the night, always with something for Pinky. But then there was also Titus, who, when he removed his clothes, smelled of herring, and she'd had to push him out the door, disappointed, pants in hand. She wanted to rise above her desires, to rechannel her lusts into words, but she was afraid of celibacy, of drying up and folding like a leaf.

She met a longshoreman named Sam one night at Jud's, when she was wearing one of her more outlandish self-apparels—her hair under a black cap that covered her forehead and ears and strapped around her chin, a piece of electrical cord wound around her neck, men's trousers with tin soldiers dangling from the seat—a statement on the war. The men with their ragged beards and worn jackets stared, and two leaned away from her as she passed through the narrow aisle strewn with tobacco bits and mud, but Sam caught her hand and asked her to join him.

He was freckled and handsome, with large green eyes and a pointed jaw. He stroked her hand, saying, "It's so soft." The calluses on his palm felt like cardboard, and when she kissed him, she tasted the whiskey on his breath and thought it was odd that he playfully slapped her shoulder afterward.

He said he wanted to take her somewhere, and they walked through the dark streets to Christopher, where he squinted at the doors, pausing before each one. He stopped before a door below street level lit by a red lamp, with a padlock hanging from the latch, but when he went down to push it open, it wasn't locked. She recognized the place. The fat woman sat in the middle of the room, legs spread under a floral skirt, grinning at the clamor around her. The same bad painting hung crookedly on the wall, the woman with a head like a pushed-over boulder. It was the place she'd gone to with Barney Fitch and Josef that night Barney had been grabbing her knee. She thought of how much she'd trusted Josef then, how she'd been willing to endure Barney's bullying for him, and now the illusion of that trust made her melancholy. She wanted to leave. Sam must have known it was a fairy joint, but she couldn't tell if he'd been mistaken or was looking for men he could beat up, to show off for her.

"Sam," she said, grabbing his arm.

"What?" He pulled her into a dark corner where beads draped down from the wall. She hadn't told him her name yet.

"I've been here before and would prefer not to remember it."

He cocked his head, smiling slyly. "Why? Did you do something you shouldn't have?" In the back there was a red curtain, behind which there seemed to be a jostling of bodies. Shoes and pants hems below the edge, jackets dropped to the floor. There were red balls of glass around candles, and red lamps hung from the ceiling on silk cords. Men with long hair lingered in the corner, and she saw the glint of pearls, a flash of lace.

Sam slammed his lips against hers. She opened her eyes as she disengaged, the room spinning a little. Then she spotted Caldwell looking at her from the next table. His curly hair was greased flat, and he wore a single dangling earring that could have been diamonds or rhinestones, and there was rouge on his lips. Through the airy bracelets of smoke, he leaned over to whisper to the man he was with. Then, with a jolt, he seemed to see her and stared as if she'd just been hit by a car, and he stood up and came over.

As Sam touched her arm and said, "What do you think?" Caldwell reached down and took her hand.

"Excuse us," he said to Sam, jerking her to her feet.

"What?" said Sam, his mouth open.

"My brother." Caldwell winked.

He pulled her outside. "What are you doing? Don't you know he isn't expecting a woman? And what do you expect he'll do to you when he thinks you've played this joke on him?"

Across the street two whores lifted their skirts at the automobile slowly passing, their faces hidden by large hats. The streetlight overhead seemed to whir like an electric bird. She looked down at her trousers, stained now with whiskey. "What joke?"

"Elsa, you look like a boy."

She'd forgotten that her hair was covered, her face bare. Her own female force directed her so obviously it hadn't even occurred to her it might not be detected beneath these clothes.

"Come on," he said, his earring glittering, as he ran, grabbing her hand to pull her down the street and turning on Charles. "Was he drunk? He isn't following us."

He was panting, then wheezing, holding his chest. "Where did you find him anyway?"

Elsa felt suddenly exhilarated, as if running a half step ahead of her body. "Jud's."

"I hope you're joking."

She considered Caldwell's prettiness, how it added a layer to his personality she had not exactly noticed until tonight.

Caldwell pulled off his earring, wiped his mouth on his sleeve, and they went inside a café. The tables were nearly empty, flecked with cigarette ash. He looked sadly faded without the glitter and rouge.

"So that's where you go all those times you leave so mysteriously at midnight," she said. "You looked quite pretty there."

"They have a rule against women except for Iris. Everyone knows that. That was how I knew the fellow must have been fooled by your pants."

They drank their gin, Caldwell telling her about the man he was with, how they had an unspoken understanding that they would meet on Tuesday nights at Iris's Place but never saw one another in the daylight.

"What's his name?"

Caldwell shrugged. "He says his name is Bill, but I don't believe it." He said this cheerfully. She thought of the elegant man she'd seen him with, his gold cuff links and unwrinkled sleeves, and wondered if he was cruel.

They ordered more gins, and she told him about Marcel's idea of the mechanical nature of sex and asked him if he agreed.

"Not literally," he said, and she saw his point. "But there doesn't have to be a lot of sentiment attached to it—I prefer it actually, when I don't fall in love, but usually someone comes along and I can't help it."

The only other people in the café were two men drunkenly arguing in the corner, and the waiter, who seemed to be falling asleep with his head leaned against the window.

"You know I love Marcel, don't you? If we had sexual relations, how could it ever be mechanical?"

"If you love Marcel, what were you doing with that character?"

"But isn't it all love? That's my point." If she gave up men, she'd have less trouble, but her poems were made of trouble. And despite everything, she wanted each of her marriages to matter, all of the affairs.

"I don't think so, Elsa." Caldwell sat up straight, tapped his finger on his glass so the gin sloshed back and forth.

"Well, I hadn't decided whether I would sleep with him after all."

"I don't know why you go to Jud's—it's an awful place. You'd do better to be a little less man crazy."

"You should talk."

"I go for long periods without, Elsa. You just happened to catch me in the middle of something."

"Don't you ever get sick of aesthetes? The men there may not know what to say about St. Vincent Millay, but I like their beards and rough talk, and periodically I like to empty myself of shame." It was something she needed to be vigilant about—because it constantly threatened to accumulate. She wanted her friends to rail against it, too, but there was always such resistance.

"What's the point of sex without shame? That's where all the excitement is." Caldwell's face was small, but his features stretched in exaggerated reflection of his talk, enlarging him. He slammed his glass on the table. "I thank God every day that I was brought up a Presbyterian—it ensured that what I do in the dark will always be sinful." He poured more gin in his glass. "It gets one high, doesn't it? I think that's exactly why you go to Jud's."

She could tell he hadn't understood her—how necessary it was for a woman to follow her desire or else she'd have it stolen from her. "You're confusing shame with titillation."

"Well, shamelessness would be a luxury for me, wouldn't it? Every time I've been caught out in the light, there's been a disaster. I never told you, did I? There was a beauty at the sanatorium—a blond consumptive. They almost threw us in jail, but we escaped on the train while they were wringing their hands over our perversity. You learn your lesson after a while." It pained her that he hadn't told her this until now, and she didn't know how to argue. Matters of the heart, she knew, were difficult for Caldwell. "Some things are better hidden. For now I'm satisfied with my Tuesday-night Bill."

"Where is he now?" She took out a cigarette, and he struck a match to light it for her.

"Waiting for me under the bridge."

32

A week later Elsa found Marcel in his studio lying on the bare floor, both of the lamps on, his hands folded over his stomach. He was looking at the ceiling and didn't move when she opened the door. "Marcel, why didn't you come to the door? Did you hear me?"

He didn't answer.

She was wearing a hat she'd made from bits of newspaper, a necklace of spoons, for him to sip from. She wanted him to see her, but he wouldn't look in her direction. For a moment she thought he was dead.

"I'm breathing," he said finally. His voice was soft, a single, flat tone, but he turned his head to her for a moment and then calmly turned to face the ceiling again. There was obviously something wrong with him, but she knew better than to ask. He resisted admitting sadness as much as he resisted her. One day she'd found herself lying with him under the bed, where Pinky had hidden her pencils, and when she put her hand on Marcel's arm, he remarked on the "fur clouds" and got to his feet. Another time he'd made one of his jokes about French drawers, and she'd offered to show him hers, but he demurred. When she threw her arms around him and kissed his neck, he laughed, wriggled away, saying, "You know, I've got so little energy."

He talked about his own laziness as an antidote to what he called her "dynamism," as if her verve might be contagious in a way that would be dangerous. He did not want to work zealously. He did not want to become excited. Of course, this was precisely why they should have become lovers, because his opposition to her worked magnetically.

She imagined taking a trip with him to a place with palm trees, silk tents, and bitter intoxicants, where they'd silently ride camels. She thought of taking him back to Swinemünde, where she'd show him the house, the marina where she'd watched the sailors, the Black Sea where her mother had tried to drown. He would be slow to take in these things, but, away from his familiar ruses and hiding places, he might finally show her his unguarded face.

If he would not have her, though, then she would have to go on loving him at a distance, taking paramours as his replacements, acolytes to him. It would be a different freedom from the one Josef had dreamed up, not a marriage, but a union of what-ifs.

Elsa sat cross-legged on the floor near him, looked at his body, slim, the stomach sunken. His gray trousers were perfectly pressed, his black shoes shined. "Do you want to go over to the Needham Gallery?"

"No. Today I'm just going to breathe."

She couldn't stand to leave him there like that, but she knew better than to touch him. He seemed to be made of air and lightness. When she was with him, she felt the spread and heaviness of her own flesh, the sticky matter of it.

She'd seen him slip out of a loft party with a woman on his arm, and once she met a woman in the morning on the stairs, still in her party clothes, and wondered if she had spent the night with him in his studio. Elsa thought, because he knew how much she loved him, he wouldn't sleep with her. He wanted the *Glass*, he told her, to be "completely impersonal," and any proximity to passion threatened that flawlessness.

"*Marcel, Marcel, I love you like hell, Marcel.*" She invented this silly poem to show she understood, to let him know that she saw the humor in herself. He smiled slightly, tapped his finger on the scratched floor. "What do you think of it? Should I ask Jane to publish it?"

He didn't answer.

"There's that Osip Zadkine show at the Needham, the one in all the newspapers. Have you ever noticed," she said, "how a certain tinsel fame can bring so many viewers to a show but dull the art? It seems to be a rule of life."

"What if it's gold-standard fame?"

"That's different." She took out a cigarette, lit it, hoping he'd sit up and ask her for one. "Did you want me to leave?"

He didn't move. "No."

"I'm not going to the show if you're not going." His stillness made her nervous, and she kissed the air with two pretty smoke rings. "Why did you decide to concentrate on breathing today?"

"It's enough of an accomplishment, isn't it? For one day?"

He was depressed, she thought, by his own disinterestedness. When the news came out in the *Sun* about the young man whose face had been blown off by a grenade, Marcel had joked, "But how will his sweetheart know it's him and not the other man she's been sleeping with?" It was an effort. She saw it quivering in the muscles around his mouth, in the twitching of his eyes. He'd made no progress on the *Glass* for weeks. And he said yes too often, even to things he didn't agree with, because yes was more charming and easier to say than no.

She put out her cigarette and lay down on the floor next to him, about a yard away.

Looking up at the waffled squares in the tin ceiling, she said, "I've got some things to show you that I found on the street." Objects had been calling to her lately from trash bins—cracked lampshades, broken chairs, cracker tins, and soapboxes. Certain crushed tin cans had a heady perfume she couldn't resist, and electrical wires and plumbing fixtures had a thin kind of singing.

"Tomorrow I'll look at them," he said. He shared her interest in the street gift and would hold the object in his hand, studying it for a long time. She suspected that his concentration on these cast-off things was a safe way for him to examine himself.

She tried to distract him with complaints about posing for Gilbert Dixon's classes, where lately her figure was reproduced in pink marzipan bundles, which made her want to take her nakedness back and hide it. "Why don't you paint anymore? I would so like to be your model," she said. She knew he didn't need her, because he worked now from thought, not sight, but she wanted to hear him say why again, to watch his face while the thought of her naked flitted through his mind.

He didn't turn to look at her and held very still. "Gilbert Dixon's paintings are bad decoration." Finally, an opinion from him. She watched the curtains flare in the breeze. A moment later he sighed and sat up, and, to her surprise, he looked not sad but rejuvenated. "Why don't you go and see my friend Man Ray? He'll take your photograph, and you can send it around to the painters."

She didn't trust the new cheerfulness, which only seemed to mask a deeper melancholy. He held himself apart, and not just from her.

"I don't have any money to pay him," she said.

"For a modern woman such as yourself, I think I might convince him to do this as a gift."

"You mean, if I pose in the nude."

Marcel smiled, quickly scratched his chin. "If you like." She wanted to kiss him but held herself back.

She met Man Ray, a small man with bulging eyes, in his basement studio, filled with crates of potatoes and lights precariously balanced on tables and hatracks. For the occasion she had fashioned for herself one of those new brassieres. She had taken two empty tomato cans, poked holes in their sides with a screwdriver, and threaded green string through them, fitted the tomato cans over her breasts, and knotted the string behind her back. When he asked her to remove them and she refused, he said, "Aren't I the artist around here?" And she said, "Not the only one."

Later, she thought he was laughing at her immodesty, that he disliked her for it, and she would have walked out had she not needed the photographs so badly to promote her business. She needed more work; in fact, she needed money immediately.

The landlord had taken to leaving red-lettered notes nailed to her door: *You'll find your little dog and bird poisoned, lady, if you don't pay for five weeks. Next time I'll empty your room onto the street.* Gilbert Dixon's classes had been canceled over the holidays, and she was almost out of food, but Jane Heap had said she could have an advance on her next poems whenever she needed it, so after she left Man Ray's basement she went over to Eighth Street to the office.

Jane Heap was the first person she could rely on to help her sustain a real artist's living, and Elsa looked forward to seeing Jane in her beads and man's suit, because it reassured her that her life was not about to unravel the way it had before. She would not have to sleep at the train station or beg Barney for money, because Jane had said, "Whatever you need. *The Little Review* wants you to write more poems." And this was almost better than having them published. It would be a delight to ask Jane for an advance, so unlike having to ask a man for a loan.

When she arrived at the office, a funeral was taking place at Capelli's downstairs. The mahogany doors were held open with black doorstops, revealing the casket, a flirtatious boa of flowers, a crepe stole. Men in dark suits stood outside on the front steps smoking.

When Elsa went into the office, Margaret's face was damp and red, and Elsa wondered if she had known the deceased.

Without saying hello, Jane, in a paisley smoking jacket, immediately began talking. "Pound's been asking about your poems, and so has Lola. She wants you to read at one of her poetry nights. You give us that tang of Europe, Baroness—and we revel in our internationalism, even if it sniffs off some people." The magenta floor was covered with blocky towers of books and manuscripts, like a miniature city. "I've been trying to finish my Editor's Notes, but unsuccessfully. I hate writing. I don't know how you do it." The office, usually tidy, was cluttered and smelled of smoke and toilet water, the bedroom door ajar, revealing the rumpled sheets. Margaret's smaller desk was covered with a pile of gold-tipped cigarettes, Jane's with papers.

Margaret, falling back on the sofa swing, began to rock back and forth, the weight of it creaking in the ceiling as though it might fall. She gave Elsa an accusing look. "Jane has apparently been out socializing so much she hasn't had a minute to do much of anything else."

"I never have been a homebody particularly." Jane nervously eyed Margaret.

"No one has ever asked you to be a homebody," said Margaret.

"Part of an editor's job is to meet people, isn't it?" said Jane sharply. Elsa had the sense that she'd walked in on some private conflict, that they were speaking in code about Sara and Jane's affair.

The tension seemed to hum in the radiator that guzzled and spit. Margaret pushed the swing faster, lifting up her ribboned high heels. "It's just even more upsetting"—Margaret seemed to choke on her voice—"when the censor is confiscating issues at the post office." She fixed her gaze on Elsa. "Do you know what they do with them?" Her usual perfectly defined lips were uneven, the red leaking from the side of her mouth. "They burn them!"

Elsa couldn't tell yet if this talk about the censor was exaggerated or not by Margaret's jealousy. Elsa thought of all those beautiful journals with their bright covers and carefully placed type. "They can't do that!"

"Every single one we sent out to subscribers," Margaret said, sighing. "Thank God we still have the bookstore orders."

The censor had already suppressed Clara Tice's innocent, spindly cartoons of nude girls, which had been on display at a restaurant, and there had been cruel raids on fairy saloons and in certain places in the park. But what could they object to in *The Little Review*?

Jane moved largely from her desk to the bookcase, taking down a notebook. "We took the chance when we decided to publish the *Ulysses* chapters. Did you read the James Joyce, Baroness? Ezra brought him to us." Elsa had followed Joyce's sentences with trepidation at first, as they wandered and made her insecure about her English. Then, all at once, following a passage on Bloom's bowels and his musings on death, she entered his body as if it were her own, and walked around Dublin, lusty and male.

Margaret fluffed herself in the sofa and stopped swinging. "Reading Joyce is like watching a bird in flight. I agree we have to publish him. Did you know Emma took a copy of *Portrait of the Artist* to jail with her?" Margaret mentioned her friend Emma Goldman at every opportunity—it was she who'd given Margaret the idea that art and anarchism had the same aims, and uttering Goldman's name seemed to comfort her in her distress.

"Why did the postmaster ever think to read our little magazine anyway, that's what I wonder?" said Jane. "The brown wrapping must have ripped somehow, and the pages must have fallen open to exactly the offending spot."

Elsa had felt *seen* when her poems appeared in the autumn issue of *The Little Review*. At Polly's she met two poets who had read the issue, complimenting her on the originality of "Blast," and at a party in a stable redecorated as living space, a woman ran up to her and said, "Are you the Baroness?" If *The Little Review* were banned, she didn't know where else she'd be published. And who would publish Joyce?

"They were offended by his talk about Bloom's body? Everyone has one, after all." She remembered the passage when Bloom lay back in a field, pleasuring himself at the sight of a young girl. "But I love the joyful body emissions in Joyce." Elsa sat beside Jane at her desk.

"That's because they occur in your poems, too," said Jane. "William said the typical *Little Review* poem was a logopoeia—a mind cry more than a heart cry. I would say a Baroness poem is a body cry as much as a mind cry."

She liked to hear Jane describe her poems, but the desperate way she stacked manuscripts on the desk and threw books on the chair made Elsa uneasy. It was possible that even Jane Heap couldn't fight this censor. "You can't be afraid of them," Elsa said. "Only a money-minded American wouldn't have the brains to see the passion in those pages."

"All those subscriptions lost, though!" said Margaret. "I don't know how we won't go bankrupt!"

Jane slammed a thick book on the desk. "Who cares? It doesn't even matter. We're not going to stop publishing what we like. Your mind is too much on money."

Margaret looked wounded. They talked more about the magazine's financial troubles, how the young poet Hart Crane had convinced his father, who owned Crane's Chocolates, to buy a year's advertisement, and Robert McSweeney, a longtime subscriber, had convinced three more bookstores to sell the magazine. But the specter of the failure of *Something Else,* a magazine branded "socialist" by the *Post,* was disheartening. "It really proves that patriotism is the vice of the age. The censor didn't even have to lift a finger," said Jane. "They simply couldn't acquire advertisers or convince newsstands to sell copies. Margaret is certain that's going to happen to us, too, unless we let Ezra take over, right?"

Margaret lifted her shoulders and sighed.

"She thinks only Ezra can raise money. But I don't want to do that. For a while we might as well have called ourselves *Ezra's Little Review.* You know, he hates it that we make so many decisions on our own—he calls us a 'gynocracy.'"

When one looked at her, so straight-backed and competent, the thought of any man telling Jane Heap what to do was patently ridiculous. "Who is this censor anyway?" Elsa said.

"John Winters is our agent's name."

"He objects to Joyce for the sexual innuendo?" The Puritanism of Americans never ceased to astound her, and it made her pity these men who seemed to wish they could go bodiless through the world, like wobbly suits of air or just words—"honor," "decency"—their women vapors of toilet water and good deeds.

Jane said, "I don't know if he even read it."

"Someone told him that it used terms from the lavatory," said Margaret, swinging again rapidly.

"Terms from the lavatory have their own beauty if they are used with feeling," said Elsa. "I'm sure that God smiles happily at our tinkles and farts."

Jane suppressed a smile. "Of course. The body is a sublime engine."

They sat in the clutter of papers silently for a moment, children screaming about a game outside on the street. Margaret stopped swinging on the couch, buried her face in her hands. As she often did, she was wearing just one glove on her right hand, the hand she said she hated (though no one else could see why). "I don't know how we can stay in print."

"Will you be quiet?" hissed Jane. "If we lose money, we'll get a less expensive printer. You don't like to think, do you? You only like to feel in a glorious haze."

Margaret screeched back, her pretty face screwed up. "You know Popovitch is the cheapest printer in the city. Besides, he doesn't know he's running a risk with the censor, because he doesn't speak a word of English. And tell me, where else will we find that kind of situation?"

Watching them shout at one another gave Elsa a familiar knot in her stomach. *The Little Review* was the only place publishing art in the middle of this war. If the magazine collapsed, what would be left? *Others? Poetry?* Those editors wouldn't want her. She shouted over them, "I have an idea!"

They stopped and looked at her. One had to resist cheap, sentimental shame. "Dedicate the next issue to the censor. Purposefully publish items that will get his notice—a little flesh, a little cursing. See if he notices. Let the readers in on the joke."

Margaret shook her head. "I'm sure he's not the kind of man who likes to be kidded."

Jane grinned, her narrow teeth flashing. "I like it. If they arrest us, all the better."

Margaret's face was red where she'd rubbed it, her eyes tired. Elsa wondered what Jane had told her about Sara.

Elsa said, "Margaret, think of it. Why not reason with the man, flatter him into learning the artfulness of what is there, so he doesn't imagine seeing what is not there?"

Jane moved a pile of papers from the desk to the trash bin, let them fall with a thud. "One can't argue with a barnyard. But if they're going to confiscate the issues anyway, why not present them on a silver platter? It will at least announce that we're being harassed, and maybe we'll get a letter to the editor in one of the newspapers. They can't burn every single copy. We still have the bookstores."

"Don't be naive. They can burn whatever they like," Margaret said.

Though Margaret remained reluctant, the three of them made more plans. There would be a photograph of breasts somewhere, essays on the matter of the body in art. "Think about it," Jane said. "Girls lean back everywhere, showing lace and stockings, wear low-cut sleeveless gowns, breathless bathing suits." There would be poems and stories meant to prick the censor's interest. Someone else was bound to take up their cause.

Elsa still had to ask for the advance, though she dreaded draining their talk down to the dregs of money, particularly now. She gave Jane Heap a sheaf of poems. "I have to ask. Do you think I might have some payment for these?"

Jane looked at her blankly for a moment, then sprang to action. "Of course, of course." She rummaged on her desk for the checkbook.

Margaret turned her head away to the window, the back of her hair matted unevenly, the bun fallen to her neck. Elsa thought she heard her murmuring something under her breath.

Later that day Elsa would write, *Kiss me / upon this gleaming hill.* With an asterisk next to it: "This line is dedicated to the censor." That would get him in the trousers. She was interested in the formalities no one used anymore, in the way they delicately banged against contemporary words. She'd pour the erotic into old-fashioned phrases, let the body's emissions lie on the tapestry and brass of cast-off antiques. *After thou has squandered thine princely / treasures into mine princely lap* . . .

It was a gorgeous Thursday afternoon, the sky luminous and soft as the skin of a belly. "Let's go out," she said as soon as Marcel opened the door. "There's a new show at 291." She'd decided that none of his other friends had noticed his depression because he always looked so elegant, smiling, saying "Yes" or "*cela n'a pas d'importance*" as often as he could. She was the only one who loved him enough to look beneath his jokes.

Shaving cream lathered half his face.

She marched in past him, noticed the drawer of ties opened, spilling out ten colored tongues. A glass bottle with an orange label rested on the table. He held a razor in one hand, a shaving brush in the other.

He puckered his lips just slightly as he did when he was annoyed. "You've caught me at an awkward time."

She glanced at the painting of her feet, which looked pinker in the new winter light. "I love shaving, don't you?" she said. "The slide of the razor against your skin, the smoothness. The tiny cuts that come almost as a relief."

He tilted his head and watched for a few seconds. "I can't go with you," he said. "I'm going to a dinner—some possible patrons."

"What do you need another one for?"

His lips looked fuller and rosier against the white cream. "Remember, my ambition in life is not to work for a living."

"You like it, too, don't you?" She took the razor from his hand, examined the glint of silver.

"What?"

"Shaving."

He took the razor back from her. "I like the sound of it—so hard to classify."

She touched his arm, which felt surprisingly hard and strong. "If you like, you can shave me sometimes—I like smooth legs." She tugged at the end of his tie. "Let's do it now."

He smiled down at her. She was momentarily mesmerized by his dimples, by the inhuman blueness of his eyes. "I have to finish dressing. We'll go see Stieglitz tomorrow."

"Who's throwing the party?" She accidentally bit her tongue, thinking of how she wanted to go with him.

"A friend of Mary's—an heiress."

Tasting her own coppery blood, she said, "I believe that woman despises me." She'd seen Mary Dryar roll her eyes when Elsa entered a party; she'd pretended not to notice when Mary Dryar snubbed her the last time at the Arensbergs'. Elsa tried to ignore her, but she kept popping up everywhere.

Marcel picked up a towel and wiped his face. "She might." He shrugged. "Is it so important?"

"Are you bedding her?"

His eyes quickly flickered around the room. "When will you get to look at Man's photographs?"

"Why?"

"He and I have an idea for you." He put the shaving brush into a cup and then took it out again, holding the bristles down and turning them in front of his face. "Mary gave me one of those moving-picture cameras."

33

In moving pictures the characters stuttered into rapid motion, the women's eyes and mouths black and emphatic against white skin, the frames followed like square tunnels through the end of the story. Theda Bara was her favorite actress, the Oriental vampire, dressed in jewels and silks, comically devastating men in the wake of her swaying hips. But Elsa felt more like pigtailed Pauline in her *Perils*, who leaped from catastrophic trains, untied herself from landlords' ropes, crawled out the windows of locked rooms, and gamely bopped her captors on the head. But Marcel and she had something different in mind. Elsa imagined herself spread out against the flat screen, her face and body huge and flickering.

It made sense that Marcel would finally touch her only in front of a camera, and, though the parts they'd written together sitting at his table were erotic, she did not assume they would make love in that dank basement, in front of Man Ray, but afterward. It was Marcel's love of jokes that made him want to play the barber, and it also gave him a ruse.

"The nude descends the staircase, to the barber waiting at the bottom," she dictated to him.

Marcel winsomely drew the diagram. She was a stick figure with a star for a head, moving in a circle, then a triangular pattern. Neither of them mentioned the censor, though the photograph of the nude was against the

Comstock laws, and the threat looped a thin wire of tension around their plans.

"I should have guessed this fetish of yours," she said. "That you like a woman smooth there."

"I'll buy a special razor." He offered her a pastille, and she popped it into her mouth.

"And afterward?"

He wouldn't meet her eyes, gulped from his glass. He drank so much whiskey because he was sad; he was sad because he maintained that happy face.

She knew that others, including Sara and Jane, for all their talk of freedoms, might be repulsed at their drama, the shaving cream and razor so proximate to sex, and his tending to her intimate parts as if they were his own. She assumed that the film, *The Baroness, Elsa von Freytag-Loringhoven, Shaving Her Pubic Hair*, would be screened somewhere quietly, shown only to Villagers at Polly Holladay's Restaurant or the Liberal Club. That made it all the more precious, available only to the eyes of the initiated. What would they see? A nude woman transformed into pure motion, and the erotic climate would heighten attention to all the objects in the room: the chair, the razor, the towel. "And will there be words to our film?" she said. "I can write them."

"That will come later," he said. "With the music."

The basement was dimmer than it had been the first time she'd gone to see Man Ray, and the crates of potatoes along one wall gave off a heavy scent. A floral printed sheet hung over a wall, where Man Ray said there had been "an ugly leak," and another wall stared back in cragged, blank brick. Man Ray, wearing a raccoon-fur coat, though it was only mildly chilly, had lined up several bottles of red wine along the potato crates, and he opened one, poured each of them a teacupful. They drank these down quickly, and he filled the cups again. Despite his hospitality, Elsa was still not sure whether she liked this short man with the frog eyes, though he and Marcel kept patting one another on the back and laughing.

Man Ray climbed a ladder, setting up high, bright lights, tying them to the rafters of the ceiling like silver suns. Nervous about being arrested, he joked in his Brooklynese, "You've heard of this fellow Comstock, Marcel, right? He's no friend of the French."

"We could devise a wonderful limerick for him," said Marcel. "There once was a man named Comstock. / He didn't have much of a long cock. . . ."

Elsa and Marcel stood near the rickety staircase of unfinished wood. He took her arm in his, the cool smoothness of his suit pressed against her wrist. The razor peeked from his suit pocket and, on the floor next to a hard-backed chair, shaving cream, a small white towel, and a bowl of water.

"It was purple and green, /" said Elsa, "From a girl named Doreen, / And so he put yours in a padlock."

Marcel chuckled. Like ice, he was unaware of his own melting. He loosened his tie, a sheen of perspiration beading his forehead. He would soon be disabused of that artistic ideal, *completely impersonal.*

Marcel and Man Ray stood commiserating on the mechanics of the camera, this long-nosed eye with a black, triangular head.

Taking another sip of wine, she set the dainty cup on the floor, shrugged off her bolero jacket, and laid it neatly over a potato crate. She unbuttoned her gray newspaper-appliquéd skirt and kicked her way out of it, then spread it flat next to the jacket. She pulled off the blouse, laid it over the jacket, and stood waiting in her red chemise and stockings.

She was aware, even in the dimness, that her flesh was not as firm as it had once been, that the surface of her upper arms and thighs had a slight uneven ripple, that all the pinkness seemed to have gone out of her nipples, though her breasts were still high and small.

"Just a moment, Baroness," said Marcel, holding up a finger. He wore his usual black suit, but it was rumpled, and the hems of the trousers looked dusty. He went into the darkness with Man Ray.

"This switch here," said Man Ray, and a lever clicked.

"And you think it will work for a continuous ten minutes?" said Marcel.

"It's supposed to," said Man Ray. "Let's try it."

"Are you ready, Elsa?" said Marcel.

"With stockings or without?" she said, imagining his warm palms on her knees.

"Whatever you please." He stepped into the light again, his face and hands white.

The one thing that bothered her was how they were going to induce Man

Ray to leave, and where they would go. On top of the potato crates? Up against that floral sheet?

Marcel called over to her. "Just think of me as an ordinary worker doing his job—as if this were an everyday occurrence to me. I'm a barber—an expert with the razor, the man with the steady, sober hand."

"I'm going to seduce you," she said. "There's nothing sober about that."

Man Ray laughed. He went under the black cloth behind the camera to fiddle with something, hunched in his fur. The camera stood there on its crossed metal legs, a box with an eye. There was something in the crouched way Man Ray held his body that she didn't trust, and his eyes wandered when she looked closely at him.

She thumbed down one strap of her chemise, then the other, let it fall around her feet. Marcel looked at her, then looked away. He took off his jacket, folded it carefully on the back of the chair, and sat down. He turned to her. "Imagine that the camera is blind. The audience is that wall of crates over there."

Her nipples stiffened. As she peeled down her stockings, her hands trembled against the smooth skin, and one stocking tangled at her ankle, so she had to tug and hop out of it.

"Shall we have some music?" Marcel went behind the camera and turned on the Victrola. A voice crooned up out of the dark: *Don't tell me love is lovely.* . . . Then the strings, weepy and slow.

She walked up the splintery steps to the door at the top. The camera made a whirring sound.

"Go!" the eye yelled. From the top of the stairs, the basement was dark, and only gradually, as she descended, did Marcel become visible, waiting for her in the chair at the bottom.

She descended into the lights, first a white foot and ankle, then a knee, then thigh, torso, breast, shoulder. She unfolded for him, planting her foot firmly on each step, one hand lightly holding the banister. She would unbutton his starched shirt, and his lips would fall onto her breast. She would bend her knee and rest it on the chair beside him.

"Stop!" yelled the eye, and there was a sound of celluloid flickering against metal. Man Ray came out from behind the velvet cloth. "Goddamn it!" He carefully turned a knob.

Marcel sat calmly, his neck rested against the chair, head tilted upward. "Do you know how to fix it?"

"Yeah. Just a second." There was movement under the drape, muffled curses.

Elsa turned and walked up the stairs again, muscles tightening in her shins. Painters had said she had a strong back with good lines, and now Marcel had seen them. Though he claimed to be immune from that kind of beauty.

"Baroness," said Marcel. "Ready?"

She began her descent, one knee slightly brushing against the other, her hand grazing the rough banister. His face looked vulnerable, lifted up to her, but she couldn't see his eyes. The camera burned and clicked in the darkness below, to her right. Of all the times she had ever made love, this would be most perfect: art and sex from the same source.

She would kneel on the floor, unfasten his trousers. She would take him in her mouth.

"Stop!" the camera yelled. "They didn't give me proper directions. Sorry," said Man Ray. He went under the cloth, and there were more clicking sounds.

She did not have enough patience. Her heart swelled painfully like a chick pushing out of its egg. There was the rapid flickering sound again, a faint burning smell.

She looked down on Marcel, hands in his lap, thumbs impatiently circling. They were becoming bodies of light powered by shadow, their transient selves flying from one side of the frame to the other. "An awkward courtship, isn't it?" she said.

"The science is new," said Marcel. "The cameras are difficult."

"When I get to the bottom, will he still be filming?" She wanted him to say, *I'll tell him to leave then.*

"That's the only way to make a moving picture—are you losing your nerve?" he said.

"Of course not," she said. They would have to wait. Marcel liked to remind her of practicalities, and she insisted on instinct. That was the charged force between them.

"Okay!" yelled the camera. "Do it again."

The soles of her feet hit the splintered wood, and she stepped down and down. She would soon have him. He would unbutton his collar first, then his shirt, and she would press herself against him, his body slight and firm, almost exactly her size. *Long must I love it, until I myself / will become glass and everything around me glassy.*

The record stopped, but the whirring continued.

She stood before him, her skin white in the hot lights. He looked up at her, his face solemn. He rubbed the sudsy lather into the small thatch of hair between her legs, swirled it into circles. She felt herself rising, expanding. He lifted the glinting razor, set it against her a few inches below her navel. One hand cupped her buttock to hold her close and steady, and the other slowly brought the razor through the foam. She felt his breath on her abdomen, smelled the mint in his hair oil, felt the cool thinness cutting the hairs.

Her knees trembled. Shaving cream spattered against his black pants. He leaned down to tenderly rinse the razor in the bowl next to him.

She put her hand on his shoulder, felt the seam in his shirt, the knob of bone.

Laughter spurted from behind the camera. "Keep your hand steady, brother. You're shaking. You look like you need a drink."

Elsa ignored the voice, focused on Marcel's face: a closed smile, his eyelids fluttering as he brought the razor back to her skin. The expectation she felt, half shaven, almost toppled her. He picked up the towel and dried the half of her pubis that was white and smooth.

The film would flicker up out of the dark, their figures endlessly moving toward one another.

"A little more," Marcel murmured, leaning closer as he scraped the razor through the foam and hairs to the delicate skin. She felt the nick, saw the bead of blood. "I'm sorry," he muttered as he smoothed the razor through the last of the lather, dropped the razor in the bowl, now milky and flecked with hairs. He brought the towel to her, blotted the tiny cut. Her skin was exquisite with air and nerves, as if this small shape of flesh were entirely new.

"Easy there," came the voice behind the camera. "Don't leave me out of this, brother."

Marcel ran his moist hand over the silkiness, circled his finger over the bare skin.

"Brother?"

She moved away from him, lazily swaying her hips, feeling the mass of herself dissolving into light. Her arms and legs and face floated up, unhindered.

The whirring sound reminded her of insect wings, bees in a hive. They would never marry. They would never grow tired of each other—they would always breathe this white light.

She ignored the laughter behind the camera. "Let me in on it, brother," said the voice.

"Turn it off," said Marcel. His beautiful mask was gone. She walked over to the wall with the smiling flowers. He followed her, and the whirring stopped. She pulled down one corner of the sheet, and he wrapped himself and her in the worn cotton. The kiss was so violent she cut her lip on his tooth.

She heard Man Ray go up the stairs, and the door closed.

34

The poplars whispered their dreams, Marcel—
They laughed—they turned themselves
To turn themselves—they giggled—they blabbered like thineself—
They smiled WITH the sun—with the same French perusal MORBID smile
like thineself—MARCEL—

She found a glass ball that had fallen off a dresser, a doorknob or decoration, which told her that endings could be solid but uninterpretable, and the roundness gave her the poem "Buddha"—*Ah—the sun—a scarlet balloon*—which might or might not enrage the censor, depending what he knew about the fairy clubs, which signaled themselves with red lights. Who was he but a man? She found a discarded shaving brush, a torn net veil, a tin pillbox, three brass buttons, the satin heel of a lady's shoe, a wooden spoon, a broken clock, seven wiped-clean rouge pots. These objects, marked by other hands, pressed against strangers' skin, sitting silent to their conversations and sleep, needed her to speak, to reply. She was having a discussion with detritus of the city, all the cast-off exquisites. And she described Marcel: a lightbulb, electricity beaming from his head; a champagne glass, the pedestal for his wit; feathers, because he needed nestling; a glass marble, which might stay cold forever unless he was brave enough to touch her again.

Already there were rumors about the film. Someone said that Man Ray had photographed Marcel and Elsa sleeping next to one another in coffins, and someone else told her that Man Ray claimed he had been the barber. Sara thought Elsa was exaggerating when she described the film and wouldn't listen, but she said, "I'll just have to see it, won't I?" Elsa couldn't help telling a few people, though the three of them had agreed that it was best to keep their film secret, to maximize the audience's surprise. But the picture mainly belonged to Elsa and Marcel, this living memory that, meant to play over and over again, would confuse time, preserve the moment of his touching her. There would be such strange beauty there that people would not know what to call it. Later they would close their eyes, but what they remembered of the film wouldn't have the right light, and they would wonder if they could believe what they'd seen.

At Polly's, Elsa and Sara drank gin and watched the contortionist, an Arab man with a girlish face, twist his body into varying poses, with a glass balanced on his head.

Sara told Elsa about Jim's last letter. "He says when he's waiting in the trenches, he thinks about me and my parents, how he's fighting for us, and then he sings to himself 'I'd Like to See the Kaiser with a Lily in His Hand,' or tells one of his buddies about the fish in the lake where he and my father go, and his legs aren't cold and cramped anymore and it's not so bad. He always was cheerful like that—a whistler."

Elsa nodded. "The baron hummed. Even when he lost."

The contortionist sat on the stone floor in his loincloth, pretzeled his legs behind his head. His angular face seemed precariously balanced on his neck, his eyes clamped shut.

"He supposedly goes into an alternate spiritual state," said Sara. "I wonder if he hears all this gossip." She rubbed her bottom lip thoughtfully. "If I didn't have a brother like Jimmy, I wouldn't believe there were people like him in the world. I was always brooding in my room, and he would go out, a bounce in his step, talking about the sunny day, the delicious bacon for breakfast. It used to annoy me to hell."

Elsa thought of the way Josef would pull the book out of her hands and insist they go dancing, and for a moment his absence felt violent again, tangled now with Marcel's new distant manner. She had not seen him except in passing on the stairs since their moving-picture-tryst, but she was still hopeful, if impatient. "I don't always trust cheerful people," she said.

"Me neither," said Sara. "I really hope to God he's lying because he thinks it will make us feel better. When he's in the trenches, I want him to be thinking of some pretty floozy—not us. It's too bleak to consider, him lying in the dirt, remembering Ohio and his chores. The problem with Jim is that he's too good." Sara drank down her gin and decisively slammed her glass on the table. "It's useful, isn't it, to have both the God and the devil? Then one can be angry and say, 'I've got to get this demon out of me.' One can empty oneself of it. Jim needs an enemy because he has no devil inside himself."

"Perhaps he does now," said Elsa.

Sara's smile fell away, and she turned the small circular pin on her jacket. "Maybe. He has no socks anymore, he said, but the letter was from months ago. I hate to think of him in that freezing rain without any socks, all this time since January with bare feet in his boots."

Elsa took Sara's hand off the glass and held it. This was a ritual they had, cursing the forces that kept the war in place, ornately blaspheming until they crumpled up laughing. It gave them some recourse against chaos, briefly relieved them of their helplessness at all those men dying and Sara's worry that Jim would be one of them. "I'd like to wipe shit all over the Kaiser's palace and piss on Wilson's motorcar."

Sara smiled. "I'd like to fill the U-boats with farts."

They touched their glasses together.

Sara's grin was so wide one could spot the longer, uneven tooth on the side of her mouth.

Elsa took a deep drink of gin, thinking, then said, "I'd like to leave Pinky's shit in each of Wilson's hats."

She wanted to do justice to the aesthetics of *The Little Review,* to make this John Winters puzzled and intrigued. She wanted her appearance to take him by the lapels and make him pay attention. Elsa strapped the birdcage to the top of her head, Fred chirping inside it as if he were a dream she was having, visible to everyone. She wore her oilskin slicker with nothing underneath except the tin-can brassiere and striped pantaloons.

As Elsa approached the censor's office at City Hall, the crowd parted for her on the sidewalk. Since the postmaster had confiscated another batch of *The Little Review* issues and burned them, Jane and Margaret had been especially upset by the silence on the matter. No newspaper reported on the scandal. Pound wrote words of encouragement but said he preferred not to write a letter to the editor of the *Post* after all. Even Caldwell regretfully said he couldn't write editorials that criticized the censorship without jeopardizing his reputation with the newspapers. Jane went around to parties and cafés, loudly complaining about their situation and soliciting support.

Elsa could not afford to agree with Jane that the censor could not be reasoned with. She couldn't afford to sit back and chuckle at America's folly, as Marcel might be inclined to do. She had to save all her ambitions and work from being burned up in some back lot.

In the first office, a blond secretary was typing at a small, crowded desk, her back to Elsa so she didn't see her at first as Elsa marched through the half-open glass door with the sign that said JOHN WINTERS, SOCIETY FOR THE PREVENTION OF VICE.

"Excuse me!" The secretary ran behind her. "You can't go in there."

A huge desk, empty except for a quill pen and holder, loomed before a limp American flag hung on the pole in the back of the large room, which echoed emptily. The brown curtains were drawn on all the windows, and the gleaming tile floor smelled of wax. She was surprised at how slight he was in his ill-fitting gray suit, a balding man who stammered, "Who . . . are you?"

"Baroness Elsa von Freytag-Loringhoven." She noticed a pink eraser on his blotter, otherwise clean.

"I tried to stop her, Mr. Winters," said the secretary, wringing her hands. "She pushed in right past me."

Elsa was prepared to hold on to Fred's cage and run, if necessary. "I am wearing this bird on my head for a reason. You'll have to listen to me to find out."

She was counting on John Winters's curiosity, on her guess that he was probably bored at his job and would like to have a story to tell about a lady barging in with a birdcage on her head. She'd seen all the profiles of Village "eccentrics" in the newspapers, understood how certain people felt stimulated by pranks they'd never dream of doing themselves. She was willing to entertain, if that could convince him to stop and she could bring back *The Little Review,* unburned and whole.

"Miss Peet. It's all right for now." He leaned back in his chair, half smiling, folded his arms. "So tell me, is this some kind of gimmick? Did someone put you up to this? I've bought all the telephones and phonographs I need, you know."

"I am not selling."

"You're German, aren't you?"

"I'm an American citizen," she lied. "One hundred percent." Marcel would love these high jinks. But she was serious, too, and believed that the only way to get through to this John Winters was to confuse the puzzle and then jigsaw the pieces into a new order for him.

He sighed, drummed his pencil on the empty desk. "All right, so you're not selling. What do you want?"

Fred, who had been quiet up to now, began to chirp loudly over her head, and she took encouragement from it. "I am a poet, Mr. Winters. Do you know how difficult it is to write a poem?"

He frowned and leaned forward, and she noticed the wispy picture on the wall—an almost-naked angel wrapped in sheets of red, white, and blue, her eyes and mouth stern. Next to this was a silver-framed diploma.

"You may not be aware of it, Mr. Winters, but your office is responsible for burning my poems, which were published so beautifully in *The Little Review.*" She wondered what Marcel would say when he heard about this, if he'd want to talk about the myriad possibilities for birdcages or the balding pattern on Winters's head and what it might indicate about his thinking.

"If the magazine was burned, then something in it was deemed obscene." He pushed out his bottom lip, folded his hands on the desk. His suit was gray, his tie gray, as was the remaining thatch of his hair, which dulled his complexion and gave his entire being a frightening flatness.

"Absolutely nothing in it is obscene," she said. "It was only misread. Words read straight when they should have been read in the round. A postmaster, Mr. Winters, unlike you or me, might not have the education to interpret a work of literature. You attended Yale, I see."

He cleared his throat, his forehead creasing, as he glanced up at Fred, who was silent now, though she could feel him hopping from one perch to the other. "I am not well acquainted with the case, but I must ask you to leave. Miss Peet!" he called through the door. "Show the lady out." There was the film to think of, too, which needed its defense in advance, the union of Marcel and her in cosmic chemistry, his hand about to touch her, her fingers resting on his shoulder. This spurred her on. She grabbed the edge of his desk and leaned forward, Fred screeching. "You burned my poems. I find that obscene, Mr. Winters."

The secretary stood next to his desk, her hands in little fists. Winters stood up and walked over to stand with his secretary. "Let me explain something, Miss—"

"Baroness."

"Yes. Well." His voice droned as if he'd repeated these lines a thousand times. "The public must be protected from the menace of obscenities. That is my mission. There are young girls in danger of corruption, white-slavery rings, women who deserve the respect of their virtue and their honor, which is proper to their feminine natures."

Everything he said was sentimental cream puff. "So art must be ruled by a thirteen-year-old girl?" she countered.

He shook his finger at her. "The laws are there for these reasons. And, birds or no birds, the law must be upheld. It's not a frivolous matter."

"And *Ulysses* is not frivolous with its use of words either."

"*Ulysses?*" He shook his head and flicked his hand as if to repel a fly. "I do not have time for this."

"Call the police? Go ahead!"

"Miss Freytag, I won't fall for the stunt." As he got angrier, his eyes seemed to enlarge. "If I have to have you arrested, believe me, the papers won't know about it."

She imitated Marcel's coolness. "You seem like such an intelligent man, Mr. Winters. Wouldn't you like to see the intelligence of Americans expanded? Do you want to deprive them? You know, there is a difference between a piece of art and a nudie show."

Fred began to chirp enthusiastically. "All I ask"—she took the magazine from her bag and laid it on his desk—"is that you read the magazine for what it is. Then you make your decision. The editors have given up, but as a poet in these pages, I cannot afford to. Do you want to kill art, Mr. Winters?" Art was human, a friend of hers and Marcel's, who liked to laugh and had a stealthy way of appearing when he wasn't expected and disappearing just as easily, a hermaphrodite with a healthy appetite.

Fred, chirping wildly, flapped his wings against the cage. Mr. Winters and the secretary gaped at her when she unbuttoned the slicker, showed him her tomato-can brassiere. The labels were a loud red, and she'd polished the tin so it glistened. "It's not a nudie show, is it, mister?"

She wanted to laugh when the secretary covered her eyes. Winters's mouth fell open momentarily, but then he closed it and gathered himself, standing straighter. "She's off her nut," he said. "Miss Peet—you have to keep these people out of the office. I've told you, I don't know how many times, the work is confidential."

"I'm sorry, Mr. Winters," she said, wringing her hands.

He was pulling Elsa so roughly that Fred's cage came unbalanced, and she held her hand there to steady it. Fred screeched as Winters pushed them out the door and slammed it.

Elsa stood there in the echoing marble hallway, Fred silent again. There was a beefy man sitting on a bench outside a courtroom scribbling on a pad of paper. Seeing her, he stood up and tipped his hat to her, and she saw the PRESS sign on his lapel. He had a pear-shaped nose that made his face appear kind. "Interesting costume you've got there, madam. Mind if I ask you what you were doing at the Society for the Prevention of Vice?"

She pulled him around the corner, to a nook where the water fountain stood, and told him everything the censor refused to hear.

The article appeared in the *New York Sun*: BARONESS TRUMPETS VILLAGE JOURNAL CENSOR DEEMS OBSCENE

> *Poet and model Baroness Elsa von Freytag-Loringhoven was heard today at the Society for the Prevention of Vice, defending the journal whose most recent cover declares, "The Little Review is an advancing point toward which the advance guard is always advancing." This Greenwich Village purveyor of new literature has been indicted by the censor on obscenity charges, the trial to be held in December.*
>
> *The baroness, a stunning, pale-complexioned woman, has been "exiled" from her husband by the war and, when she came to America, was induced to become an artist's model by various artists. She appeared at City Hall wearing a birdcage on her head, with a live chirping canary*

inside it, a raincoat, and an unusual costume beneath made from tin cans and string. The beautiful adventuress declared that the Irishman James Joyce had written "a masterpiece," a novel called Ulysses, *which has appeared in serialized form in the journal in question. The baroness believes that the censor has banned the material only because he has not read it properly. She paid a visit to his office in order to "educate" him but said she was unsuccessful.*

Mr. Winters, the agent for the Society for the Prevention of Vice, explained that the issue in question was declared unmailable by the postmaster, not only because of the Ulysses *episode it contained but also because of the whole tone of the magazine.*

The Teutonic baroness, though, would not be cowed, declaring, "Never mind the delicate soul whose sanctimonious ideas are violated: their perfumed dresses need an airing on the clothesline. They suffer from a hatred for nakedness, for anything that steams, boils, wails, and retches."

The editors of The Little Review, *Jane Heap and Margaret Anderson, who were not previously made aware of the baroness's official visit, made this statement:* "The Little Review, *in our estimation, has provided a good answer to the censor's strictures, those too-long-upheld laws of Comstock. A good answer deserves a good question."*

35

Marool had cut out the article from *The Sun* and pinned it to her door alongside a bird feather underlining the words "Baroness Trumpets." Though he seemed to love the mettle in her that confronted the censor, he did not seem to love *her* any more than he had before. She went upstairs one night, nude under her oilskin slicker, and when she suggested they make love, he seemed afraid to touch even the sleeve or hem of her coat. It was impossible that he'd turn out in the end to be like August—he had an even more distinct *sexpsychology* than that. But she wondered if her fervor had frightened him, the way she bit at his ear and shoulders, squeezing his hand, or if he had been afraid of the force of his own need. The night of the filming, his mouth had tasted of sour wine as he'd pressed her back against the wet brick, lifting her thigh in his arm, and she thought she smelled his loneliness.

With the silence on *The Little Review*'s suppression finally broken, Jane Heap met indignant people at parties who wanted to argue for the free circulation of art, and she seemed to thrill to the speeches, despite the men who admired Joyce but considered her and Margaret "knuckleheads" for trying to publish *Ulysses* in America. Less brave than Jane, Margaret Anderson asked the Baroness, "Please, do not try to speak for us again, with or without a birdcage," but Elsa could tell by the way her smile spread around the word "birdcage" that she had enjoyed the escapade and was maybe even hopeful again.

The Arensbergs had invited a smaller crowd that night. Marcel sat in the corner playing chess with Walter. There was a young woman lying back on a chaise longue, one Frenchman kissing her feet, another rubbing her thighs, a third with his fingers nudging the top of her voile gown. Earlier in the evening, she had loudly pronounced that she wanted to lose her virginity, and the Frenchmen, all painters, vied for the opportunity. Louise Arensberg had just returned from the opera *Rigoletto* and was traipsing in and out of the kitchen, calling instructions to the cook. Sara and Jane sat on the velvet sofa cooing and stroking the weave of Sara's skirt. A week before, Sara had finally confided to Elsa that she was smitten with Jane, and she seemed surprised when Elsa said she'd known this for a long time.

Elsa, her recently hennaed hair gleaming red, wore harem pants strung with Wrigley's gum foils, and her postage-stamp beauty mark. She studied the new Brancusi sculpture that the Arensbergs had recently acquired—*Princess X*—a woman's face in the form of a phallus, eyes and mouth secreted in the smooth, gilt shaft, breasts in the place of balls. Elsa thought of the room she'd invaded in the Naples museum, the lovely platoon of male genitalia. A man suddenly stood beside her. "I like your poems." He smiled shyly, a man in a brown suit who seemed to shrink back when she returned his gaze. "It's free verse but beyond, isn't it?" He had round, moist eyes, a strict mouth, and her hunger to believe the praise threatened to muddle the clarity she'd finally found, wanting to write outcries and records. She wasn't sure poems should be pleasing anymore—that was the old way.

"What did you like?"

He cleared his throat. "Uh, the way the words run down the page so unexpectedly—the reader has to chase them." He nodded to the Brancusi. "What do you think of it?" She thought now that he had only been making conversation, that he might even be a poser, though the Arensbergs usually didn't invite artists with nothing to show for themselves.

"It's a female phallus—*Princess X* doubles one's pleasure. I wish I had one for myself."

If we can get the Baroness to recite her poems for the guests . . ." Jane was saying as Elsa walked near. She sat down on the couch next to her. Even though Sara and Jane's affair was no longer secret, Margaret and Jane still worked together at the apartment every afternoon. Sara felt guilty, she'd told Elsa. But Jane said that she couldn't think properly when she was with Margaret. Elsa felt strangely panicked whenever she saw Margaret sitting alone at a party, or looking ruefully at Jane. She knew Margaret did not want to be seen as Victorian, and so of course, she made accommodations for love, but the pain was stamped on her face.

Elsa wondered if *The Little Review* would begin to be different now, if there would be a battle for power and, if so, whose taste would win. But the festive lamplight and conversation and clinking glasses made her dismiss this worry, when she glimpsed Sara's and Jane's clasped hands beneath the drape of Sara's skirt.

"That's it," said Sara, who wore the celluloid bracelet Elsa had stolen from Woolworth's and given to her as a present. "We've been talking about a costume ball, Elsa. To raise money to make up for all the money lost to subscribers who had to be paid back after their issues were burned. Would you be willing to perform?"

Elsa didn't know why Americans were so enamored of the costume ball. It seemed the only kind of revelry with a guaranteed success and had something to do with the masks, the covering of the face, which made one drunker than the booze.

"I'd be happy to perform," Elsa said. "I've been performing for months now."

"In costume," said Jane. "What will you invent for that occasion—fireworks? Working wings?"

When Jane let down her screen of intellect, there was a zany girlishness in her. She laughed easily, and her mouth and eyes pulled apart from one another in cartoonish expressions.

"But Marcel and I have a performance already recorded." Elsa couldn't keep the secret any longer. She needed to talk about the film, nest it in reality, and she'd already given Jane the details. "Why not show the moving picture?"

Jane fingered the beads around her neck. "If it's what you say it is, the vice department would be there in a second. They'd close us down before we raised any money. Is it really that, Baroness?"

"Ask Marcel. Maybe he'll tell you." She wanted to know how he would describe it to them. She couldn't be certain, but she thought he was avoiding her now, as if she were some nincompoop who'd insist that he marry her; and even her own romantic nature annoyed her—why did he have to be the one she loved?

Walter and Marcel were still at their chess game, Marcel scratching his head, Walter scooting a piece across the board, both of them oblivious to the party, as if they were the only men in the room. Elsa wondered how they managed such concentration in the midst of all the laughter and flirtation. This was only more proof of Marcel's hard, cool surface, along with the fact that he had not spoken to her all evening. He was glass, and she was fat, yellow clay, and she was trying not to be hurt, though he'd cut her.

"Are they going to play all night?" asked Sara.

Finally Marcel stood up and walked across the room, wobbling slightly, a whiskey in his hand.

Jane tugged at the hem of his suit jacket. "Is it true what we hear about this moving picture, Marcel?" said Jane.

He dipped a match into the bowl of his pipe and sucked on the stem. "Is what true?"

"Is it as bawdy as the Baroness says it is?"

She would write the script to accompany the images, the words thought but not said. *Yet BEFORE thou lovedst the straight yellow / highways—the whirring poplars / —the fat color of clay—and thou lovedst it beyond measure!* She waited for Marcel to drop a hint—though she knew he'd only be elliptical.

"Is it Cubist? Is it Futurist?" asked the man.

Marcel pulled his pipe from his mouth. "Look at her!" Marcel said. "The Baroness is not a Futurist. She is the future." She resisted the thrill streaming up her spine. Was this a promise? Or was he only asserting her distance from him? Oddly, the more he moved away from her, the more ideas and phrases shook in her head, and the line of her desire tautened.

She sat at her dressing table, absently petting Pinky, listening to the traffic and voices outside her window, aware of her hunger, aware of her breath. When she did write, it was meaningless. So she gave it up, but the poems came again, each one wired to him in a phrase or a tone, and finally she decided to address the poem to him directly.

Love—Chemical Relationship
Un enfant français: Marcel (a futurist)
Ein Deutches kind: Elsa (a future futurist)
Poplars—sun—a long highway . . .

Lately she'd had dreams in which she was flying. Her feet would churn in the air as if she were cycling or treading water, and she rose up over sidewalks, streets, green lawns, hovering just above the heads of people, dodging the trees and roofs. It was not effortless—in the dream she could feel the muscles tense and churn in her thighs—but it was not arduous either, and there were never any pains.

The young poet who lived above the offices of *The Little Review* had given her his typewriter to use while he was away, and she set it up on the dressing table. There was something satisfying about pounding a letter with her index finger.

She studied the complicated turns of Pinky's tail, the patterns of feathers that fell to the newspapers at the bottom of Fred's cage, the white blobs over Pershing's face and the word "Garden," the smattering of face powder against the deal dresser, the gather and sway of the tapestry coat she'd hung over the closet. She looked at these things, and after a while the voice came, whispering to the back of her ear at first and then in a howl like the horn of the merchant ship as it came into the pier. These howled lines were meant to be shouted, and she denoted them by using capital letters.

She typed a good copy of her new poems for Jane Heap, picking out each letter on the machine as if choosing chocolates from a box. Outside, the snow was melting in little islands of white against the wet cement, and there was a drama between a woman who'd lost her cat somewhere on the fire escape and a man who had spotted it up near the roof. Elsa could hear their voices below her. "I would offer to climb up, miss, but I've got a bad back. I saw the tail—is it white?"

"White with orange stripes. Oh, dear."

"I would offer to climb up."

"No. I'll ask my neighbor. Or I'll put out some fish."

Sometimes while she was writing, a slip of one of these street conversations insinuated itself into a poem, and what had been fleeting and anonymous was set down in print. So much of writing was about *not* saying this, *not* saying that, the obvious crossed out, whole pages of notes not used, and then, purely by chance, a stranger's talk suddenly mattered. Unpredictably, a scrap of the world seized up and glowed.

Across the hall the illustrator's telephone rang, and no one answered it. The couple upstairs screamed at one another in Russian. Pinky trotted to the window, wagging his tail.

Days like this, empty except for work, had been pleasant with her husbands, domestically enclosed so the time felt endless, but they were happier now that she was alone, when she could court the voice, take it into her body and sleep with it, when it would tell her things she would never write but were thrilling and necessary anyway, the way it led her burning through the Wintergarten and Swinemünde, faces aflame, and her own body so electric it hummed and sped through years: a restaurant with round tables, the dull wood of August's hashish pipe, Paris alleys, Franz's mercenary eyes, the chicken-scratch dance, Josef's trousers, and his delicate knuckles, and the red mark on his cheek like a rouged kiss or a warning. She didn't want to marry Marcel, or anyone, ever again, so the voice could go on and on. The emptiness she'd feared all this time formed the windlike pressure behind it.

The other day the voice had been so quiet she had to put her ear to the dressing table to hear it, but the words came steadily marching. The sun, high and strong in the window, seemed to fade immediately to a weak orange light, when she found herself, pencil in hand, out on the fire escape, legs dangling in the air, and caught herself on the railing just in time. She'd fooled herself too well. Days later she'd stalked the voice, which hid from her and then boomed out a single word in hourly intervals. She stalked it all the way to the basement, which smelled of sewage, and among all the discarded furniture, in the rat's nest she found under a table, there was the word she had been waiting for. When she went to leave, the door was locked, and she screamed and pounded the door for two hours before anyone heard her. When she finally returned to her room, there was the rat's snout and mouth on her face in the mirror. Only after she scoured her skin with her hands did her own features emerge again.

The lost cat sidled down past her window, white paws, orange body, and the woman below said, "There, now. There, now." Elsa finished typing, pulled the paper out from the machine, which gave the poems a false sheen she didn't trust. She would lay the poems under the bed and read them again in the morning before she made changes.

When she knocked on the office door, Margaret answered, and she seemed flustered. "Oh, hello, Baroness. Come in. Forgive me. I've lost a receipt that I simply must find within the hour. And Jane is out talking to Popovitch—he overbilled us for the reproductions."

"I have poems."

The sun came through the window in a white shelf. Margaret had already turned her back and was rustling through papers on a table. "Oh," said Margaret. "Will you put them on the desk there? And will you stay for a cup of tea? If you can find something to read, I'll have it ready in a moment." Jane's paintings, which she never mentioned, were hung on the wall: a depiction of a woman getting out of a taxi, a painting of a series of blue planes like blank playing cards scattered on a tabletop. Elsa imagined she considered her real art conversation—the paintings only rushed and fragmented, angry sketches of what she wanted to say.

Elsa sat down in front of the cluttered desk—this was where Jane usually worked. She thumbed through the new books on the shelf, *Birth* by Zona Gale; *Treat 'Em Rough* by Ring Lardner; Conrad Aiken's *The Charnel Rose*—and then she idly glanced at the papers on the desk, when her own name caught her eye.

Elsa von Freytag-Loringhoven, in my opinion, has walked perilously near (if she has not passed over) the edge beyond which the vision of delirium melts into the blank self-enwrapped exaltation of trance. The psychology of the author is that of a madwoman. I feel an intense, horrid, and even beautiful obliviousness to all but the dominating emotion. . . . It is only in a condition of disease or mania that one may enjoy an absolutely exalted state, that numbness of the sensibilities toward everything outside the single inspiration. Evelyn Scott.

Who the hell was she? Another letter lay beside it.

Art cannot be written by persons who are mad—it is one of the golden rules. Elsa von Freytag-Loringhoven is to me the naked oriental making solemn gestures of indecency in the sex dance of her religion.

That note was from a Gregory Bowlin. In the back of the room, a tea-spoon clinked against a glass. Then there was the sound of liquid being poured. She found another letter beneath Bowlin's. *Dear Miss Heap. Is* The Little Review *hypnotized so it now prints the ramblings of maniacs?*

Elsa moved her folder of poems away from the letters, fingers trembling. She pushed the letters to the back of the desk and laid an open dictionary facedown on top of them. Elsa took her sheaf of poems, held them to her chest, trying not to remember how she'd almost fallen from the fire escape, how she'd almost become a rat. She brought a fist to her lips and imagined what she would say to each of the correspondents. After all, whatever madness she had in her, she'd made good use of—one could not control a poem any more than one could control thunder or wolves or spring. But their thinking was the old way, and it wasn't her job to give them a new brain.

She would read the poems again before she gave them to Jane, but she would not let Margaret touch them. She suspected that Margaret blamed her for introducing Jane to Sara, and she had never quite trusted her arch friend-liness anyway.

"You like milk and sugar, right?" Margaret said, carrying the tray over to her. When she saw where Elsa was sitting, she looked guiltily over at the desk. She set down the tray on the table next to the sofa swing. "Why don't we sit over here? There's something I want to show you." Her coif was a perfect pile of curls like brown grapes, her face powdered so white it appeared flat. She patted the seat of the sofa, and Elsa, seeing through this ruse, nonetheless moved, because she hadn't decided yet what to do in her own defense. Margaret opened the drawer of her desk and thumbed through some papers.

Elsa kept quiet, though it was difficult. She would not ask what those let-ters were doing there, so neatly arranged on the desk like doilies. If Jane were there, she might ask, but Margaret would tell her, in a fake sad voice, that yes, they had come and yes, they had to be printed, because *The Little Review* had a policy of printing every letter from its readers.

Margaret turned back around, holding an engraving. "What do you think of this? Should we use it?" Elsa had seen the original piece at 291. The reproduction depicted a painting by Man Ray—a portrait of Stieglitz, his face merged with the lens and cabinet of a camera, a man and his work. It was more camera than face, erasing the sympathetic lines around Stieglitz's mouth, the thoughtful wrinkle of his nose.

"There's so much he left out," Elsa said. "But the censor won't complain."

Margaret abruptly turned her face in a way that suggested surprise. "I rather like the statement myself." She used the silver tongs to drop a lump of sugar in her cup, then picked up a small teaspoon to stir. "The bookstores won't carry the issues anymore—except, thank God, for Washington Square Books. We need to convince them that we're worth the risk—will you ask after us when you go into a place?" She stirred so rapidly that the spoon violently clinked against the cup. "And I must ask you as a favor, Baroness—see, it's in our best interest to seem dull to him, school-marmish—to please keep your distance from Mr. Winters."

Elsa felt as if the floor were slipping away beneath her, an uncontrollable sinking, as if any moment she might fall through into the undertaker's room below her. It was the letters that had made Margaret undervalue what she'd done. "But Jane told me people have never taken as much interest as they do now."

"Yes, but talk alone won't keep us in business. There are limits."

Margaret was only a parlor anarchist, going on this way about limits. The time had come for barriers to be happily destroyed. "Well, what are they, then? I thought *The Little Review* was bent on pushing them forward."

Margaret pursed her lips so the red lines lay perfectly still.

They would print the letters, and then Margaret would throw up her hands and say, what could she do? They couldn't possibly publish any more of Elsa's poems.

"We have to be strategic in our dealings—he's not going to reward us for games." Margaret nodded to herself as she stacked the teacups, and the clink of spoon on china was unbearably loud.

Elsa thought of the game her mother had invented in the asylum, a playing board of newspaper, a lost button and a spool the pieces, how the object of the game kept changing, though her mother had not seemed to notice and didn't mind that nobody ever won.

Margaret had a duplicitous smile, her skin deceptively flawless. "This moving picture you've done with Duchamp. When will it be developed? We're considering a forecast, or a review." If the mind was a landscape the artist pioneered, the wilderness crept up quietly and suddenly in all its wildness. She loved wandering that uncharted, rocky territory, and so did Marcel. But no one would call him insane.

"I don't know yet," said Elsa.

36

S he decided to break into the office and take the letters. Who could print them if they disappeared?

Elsa knew that on Tuesday, in the afternoon, Margaret and Jane would be at the opening at Lafitte's Gallery, where Charles Demuth, one of their artists, was displaying his work. That would be a time when the alley with the fire escape would be quiet, before people began preparations for their meals or headed home from work. The side window was usually left open.

She wore her black dress, her flat black slippers. She walked past the people rushing into stores, the Patchin Place courtyard, the looming steepled clock tower. Her nerves jangly with hunger, she wondered again how easily Margaret and Jane could be convinced to go against her. She had to get into the office somehow. If the window were locked that night, it would have to be broken. She picked up a brick in a drive behind the cheese shop.

When she got to their building, there was nothing in the alley except trash and half an abandoned carriage like a small crushed house. She started up the fire escape. The most difficult part was jumping up to the first level, where there was a gap but no stairs, where, if one was escaping from a fire, one only had to fall. Stretching her arms above her as high as she could, she leaped up and grabbed the railing, heaved her torso over the landing, the waffled metal pushing the breath out of her. Just as she gained her footing, two boys ran into the alley chasing a ball.

She crouched, pushed up against the dark window, hiding from the boys.

"Where'd it go?" said one boy, swinging his bat.

"Don't know," said the other, one hand posed on the brim of his cap. He lifted a trash bin and searched behind it.

"I see some rotten fruit with green mold for you to eat."

"Sure, I'll eat it. Hah! There it is!" Both of them ran to the edge of a building, picked up the ball, and ran out of the alley.

Just then a light went on behind the window. As she leaned away from it, she realized this was the undertaker's room. Inside, on a gurney, lay a body, the flesh grayish, supernaturally still. The corpse's hair was a wiry red, the breasts spread on either side of the torso, the mottled belly sunken below white hip bones. Elsa was transfixed—one could see the lack of breath, which made the form seem neither male nor female but simply dead.

A shadow moved across the floor in the room, so Elsa climbed up, the cold metal pressing through the thin soles of her slippers, her hands raw on the railings. Through the window on the third floor, she saw a man in a kitchen, slicing onions in quick, violent thrusts. She continued to climb, hoping he wouldn't look up. She smelled cabbage cooking and, somewhere, laundry soap.

When she finally reached the third floor, books and papers pressed up against the window glass. She felt a curl of fear that either Margaret or Jane had stayed behind and was lying in the back bedroom, sniffling or reading. But there was no sign of anyone in the larger room. She knew they must have gone to Lafitte's. They went to every opening, because Margaret charmed the artists into letting them print the reproductions—and sometimes she convinced the galleries to pay for the engravings.

Elsa pushed up against the window frame, but it wouldn't budge. Glancing down at the alley, which was silent, darkening, she pulled the piece of brick from her pocket. She heard traffic out on Eighth Street, a horn, a train screeching. She bashed the brick against the glass until it cracked in a kind of sun ray, then pulled the shards away from the wooden frame, stacking them on the fire escape, until there was a space large enough for her to crawl through. As she stepped into the room, the books resting on the windowsill fell on the floor.

There was a smell of pencil dust and paper, and, in the dim silence, her aloneness was a thing suddenly solid, like a chair in the room she hadn't noticed before.

Margaret's reading glasses lay on the table next to Jane's string of beads. On the swing sofa, the velvet pillows lay piled in a mound that seemed almost animated like some kind of luxurious pet. A half-sewn blouse lay on an easy chair with a spindly pincushion. Elsa wondered if either of them had even considered telling her about the letters. She suspected that Margaret might have been false with her all along, only pretending to admire the poems. Margaret, with her dainty cigarette holder carved with flowers, which now sat on her small desk, catty-corner to the box of perfumed stationery.

Elsa turned on a light, went to Jane's desk. The poems were not in the spot where they had been. There was a compact of face powder, a tin of mints, piles of page proofs, a note from a Susan inviting Jane and Margaret to supper. Each drawer stuck slightly as she opened it. The bottom one held paper, the middle one a folder of manuscripts, the top one a silk pouch filled with auburn hair. Elsa went to the bookshelves, rifled through the papers and manuscripts, then to Margaret's desk, where she found only pencils and old issues in the slats underneath. She was frustrated, trembling. If the letters had already been sent to the printer's, she would have to go to Popovitch's and invent a story. "Jane Heap asked me to retrieve some copy." But he didn't speak English, so she'd have to find someone who spoke Armenian—maybe the grocer on Horatio. She stood in the middle of the room, walking in a circle, her heart chugging like a train. She spotted papers on the little table near the sofa swing, heard footsteps in the hallway, the creak of old floorboards. Then she spotted the letters stacked next to a half-peeled orange, her name in type that seemed larger but wasn't.

The key turned in the latch. She grabbed the letters, just as the door behind her banged open. She wheeled around and screamed.

The policeman, a large man with a hefty mustache, lunged forward, holding out his club. "Put that down, miss." He grabbed the letters, tossed them on the desk. "If you have jewels or money on your person, you'd be better off handing them over now rather than waiting for them to search you at the station."

He gripped her by the arm. She jerked away, but he grabbed her again. "I don't have anything, so let me go. The ladies who live here are my friends."

"Oh, yeah? Then why crawl through the window?" She tried to pull her arm away, but his fingers dug into the muscle. "This must be some kind of office?" he said, his eyes alighting on the sofa swing. "But what kind? What were you after there, the cash box?" He raised his eyebrows and pulled her closer to him.

"Take your goddamn paws away!" She tried to think of a reason she'd need the letters, but she didn't know how to explain the broken window. "It's a magazine, and I am one of the authors. I told you, the ladies are my friends, Anderson and Heap."

He shook his head. "I don't see any printing press." He stepped behind her, grabbing her wrists. "Let's go now." Walking behind her, holding her forearms, he pushed her forward like a wheelbarrow into the hallway. Her wrists stung in his grip, and she contemplated giving him a backward kick, but he was too close behind her.

When they got outside, she saw Margaret and Jane huddled together in the street, an aproned woman next to them pointing up at the fire escape. Jane, in her opera overcoat and top hat, took a step forward. "My God!" Margaret, in a shimmery black dress, covered her mouth with her hand.

Defeated, Elsa nodded in their direction, trying to keep her dignity. There was a paddy wagon at the curb. The policeman clicked open the lock at the back and opened the door. He pulled down a small set of stairs and pushed Elsa up into them. Jane came around calling, "Wait! We know her! Wait a minute!"

He slammed the door. Elsa could hear them talking loudly outside. She couldn't make out Jane's words, only the policeman's. "I don't know what you Villagers do—but as far as I know, a burglar is a burglar, whether you know her or not. What would your boss say, after all?"

Elsa banged on the door as the paddy wagon began to move. She imagined Jane saying to him that it was *their* home and *their* friend and, because Elsa was clearly not a burglar, it was up to *them* to decide what should be done about it. But the policeman must have been fetched somehow, by either Margaret or Jane or a neighbor.

There were two whores sitting on the bench in the back, one in a red dress and one in a purple dress who wore a blond wig that had gone askew. "What did you do?" the one in red said.

"I was trying to visit friends," Elsa said.

"Us, too," said the purple one, clearing her throat in a hack. "If you cry, and you get Judge Moore, he'll let you off," said the woman in red. "I say, cry every time."

"I don't cry," said the purple one. "I can't anymore. There's not enough tears in the world to—"

"Oh, shut up," said the other whore.

The back of the wagon rattled as it began to move forward, the wooden walls creaking. Elsa's spine pressed against the side, jostled as they went over cobblestones. "We should have avoided Gansevoort, I told you," said the red-dress prostitute.

"Silly Betty," said the other. "If they don't find you on one street, they find you on another."

Elsa heard a metallic whine and clatter at the door and looked over at the latch, where the door opened slightly, revealing a thin line of light. The brakes screeched, and it slammed shut again. The woman in purple lurched forward. "Jeez, you'd think they'd drive less rough with ladies in the back."

Elsa slipped to the end of the bench and then crouched near the latch, the appearing and disappearing vertical line of light. She had to get out. Someone had to feed Pinky and Fred, and Marcel was expecting her at eight o'clock. Besides, she couldn't stand to stay in the jail cell—the odor ate away at her brain. From behind her, she heard the woman in red's voice. "What are you doing there?"

"Shut up," said the other woman.

Elsa pressed the latch. The door opened again slightly. She squeezed her hand through the space, her wrist between the bouncing door and the wall of the wagon. She could just reach the lock outside dangling from the latch, which hung loosely on a metal ring. She lifted it, pulled it off its ring so the door fell open. She held the lock for a moment, then let it drop to the street, and pushed open the door slightly.

Behind her, one of the whores was laughing. "What is she doing?"

Holding on to a strap over the bench, Elsa poked her head and shoulders out the door.

The air and soot whisked against her face, blew back her hair. Holding the door ajar, she looked down at the street rolling beneath her. She opened the door far enough to see the automobile behind the paddy wagon.

Through the windscreen, she could make out the couple in the front seat, the woman's mouth open, the man leaning over the steering wheel. She looked down at the street, the road moving faster now. She only had to do it. She felt the push in her knees. She imagined feeling her feet hit the ground. She took a deep breath of tar-smelling air and leaped. When she hit the asphalt, her knees buckled, and she landed on her hands and twisted ankles. The automobile that had been following the wagon screeched and swerved to the other side of the street. She pushed herself up into a squat, horns honking all around her, and stepped over to the sidewalk. The police wagon went on. It turned the corner quickly, the back door banging open and shut.

She heard someone yell, "That woman! She just jumped!" Horns honked.

She ran into an alley, ducked behind some trash cans. She was shaking. She smelled potato peels and something oily. She watched a cat sidle against a building, its tail a ragged nub. She watched a milk bottle roll past a brick wall, then snag on a pipe. She was expecting police, indignant bystanders, but no one came down the alley except a staggering drunk who sang, *Nella, Nella, capturer of fellas*. Her knees throbbed. She fell back to rest on her buttocks and hands, landing in something that felt like a soft banana or shit. She sat there, hardly moving. She saw the blood soaking through her skirt, where she had cut her knee.

When she got home, there was still time before Marcel was supposed to come down to the room. She sat in front of the mirror, examined the cracked lines of her lips, the rakes of fine lines above the temples. When she moved the lamp, the light spilled around the beaded pot holder and caught on the shellac of the whistle, in the sheen of the beads. The tweed was smeared now with paint, dirt, and ink, but this somehow made the adornments more glittery and mesmerizing. Her eyes followed the design of beads around and around like a puzzle or some kind of rosary. There was beauty in the worn-ness and tears, so optimistically held together by beads and crude stitches, crosshatched and purposefully uneven. Her mother had handed the pot holder down to Elsa like a ruby ring or a set of china, and thinking it was all she had now of her, Elsa felt the creep of grief.

That night Marcel kept his distance again, and if she were to accuse him of any kind of cruelty, he'd say she was being sentimental. There was nothing more to their touching than a wheel against a track, a lever in a pulley, he'd say, and all that talk of romance was for women less intelligent than she was. She was modern and should know better than to attach any meaning to sex other than the pleasure itself.

It wasn't as if she had any rational argument against this, but she still believed he was attracted to the force of her desire for him and wished he'd admit that it was rare. He turned to her dressing table, fingered her mother's gift. "What is this?"

"Isn't it ugly?"

"Not at all! How did you make it look so old?" She wanted to draw his face close to hers, feel his breath on her cheek.

"It *is* old. My mother gave it to me."

Marcel beamed. He rubbed the tiny beads, smelled the fabric. "I find tools that are useless fascinating. They require more skill."

Fred chirped at Marcel, small bleats of curse words. *Damn! Shit!* Marcel smiled and sat on her bed, his body thin beneath loose black trousers and white shirt. "Have you found anything lately for your collection? That lever there, I don't like it anymore—I think you need to find objects that go beyond good or bad taste."

She realized that when she was with him in this mood, she felt most alone.

He said nothing. She wondered if Jane Heap had gone looking for her in the Tombs. Someone had seen the broken window and panicked, but surely Jane wouldn't have had her arrested if they'd known it was she who'd done it. She wondered if they guessed what she'd been after. Otherwise they would assume that her burglary was proof of the letter writers' accusations. She was her own worst advertisement, like those signs that promised a beautiful complexion, where the girl's face has been worn away into the underlying brick. She lifted up her skirt and showed Marcel where she had scraped her knee.

"How did you do that? Dancing?" he said.

She didn't want him to know about the letters because he might become afraid of her again. She told him she'd been trying to steal subscription checks because she needed the money. "Can't we get a patron for the moving picture, so I can pay my rent, buy some new things?"

His long noble nose lifted in the air as he tilted his head back to study the ceiling, and for a moment she thought he didn't believe her. "We can't, I'm afraid. A shame. *Cela n'a pas d'importance.* The picture was ruined in production."

"What?" Her stomach lurched.

"Our friend said the strips stuck together in the chemicals." He shrugged. "*Il n'importe pas.* It was an experiment. The technology isn't ready for us, apparently."

The film had always felt tenuous and hypothetical as long as it remained to be seen. But she was still crushed. All of that lost, her descent to him, his tending to her, that erotic climate, and the nude's transfiguration. It was as if none of it had ever happened, as if Marcel had never laid his hands on her.

"Luckily, two frames survived," he said. "You are dancing in them."

37

The *e* on the typewriter was stuck, and she realized how many words in English included that letter, the workman of the alphabet, the pest who insisted on being joined to the others. Then, in frustration, she opened the cabinet, seeing the fan of metal rods that gathered at the single hinge, and when she reached in, the ribbon caught on her finger and ripped.

There had been no poem all day, just words, but she'd been finding solace in just typing them over and over, hoping one fragment might take interest in another like a man and a woman in a dance hall, but they were all wallflowers. She'd been having problems lately hearing the voice, troubled as it was by the insults of the letter writers. She wondered if there was something she could learn from their outrage. She wanted her work to move between *inside* and *outside,* to obliterate those boundaries. Precisely because people protected them, they needed to be broken. To be permeable was human, thrilling.

A quick, curt knock on her door, and then it swung open and Sara was there, in her loose dress, her kitten eyes screwed up. "Why the hell did you burglar them?"

Pinky was barking, his little body leaned forward, tensed as if held by a spring. Elsa scooped him up in her arms to soothe him, his moist nose against her neck.

"Jane went to look for you in the jail, you know, but she's furious. I honestly don't understand why you would do it. You manage to offend every single person who might be able to help you." Sara's voice was unusually staccato, her forehead drawn together. "How did you get out anyway?"

"I jumped out of the back of the wagon."

Sara sighed in a way that let Elsa know she didn't believe her. Sara believed her less and less these days, and Elsa sometimes gave up on trying to explain herself. Reason was overvalued. One had to use words off-kilter to say *Here, try to see the connection.* Besides, she didn't know anyone who could truly explain themselves. "If you aren't going to believe me, why even ask?" Pinky jumped down from Elsa's arms and trotted over to sniff Sara's brown leather shoes.

Sara wore a peasant dress that had been home-dyed, the blue leaking out from hand-shaped spots. "Margaret said you even stole a roll of stamps once when you were there. She thinks it's a neurosis of yours, but she may not forgive you for this."

Elsa didn't remember now why she had taken the stamps, only that she could not stop her hand from reaching for them. It had something to do with what Margaret had said about Williams's poems being precisely *American*, and then the way she'd looked at Elsa as if she weren't giving them enough of herself. "The real reason she is angry is because she blames me for you." She knew it was cruel as soon as she said it, and Sara took a step back, but it was satisfying to name the thing that Jane and Sara had done, to fling it in the air like a black moth or a bat. She was not the only one whose passions had consequence.

Sara was quiet for a moment, her little mouth bunched together. "Okay, tell me why you did it. I'm listening."

Elsa picked up a rusted metal ring she'd found yesterday, some kind of plumbing fixture. It was the size of an orange, with a diamond-shaped rivet on the top like a giant wedding band. "There were some letters that attacked me. I knew they were going to be printed, and I wanted to burn them."

Sara's hair was pulled back, pieces falling in unflattering outline of her full cheeks. "Was it really only that? I thought Jane mentioned them to you."

Elsa warmed the metal between her hands and shook her head. "I found them on her desk—I don't believe they were going to tell me. They were going to let me find them when I opened the magazine—*Letters About Our Crazy Baroness*." It hurt her to even consider it.

"They think you were looking for money."

"God knows I do need it. I haven't paid the landlord all month."

Sara had thrown out all of her paintings now. If she didn't gather herself up, she would lose the rest of herself to Jane, or perform some dreary act of resignation like returning to Ohio or marrying a bore. Sara herself knew none of this, but Elsa did from the way she held her head forward, her diffident posture.

"If only you had asked about them, you would have discovered that Jane happens to be composing a long defense of your poems and your mind. She was raised next to an insane asylum—for Christ's sake, her father worked in one—she knows the difference." Sara slowly stomped over to the window and looked out. "You annoy me, do you know that?"

"Did you read the letters?"

Sara looked away. "Yes."

"And what did you think?"

Sara picked up an old sandwich from the dressing table, then dropped it. "I think you cultivate this . . . this *state*. And it gives you the poem. But you take it too far. You have to stop this. Otherwise, what's going to happen to you?"

There had been a moment all those years ago near the fireplace, when her father, stripping her mother of her wet clothes, had said something similar, and it was one of the only times Elsa could remember him being tender. She pictured her mother, walking out of the half-frozen sea, her face and arms blue with cold, then hid the image from herself the way one flings a photograph into a drawer.

"Every artist has to cultivate his state—you know that. He's the king of his own country."

"But there's a separation between the work and the life—don't you see that?"

Elsa remembered the time her mother laid her clothing down the staircase and hallway, spread forms of dresses, funnels of stockings leading to the window, where there was a view of a bird's nest with two bloody chicks. She told Elsa the cat had eaten the mother.

"For me there isn't," Elsa said. "Of course art and life cohabitate. How else can one get the necessary infusion?"

"That's just a beautiful dream," Sara said. "One can take risks in one's work that are deadly in life. God, that's what we need our work for—to get away from the everyday. Elsa, I know a dozen poets, and none of them acts the way you do."

"None of them is me," Elsa said. "I don't know how to pull life and art apart."

Sara stared at her.

"If that makes me mad, I don't want to be sane."

"Elsa, you don't mean that. You're not a lunatic. I only wish you would be more . . . more politic." She glanced at the objects in the corner. "What's all that?"

Her collection: artifacts from various alleys and the gutter. A whip of torn electrical cord, a rusted wheel, a tangle of colorful wires. A bright gold wad of foil that she was thinking about attaching to a belt.

"I'm considering these things."

"Considering what?"

Elsa went over to Fred's cage, opened the fragile little door to look in on him. His tiny eyes pierced her. "Whether there's any life in them."

Sara rubbed her chin. "I like the wheel—I suppose." She paused. "But you have got to clean up this room! It's beginning to smell."

Sara plopped herself down on the bed and crossed her legs, sighing. "And what does Marcel think of all this? I suppose he finds it amusing. Does he want you to play a burglar in his next moving picture?"

Elsa saw the lost frames, the camera following her feet, knees. Marcel, sitting in his black suit, lifting the razor so it glinted in the light. The music: horns and piano. All of it vanished, dead.

"Just behave yourself, will you?" Sara said. "Stop acting like people are against you. Do you have a cigarette?"

Elsa took two from her case, and they sat on the bed smoking in silence until Pinky came over, whimpering because he had to go out.

She wrote an apology to Margaret and Jane: *I am sorry I broke your window to get inside the office. I should have simply asked for the letters, which belong to me in the first place, though Sara has told me you hate them as much as I do.*

Please understand, like any person I wanted to protect my reputation, and I ask that they not be printed but, if they must be printed, that you at least allow me a rebuttal.

She walked up Bleecker Street in her plain shirtwaist and proper-lady hat, passed a sign that said SALLOW SKIN IS ONE OF THE GREAT FOES OF WOMANLY BEAUTY. IT CAN QUICKLY BE CORRECTED WITH BEECHAM'S PILLS. There were many foes of womanly beauty—hard, steely points that came running at you, aimed at the heart, the brain, guns that went off while one slept.

In front of the pharmacy, a writer with a scraggly black beard said, "Hello, Baroness," nodding to her, and she nodded back because she couldn't remember his name. She remembered the poetry reading where they'd met, how the dust formed swirled patterns on the floor and the poster on the wall for the International Workers of the World, a cartoon man raising his rocky fist, and how the writer had sat very straight in his chair and talked to her about elegies, musing about whether a poem mourning death had a moral imperative not to be funny. She remembered all of these things, but not his name, and he looked at her quizzically as if she should have had more to say to him, but she didn't, so she just nodded.

She was going to make a peace offering to Margaret and Jane by visiting the bookstores where she knew the owners and asking them to carry *The Little Review*. The latest issue was the one they'd dedicated to the censor, opening with the bare-breasted photograph of the Baroness in her beads, Mina Loy wearing Elsa's thermometer earrings. She thought readers were bound to take notice, and they needed only one or two powerful people to take up the cause. She would go to Francis at Book Leaves and McAdams at Charles Street Books, whom she almost considered friends. Up to this point, only Washington Square Books overtly sold copies, but a few other bookstores kept them hidden behind the counters.

At Seventh Avenue she crossed at a diagonal, making her way through a passing crowd of Italian women in dark, sacky dresses and boys in cockeyed caps. At the store that sold Victrolas, a ribbon of music ran through the open door just before it closed. The hat cleaner was crowded, a line of irritated faces near the entrance. A woman wearing a filmy veil over her bonnet came out of the perfume store and paused to button her jacket. Elsa walked past the bakery window, the breads lined up, a momentary smell of yeast and flour; past the candy store, jumbled jars of pastilles and licorice; past the cheese shop, where an aproned man carved into an orange wheel. The shops with their daily activity, their frank reply to hungers, were a comfort to her.

Why couldn't she be more practical? Even in the liberty books, the lists of good deeds every citizen could do for the war effort, she had noticed a beautiful expedience. Families were asked to save their peach pits. Across the country they accumulated in empty meat cans and candy tins, dried wooden eyes that clanked against the metal and then grew heavy. The mother would serve peach pie, peach cobbler, peach salad, and though peaches were expensive, her husband would say nothing. The children, who became sick of the sweetness, would not complain. The mother would send the peach pits to an address in Virginia, where they were ground to a paste and used to make the filters for gas masks that pressed over a soldier's mouth and nose.

Overhead the blue sky was scraped with clouds, and she heard the clamor of the train.

She would make an effort to keep a routine—breakfast, lunch, and dinner, regular walks with Pinky. She would be frugal and shrewdly ascetic like Marcel. She would wear black and gray skirts. That would make the letter writers look like liars. She could write poems at leisure, the way Marcel worked on his *Glass*, allowing the passage of time to corrupt the process. She would give up on love, which only drove one's mind in circles, and maybe she would denounce men altogether, as her mother had suggested to her years ago.

She stopped at each bookshop on Eighth Street, and each time she asked the clerk about *The Little Review*, the man shook his head and said they were careful about their stock, there was a limited readership, they were good Americans.

She went into Book Leaves, where most afternoons the owner, Francis, sat in his fishing cap, reading from old tomes, and Elsa sometimes sat in the dust talking to him about Hamsun or Shaw. She was sure she could persuade him, but when she asked if he would stock the magazine, he shook his head sadly. "I'd like to, Elsa. Honestly. I know, your poems are published there.

But I don't want any trouble. I'll keep it under the counter for people I know, all right?"

As she left the store, she spotted Mary Dryar in a stiff felt hat, coming out of the French bookshop across the street. As she looked in Elsa's direction, Elsa thought she saw a sneer.

38

They had finished dinner—lamb chops with mint-leaved pota-
toes—and now they were finishing the gin. Polly had changed the
tablecloths to a brown-and-orange calico.

Jane had avoided the subject all evening. There was a long talk on the
problems with those artists associated with Greenwich House, where immi-
grants were taught to read and the hungry were served soup and the painters
wrongly considered their paintings revolutionary. And Jane wouldn't
exactly look at her, until finally she settled in and said, "You know, Elsa, it
was a damn pain to have to get the window fixed and clean up the mess.
And, my God, we felt awful having you arrested. Couldn't you have asked
me about those letters?"

"I didn't think you would listen."

"Obviously not. I've put the entire episode behind me, but Margaret's
still furious." She traced the bright red line of her lower lip. "Do you know
what they said about all the Cubists' work? That they were pictures from
deranged minds. You needn't have taken it so seriously. An artist evoking
his consciousness at a higher power on some piece of work will of course
appear to be callous and stupid or a wild man to the layman."

Jane spoke so sensibly that Elsa felt silly now that she hadn't trusted her
to take her side. "I suppose I do go insane for a time when I write," Elsa
said. "It's like steam pressure on the teakettle. When it whistles, it's over,

but I am more sane than ever after that." Elsa did not tell her about the times when the kettle had not whistled soon enough. The other day she had accidentally sipped at a bottle of shampoo and that night found herself standing in the hallway naked except for her shoes.

"That's different," Jane said. "The people my father looked after had no real purpose—you are all purpose."

Elsa remembered her mother's room in the asylum, how clumps of blond hair lay on the dusty floor, bars on the window that checkered the light, a smell in the common room like stale cookies and sweat. "But asylums are just rooms of futility."

"I don't think so, Elsa. My father was intent on art and literature and music—it had meaning insofar as there ever is any."

Robert, a sculptor whose work had been reproduced in the last issue of *The Little Review*, joined them uninvited. His floppy dark hair veiling one eye, he ogled the women. "That one there," he said. "She has an appealing walk. And that one there, with her curls, makes me want to snuggle into her bosom."

Jane rolled her eyes. "You're boring me."

Since the incident, Margaret would not even speak to Elsa. At the opening at 291, Margaret had walked right past, and Elsa pretended not to notice. But Jane was her champion. She had written a long editor's note that said, *When a person has created a state of consciousness which is madness and adjusts (designs and executes) every form and aspect of her life to fit this state, there is no disorder anywhere*. Elsa knew that for as long as Jane cared about her, her poems would have a place in *The Little Review*. She'd promised her that. But it would still be disastrous if the magazine went bankrupt—poems like hers were not part of the marketplace but outside of it.

Tonight there was a frenzy at Polly's, something contagious in the lamb chops that had made everyone so happy. Even the surly waiter, Hippolyte Havel, had taken off his apron and joined a laughing group at a table for a drink, and there was a couple dancing ragtime to the Victrola in the corner.

Elsa was glad she had worn her pantaloons with bells, which, when she walked, made her feel like the Pied Piper, the way men followed her or smiled. She wanted to dance and would have asked Robert, but he was so bleary drunk that his body seemed collapsed in a puddle of lust. "That one there, with the cute waistline—I'd like to see her legs."

His eye was drawn by large lips, slender skirts, but he winced as he admired them, showing his teeth as if the sight of them made him angry. Julio the sculptor sat down with Jane, and she began a harangue about the overly zealous sincerity of that crowd associated with *Others*, how it kept them from seeing pieces clearly and limited her interest in their pages, not because they were bent on making American literature but because they were bent against Europe, and also too influenced by Williams, though she adored him herself. Julio listened as if she were giving him some kind of transfusion.

The crowd of "hobohemians" straggled in—the poets who usually refused to pay for a drink and always had some scheme for convincing someone else to float them. Their hats were askew, and they waved papers and bottles in the air as they headed for a table. Elsa had never seen so many of them together at one time. The burly one whose name she'd forgotten, his flannel shirt untucked over dirty pants, moved away from the door, and then Sara walked in.

Her hair hung around her plump cheeks in wild loops, and she'd badly misbuttoned her jacket, so a tail stuck up near her neck. Her face was stricken, as if part of it had been erased, her eyes strangely inward and blank. Her hands in fists, she weaved through the jumpy dancers and came around the side of the bar.

Elsa stood to go to her. She passed the quarreling poets, ignoring their slurred calls. She stumbled on the leg of a barstool and righted herself. By the time she reached Sara and saw the crumpled letter in one fist, she knew what had happened.

Elsa and Jane took Sara back to her room, where she lay facedown on the bed, the pillow wrapped over her head. After a long time, she sat up, threw a drinking glass on the floor, and cursed the president. "When he comes to New York, I'll throw dead rats at his ass and pay the drunks to piss on him." Jane smoothed back Sara's hair. Elsa took her hand, hot and trembly, in her own. There were no sufficient words, though Sara went on cursing.

Sara would not leave her room for two weeks. She lay on her bed, and Elsa and Jane brought her toast and boiled eggs and wine. At first the official announcement was that Jim had died in combat, but one of his friends had written to his mother and told her the truth. It had rained so much in the trenches at Paschendale that Jim had drowned one night, while he was asleep in the mud, his gun notched under his belly. Because of the rain, most of what the soldiers did was wait, and he had not been the only one to die this way, taking mud into his lungs. They had found sketches he'd done folded in his undershirt against his chest, a cameo of his mother in his pocket. Sara refused to go to Ohio for the funeral and said if her family wanted to see her, they would have to come to Manhattan. She would not go out, she said, until people put away "all those goddamn flags."

Elsa sat in front of the mirror at her dressing table, holding the razor. She had suffered a bout of ringworm the week before (acquired, she thought, from sharing food with Pinky), and there were patches where her hair had fallen out. She'd decided to shave it off. She ran the razor through her hair, careful at the back, where she couldn't see what she was doing, and hurriedly in the front, nicking her forehead. The hair fell in clumps into her lap as she watched her face in the mirror gradually come to a new focus—eyes huge, mouth wider, ears poking out on either side like seashells hinged to her scalp. She'd shaved away all the hennaed red, and her natural color appeared in the stubble—gray flecking the light brown.

Caldwell had sources that said the war was ending, and he wanted to go to Paris as soon as he could. In France there were places where one could go and watch beautiful men bathing, rooms one could rent without questions, and he knew a rich woman who claimed she was interested in reviving *LET-TERS*, but not in New York, which "had lost its juice."

Elsa thought of the buildings in Paris with their lacy, lingerie edges, the silver air and wide boulevards. She vaguely remembered being happy there, before Franz became so embittered and then passed the bitterness to her. The smells of pungent cheese and fruit pastry, the statue of Chopin near the Jardins du Luxembourg, a boutique where she had bought leather gloves with red buttons—all of this took on a different cast now that she loved Marcel. He had been a librarian there, which she could only barely imagine, his slim form haunting the stacks, sitting for hours behind the desk, stamping the backs of books. It seemed that could only have been another Marcel, not the one she knew. In Paris, away from the scolding finger of the censor, away from stars and stripes and eagles and the shouts of her landlord, she would feel less constantly afraid. She would be able to write without the large mouth that sometimes appeared now beside her dressing table, the tongue huge and wet like a pink seal, the lips red and wooden.

But the war had not ended, and she couldn't go anywhere for now. She had tasks to accomplish anyway, things she had to do while Sara hid in her room. First she was going to play a grand prank.

She studied her face in the mirror. The tiny hairs on her scalp wouldn't take to the henna, so she had the idea of using paint. She brushed vermilion over the dull lawn, carefully wiped the edges of her hairline with a handkerchief. Afterward she thought she looked astral, planetary.

She put on the blue dress with the *Limbswish* piece she had made. It was a curtain tassel that she had gilded silver and topped with a tin cup that she hung like a bell. She wanted to gird herself, a female soldier against the war. She slung this over her waist, and the tassel was heavy at her hip, like a gun in a holster. She tore off the shoulder of her blouse and drew in a tattoo with black ink.

Elsa had seen enough examples of the male genitalia to make her own model look passably real, despite the fact that she had not had sex for weeks. She'd bought some artist's clay and sculpted it to the best of her memory—the shape of Josef's, but with the girth of a man's she had been with in Berlin. She stood it up on the windowsill and let it harden in the sun. She wanted to disrupt the cheery-faced patriotism, to force a pause in the mindless machine that kept the war at pace, and she'd thought for a long time how to do it.

In the newspaper she'd read about the Daughters of Democracy benefit, advertised with the pretty faces of the patrons, a ribbon banner that said, TO SUPPORT THE BRAVE AMERICANS. Already she imagined reporting her performance to Sara. Though Sara was still too distraught to leave her bed, she would appreciate the novelty of Elsa's intent—taking their private cursing game to a new level, bringing it to a crowd. People didn't always know what they needed until it arrived.

On her way to the Brevoort Hotel, horns honked at her. A man, staring at her while she passed, banged his head into a lamppost. A mother covered the eyes of her two small girls. Two boys with dirt on their faces threw pebbles at her from a schoolyard, where other children pressed their faces against the fence to watch her. As they called out to her, "Lady! Lady!" their mouths squeaked. She watched their lips and tongues round into wooden spools. Long yellow yarns wound between them so they spun clockwise and counterclockwise, the yarns turned, threaded onto the black spokes of the machine, its engine wailing louder and faster every second. Afraid of getting tangled in the yellow strings spouting from the machine's mouth, she went to pull the lever. Before she could touch it, the machine screeched to a stop.

"Miss!" the schoolteacher was calling to her. "Keep away from the children."

Confused, Elsa looked at the woman's indignant, spectacled eyes, her arms gathering small shoulders close to her. A girl in a pinafore was sobbing.

Elsa turned away, shaking, and walked toward Fifth Avenue. Her legs were tired, her bare shoulder chilled, but there was something she still had to do. As she kept walking, gradually her thoughts condensed, and the trees and paved roads stopped fragmenting and remained still.

When she arrived at the hotel, a large man holding a fan of cards gaped at her and stood up from his stool when she approached the door. "It's a private party, madame."

"And I'm a guest," she said, thinking he must have assumed she was a vagrant, someone who wandered the streets in rags, though they weren't rags exactly, and that must have puzzled him.

"Do you have your invitation card?"

"I forgot it."

She could see just inside the door, two ethereal women in long gossamer gowns gliding across the floor. A waiter carried a tray of crystal goblets past a Japanese screen. Standing next to the screen's chinaberry tree, she recognized Mary Dryar in a chic green dress and tiara, squinting at the doorway. It was not the kind of party Elsa would have usually attended—wealthy society ladies and men who owned steel companies and oil concerns, their festivities minutely recorded for the newspapers.

"Why not just let a lady through?"

"Can't do that, I'm afraid." The man shrugged apologetically. She shrugged back at him and turned toward the sidewalk.

She circled the building and went through the alleyway to the other side of the hotel. She saw a maid step out of the service entrance and dump a bucket of water outside near the trash cans. When she went back inside, Elsa tried that door, but it was locked. She knocked, but no one answered.

About ten feet from the door, clouds of steam puffed from an open window. She went over and hoisted herself up on her hands to look inside. Through the vapor she saw that it was the kitchen. A big pot was boiling just below the window, and a man was stirring something liquid in a bowl.

"Hello in there!" she called to him.

He looked around the room and then saw her with a start. "Yes, ma'am."

"Can you move this stove so that I can climb in there?"

"No, I can't," he said. He returned his attention to the bowl, stirring faster. "There's a door just down the way."

She fell back into the alley, and in a few moments the service door opened. The maid stepped out. "Is anyone there?"

"Here," Elsa said.

"We're not supposed to use this door for guests, but John said this was an emergency? Are you sick? What happened to your dress?"

"Oh, it's a Poiret, a new one. I am the Baroness von Freytag-Loringhoven."

The maid took in a breath, and Elsa scooted in past her. She stood in the dingy hallway, heard the clattering in the kitchen, a woman singing, and farther down the hall she heard the tinkling laughter and muffled voices of the crowd at the party. At the end of the hallway, she found a small back staircase, which she followed to the bottom, and when she opened the door, she was in the candlelit lobby with all the guests.

The women wore lace or silk dresses, cut into low triangles at the back. The men wore black suits. Hazy landscapes in garish colors and portraits of pink-complected faces lined the walls, the frames arranged with all the grace of cars in a parking lot. Elsa took a drink from the waiter's tray. She turned one of the paintings—a sea storm—upside down.

Moving into a circle of guests, she met the Countess München, who, recognizing the name von Freytag-Loringhoven, assumed that the Baroness was acquainted with her nephew in Munich. The countess must have been farsighted, because she commented on the Baroness's ensemble as if it were one of the more outlandish designs from Paris.

Elsa went along with the charade.

"You must know the von Stickels." The countess grinned and blinked extravagantly. What was a German countess doing at a fête for the war?

"Oh, yes," the Baroness said. "Their sticks!"

"What was that, dear?" The countess had a pretty mole below her eye, like a second iris. She must have needed to demonstrate her patriotism some-how—or lose her parties and teas.

"I know them well."

"And the Baronin Freudenberg?"

"He was my first dance."

"Oh, that Lars," the countess chuckled. "We have so much to discuss, the von Leipzigs, the Baroness Fincke. Everyone's in exile, of course. Why have we not met sooner?"

The Countess München's husband stared at his wife and the Baroness, who was wiggling the *Limbswish* at her hip so it clanged back and forth.

"How amusing," said the countess.

When Elsa noticed the count's fingers twittering at his wife's shoulder, she excused herself. The countess protested, insisting that she return so they could discuss the von Struehls, who'd had such a fright since the war. Elsa walked through the crowd, the phallus in the pocket of her skirt, pressed against her thigh.

Next to a statue of a nymph, Elsa waited for the waiter to come past with his tray of drinks. The nymph's hair was festooned with bulbous flowers, and her breasts were tiny and squared off like thimbles. But her face, with its turned-down mouth and sentimental eyes, was all wrong—a nymph should smirk and wink.

There were women with feathers in their turbans, women wearing tiaras and glittering jewels.

She saw Gilbert Dixon squiring a redheaded woman to the corner. She saw a tall, gray-haired woman whom she'd met through Sara—an heiress who wanted to find an artist to sponsor but was waiting for "the right situa-tion." Two men passed by, gingerly holding their drinks, ostentatiously not staring at Elsa. People who noticed her in the crowd would stare and then quickly look away, blasé expressions pasted on their faces. It amused her how much the rich resisted expressing surprise.

There were women laughing and adjusting. They fixed the combs that held up their coifs, pulled with a thumb the strap of a gown, lifted a shoe to rebutton the latch across the ankle.

She passed by the table at the entrance and read the sign: THE DAUGHTERS OF DEMOCRACY IS AN ORGANIZATION DEVOTED TO THE SUPPORT OF AMERICAN MEN FIGHTING OVERSEAS. PLEASE MAKE YOUR DONATION. A wooden box stood waiting at the end of the table, a woman standing behind it. In the center of the room stood a five-foot-tall arrangement of roses, dyed red, white, and blue, the blossoms packed close together in horizontal stripes and finished at the top with a papier-mâché American eagle, the entire assembly resembling a miniature parade float.

The room smelled of soaps and hair pomade, cigarettes and whiskey, the music drowned in talk. One woman hissed angrily at the man next to her, his head bowed to take his punishment. A blond young woman stood before three men, turning to each one as she spoke as if they wouldn't be able to hear her if she weren't looking directly into their faces. A large woman in a peacock blue gown leaned to have her cigarette lit by a man wearing medals who seemed pleased to flick his lighter. The voices wove in the air, silken with rough strands.

Elsa stood in the middle of the room next to the patriotic sculpture of roses. A few faces turned to peer at her dress. One or two men gazed at her and shook their heads. In the corner Mary Dryar rose up on her toes and craned her head over the crowd.

Elsa knew she wouldn't have much time, that her moment had come.

She pulled out the phallus and lifted it over her head. The crowd began to hush. She turned in a circle to display it, and people stepped away from her, making room, stray bits of conversation left in the silence: "And nothing we can say——" "Susan wanted the children to go to the park." There was the delicate clink of wine goblets, a cough.

Elsa stared back. She suspected they could not quite fathom what it was yet that she held in her hand. A woman with earrings that dangled to her shoulders frowned. A long-faced man opened his mouth to a perfect O. A doll-eyed woman shook her head.

"Ladies! Ladies!" Elsa called out. "Daughters of Democracy! Here is the actual tool!"

A woman in a silver dress pressed her hands against her ears and closed her eyes. A woman wearing a black-jeweled tiara turned her back. The crowd began to murmur.

"Have a look!" Elsa said. "Imagine if every single one of your members had this member. Imagine your pleasures." She raised the phallus higher, and people backed away as if it were emitting smoke. She heard gasps and sighs.

Scraps of indignation flung up out of the murmurs. "What is that horrible thing?" "Who is she?" "Is that Louis's daughter?"

In a moment she would make her speech about the obscenity of the trenches, pocked with her curses so they'd listen. Now that she had their attention.

Her arms swimming through the crowd, Mary Dryar pulled forward. "Baroness, I'm afraid this party is closed to nonmembers. I must ask you to leave." Her toffee-colored hair gleamed in a swirled tunnel punctuated by an orange feather. Her elbow-length gloves were dotted with pearls. She wore a chic, loose silk dress, Oriental inspired. Pretty Mary Dryar was the worst person to have to contend with when one was trying to give a performance.

Elsa slowly stirred the phallus in the air, delighted that some of the people were still watching. "Think of your pleasures, ladies." Her lungs swelled as if her breath were heating up for this. "*No spinster lollypop for me / Yes we have bananas!*"

Mary Dryar turned to the people around her and said, "You've heard of the Baroness—she's famous by now. Would anyone care to escort her to the door?"

The waiter coming around the corner tripped, and a plate of sandwiches flew up in the air, cucumber disks, sausage slices, and bread triangles flung everywhere. The electric light flickered, and the Victrola crooned in the corner. *He made her love him. She didn't want to do it. She didn't want to do it.*

Mary Dryar moved closer, and Elsa gazed at her small face, the delicate, sharp nose. Elsa brought the phallus down and stroked the smooth, hooded head. In a moment she would have her say. "You want this more than anyone here, don't you, Mary?"

Mary Dryar's eyes blazed.

Elsa turned to the crowd behind her. "What looks obscene really is not, ladies. The real obscenity is hidden to us." There was something afoot in the flower arrangement, a squirrel or a bird skittering beneath the blue, as it bulged forward. Elsa's attention was drawn away by the moving roses, though she tried to focus on what she wanted to say. A few of the blue blossoms lost their heads and dropped to the floor, petals scattering. The arrangement itself shook off balance, shivered as if it might topple or explode.

Mary Dryar continued. "She's confused, our Baroness. We don't know what happened to her hair."

A portly man in a red bow tie bucked into laughter, tipping his head. A stately woman in a black dress and pearls rolled her eyes and turned her back. The crowd grew louder as more people came to look at her, and she felt suddenly trapped and hot. As she turned, the faces blurred into squashed pieces of flesh, rictuses of screams and laughter. She had to say what she'd come to say, though she was having difficulty remembering it, and it had to be ardent and clear. She had to modulate her voice.

The smell of a burning electrical wire came from the flower arrangement, a low, thin hum. The arrangement tilted forward, as if something pressed behind it.

"This woman wants to throw me out of here," Elsa said. "Because she's afraid of the truth."

From behind the display of roses, a sweep of skirt, a cough, and then gradually Elsa's mother appeared, laughing, wet hair plastered to the sides of her face, ice sequining her dress. A single icicle hung from her earlobe to her neck. Her face was chapped and blue. Elsa dropped the phallus on the floor and began to tremble, suddenly very cold. Though her mother's eyes were invisible behind black swaths of felt eyelashes, her mouth moved purposefully. "Go away," Elsa murmured. "Not now." People stood around her screaming, but she heard only garbled noise. She covered her ears, just as two men took either of her arms, as if beginning some kind of folk dance, and they turned her around and led her to the door.

39

A few days later, Sara finally got out of bed and left her room. She'd heard about Elsa's escapade at the Daughters of Democracy benefit, even before Elsa had a chance to tell her, and now she was more quiet than usual. On their way to Polly's Restaurant, she moved in an overly careful way, as if afraid of falling.

Polly's was nearly empty, and they sat down at the corner table near the fireplace. "At least I disrupted their toilet-water-stinking pretty benefit," said Elsa. "The ladies were shocked." She smiled, remembering one who dropped her punch glass, splashing red on her yellow gown. "Appalled."

Sara's black dress was frayed at the collar, a small cigarette hole in her sleeve. "Of course they were. All I hear these days is talk about the penis you sculpted and whose it might be modeled upon, and how Mary Dryar slapped you in the face." Her voice was sharp, but Elsa didn't understand why she was angry.

"That woman hates me because she's afraid I'm the one Marcel loves."

Sara threw her fork down on the table. "Why do you have to act like you're in the circus, Elsa? You know, sometimes it's not very easy to stand by a person who spends her time thinking of ways to get people's goat. I don't care what you look like, but I wish you'd think for just five minutes before you wrecked your chances at getting patrons—and maybe even mine, too."

Elsa was stung. She'd thought Sara, of all people, would have understood her intentions, and though the hallucination of her mother had so shaken her she had not been able to finish her speech, she had nonetheless believed that she'd done some good there—that the matrons would reconsider before they bought more Liberty Bonds. "I did it for Jim," Elsa said.

"Jim!" Sara groaned, then laughed. "Jim! Do you know how much he would have hated that? He's from Ohio, for Christ's sake! He would have taken one look at you and run the other way."

Jittery, Elsa took the salt and pepper shakers in each of her hands and juggled them back and forth on the table. She kept her hands moving so as not to feel hurt. Ordinary language failed in cases like that, didn't Sara know? One had to use a slant tactic, not the same words used in war slogans. "But don't you think it was the most electrifying protest? If only you had seen it."

Sara shook her head. "No, Elsa. No one saw a protest."

Purposeless. Her father had accused her of it as she lay in the tree tracing the grain of the bark or stood by the window watching the shiver of the leaves. She tried to swallow her meat but choked on it.

"People saw a male sexual organ in your hand," Sara went on. "That's all. No message. And if you don't stop, it's going to ruin all your chances, because people will misread the poems."

"If they don't know how to read, that's their problem." The ideal reader would see the map of thought, the rivers and byways, the places where she'd been lost and the landmarks that oriented her wandering. "But once I had the idea, Sara, do you understand? I had to do it—to see what might happen, see the trouble thrown back at me. I saw the announcement in the newspaper, and from that moment on, there was nothing else I could do. I had to act."

"Malarkey! They escorted you out of the building, didn't they?"

"Yes, but they weren't talking anymore about the war effort—by the time I left."

"No, they talked about how you were crazy."

The word stung, but only for a moment, because she had known what she was doing until the apparition of her mother had appeared. "If it were genius I displayed, they wouldn't even recognize it."

Sara blew out a sigh. "You don't give a damn what they recognize. That's the problem. As long as you have your *purity*."

Sara, sitting across the table, touching her throat, seemed very far away. Elsa could only look at her face. It seemed it would take years to be able to cross the flat wood plane of that table.

In the blank afternoons, Elsa put on her coal-scuttle hat and walked Pinky in scalloped lines through Washington Square. Now and then someone would recognize her and call out her name, but she often ignored them because it took so long to cultivate a work-worthy solitude, and she'd pull Pinky through the winding paths. Her poems appeared again in *The Little Review*, and Jane sent on the letters that praised her. They said she'd completely broken with the past, that she'd found a way to take words down from the planets and stars, but the praise sounded false to her, and tepid, and posed certain dangers.

Man Ray's photographs of her had been a success. George Biddle and Robert Henri had called on her to pose, and she earned enough money to pay rent through March.

On painfully quiet nights, she went to Jud's and gave one of her performances—new poems delivered in growls and shouts, Fred accompanying her, his cage worn either as a headdress or as a pendant to a necklace. The regulars tolerated her because she was entertaining, and even with her bald head and dresses strung with garbage, she picked out a lover now and again. She wanted to give up men, but sometimes she couldn't help herself.

In the mornings she slept or tried to conjure the voice back. She could not levitate to the words then, because someone was always shouting or cooking cabbage, singing and walking down the hallway. The grassy smell of mold, the torn striped wallpaper, and the tin ceiling pressed toward her, and there were no words for any of this—it resisted words. The mouth appeared, mocking her, teeth white and square around the wagging tongue, and she put her head inside it, stared all the way back to the maroon throat and mammary tonsils.

Elsa walked past the white of the Biltmore Hotel, where a crowd had gathered near the entrance, young people carrying books and women in outlandish hats with garish feathers and openmouthed flowers, men in gray suits without overcoats now that it was warm again, all of them waiting for a famous actress apparently, or maybe Isadora Duncan, who had recently danced at the Metropolitan Opera House wearing a flag that she removed in the end—the wrong use of eros, Elsa thought, too pat and entertaining, even if one ignored the nod to recruitment.

She kept walking, past the knife grinder's cart that moved slowly, waiting for people to flock out of the buildings with scissors and knives flashing for him to sharpen. The automobiles went around the cart, and the horse moved lazily, blinking at the exhaust.

When she neared her building, she saw him standing on the side of the street, his red hair and beard ghosting out of the past. She felt something sandpapery in her throat because of the way Barney Fitch looked, officious gray hat and suit coat. Here he was, still pursuing her as if she were owed to him, though surely she looked less valuable to him now with her head shaven. Her legs worked reluctantly.

As she approached, she saw his eyes go wide. "What happened to your hair?"

"What does it look like?" She was glad to see that her hairlessness frightened him.

"Are you ill?"

"That's a matter of opinion." Pinky strained on the leash, barked frantically, his tiny body quivering. Barney stood there looking at her in a strangely pious way. He shouted over the barking, "I have something to tell you!"

Men like Barney were good at fooling themselves—he still believed he was the one who could save her. "Whatever arrangement you made with Josef doesn't concern me," she said. "Why are you here? I don't want you to be here."

Barney swallowed, his red eyebrows bald at their ends so they resembled two short rust marks. He took her arm, still shouting, "Elsa, be quiet!"

She wanted to ignore him, but the imbalance in his face made her listen. There was something so odd about his expression, puzzlingly lopsided.

She led him up the dingy hallway, where someone had spilled an oily substance on the stairs. She opened the door to her room, watched his eyes register the decrepit furniture, the peeling wallpaper, the crack in the window, the jumble of papers on the floor. She did not want him to sit anywhere that might make her remember his presence later, so she stood by the window, holding Pinky in her arms, petting his bristly fur. "What is it, Barney?"

He blinked rapidly a few times and began to say something but stopped. His suit was tight at the waist, his body a bulging apple beneath it, and he wore a ridiculous green tie. "Why are you here, Barney? I don't want you to be here."

"Josef is dead." Only in the silence that rang out after the words did she fully understand him. "The letter came from his brother yesterday—they found my address in his business papers."

She meant to ask what happened, but there was a rush of Josef—his smell, his hands on her face, the way he said American words like "sizzled," and how much she'd hated him for the false sightings on the street.

"No one knew where he'd been this past year because he was captured by the French when he tried to cross the border. They finally let him go when they figured out he couldn't help them. The family had been expecting him to come home. He hanged himself in a hotel room. He was in Switzerland."

Barney's eyes were slow and unblinking in a way she hated, his cheeks pouched over his beard. "Switzerland?" she said.

Looking down at the grain of Pinky's fur, she remembered how tall Josef had seemed at first, how he'd made her laugh. *Calm down,* he would say to her now. Barney cleared his throat. Her vision blurred, and he suddenly appeared shorter, his beard a hundred pinkish worms. "What was your arrangement with him?"

He shook his head. "A small thing—he had some silver hidden in his shoes and in the lining of his trunk."

"Why did you think it would be easy to have me?"

He took a step away from her, shaking his head.

She felt a swell of nausea. "He never pimped me to you, did he?"

"Of course not."

She looked down at her shoes, the leather cracked and worn. Josef had left, so fleet-footed and sure of his own luck, pulling her into that closet on the ship, his breath on her neck, hand between her legs. "His father would have blackmailed him into the military, isn't that right?"

She stared again at her shoes, the patent leather scuffed to blue patches. She'd worn these shoes the night she and Josef had gone for a drink in five

different nightclubs and played the game when they each had to reveal a
secret before finishing the glass. She'd had on those shoes the night he'd told
her she had a laugh like rain.

Barney's voice returned to its even cadence, which sounded derangedly
content. "I think the family believes he betrayed them, that the French
forced him to reveal information. Who could blame him? You can't imagine
what they do to prisoners of war." His pretense at knowing Josef started the
anger growling in her. She knew Josef down to the hairs in his crotch, his
snoring, fruits that disagreed with his stomach, ties that suited his eyes,
books that bored him, the taste of his mouth. "Get out," she said.

"I want to help you." She heard him rustling in his pocket. *Calm down,*
she heard Josef saying to her, but her heart, expanded in her chest, was a
painful fist.

"I'll start to scream."

"Elsa, please. You can't be alone here."

Josef linking his arm in hers, Josef's hands on her face. Josef's feet dan-
gling near a strange bed. She heard the door slam, and she fell back against
the window, her throat burning.

Outside, from the street, objects serenaded. A tin can, crushed by the
wheel of a truck, beets still leaking from the seams. Its shape was an uneven
oval, not quite an eye, not quite an egg. It wanted her to save it, take it up to
her room and study it. There was a thin scrap of wood, broken unevenly at
the top, waiting for her on the lid of a garbage can. The wood had chipped
along its grain in delicate and precise serrations that looked deliberate but
weren't, a shape like the top of the Woolworth Building, the cathedral that
absolved her of all her mistakes, all her pessimisms. The objects needed her.
She stood by the window for an hour, thinking about them, until the news,
in painful intervals, returned.

Later that day she went up the stairs, running her hand along the dusty ban-
ister, an explosion of pale yellow mold on the landing. Marcel was suddenly
the one person she wanted to tell. He would keep her focused on the practical:
a dinner of spaghetti, sleep helped along with red wine. He would offer some
witticism about why someone would hang himself rather than use poison or
a gun, and it would show her how to detach herself. Perhaps this could work

retroactively, erase her suffering. Marcel's policy of staying apart from the world now seemed as sensible as locking one's doors at night against the murderers and thieves. The problem was, she didn't know how to detach herself from the world and all its flowers and garbage, its storms, chimneys, crowds, and moths. She'd fled her room, populated by a hundred of Josef's faces—in the mirror, on the pillow, peering out from under the bed.

She pounded on Marcel's door. She heard his scratchy Victrola, footsteps, which might have been coming from another studio. She pounded again.

Finally the door opened. Mary Dryar, her hair lank, her sweater half unbuttoned. "What is it?"

"Is he here?" Elsa walked past her into the room. There were wine bottles on the floor, ashtrays full of cigarette butts, the Murphy bed down, a swirl of sheets.

She felt her heart thinly beating. As she stepped to the center of the room, the window light caught on the *Glass*. There were the spare, cunning hieroglyphic marks. There was the female figure like the bottom half of an insect penciled on the cold surface, opaque with sun glare. The painstaking, precise lines of paint. Outside, a jackhammer cackled.

"Marcel went out." Mary Dryar backed away toward the window. "You haven't got that awful thing with you, do you?"

That night after the film Marcel had said . . . what? "I must respect the nude," as he pulled her closer—just another of his witty remarks, but at the time it sounded sincere, his skin startlingly soft as he held her there against him.

There was the drone and screech of automobiles. Elsa grabbed the bottle and swung it overhead, red wine trailing from the lip as she brought it down against his *Glass*. The *Glass* cracked, held a moment between the sawhorses, then shattered in glittering pieces at her feet, one long shard at the top of the pile.

40

Jud's was quiet that night, a table of men playing cards, the bartender Timothy wiping glasses, studying each one before he stacked it on the shelf behind him. She sat down, wearing her dress appliquéd with newspaper scraps and the cap with four different feathers and a spool. She ordered a whiskey.

Timothy didn't argue with her anymore and took out a glass and poured. She'd discovered he was a German, too, but had pulled away the leaves of his accent and changed his last name from Schein to Shin. Sometimes they talked about music.

He set down the glass in front of her, and the whiskey splashed up around the edges. "You can go ahead tonight," he said. "But if they don't like it, stop. Don't chase away the customers."

"I am not in the mood tonight anyway," she said, lighting a cigarette. He nodded and went to the end of the bar to serve a man. There was a bowl of goldfish behind the bar that had not been there before, and she watched the bright orange flick of their tails. Perhaps she would be more free now, a nun for the sake of her art, all desire trained upward. She heard the *Glass* cracking again, felt the weight of it crashing to the floor.

When Sara happened to stop by the night after Barney delivered his news, Elsa had put on the trousers and shirt that Josef had left behind. She'd unraveled the hem in the shirt and was trying to tear off the cuffs.

"What are you doing?" Sara said.

Then Elsa told her about Josef, finally ripping off the right cuff.

"I'm sorry," Sara said, grabbing her hand. "Too many things like this happen, without any reason."

"And I broke Marcel's *Glass*."

"No you didn't."

Elsa didn't have the energy to convince her. She began to work at the other cuff.

Elsa had run down to her room after Mary Dryar screamed and later heard Mary Dryar yelling to Marcel as he ascended the stairs.

Now it was the next evening, and she still had not spoken to him. She asked Timothy for another whiskey.

A little later someone came and sat on the stool next to hers. He was a British man with an easy smile, crooked teeth she could not stop studying. He had been in the navy, he told her, but had been wounded in an accident and discharged, and he had come to New York as a "seaman."

"I met a man at a pub one day, and the next thing I knew I was here. How did you come to New York?"

"I married a thief, though I didn't know it at the time. He disappeared, and so now I'm stuck."

"You're stuck, all right," he said, laughing, too, and drinking. He had dark eyebrows that streaked across a narrow forehead and red lips that looked almost triangular. She couldn't help thinking about how he would take her to bed, hands scurrying for buttons.

Though she wanted to resist, she felt herself leaning toward him, studied the pattern of stubble on his chin. Certain oval-shaped faces, when she lowered her eyes in the dark, could become Marcel's. Others couldn't. She didn't know which kind his was yet. "I like seamen *and* semen," she said. He laughed and clapped his arm over her shoulder. His eyes were the color of hay. In the dark, if she kept her hands on his hard shoulders, it would not matter so much what he said to her.

The bartender poured them both another whiskey. "I like the way you talk," she said. "All British men sound like gentlemen."

"We do, do we?" He tickled the top of her arm with his finger, purling up a shiver. "I'm leaving tomorrow for the Canary Islands. But there's a place I could show you." She could not refuse him. She was too lonely.

When they left the chophouse, Eighth Avenue sloped, and she caught herself just before she tripped on a stone. He did not offer his arm to steady her. He was pretending not to notice that she was drunk.

"Just this way," he said. They turned a corner into an alley. There was a pleasant smell of orange peels, laughter through the windows above them, the clanging of pots.

"Wherever we go, I'd like another whiskey and two more cigarettes." She paused to look at a broken-down piano standing there with the trash. Half its keys were missing, but the wood frame gleamed. She bent to touch the curled letters, *Steinway*.

Something slammed into her stomach. An animal. A mallet. She stood up, looked around her, reached out for him.

He hit her again. She fell back onto a pile of boxes, and her head pounded against a brick. The lid of a trash can clattered.

He knelt over her, his chin and chest suddenly larger, and slapped her face. "I told you you were stuck," he said, unfastening his pants. She wanted to kick him, but her legs were as wobbly as trees in watery reflection.

He pushed up her skirt, tore off her garters. She spit in his face, and he thrust inside her. Her buttocks pressed against sharp tin, the edge of something broken. He pinned down her shoulders, and when she reared up against him, she couldn't breathe.

She lurched up and spit again. She studied the gleam of it running down his temple. "Get off me," she said, and his knuckles pounded her in the brow.

When she could see again, he was yanking the paste jewels from her neck, four strands of them, and then wriggling off the celluloid bracelets. He looked in her bag, fished out a couple of dollars, and threw it on the ground. His pants were still open at the crotch, his belt buckle clanging loose against his leg.

She wanted to kick him, but she couldn't move. He took out a knife, wiped each side on his pants. She could barely make out the body and hand that carried it toward her in the dark, silver and sharp, choosing her like an arrow in a diagram.

The cool metal pressed at her throat.

"You're not going to touch me, *blöde Kuh*," she said, in a voice that startled her. She heard a ship's horn in the distance, languorous and nasal.

He put away the knife, stood up again, and walked off. His laughter echoed down the alley.

There was a heavy smell of roses.

In the hospital room, iron beds on either side of her, green sheets or white sheets on the beds. Hourly, the nurses came in with a stack of bandages.

She went over to the window, barefoot, sore, and watched a parade of recruits, late to the war, the marching band's shiny tuba like a bright sea creature and the silver flutes winking in sunlight to the offbeats of the drum.

"Come back here, Miss Freytag." That was the nurse with the face of a kind fish.

"I am not a 'Miss.'" She clung to the window, watching the ladies who followed the soldiers, waving flowers and smiling. The uniforms looked snug and square on the young men's bodies, their faces clean. She could hear the bouncy music, the soldiers' legs snapping to cheerful rhythm.

"Come back here, then, Mrs. You are not being a very good patient—*that* I know."

"I'm not patient," Elsa said. The man's smell came back to her, the acrid breath and sharp odor of his armpits.

The old woman in the bed next to hers wept constantly. The other woman had had her appendix out and warily watched the doctors and nurses as if afraid they might take out something else that she needed.

Elsa's ribs were bruised. The left half of her face was raw. Deep, pear-shaped bruises mottled her arms and legs. And there was a secret bleeding, an ebbing away of herself from a source she couldn't pinpoint.

She lay under crisp sheets, staring at the white ceiling, now and then writing down a single word on the scrap of paper next to her bed—*storm, girl*. She concentrated on the joke that he'd thought her Woolworth jewels were valuable, pictured the pawnshop owner laughing when he tried to sell them. The nurses gave her hot milk and stewed potatoes.

The doctor had curly black hair and eyes like burning coals. He said there were no broken bones, only a sprained arm and lacerations they wanted to watch.

On the second day he came to examine her, he wanted to draw blood. When he asked her a list of questions about her history, she told him about the syphilis. She thought he would give her mercury pills, and then the visions might subside.

He stepped back a few inches and looked at her again, lying in the bed. "Have you been experiencing any unusual pain?"

She grinned. "Have you taken a look at me, Doctor?" She felt the sharp gouges in her back, and when she closed her eyes for a moment, saw the fist coming toward her.

The doctor touched her arm. "I mean before the incident." His voice sounded cruelly disinterested, but his face was kind.

"When I walk, it's in my bones sometimes, sharp little stings and pricks like ant bites."

He had a delicate nose, a tiny tip, palely flared nostrils. "It's likely the symptoms are recurring. You were treated with mercury?"

"Yes, yes. So many years ago. I was a girl, and they cured me." She had the sense that if she acted annoyed, then it would be true, that syphilitic blood thinned at the sign of anger. "Do you have those little blue pills for me?"

"I'm afraid at this stage they won't do much good." He stared at her a moment, then wrote something down. "Baroness Freytag, you must try to answer me as honestly as you can. Have you experienced any false vision, or have you heard voices?"

A small thing leaped between her heart and her throat. She looked at the blank white walls, at the almost imperceptible egg of pale green beneath the paint. She wondered what he would say if she told him the truth, if he'd begin talking about sending her "someplace safe." "I'm a poet, Doctor. I often have visions. Writing into the night. Calls from the moon."

His face was smooth shaven, a very pale olive color, and she wanted to touch his cheek, feel its texture, the slight oiliness and warmth. "Not that. Hallucinations. Ghosts."

If there were no good pills, then he couldn't do anything for her. Her mind was hers to hold. "I'm not crazy, if that is your insinuation," she said. "I was beat up, fair and square. I didn't invent this."

"Yes, well, then. The disease doesn't always progress that way." He looked relieved, smiled, and patted her arm. "Try to rest." He turned and went to the old woman's bed.

Sara, arriving with Jane, had smuggled Pinky into the hospital inside a hatbox.

"What happened, Frying Pan?"

Pinky clamored out of the box, his paws scratching the cardboard, and landed on her lap, licking at her neck. "In the bar he looked handsome, and, I don't know, I was feeling spunky." The old woman who'd been given morphine, started to sing. *They're all in the old trees now, Harry and Jerry and Simpson and Sue.*

Jane, who drew into herself under her coat, said, "Do you have to listen to her all day?"

Sara's skin seemed awkwardly stretched away from her features. "Didn't I tell you to stick to our places?"

"He suffered for it, believe me." She had to give herself something. Jane cocked her head, and on Sara's face there was a slight tremor of a smile. "I kicked him in the balls, and I was wearing my heels." The smell of the hospital made her desperate to brag, to remember how her body had felt before it hurt.

"Well." Jane put a box of candy on the nightstand. "I'm sure you gave the fellow what he deserved, but now we're concerned for you. Are you in terrible pain? What does the doctor say about when you can leave this place? We still want you to perform at the hall—one of these chophouse performances you've been keeping secret from us. Sara's going to make the posters. So we want you to get well as soon as possible."

Elsa worked at Pinky's fur, looking for ticks. It was hard to believe there were any in the city, but she'd found one on his neck just last week. His huge eyes stayed fixed on her face, patient.

Sara drew the curtain around Elsa's bed. "I didn't even know about these performances until Caldwell told me. Why Jud's?"

"It's nicely located, just down the block. I can go whenever the inspiration hits me."

"When are you going to learn, you're not a boxer or a longshoreman?" Sara said. Her face was more timid since Jim had died, her eyes smaller and less bright, her mouth pale.

"I kicked him where he was softest—I told you."

Sara sighed, adjusting the blanket at the edge of the bed. "I never said you didn't."

"We've begun the announcements," Jane said. "Peggy donated the liquor. Robert knows a band."

Elsa nodded, a stinging in her eyes. She'd get away from the memory of that weight on her, the blows against her ribs. But even with Jane and Sara, she felt tiny and invisible in this bed, exiled from the world as punishment for not being able to detach herself. She heard the creaking wheels of the nurse's little cart, the clink of glasses and syringes. There was a smell of rubbing alcohol even in the food they served.

"How are they treating you here?" said Jane. She looked bulky and uncomfortable in all the white efficiency.

"The doctor is handsome. The nurses think I'm contaminated."

With a whoosh the curtain pulled aside, and the nurse, sounding an alarm with her voice, said, "Get that dog out of here."

Pinky barked, and suddenly there were ten nurses screaming about the dog. Elsa watched Sara stuff Pinky back inside the box. Jane protested, "But you see he's just a little dog. We thought he might cheer up the patient." They hurried out, Sara and Jane waving, Pinky barking, only his snout visible above the cardboard.

There were irises that Caldwell had brought on the nightstand, a notebook and pencil, where she had written, *life's beggar truth*. Caldwell had scolded her for choosing the wrong sort of man, but halfheartedly, because he knew how difficult it was to see a man's character in the dark. Mainly he'd tried to make her laugh. He told her what Jane had said about the writer Robert McAlmon, calling him "an epileptic without enough gumption to have fits." And then about the night he'd spent at the Arensbergs', when a drunk Frenchman, whom nobody seemed to know, mistook the staircase for the lavatory and urinated down the carpet runner. While she was still laughing, he squeezed her arm and said, "Seriously, Elsa. Think about it—a minute or two of pleasure—what's it really worth?"

She did not expect Marcel to come at all. "The *Glass* saves me by virtue of its transparency," he'd told her. He'd made a hundred diagrams of his plans but wanted to wait to work them out slowly. He had so much patience. This was the reward for his denial: the passing of time itself a pleasure. She saw again the cracks fissuring the *Glass*. Marcel's carefully calibrated marks fragmented on the floor. She wouldn't blame him if he never forgave her.

When Marcel came to see her on the third day, wearing a black suit and starched white shirt, his hair gleaming, he was smiling. He brought her a pair of dice, and the two of them took turns tossing the cubes against the green-tiled floor.

"Who did this to you?" he said, polishing the dice with his shirttail.

"Oh, one of my acolytes." She didn't want his pity. "I told him I wanted a little pain, but he could not restrain himself. I should have taken the branch to his back." What was wrong with being alone? There wasn't any reason her passion had to go wrinkled and flabby without him.

Marcel didn't smile. He handed her the dice. She blew on them in her hand until the marble was warm, then flung out her palm and followed the rattle on the floor. A two and a three.

"The mechanical theory of sex," he said. "It doesn't usually work for women. Didn't I warn you?"

"Who said it was mechanical?"

Marcel got up from the bed, drew the curtains closed, and traced a finger along the iron beam that held them up. He stood very close to the bed. She could smell the cold spring air on his clothes.

"The baron died," she said. "He hanged himself."

She waited for Marcel's joke. The picture of it in her mind was absurd—the feet dangling above the floor, one shoe fallen off, the lucky blue charm in the trouser pocket.

He said nothing and stood there looking her over.

"I wanted to tell you," she said. "And when you weren't there, I broke the *Glass*." She did not know what else to say.

He pursed his lips, and she studied the angles of his face, the lovely bump on his nose. "I suppose I am grateful to him, then. As it happened, the old *Glass* was exhausted. I needed a new one all along."

She pulled the covers down, exposed the ugly flowers on the hospital gown. The nurses whispered together beyond the curtain, and she smelled the gluey stew they were about to ask her to eat. At first she thought she saw water welling in his eyes, but when he turned his head, she saw it was a trick of light.

"Amazing," she said. "Even now there's not a hair out of place, not a tremor in your voice. What would it take, Marcel? How much would it cost you to show that you cared at all?"

He fixed his eyes on her.

"What are you made of?"

He sighed. "One has to choose—either liberty or restraint." For once his lips weren't shadowed by a smile. "I want to remain in myself, do you understand? I refuse all kinds of things—meat, parties, cognacs, marzipan. If I refuse you, too, who is to say I didn't want you?" He seemed deflated after he said this.

"You don't have to refuse." Busy shadows moved beyond the curtain.

"But I do, Elsa." He touched the curtain railing, wrapped his fingers around it, swung forward slightly. She wondered how much longer she would have to love him.

41

Elsa walked past the USA Sugar Company, past the hotels and piers, where men were unloading cargo from a ship. She turned and walked up Christopher Street, past the flower shop, the grocery. There was a group of black-clad Italian women gossiping on a stoop, their voices low and musical. A red-haired woman in a yellow dress came toward her, walking in a half-tripping, half-dancing way, a book tucked under her elbow. Elsa looked past her at the flowers sprouting out of a window box, loud and hysterical, purple and red protrusions.

She walked all the way to the Seventh Avenue train station, went up the platform steps, and stood on the wooden planks, listening for the train. Two women stood beside her, talking excitedly about buttons. "If they're too large, they look cheap—and they make your torso look puny."

"If they're too small, Liz, then I can't get my fingers to do them all, especially if I'm in a hurry."

"Smaller is always more elegant," the other woman muttered.

They looked suspiciously at Elsa in her ratty old fur coat, the hem stained where Pinky had peed on it. She knew she looked haggard and sick, a bruise like an eggplant still on her temple, her eyes rheumy and veined as an old woman's. But she didn't care. Elsa walked to the other side of the platform. The wood began to shiver under the soles of her shoes. She leaned over the edge, studied the boards laddering all the way into the distance, the parallel metal tracks where a rat skittered just under the partition that curved. Last week a woman had laid herself down there, folded her arms, and waited for the train. The papers said her husband had left her for another woman. The train squealed a few blocks away. Elsa felt the sorrow of gravity pulling her, her feet precarious on the platform.

She thought of all that time Josef had been imprisoned. She wondered what he'd eaten, if he'd had to sleep on a cement floor or if they'd given him a cot. She wondered if they'd beaten him to get information he didn't have, and if he'd had to lie to save himself. At what moment had he decided it wasn't worth it to return? He'd seen the war and perhaps couldn't imagine going even closer to it, as he would have had to do. And how else to respond except with an act of negation, subtraction?

When the world went mad, one had to turn one's head away and refuse. The day after her mother had tried to drown herself, Elsa was afraid to leave her room, afraid of the next day's chirping birds and sunlight, which would confirm what she already knew—that her mother was becoming not-her-mother. Elsa understood now why her mother hadn't seemed sorry—there were times when *No* was the only way to answer.

The train wheeled to a stop in front of her. Doors swung open, people rushing onto the platform, their faces desperately in search of the place they wanted to go.

There were so many words to get down. She did not leave her room, her hunger sated by crackers and water. She and Pinky used the window box for a toilet, dropping the contents each night into the alley. Unbathed, she began to smell floury and sweet, of salt and milk. It was her own smell, and she did not mind it.

Sara knocked on the door and called to her, "Frying Pan, you there? I hear you, I think. Come on, answer." Pinky barked, jumped at the door. Elsa lay on her bed, staring at the raked lines of veins in her hands. After a while Sara gave up. She came back the next day, rapped rhythmically on the wood as if tapping out a tune. "Elsa, please. Open the door. I have news for you." Elsa continued to write ecstatically, words wrapped in spirals down the page. Marcel knocked delicately and never spoke. She could tell by the evenness of the knocks and the lightness of footsteps afterward. He gave up trying after Thursday. She was writing entire books of desire, words with colors and smells. Caldwell pounded on the door until Pinky barked at him, and slipped notes through the seam between door and floor.

There's a party on Charles Street. Why don't you come?

Dinner with Sara and me? Polly's, 8:00.

Once the illustrator across the hall rapped lightly and said, "Phone."

She did not want to hear anyone else's voice in her mind. She had so much work to do. There were whole plays coming to her in verse:

On a podium, in a dynamic attitude stands the nude.
Man in knickerbockers enters—briskly—eases to slouchy leisure.
MAN: Lonely?
NUDE: Lost.
MAN: Where is he?
NUDE: Snuffed.
MAN: Dead? Is he now!! Cluk Cluk Cluk!

There was a philosophical treatise, called "Life's Beggar Truth":

Desecrated to Marcel:
Change is life's mechanical constant stimulant.
(consider money!) Erupting skin—
evolutionally rendering it tough—sinuous—callused—
piloteye glued to immediate corners—
ghostily repeating youth's prancing kick—
money is exhilaration—substance—lungs—
without which destitutes of conventional means
life dynamo is complicated.
Hence to say:
Nobody has not been choked purple.

Someone slid posters beneath her door: COSTUME BALL FOR *THE LITTLE REVIEW*, A NEW-FASHIONED HOP, SKIP, AND JUMP, AT THE ULTRA BOHEMIAN, PREHISTORIC, POSTALCOHOLIC WEBSTER HALL. SEE BARONESS ELSA IN PER-

FORMANCE, MAY 29. There was a picture there of a mask, long ribbons trailing around the letters, a note scrawled at the bottom: *We hope you will still perform. Call on us if you need anything, JH.* She resented the intrusion.

Words were everywhere now—under the radiator, wrapped around the doorknob, pressed against the windowpane—and all of them were the right ones. Her conversation with the objects intensified. The faucet, sneezing, wanted her to dance the monkey trot, as she had all those years ago at the Ritz, and then to float out the window, stiff as a board. The hairbrush, so easily insulted, unused, sulked, and would have preferred a recitation of particulars. Angry, the jars clanged together so loudly she could not reply to them, and there was no poem that day, though the next afternoon, when she opened the cookie tin, there was a poem there, pressed against the edge.

Her mother, who appeared in the sheen of the windowpane at night, looked down on her while she slept and read the new poems aloud in a hushed rumble punctuated by sneezes.

Elsa was comforted by this but puzzled when a baby kangaroo appeared in her room, hopping between door and window, though there was nothing in his pouch, and when she opened the door, he refused to leave. On the day the kangaroo finally left, a yellow star appeared in the upper right corner of her room, flickering bright and smaller, bright and smaller, day and night.

The beaded pot holder seemed haloed with gold light, the beads worn to a tarnished silver sheen. She saw the exact place on her father's coat where the scrap had been cut from—just next to the lapel, above his heart. A breeze blew through the whistle so it emitted a thin, high-pitched sound, and then she knew it was time for the ball.

That night, as she gathered her costume, the items in the room did not jumble and rearrange themselves into an order she could not follow, as they'd threatened; Pinky and Fred did not hide from her as they had before but sat quietly watching her prepare; and the mouth kept its distance, hovering somewhere just outside the window, wooden lips making a racket as they banged against the fire escape.

Out of an old fur collar and birthday candles, she created a headdress: *animal and light.* She put on her teaspoon earrings and five purple anklets that clattered on her shins as she walked. She cut one of her dresses just below the knees and covered it with round disks of tinfoil.

Refashioning herself, she prepared to leave her room again, though her

poems were alive there, and she hated to leave them. One hid beyond the
cloak inside the closet, several lay under the bed, two curled up against Pinky,
another was growing slowly in the heat and mold on top of the radiator. As a
girl she had not expected her poems to come to her this way but imagined
them like strikes of lightning, airy envelopes that would float down like snow.
But that was all before she could see the numinous charge in garbage cans,
before she fixed her attention to the wail of metal against wheels and water
gurgling in pipes, that music that turned inside out, somersaulted, and bur-
rowed into the light. Before she finally saw the way her mother's gift skirted
something holy. He had not loved her, yet she'd made a gift from this lack.

She sat at the dressing table and explored her reflection: eyes so pale they
resembled bubbles, lips cracked unevenly at their edges, nose long and
strong. There was hardly a ghost of the girl she had been at the Wintergarten,
and now she had to draw a different beauty onto her face, ageless and elastic.
She painted her cheeks yellow, outlined her lips in black. She dipped several
of Fred's feathers in gold paint and carefully glued them to her eyelashes.

The New York Sun, May 28, 1918

WEBSTER HALL COSTUME BALL—*THE LITTLE REVIEW* AND ITS
BARONESS

*Revelers will don costumes Saturday night for another of the Vil-
lage's infamous balls. The occasion? To raise money for the magazine of
new art and literature,* The Little Review, *which has suffered recently
from the scoldings of the Society for the Prevention of Vice. Each of its
last three issues has been confiscated by the post office and burned.*

*The Baroness Elsa von Freytag-Loringhoven is slated to perform at
the ball, along with the dancer Isabella Mitchell.*

*To understand why the censor objects, one might read the baroness's
verse printed in* The Little Review. *To this reporter's ears, her poems are
only words strung together in half-sense, but such is so much of the art
coming out of the Village these days. Who knows? She may be our next
genius. Jane Heap, one of the ladies who edits* The Little Review, *has
said, "The Baroness is the only person anywhere who deserves the epithet
extraordinary." The Baroness was reportedly seen in performance last*

month, wearing a skirt donned with tin soldiers, her skin painted yellow, her lips black, as if she were reciting out of the mouth of a corpse.

The huge chandelier hanging over Webster Hall sent specks of light onto the revelers: cats, kings, savages, and fairies. The band—two brass horns and a piano—played from the stage, and in front of them, a group was dancing, arms sawing the air, feet frantic. The place smelled of perfumes, spilled wine, and cigarettes. Now and then a hat or a scarf would be flung up toward the ceiling.

When the Baroness arrived, the crowd parted around her. For a moment she felt a surge of fear and even wondered if she might have lost her voice without knowing it. "Will you look at that?" she heard a man say as she passed.

"That's her," said another voice.

Pushing out of the crowd, Sara emerged, wearing tiger's ears and a long tail, whiskers drawn in kohl over her mouth. She hugged Elsa. "I didn't know if you were ever going to come out."

"I didn't either," said Elsa. "I've been working." Sara needed to feel her own strength again, and if Elsa could get her hands on a goddamn white dove, she would give it to her. Sara would at first say, "What's with the bird?" but in a little while she would listen and feel sturdy again, limber.

Sara looked down. "I knocked on your door. You couldn't even answer?"

"I didn't hear you, dear," Elsa said.

Next to Sara, Jane appeared, tall in her King Cole crown and velvet robe, her cheeks and nose rouged for merriness, gray cotton patched on her chin. Her lips were quickly moving, her eyes melancholy. She'd have to learn to talk less rapidly, so that heaven could hear her. Even now the brassy music was too loud for Elsa to fathom what she was saying, until Jane leaned forward and said, "Where have you been?"

There was no truthful answer, so she asked for champagne.

With Jane and Sara on either arm, she walked grandly to the bar in the back of the hall, passing a pirate, an Egyptian princess, a harem girl with glitter on her small bare breasts. Behind the bar, along the wall, giant goddesses presided, their forms pressed out in gold plaster. Females in the midst of becoming something else: a woman sprouting wings from her shoulders;

a torso with bosom attached to a bird's head and beak; a woman with horse's legs carrying a sword.

Handing out the goblets of champagne, Jane said to Elsa, raising her cotton eyebrows, "Some of the guests here have been asking about you for months. People who've admired you from afar, who've wondered about the woman who wrote *those* poems!"

Elsa tried not to look in the corner, where the revelers' faces seemed to be melting off of them, flesh puddling on the floor like pink milk. But when she looked away, in the direction of the columns, there were three men in suits each missing a nose. And next to them, there were three faces without lips or eyebrows. She wanted to restore these features, draw them on with paint.

Sara took Elsa's hand. "I refuse to let you out of my sight. What possessed you to disappear like that? God, don't you realize how much you missed? There was an opening at Lafitte's and a grotesque party at some sculptor's loft, but Djuna got into a stimulating argument with Harrold. And Caldwell and I went to a party where everyone was talking about Paris. I'm going as soon as the war is over. That's the one place in the world, I think, where I could maybe do something worthwhile. Then there was a big mess with Margaret, when she drank too much one night and followed me around Polly's, hissing, 'I hate you, I hate you,' but I suppose we're reconciled. It had to be said." Sara's tiger face suited her, black and gold paint striping her forehead and cheeks. Her whiskers worked over her smile like black sun rays. "And I tore pages out of a liberty book and wrote down every obscenity I could think of, and mailed them each in separate envelopes and signed Jim's name to them."

"Herzlichen Glückwunsch!" So Sara was safe. She would not go back to Ohio.

They were moving through the crowd, up toward the stage, chandelier light dotting faces and masks. Sara put her mouth close to Elsa's ear. "Don't disappear like that again. I might not forgive you."

Elsa touched the yellow felt of Sara's tiger ears. How could she promise that she would not? There was so much work to be done.

Caldwell bounced out of the group of dancers, dressed as a page—blond wig, harlequin tunic and tights, pointed gold shoes. "You've come out!" he said, stepping back to admire her costume. "How did you ever manage such eyelashes? You look as if you might stare beams of gold filigree."

"I will," she said. In his pretty yellow wig, with his lips so pink, his loneliness was clear, but lovely, like a single flower in a wide field.

Jane said, "Is that our Mr. Caldwell? Well, you look so pretty!"

Caldwell folded his arms and slumped slightly, nodding. Elsa wondered if his Tuesday night Bill was somewhere among the revelers, dressed as a prince.

The drum rolled. Jane sauntered up to the stage and flung out her hands for silence. "I wanted to give a speech, to say that *The Little Review* represents the best creative work that is being produced here and in Europe, written without an eye on the established publisher and not garbled in editorial rooms either, to meet the taste of the average mind. But I've decided, finally, to let art speak for itself." As she announced the first performer, a dancer in tights, yellow veils, and a blue mask, Sara leaned closer to Elsa and whispered, "She's depending on this night to save the magazine." The music jangled from the small band of instruments gathered near the curtain. The dancer moved her body as if it did not belong to her but to some cloud, her feet paradoxically pounding the wood of the stage.

Someone touched Elsa's shoulder, and she turned to see Marcel, wearing no costume except a dunce's cap and reeking of whiskey. "Is it Elsa or something else?" He kissed her on both cheeks and murmured something French into her ear that sounded erotic. She smoothed a stray piece of tinfoil on her skirt, pleased with its glimmer. Then he stepped back, his cheekbones sharpened in shadow, his blue eyes rapidly growing the black lashes that turned them into the eyes of her mother. Of course he and her mother had the same cold delicacy. Why hadn't she seen it before? But unlike her mother, he would never allow anything to muddle the sheen of his brain—only whiskey gave him permission to lose himself.

He pointed to the ceiling. "See that rafter? I found the ladder. I'm going to climb up there and watch you."

"You're too drunk for that, my friend," said Caldwell. "We don't want you splattered all over the revelers."

"But yes. I need a good view for the Baroness's performance." His voice wove in and out of muttering as he chattered about how he would climb up to the ceiling, the ladder he'd found in the alcove, the ledge he'd spotted.

Looking at his red-rimmed eyes, she had to forgive him for his glassy nature. She took his face in her hands and kissed him. *"Marcel, Marcel, I love you like hell, Marcel."*

He stepped back, laughing, his dunce cap askew. "If only," he said.

The dance was almost over. Elsa turned to Sara and handed her a book of matches. "Light the candles for me, please." She lowered her head while Sara touched the match to each candle in the headdress, her head expanding in luminosity.

Jane announced the Baroness as "a woman of brains, of mad beauty and *elegantes Wesen*." The musicians laid their instruments in their laps, and Elsa took the stage.

The mass of the crowd before her blurred into shadowy mounds of flesh and sequin, though Sara, Jane, Margaret, and Caldwell stood just below her, tiger, king, slave girl, and page. She felt the head of the candles above her, a trickle of wax down the back of her neck.

After all is said—done—ardortasted—faith digested—postsex compromised
Youth mask's blandishments a mortal grimace—shredworn—
Abased in spectral spooks' macabre mockmimic—too testical—
In hapless copulation tangle feeding gracelorn shell of ghostly repeating youth!
To shrug—shudder—weep—grin—hoot—ironically dash lurking mites
Of earth's dignity to hell-larking smithereens—

She saw Marcel at the top of a ladder he'd moved against a pillar, which he hugged as he shimmied upward. Jane raised her sequined King Cole scepter, twirling it in the light. In the back, a man wearing just a towel heckled her drunkenly. "What is that language you are speaking?" The question made them lean closer, wanting to hear the broken song, to find out if it would shimmer in the forehead, or go back into silence.

Above her, Marcel struggled to swing himself onto the rafter. She could not help loving him, even at this distance, though she saw how he needed to oppose her. Below her, Sara leaned onto the stage, her feline face completely encircled in light, ears opened.

Elsa began another poem.

City stir on eardrum—
In night lonely
Peers—:
Moon—riding

Pale—with beauty aghast—
Too exalted to share!
In space blue—rides she away from my chest—
Illumined strangely
Appalling sister!

Elsa's head fell back, and she closed her eyes, the feather lashes heavy on her lids. When she opened her eyes again, looking up, there was Marcel on the rafter, waving. Behind him on the beam, the velvet dress, the patent leather slippers. Her mother pressed against his back, arms wrapped around his waist, the ice on her dress melting. Water rained down on the revelers, plinking on the hard floor. A large drop shimmered on Caldwell's head, a silver wash over Jane's and Sara's faces.

Elsa's feather eyelashes made a gilded, fringed frame of the crowd. All those needy faces looking up at her with quizzical eyes. They did not know what they wanted from her, but she felt their longing. She wanted to give it to them. She wanted to give away all of herself.

EPILOGUE

PARIS *1927*

Sara rushed through the damp air and strange quiet, having waited all afternoon, the city loud with rain. She crossed the street and turned south toward the broken-down buildings, the basement hovels of morphine addicts, and alleys where whores wore mattresses strapped to their backs. Elegant shutters swung half torn from windows, and doors were padlocked or missing. This was the far side of Paris. As usual, Elsa had managed to make her aloneness huge, and no one came down there to the Grand Hotel, with its one-franc rooms, except to see her. Her solitude was like a whirlwind, and one never knew what might blow out of it.

The questions turned in Sara as she walked the slick, gray streets, puddles like broken mirror shards, an automobile hissing past. If she were going to kill herself, Elsa would have thought she at least owed her friends a flourish. But what happened was like a joke without even the decency of a punch line. No one even knew why the oven door had been left open, or why the gas jets had been switched on.

Sara walked past a bench where an old woman pressed a rosary to her lips; past a crowded, noisy café; past a building where a tired-looking woman hung out of a window, her arm limp against the stone. She watched the stores beginning to close up, the padlocks hooked on the doors, windows covered, awnings rolled away. She saw a woman go by wearing a hem as high as her knee—stockings falling down her ankles. Legs everywhere now, scissoring past, and suddenly every other woman, even this sad prostitute, was wearing a cloche hat, and if Sara squinted her eyes, it looked just like the coal scuttle Elsa used to wear on her head.

Sara had finished with weeping, but Elsa's absence seemed unreal and cruel, like a cosmic mistake. Crossing rue Barrault, Sara stepped in an oily puddle and soaked her shoes. In a wet shop window, there was a tidy pyramid of canned meats. A bus screeched at the corner, letting out three men in gray coveralls and a tiny woman lugging a fishnet sack of vegetables. She remembered that she owed rent, just as a hand flipped the sign in the bakery window to *Fermé*. Already, she felt the assault of the ordinary.

She went into the hotel and ran up three flights of stairs to the room where she'd found the baroness lying in her bed two days before, her face still fierce, as if she were a soldier marching, eyes closed, into battle. Pinky lay behind the doorstop, curled around his tail.

Sara was the only one who did not believe there would be a note somewhere. During the wake, people cursed in the Baroness's honor. Lo hung her head out the window in the thunderstorm, and Robert arrived holding the death mask over his head like a crucifix. Because everyone else was still drunk, they wanted Sara to go back and get Elsa's things.

Elsa had just had a hundred flyers printed to advertise her new modeling school. ARE YOU ASLEEP WITH SOMNOLENT MODELS? WAKE UP IN CREATIVE *CRO-QUIS!* THE BARONESS, FAMOUS MODEL FROM NEW YORK, PUTS ART INTO POSING, BODY EXPRESSION, SPIRIT PLASTIC. She had not modeled since she'd left Manhattan, but already had the attention of a gallery owner here in Paris. With a huge grin, she told whomever she met that her poems were being published in *transition*. And she was still pulling pranks. The other night she had shown up at Le Dôme wearing nothing under her oilskin slicker, poured sugar into a man's beer because he was "acting sour," and, when she ran out of money asked the waiter if he would invite the bearded gentleman at the bar to pay for her—then ducked under the table and scooted out.

Sara suspected that what happened had something to do with one of the rangy, unshaven men that lately Elsa had a habit of picking up at Lumière, the café with a cigar-store front. Elsa had been flirting again with hoodlums and vagrants—one of whom might have found it amusing to kill her and take what little money he could find.

The window had been left open. Tattered curtains blew in over the rain-soaked bed. There was a pot on the stove, a half-drunk bottle of vermouth on the table, a dull glisten on the green glass. Sara felt dizzy, as if her head were separating from her neck, and didn't want to weep again because she had to get it all packed, before the proprietress threw everything away.

She dropped the baroness's trunk in the middle of the floor and opened it. Inside was a tangle of clothes, feathers, tin soldiers, squashed, gilded fruit, screws and eyes, a harness, flecks of gold paint, and teaspoons.

Against the wall the things Elsa had collected from the streets—a piece of rubber torn from a tire, several foil wrappers, a wire clothes hanger. There was also a half-finished assemblage, a rusted chain that she'd hooked to a wooden box with a design on the lid of a woman chasing a cat. Sara would take that for herself before Marcel got his hands on it.

Sara searched under the bed, inside the oven, even into the drain of the sink, but just as she'd suspected, there was no note. Sara collected the objects from the dressing table, where books slanted against a mirror, Nietzsche lay against a perfume bottle, and Oscar Wilde under a box of face powder. Rifling through the books, she found scraps of butcher paper with sketches, and a lingerie bill. In the drawers she found the passport with German and French customs stamps—Elsa, in her photograph, wore her hair slashed short on her forehead, her eyes furiously bright. She discovered notebooks and unwritten bank receipts—hundreds of them Elsa must have stuffed in her pockets—with fragments of poems scrawled on the backs. Sara read one:

> *Here*
> *Crawls*
> *Moon—*
> *Out of*
> *This Hole.*

The proprietress, a skinny, hawkish woman, suddenly at the door shaking out her umbrella, said, "Remember, the furniture wasn't hers. It belongs to me."

Sara, packing the notebooks into the valise, said, "You must have some idea who she brought up here."

The woman shrugged, backing into the hallway. "I don't know—it looks like an accident to me."

"Isn't it a happy accident?" Elsa would say when she showed Sara one of her poems. "I didn't expect it to happen this way at all."

AUTHOR'S NOTE

Holy Skirts is a fictional reimagining of the life of Baroness Elsa von Freytag-Loringhoven. The character of the Baroness and most events in the novel are based on original sources, but because of wide gaps in what is known of the Baroness's life and the necessities of the narrative, certain events and facts have been changed. For example, the film of the Baroness by Man Ray and Marcel Duchamp was actually made a few years later than as portrayed in the book, and the barber in the film was probably Man Ray, not Duchamp. Similarly, the obscenity trial over James Joyce's *Ulysses* in *The Little Review* also occurred a few years later, and the Baroness's visit to the Society for the Prevention of Vice is fictional, though there is evidence that she was virulently against the suppression of the novel and *The Little Review*. To preserve the story, I have also compressed time, changed the names of her husbands, omitted certain episodes in her life, and moved incidental locations (for instance, there is evidence that the Baroness lived in the same building as Duchamp for a period, but not at the Fourteenth Street building).

Because the story is told from the Baroness's perspective, I have often recast events as she might have seen them. As such, the portrayal of recognizable figures is always fictional and never meant to be factual, even when drawn from sources. *Holy Skirts* is not intended to be a historical document. For biographical facts on the Baroness Elsa von Freytag-Loringhoven, readers should seek out the recent, excellent biography *Baroness Elsa* by Irene Gammel.

The historical Baroness Elsa von Freytag-Loringhoven wrote numerous poems and an unfinished autobiography. The poems and fragments that appear in the book are either taken directly from her papers or modeled closely on the poems there. Similarly, the autobiography was a major source in my exploration of the fictional Baroness's inner life. For access to the Baroness's papers, I am indebted to Special Collections (papers of Elsa von Freytag-Loringhoven), University of Maryland Libraries, and to the Special Collections Department at the Golda Meir Library at the University of Wisconsin-Milwaukee, where the papers of *The Little Review* are housed. For access to precious old copies of *The Little Review*, I am grateful to the Fairleigh Dickinson Library on the Madison Campus.

ACKNOWLEDGMENTS

I am indebted to the Professional Staff Congress–City University of New York Research Foundation, which awarded me two grants that allowed me time to write and provided funds for travel necessary for my research. I am also grateful to Fairleigh Dickinson University for release time, which helped me to make progress on the book.

Many books were indispensable in my research for this project, especially the following. On Berlin in the early twentieth century: *The Germans,* by Gordon A. Craig; *Faust's Metropolis: A History of Berlin,* by Alexandra Richie; and *Berlin,* by David Clay Large. On World War I: *The First World War,* by John Keegan; *The Great War and Modern Memory,* by Paul Fussel; and *World War I at Home, Readings on American Life: 1914–1920,* by David F. Trask. On Greenwich Village in the 1910s and 1920s: *Strange Bedfellows: The First American Avant-Garde,* by Steven Watson; *American Moderns: Bohemian New York and the Creation of a New Century,* by Christine Stansell; *Greenwich Village, 1920–1930,* by Carolyn Ware; and *Greenwich Village: Culture and Counterculture,* edited by Rick Beard and Leslie Cohen Berlowitz. On

Margaret Anderson and Jane Heap in particular: *Four Lives in Paris,* by Hugh Ford. On the Dada movement in New York, the Whitney Museum's catalog of *Making Mischief: Dada Invades New York,* edited by Francis Naumann, was most helpful. I also consulted *New York Dada,* edited by Rudolf E. Kuenzli.

Several phrases and ideas attributed to Marcel Duchamp are borrowed from *Dialogues with Marcel Duchamp,* a selection of interviews, by Pierre Cabanne. Calvin Tomkins's biography *Duchamp* was also helpful.

Several phrases and ideas attributed to the Baroness are taken from her autobiography, a published and edited version of the autobiography found in her papers, *Baroness Elsa,* edited by Paul I. Hjartarson and Douglas O. Spettigue. In addition, though my research began before the book was published, Irene Gammel's biography *Baroness Elsa* was a helpful source later in the project, as was our correspondence and conversation. The exhibit of the baroness's work at Francis M. Naumann Fine Art, LLC, was inspiring, as were conversations with Francis Naumann.

The excerpts of Mina Loy's poems are from *The Lost Lunar Baedeker,* edited by Roger L. Conover (New York: Farrar Straus Giroux, 1996). The quotations in English translation from Goethe, Novalis, Brentano, and Fontane are from *Great German Poems of the Romantic Era,* translated and edited by Stanley Appelbaum (New York: Dover Publications, 1995). The first epigraph is from George Biddle's *An American Artist's Story* (New York: Little Brown, 1939). Some of the letters regarding the Baroness's poems are taken from *The Little Review,* though in certain cases the names have been changed.

For their careful readings and insights, thanks to Elizabeth Mitchell, Darcey Steinke, Natalie Standiford, Karen Wunsch, Rita Signorelli-Pappas, Walter Cummins, Tim Houlihan, Dannielle Thomas, Sharyn Rosenblum, and Tim Thyzel.

I am also grateful to Ira Silverberg, Carolyn Marino, and Jennifer Civiletto. And finally a big thanks to my family and to Craig Marks, who read this book in all its incarnations.

About the author

About the book

Read on

P.S.

Insights,
Interviews
& More . . .

Meet René Steinke

Marion Ettlinger

RENÉ STEINKE was born in Richmond, Virginia, and raised in Friendswood, Texas, between Houston and Galveston. Her father is a Lutheran minister, her mother is an artist. She is the eldest of four children.

Her early days call up vivid memories of Texan sun and Gulf tempests. "We used to ride our bikes through the oil fields into town, the heat beating down on our heads," she says. "The creek near us would occasionally flood the streets. In the mid-1970s, there was a hurricane and the first floor of our house was completely flooded. Tables, chairs, toys, and clothes went bobbing down the creek, and for months, the whole town smelled of mildew."

"Friendswood was a small town, originally settled by Quaker people," she says. "But social life revolved around the football team, the Mustangs. My first published writing appeared in the local newspaper, a column about high school news called 'Mustang Mania.'"

She holds an MFA from the University of Virginia and a Ph.D. in English from the University of Wisconsin-Madison. While pursuing the former degree, she studied writing with George Garrett and Charles Wright and became close friends with cousin Darcey Steinke, a fellow student and (now) novelist.

"We were both waitresses at Miller's Restaurant, a bar and burger place where a few other budding artists and musicians worked. When it was slow, we sat talking or reading novels in the wait station."

She continued to waitress throughout much of her early twenties. "I used to be very agile," she recalls, "and could balance three plates on one arm. And for some reason, I kept getting jobs at places where you had to light a cocktail or a plate of cheese on fire and serve the flaming thing at the table."

Her poems have also appeared in *TriQuarterly, Southern Poetry Review, Cumberland Poetry Review,* and *Carolina Quarterly.* She is the recipient of an Academy of American Poets Prize. Her favorite poets are Elizabeth Bishop and Rainer Maria Rilke. While she hasn't written poetry "for years," it was poetry that drew her to Baroness Elsa von Freytag-Loringhoven. "I thought I could imagine that part of her creative life," she says.

Her writing has also appeared in *Vogue* and the *New York Times.*

Her first novel, *The Fires* (2000), tells the story of twenty-two-year-old Ella, a sympathetic arsonist. *Publishers Weekly* called *The Fires* a "sensitive, eerie" debut, its "rich, sensuous prose . . . studded with arresting imagery."

She describes her writing habits thus: "I write in longhand, and go through several drafts before I type anything on the laptop. Then I work on a typed manuscript, make notes, revisions, and additions, before typing again. I write in the mornings, as many days as I can, in my study at home."

She teaches fiction writing in the graduate and undergraduate programs at Fairleigh Dickinson University.

She is editor-in-chief of *The Literary Review,* in whose pages she was of late most pleased to publish "three very short stories by Lydia Davis, an excerpt from Lynne Tillman's recently completed novel, two poems by Charles Wright, and a poem by Frank Bidart."

She plays keyboard in the rock band ▶

> ❝ I kept getting jobs at places where you had to light a cocktail or a plate of cheese on fire. ❞

Meet René Steinke *(continued)*

Ruffian, a thumpingly literate quintet comprised of four writers and a documentary filmmaker. "When Ruffian began," she says, "none of us knew how to play our instruments, so we had to have a certain amount of punk-rock moxie. I play a vintage Farfisa keyboard, which has a 1960s, slightly plaintive sound. . . . We have a song called 'Lefty,' about a bad self-righteous boyfriend; a song called 'Monica,' a sympathetic, cautionary address to Monica Lewinsky; and an anthem to the horse Ruffian ('Undefeated'), the famous filly racehorse who died heroically in the 1970s."

In her case, the rocking nurtures the writing. "Creating music has been strangely good for my writing," she says. "Having to compose songs from scratch has taught me things about composition, rhythm, and form." Moreover, she notes, "performing onstage has given me some insights into some of the Baroness's exhibitionist tendencies."

Asked whether she ever made a fashion statement of baronial proportion, she replies: "I once wore a bright lime-green polyester suit to the MTV awards at Radio City Music Hall, hardly in league with the Baroness's creations, I'm afraid."

She lives in Brooklyn with her husband and infant son.

She is at work on another novel, set in Texas. ❧

❝ She plays keyboard in the rock band Ruffian. ❞

René Steinke on Writing *Holy Skirts*

THE STORIES of early New York Bohemia have always fascinated me. The Baroness was this outrageous figure who kept walking through various biographies of the period wearing crazy outfits—a dress with a taillight, a birdcage necklace—alternately seducing men or causing them to take up boxing to defend themselves from her. I was leafing through *The Little Review,* a literary magazine circa 1920, and I came across her poetry, which struck me as way ahead of her time, almost proto–punk rock. Then I discovered that she was a friend of one of my favorite writers, Djuna Barnes; a muse figure for Marcel Duchamp; and a model for Man Ray. Several of her collages and assemblages were featured in the Whitney Museum show "Dada Invades New York," and I met the curator, Francis Naumann, who was also a Baroness fan. I was so intrigued by the Baroness, I could not believe no one had yet written about her. She seemed the precursor to contemporary figures like Madonna, Björk, and Courtney Love, and her struggles in love and art mirrored the struggles of many women I knew. I was hooked.

When I began the research, there was very little information on the Baroness's life, aside from her cameo appearances in various biographies. Her unfinished autobiography was available at the New York Public Library (published by a small Canadian press) but out of print, and the chronology only reached the point in her life when she was married to her second husband. In order to find out more about the Baroness, I had to look at her papers, which were available in the archives at the University of Maryland at College Park, and in the papers of *The Little Review,* at the library at the University of Wisconsin-Milwaukee. Spending several days in these libraries, I read her letters, poems, and plays and looked at her drawings and notes. At the time, I lived in Greenwich Village near the Baroness's old haunts, but I also visited Paris, Berlin, the Amalfi Coast, and other places where she lived. ∾

> ❝ I came across her poetry, which struck me as way ahead of her time, almost proto– punk rock. ❞

Outtake: A Bizarre Tale Not Found in *Holy Skirts*

THE BARONESS Elsa von Freytag-Loringhoven led a life full of unlikely adventures. Not all of them fit into the structure of this novel, such as the story of her unrequited love affair with the doctor and poet, William Carlos Williams.

I first discovered the Baroness in 1989, when I was writing about Williams and wanted to find out what the critics had said about his book of poems, *Kora in Hell.* I was in the library, reading dusty old copies of *The Little Review,* when I came upon a review of Williams's book written in the form of a prose poem: "Hamlet of the Wedding Ring." It critiqued Williams's appearance ("you wobbly legged, business satchel–carrying little louse"), his American-ness (his infatuation with "factory-girl America"), his integrity ("sour-apple cider plus artificial bubble–chemical spunk"), and even his virility, all in the context of his poems. The review was written by the Baroness, and I was immediately drawn in by her fierceness and loudmouthed lyricism. In 1921, it was unheard of for a woman to write such a damning critique of a male writer—and in the form of a poem, at that! Reading Williams's autobiography, and later, the Baroness's correspondence, I soon discovered why she was so miffed.

Williams lived in Rutherford, New Jersey, with his wife, Flossie, but would frequently visit New York City for a taste of bohemian parties and intellectual banter—he was rumored to be a bit of a womanizer. One day, while visiting the editors Margaret Anderson and Jane Heap at the offices of *The Little Review,* he saw an artwork by the Baroness under a glass dome. He described it as "a piece of sculpture that appeared to be chicken guts, possibly imitated in wax."[1] When

> " In 1921, it was unheard of for a woman to write such a damning critique of a male writer—and in the form of a poem, at that! "

---

[1] William Carlos Williams, *The Autobiography of William Carlos Williams* (New York: New Directions, 1967), 164. Williams's friendship with the Baroness is discussed on pages 163–169.

he later wrote to the editors that he wished to meet the artist, they enthusiastically agreed, but noted that he would have to wait until she was released from the Women's House of Detention, where she had been jailed for stealing an umbrella.

On the day of her release, Williams met her at the jail and took her to breakfast. The two poets had a sparkling conversation, and sometime that morning or soon after, Williams announced that he was in love with her. Much later, he wrote that she reminded him of his "gypsy" grandmother, implying this was the reason for his surge of affection, but one wonders whether he only felt the need to make an excuse after their relationship soured. In any case, the Baroness took his declaration seriously.

Writing in retrospect, Williams seems squeamish about his initial attraction to Elsa, and gives a rather mean-spirited description of their first kiss. "Close-up, a reek stood out purple from her body." [2] What's puzzling is why, if he found her so repulsive, he visited her studio apartment, invited her to visit him in Rutherford, and even left a basket of ripe peaches in front of her door as a gift. He resisted her sexual advances, according to both of their accounts, but Elsa claimed to be in possession of two love letters from him. [3] In one of her attempts to seduce him, she supposedly suggested that they have sex, so he could "contract syphilis from her to free [his] mind for serious art." [4]

One night, with a male sidekick, the Baroness went to Rutherford. The man phoned Williams, saying that a baby was about to be born, and his services were needed. As Williams rushed out of his house, the Baroness, waiting in a parked car, grabbed him and said, "You must come with me." When he resisted, she hit him. The event left Williams so shaken that he took boxing ▶

66 Writing in retrospect, Williams seems squeamish about his initial attraction to Elsa, and gives a rather mean-spirited description of their first kiss. 99

[2] William Carlos Williams, "Sample Prose Piece, The Three Letters," *Contact 4* (Summer 1921): 11:12.
[3] Irene Gammel, *Baroness Elsa* (Cambridge, Massachusetts: MIT Press, 2002), 266.
[4] Williams, *Autobiography*, 165.

Outtake: A Bizarre Tale Not Found in
Holy Skirts (continued)

lessons to protect himself, and the next time he ran into the Baroness on Park Avenue, he "flattened her with a stiff punch in the mouth." Somehow, he had a policeman arrest her, and she screamed after him, "What are you in this town, Napoleon?" [5]

Finally, despite their combative history, Williams praised the Baroness. "The Baroness to me was a great field of cultured bounty in spite of her psychosis, her insanity. She was right. She was courageous to an insane degree," he wrote. "I found myself drinking pure water from her spirit." [6]

> 66 The event left Williams so shaken that he took boxing lessons to protect himself. 99

[5] Williams, *Autobiography,* 169.
[6] William Carlos Williams, "The Baroness Elsa von Freytag Loringhoven." *Twentieth-Century Literature* 35.3 (1989): 279–84.

The Baroness's Collages and Sculptures

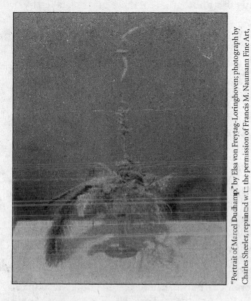

"Portrait of Marcel Duchamp" by Elsa von Freytag-Loringhoven; photograph by Charles Sheeler, reprinted with the permission of Francis M. Naumann Fine Art, New York

THIS IS THE PIECE I imagine taking shape in the Baroness's imagination at two points in the novel. At the end of chapter 27, just after she meets Duchamp at the Arensbergs' apartment: "She caught sight of Marcel across the room. He lifted his champagne glass to her. Out of the bubbles sprouted something like a bird-plant, chirping and blossoming, a thing only the two of them possessed the insight to see." And at the beginning of chapter 34: "And she described Marcel: a lightbulb, electricity beaming from his head; a champagne glass, the pedestal for his wit; feathers, because he needed nestling; a glass marble, which might stay cold forever unless he was brave enough to touch her again." In the Baroness's correspondence and poetry, Duchamp is often associated with lightbulbs (his brilliance) and glass (his brittleness and beauty), and this assemblage also reflects those motifs.

Unfortunately, like many of the Baroness's ▶

> **Read on**

> 66 In the Baroness's correspondence and poetry, Duchamp is often associated with lightbulbs (his brilliance) and glass (his brittleness and beauty). 99

9

The Baroness's Collages and Sculptures
(continued)

artworks, the original piece has been lost, and only this photograph of the sculpture, taken by the artist Charles Sheeler, survives. Some of the Baroness's pieces were made with perishable items—fruit, gilded vegetables—which is presumably why they eventually disappeared. Others seem to have been lost by accident. Years ago, one of the owners of a few works by the Baroness had sold them and was delivering them by train to Mark Kellman, a collector in New York City. Unfortunately, one piece, stored in an ancient paper bag (where Elsa had originally kept it), was left behind on the train, never to be seen again. It makes me wonder which other concoctions of light bulbs, wood, feathers, wire, plumbing fixtures, and tin may have been left in basements or attics around the Village—the Baroness was very generous in giving away her art. Who knows? Perhaps there are more of her pieces yet to be discovered.

The Baroness's collage, "Dada Portrait of Berenice Abbott," can be found at the Museum of Modern Art in New York. Her assemblage, "God" (with Morton Livingston Schamberg), is in the collection at the Philadelphia Museum of Art. Her collage, "Portrait of Marcel Duchamp," belongs to the Vera, Silvia, and Arturo Schwarz Collection of Dada and Surrealist Art at the Israel Museum in Jerusalem. Other pieces by the Baroness belong to the Mark Kellman Collection in New York. ∽

The End of the Baroness's Life

IN THE SPRING of 1923, friends took up a collection to pay for the Baroness's boat fare to Germany. Poverty had worn her out, and she blamed her depression on America's materialism. During her last month in New York City, she camped in Fort Washington Park.[7]

She landed in a war-ravaged Berlin, and moved into a small, unheated room. According to *Baroness Elsa* by Irene Gammel, the Baroness contacted the Baron's family, expecting financial assistance. But they only sent her (via their lawyer) a few of the Baron's belongings and ignored her other letters. Then in July, her father died in Swinemünde, and she discovered that he had disinherited her. Other family members, comfortable in their middle-class conformity, were cold and uncharitable. In order to survive, she was forced to sell newspapers on the street, calling out headlines to passersby.[8] By chance, when he was visiting Berlin, the Baroness's old friend, the poet Claude McKay, ran into her. "It was a sad rendezvous," he said. "The Baroness in Greenwich Village, arraigned in gaudy accoutrements, was a character. Now in German homespun, she was just a poor pitiful *frau*. She said she had come to Germany to write because the cost of living was cheap there. But she complained that she had been ditched. She didn't make it clear by whom or what. So instead of writing she was crying news."[9]

For three years in Berlin she lived in abject poverty, working nonstop and still unable to furnish herself with the basic necessities of clothing and food. She wrote often to friends in America, asking for help, especially to the novelist, Djuna Barnes, and to the photographer, Berenice Abbott. Both ▶

> " During the Baroness's last month in New York City, she camped in Fort Washington Park. "

> " For three years in Berlin she lived in abject poverty, working nonstop and still unable to furnish herself with the basic necessities of clothing and food. "

[7] *Baroness Elsa*, 311.
[8] *Baroness Elsa*, 316–320.
[9] Claude McKay, *A Long Way from Home* (New York: Harcourt and Brace, 1970), 105, 241.

The End of the Baroness's Life *(continued)*

Abbott and Barnes helped her with gifts and small amounts of money. But it was Barnes who became Elsa's "second mother," and Elsa's letters to her are heartbreaking.[10] The Baroness lived for a short while at a home for destitute women, and later, she lived in a mental institution, though the authorities wrote, "Even though she cannot be considered mentally insane in the full meaning of the word, her attitude toward the world that surrounds her is so strange that we have to judge her like an abnormal person." But she was dismissed from the mental institution soon after going there.[11] During this time, in her letters to Barnes, Elsa began to write her autobiography, which Barnes agreed to try to get published (along with a book of the Baroness's poems). Elsa focused her efforts on getting to Paris, where by now, many of her American friends—Barnes, Duchamp, Man Ray, and Abbott—had emigrated. She put on a show for the French Consulate, where she went to request her visa. "I went to the consulate with a large sugarcoated birthday cake upon my head with fifty flaming candles lit—I felt just so *spunky and affluent!* In my ears I wore sugar plumes or matchboxes—I forgot which."[12] In the spring of 1926, she was finally granted her visa, and through a small inheritance from one of her aunts, was able to purchase passage to France.[13]

In Paris, she first lived at the Hôtel Danemark, in Montparnasse, and her fortune began to turn. Probably through the help of Peggy Guggenheim and others she secured a studio and planned to open a modeling school. Two of her poems were accepted for publication in the esteemed literary magazine *Transition*.

> 66 In Paris her fortune began to turn. 99

---

[10] Elsa von Freytag-Loringhoven Papers, Library, University of Maryland at College Park.
[11] *Baroness Elsa*, 352.
[12] *Baroness Elsa*. Autobiography and excerpts of selected letters. Ed. Paul I. Hjartarson and Douglas O. Spettigue with an introduction by the editors. (Ottawa: Oberon Press, 1992), 214–217.
[13] Gammel, *Baroness Elsa*, 360.

Though she tried many of her friends' patience, she was reunited with many of those she had known in New York.

At the end of *Holy Skirts*, I've fictionalized the mystery of the Baroness's death in December 1927. It was never determined whether she had been murdered by a cruel paramour or chose to commit suicide or was simply the victim of an accident. Djuna Barnes commissioned a death mask and wrote an obituary, calling the death "a stupid joke that had not even the decency of maliciousness." [14] But the Baroness's high jinks continued even after she was gone. On the day of the Baroness's burial in a Paris cemetery, Djuna Barnes went with her lover, Thelma Wood, but couldn't find the gravesite. They went to a bar to get drunk instead, and when they returned, they had missed the funeral. Years later, when Djuna Barnes opened one of her closets, the Baroness's death mask tumbled out and hit her on the head. [15]

[14] Djuna Barnes, "Obituary," *Transition* 11 (February 1928): 19.
[15] Gammel, *Baroness Elsa*, 384.

The Baroness's Legacy

FOR DECADES, most of the Baroness's poems, collages, and assemblages were lost to art and literary history. This was partly a result of conflicting attitudes toward the Baroness during her lifetime. "Take her as a joke," said the writer Robert McAlmon,[16] and many people did, unfairly dismissing her. Jane Heap and Margaret Anderson championed the Baroness, but after the dissolution of their relationship and the end of *The Little Review,* their interest in the Baroness's poetry waned. Berenice Abbott placed the Baroness "somewhere between Shakespeare and Jesus,"[17] and Marcel Duchamp said of the Baroness, "She is not a futurist. She is the future."[18] But even these praises and the efforts of Djuna Barnes went in vain. Barnes, after the Baroness's death, struggled to write a biography of her. One passage on the Baroness's time in Berlin reads, "Because she is strange with beauty, because she is high with fear, her heart is going down."[19] Barnes continued (without success) to try to get a volume of the Baroness's poems published. When Barnes was in her eighties, she told her friend Hank O'Neal that she still felt regret that she had not been able to get the poetry published, as she had promised to do. [20]

In 2002, the Baroness's biography, *Baroness Elsa* by Irene Gammel, was published. Only recently (2005), in Berlin, was a collection of the Baroness's poems published *(mein Mund ist lüstern / I Got Lusting Palate,* edited by Irene Gammel). In the spring of 2002, the Francis M. Naumann Fine Art gallery displayed an exhibit

---

[16] Robert McAlmon. "Postadolescence: 1920–1921." In McAlmon, *McAlmon and the Lost Generation: A Self-Portrait.* Ed. Robert E. Knoll. (Lincoln: University of Nebraska Press, 1962), 116.
[17] Gamell, *Baroness Elsa,* 393.
[18] Marcel Duchamp, quoted in Kenneth Rexroth, *American Poetry in the Twentieth Century* (New York: Herder and Herder, 1973), 77.
[19] Papers of Elsa von Freytag-Loringhoven.
[20] Interview, private letter from Hank O'Neal.

of artworks by the Baroness and portraits of the Baroness by artists such as Man Ray, George Biddle, and Theresa Bernstein. But the Baroness's most brilliant work of art was herself, which is why she was such an awe-inspiring subject. ᘉ

66 Berenice Abbott placed the Baroness 'somewhere between Shakespeare and Jesus,' and Marcel Duchamp said of the Baroness, 'She is not a futurist. She is the future.' 99

Have You Read?

THE FIRES

Ella is a connoisseur of fire, a woman enthralled by it as other women are by love. She savors the seductive promise of a spark, the caress of a curling wisp of smoke, the all-consuming hunger of a spreading blaze. Ella's heart seethes with a rage that can be spoken only with tongues of flame.

In her remarkable first novel, René Steinke has created a narrator so lyrical and lucid in her madness as to raise the book to the level of romance. Trapped in a sleepy Indiana town, torn by inner demons that drive her to pyromania and promiscuity, Ella is at once entirely original and unforgettably real.

As she struggles to come to terms with her family's tormented past and her own uncertain future, she draws the mesmerized reader ever deeper into her scorched soul, revealing a sensuality that will spiral into final, fiery destruction—unless it can be quenched by love.

"An intriguing . . . insight into a diseased soul. . . . Steinke has a knack for the macabre."
—*Kirkus Reviews*

"Hope is fragile in this darkly compelling and beautifully written story." —*Booklist*

D on't miss the next book by your favorite author. Sign up now for AuthorTracker by visiting www.AuthorTracker.com.

Read on

16